JONATHAN
NEFF
POWER PLAY

To Bob —
Thanks for your
support — Jon Neff

JONATHAN NEFF
POWER PLAY

HAWK
PUBLISHING
G R O U P

TULSA

LIBRARY OF CONGRESS CATALOG IN PUBLICATION DATA

Power Play / Jonathan Neff

[1. Neff, Jonathan C. - Fiction-United States.]

Hardback ISBN 1-930709-56-0
Trade Paperback ISBN 1-930709-54-4
Library of Congress Control Number: 2004117529

Published in the United States by HAWK Publishing Group.

HAWK Publishing Group
7107 South Yale Avenue #345
Tulsa, OK 74136
918-492-3677
www.hawkpub.com

HAWK and colophon are trademarks belonging to the HAWK
Publishing Group. Printed in the United States of America.
9 8 7 6 5 4 3 2 1

Dedication

*This is for Patti, whose passion for life,
commitment to family and abiding love
has come to be my firm foundation.*

Acknowledgments

I wish to acknowledge David and Sherry, who undertook the trying task of reading and commenting on my first unedited manuscript; Margie, Ashley and Aubrey, whose encouragement raised my spirits when the work seemed endless; and Bill and Jodie, who believed in me when I most needed it. Thank you for your love and support.

Nothing will ever be attempted, if all possible objections must first be overcome —
Samuel Johnson

Prologue

Wilson Rogers pushed through the heavy glass doors of the state office building and stepped from the empty foyer into a bitter north wind. He stopped long enough to turn up the collar of his knee length wool overcoat and pull on leather driving gloves. Across the street, falling snow swirled around the dome of the Capitol. It was nearly five o'clock on Friday afternoon, and the bare elm trees on the mall cast long shadows as they bent in the wind. Snow was beginning to coat the nearby patch of lawn, and all too soon the pavement would become treacherous. The aging Public Utility Commissioner wasn't looking forward to the two-hour drive home, which could easily turn into four hours or more, if conditions continued to deteriorate. He hoped that the brunt of the storm would hold off a little longer.

As he turned from Lincoln Boulevard onto the expressway, Commissioner Rogers cursed himself for ever even thinking about going into politics. Three years ago, the office of Public Utility Commissioner had looked easy. Traveling statewide for meetings with business leaders, dealing with the public utility companies and helping establish government policy had allowed him to represent the public interest. And at first, he and his wife had enjoyed being on a first name basis with the Governor and the rest of the state's muckety-mucks, which was a big step up from the twelve years he'd spent serving as a rural County Commissioner. But now, Wilson Rogers wished he had stuck to repairing gravel roads and hiring his nephew to paint the county courthouse every three years.

As he guided the nondescript government sedan onto the turnpike, he considered how much things had changed. A small but vocal constituency was holding his feet to the fire, and business interests with the power to make or break his political career were far too involved for comfort. At the commission meeting earlier, he had dutifully represented a constituency that vehemently opposed construction of the new power plant. Keeping his promise, he had doggedly argued against the project, just as he had done at the last three meetings, even though he was the sole commissioner to oppose it. Huntington's hostile expression, coupled with the dark mood of the men sitting with him in the gallery, had sent tendrils of fear creeping up his back. They were so intense that he had momentarily clutched, weakening his closing comments to the point they were all but useless.

Damn it! Frustrated, he hit the steering wheel with both palms. Maybe it was time to call it quits. The situation was out of control. If he could find a way to assuage Huntington's wrath, then claim health problems, he might be able to take early retirement. There had to be a way out of this debacle without totally capitulating to their coercion. He decided to think about it over the weekend, then first thing Monday morning take decisive action.

Ten miles out of town, the snow was coming down harder, but the rapidly falling temperatures and stiff wind kept it blowing off the road, leaving the pavement relatively dry. Checking his watch, he accelerated a little, eager to be home where a cheery fire and a good dinner could quell his anxiety.

Rogers glanced at the rear view mirror. A moment ago no one had been in sight, but now a black Mercedes was rapidly approaching. *Whoever that is,* he thought, *he must be doing at least eighty-five, way too fast for this weather.* In the darkness with the snow slanting across the highway, he instinctively tightened his grip on the wheel.

The Mercedes quickly closed the gap, then moved into the left lane. Rogers divided his attention between the road and the other car, hoping it would speed up and pass him before they crossed Keystone Dam, which was just a few hundred yards ahead. As the road began to narrow, he slowed to let the Mercedes pass.

When the car pulled fully alongside, Rogers glanced to the left and was momentarily paralyzed by the image of one of the men who had been shadowing Huntington at the last two commission meetings—a tall, dark man with long, black hair and an unpleasant demeanor. He seemed to emanate hatred as his eyes flared with a wicked ferocity.

Without warning, the Mercedes swerved into his car, hit it hard, then instantly corrected. As the sedan flew over the guard rail and plunged fifty feet into the dark waters of Keystone Lake, Rogers felt a terror unlike anything he'd ever experienced. Rolling, the car struck the lake upside down, breaking the windshield so that icy water instantly began to flood the passenger compartment.

On impact, Roger's head slammed against the window, then the ceiling, stunning him into a deeper state of shock, but the rush of frigid water quickly brought him back to full consciousness and he gasped for air. With the car slipping deeper into the water each second, he knew he had to get out fast!

Upside down and submerged in freezing water, Rogers struggled to free himself from the seat belt and open the door. Surprisingly, he was able to do both in a matter of seconds, but by that time the car had fallen more than ten feet into the murky depths. Vertigo added another layer of confusion as he frantically tried to sense which way was up. Pushing out of the car, he shoved off in the direction of the escaping air bubbles, and three hard, quick strokes brought him to the surface. With lungs bursting, head and heart pounding, he gasped in the frigid air.

Overhead, a row of lights shone atop the dam. He was only thirty feet from the dark concrete wall, and painfully, he stretched his cramping muscles to swim.

Intently focused on his goal, he didn't think to kick off his shoes or slip out of the jacket that was restricting his arm movement. With the wind whipping the water to whitecaps and snow swirling in the yellow glow of the dam's lights, his only hope was to get to dry land with the little strength he had left.

With a thrill of desperation, Rogers stroked hard and reached the concrete monolith in less than thirty seconds. Fighting to stay above the surface, he searched the smooth, vertical wall, but found nothing on which he could gain a purchase. Dog-paddling for a precious minute, he tried in vain to find some way to climb the fifty feet to the top of the dam. Turning toward the shore, he realized that it was almost three hundred yards away.

Rogers had never been a strong swimmer and for the first time in his life the threat of imminent death crept into his consciousness like a wraith. It was a new concept and his mind, numbed by the events of the past five minutes, did not entirely grasp the finality of the situation. Although he wasn't a deeply religious man, something in his childhood training took hold, and he fervently prayed for the strength to reach the shore. After swimming as hard as he could for a minute, two minutes, three minutes, he knew it was no use—he had only made it a third of the way.

Completely exhausted, he stopped, gasping for breath, his head pounding, his chest aching. Pains began shooting down his left arm and up the side of his neck. His face felt hot, not cold, and the stabbing pains in his chest declared that his laboring heart was the weakest link in the chain.

Wilson Rogers rolled onto his back and floated, trying to breathe deeply against the intense and spreading chest pain, but air would not come fast enough. He felt as if he were suffocating. With an odd detachment, he watched a small snow devil swirl only fifty feet away and thought that fifty feet was really not very far at all. He could easily walk that distance in a few seconds.

Suddenly, the pounding in his ears faded. His eyes widened as the searing pain in his chest abruptly ceased. As the white fog of his last breath curled into the night air, his limp body silently slipped beneath the waves.

Chapter 1

The two men eyed each other warily over the white linen tablecloth. A thick report lay on the table between them. The elegant crystal water goblets had not been touched. A discreet tension filled the air, discouraging the waiter from approaching even though the country club's small dining room was nearly empty. Outside, the mid-afternoon temperature at the swimming pool was nearing one hundred degrees.

Tom Huntington sat on the edge of his chair, leaning slightly forward, both hands palm down. The immaculate cut of his clothes and his posture hinted of a military background. His broad, craggy face held the certain assurance of one in command, and his square jaw was set. Staring at the younger man through steel-grey eyes, he remained silent.

Tony Angelletti scowled as he looked hard at the report. His curly black hair brushed the collar of his charcoal grey suit as he abruptly glanced up. With a look of determination verging on defiance, he drew a deep breath and said, "I can't do it, Tom. I *won't* do it. Whatever was said before, whatever you or the others may have thought about my position on this project, I won't go along with it." His clear, dark eyes were apprehensive, but his voice remained steady and firm.

Leaning forward, Huntington's eyes narrowed. "Don't be stupid, Angelletti. You know what this means to the company. What's good for Southwest Energy is good for the state. What's good for the state is good for the Governor. And you could *be* the Governor, boy. Don't let a little success come between you and your friends." His deadpan gaze was anything but friendly.

Angelletti shrugged. "I have a career to consider, Tom. This data is phony, and it's obvious. The figures are weak—they're simply not believable. We won't need this much power generating capacity for decades, if ever, and there's no good plan to pay for it. This project would be an unnecessary burden on the ratepayers. Sponsoring it could be the end of my political career."

Huntington had long ago perfected his threatening glare and tone of voice. "*Not* voting for it could be the end of the road for you, boy. Do I have to spell it out? *I* put you in office and I can just as easily take you out." A cynical half-smile crept across his face. "Besides, the newspaper is with us. The Governor's onboard. Everyone who counts will support this project. There will *be* no opposition. It's all set."

With absolute conviction, Angelletti calmly replied, "No, let *me* spell it out for *you*, Huntington. I swore an oath to the people of this state. This project is totally bogus. We both know it. I don't care who you've lined up to support it. *I* won't support it, and *I* won't sign the commission order. Period. End of story. Go find yourself another patsy."

The older man blinked twice in disbelief before pushing himself up with both hands. Leaning forward, his bulk was menacing and close, his voice filled with anger. "You're a *fool*, Angelletti. You're *done* in this state." After a brief hesitation, Huntington turned on his heel and strode out of the dining room.

* * * * *

Moments later, Tom Huntington, managing partner of the law firm of Huntington, Bandini & Fane, stepped into the backseat of a stretch Mercedes Benz waiting in front of the country club. He settled into the leather seat, glancing out the window at the golfers putting on the eighteenth hole. The man in the front passenger seat appeared to be ten years younger than Huntington, but was equally well-dressed in a finely-tailored navy suit. Graying at the temples but still athletic in build, Gino Bandini was the very image of the conservative downtown business lawyer. The young driver, Wilbur Olsen, bore a strong family resemblance to Tom Huntington.

As they pulled away from the clubhouse, Bandini turned toward Huntington and ventured, "Any luck?"

"He's an idiot," Huntington growled. "He won't play. But that thickheaded prima donna will wish he had. He could have been Governor."

Bandini chuckled. "This town turns out a fool a minute."

"What the hell are you laughing about, Bandini? You're in this deep enough yourself." Huntington's tone of voice would have stopped a charging bull in its tracks.

"Don't take it so seriously, Tom," Bandini replied. "I know you had high hopes for the boy, but I told you he has a dangerous streak in him. He ran with the wrong crowd in law school. Spent too much time talking about the public interest and the public trust. Too independent. Not greedy enough. Better we find that out now than after we make him Governor."

Huntington glared at Bandini. "That farm boy will never be Governor. And he's not going to blow this deal for us, either. I've been running this state since long before he was born. Without me, he's finished."

Bandini's ever-present smile played across his thin lips. "There's more than one way to skin a cat, Tom. He'll eventually cave in. He's a politician and you know politicians—they're like bananas. First they're green, then they turn yellow, then they turn rotten." He chuckled at his own joke. "Angelletti just needs a little more persuasion. Maybe it's time to call Aberson."

Huntington's frown gave way to a look of dour determination. As the Mercedes wheeled through the massive gates of the posh country club, Huntington said to the driver, "Wilbur, get Aberson on the phone. Tell him to be in my office in half an hour."

* * * * *

Pug Aberson was an eternal fixture in the small world of Oklahoma politics. He had been heavily involved in every gubernatorial campaign for longer than anyone could remember, not to mention the campaigns of state representatives, congressmen, senators and judges. For years, Aberson had always answered direct questions about his background with evasive, jovial responses. His involvement in politics and influence-peddling was so complete that most people had forgotten that he had once been a country lawyer and state legislator.

For more than forty years, Pug had haunted the halls of the Capitol as a lobbyist, consultant, and power broker. During his prime, the short, rotund figure had spent nearly every afternoon in one of the exclusive luncheon clubs atop the tallest buildings in Tulsa and Oklahoma City, working deals. Even at seventy-two, he was still capable of dodging every bullet that came his way. Some thought that he was past his prime, but not Pug. Asked if he ever intended to retire, he would flash a winning grin and respond, "Not as long as I can be of service to the fine citizens of Oklahoma!" But exactly how he served them was never quite clear.

After the secretary announced his arrival, Aberson ambled into Huntington's spacious office on the twelfth floor of Southwest Plaza. He stuck out his hand as Huntington rose from the leather couch. "Tom Huntington, *my* it's good to see you again. Why, you look just as strong as a bull. You must be getting younger every day! Still chasing the young heifers, too, I'd wager."

Huntington's granite face cracked as he raised one corner of his mouth into a half-smile and briefly shook Aberson's hand. "Pug, you're an old rascal and just as ugly as ever. Sit yourself down and tell me who's catching the heat this week." He ushered Aberson to a pair of overstuffed leather chairs by a large window that overlooked a graceful bend in the Arkansas River and the expanse of oil refineries beyond.

"Aw, Tom, you ought to know me better than that by now," Aberson laughed, as he slowly settled into a chair. "I'm not one to kiss and tell. Besides, you've got ears on both ends of the turnpike and more eyes than a bushel of Idaho potatoes. You probably know who half the state senate slept with last night. Why don't you tell *me* something interesting?"

Huntington emitted a guttural sound that passed for a laugh. "Pug, years ago when I was just starting out, an old hand told me that it's not *what* you know, but *who* you know that counts. I took that to heart then and it served me well for a while. But once I knew everyone in the state worth knowing, I learned that it's not *who* you know, but what you know *about them* that puts you ahead of the game."

"I always did like the way you get right to the heart of things, Tom. That's a lesson that doesn't come easy. But it's a good one to know if you're messing around in politics. And Lord knows, we've both done some of that over the years, haven't we?" Aberson laughed and tapped his cane on the marble floor, letting a few seconds slip by before getting down to business. "Now tell me, Tom, what can I do for you today?"

Huntington got straight to the point. "Pug, it appears that there is a need for your services."

Aberson smiled. "Of course, Tom. How can I help?"

"You're aware of the Greenleaf Project that's currently before the commission?"

"Of course I am, Tom. It's been bouncing around in the commission since last summer. I haven't followed it closely, but it seemed to get sidetracked after Commissioner Rogers died in that accident last winter. That was real sad. I always liked Wilson Rogers."

Huntington scowled, withholding comment on Rogers' unfortunate early demise. "You know this project is very important to the company and the voters. I think it's been on hold long enough. Stallings and Barker both resisted the idea at first, but they came around easily enough with a little persuasion. Angelletti, however, is a problem. He's the new kid on the block, filling the seat Rogers vacated, and he's refusing to cooperate. In fact, he's taking an even harder stance than Rogers did." Huntington paused, lowering his voice for effect. "Pug, the company has put a lot of time and effort into this project. Management wants it to go forward—it needs to get through the commission very soon."

The conversation then dropped into a familiar dialogue that had taken place between the two men at least a dozen times over the past thirty years. Pug's watery blue eyes opened wide with a look of great innocence. "Gosh, Tom, I always want to help do what's right. What's your plan?"

Huntington stood and crossed the luxurious office to his inlaid teakwood desk. He unlocked the right top drawer and removed a large manila envelope. Placing the envelope carefully in the middle of the coffee table between them, he said, "This might help change some opinions about the project. Down deep, the commissioners know it will be good for the state. Sometimes they just need a little extra encouragement."

Pug eyed the thick envelope with suppressed excitement, mentally weighing its contents. Based on past experience, it contained not less than a thousand one hundred dollar bills—just enough to make sure that the job was done, but not so much that the commissioners would make unreasonable demands in the future. Pug wasn't familiar with the details of the Greanleaf Project, but he knew that certain individuals stood to make millions. Three commissioners at $10,000 each, maybe $20,000 tops, if they were stubborn, left a tidy sum for a guy with no overhead.

Huntington stared at Aberson, never quite sure about the man he had known for decades, but still willing to take the risk. "Pug, I don't care what it takes to get the votes, and I don't want any of this back, as long as we succeed. How it happens is your business. I have great faith in your ability. Just get the votes, and do it fast."

Pug smiled broadly. He was in familiar territory, completely at ease, truly enjoying the opportunity to productively use his talents. He leaned forward and hoisted himself up with the help of his brass-headed cane. Slipping the manila envelope into a worn leather satchel, he tucked it under his arm and said, "I always try to do what's best for the state, Tom, you know that. And if you say the Greanleaf Project is what we need, well, your word is good enough for me. Get out your ground-breaking shovel, because this deal is as good as done!"

* * * * *

Tony Angelletti had purposely avoided contact with Pug Aberson during his campaign. Although he did not know much about Aberson, he was well aware of his reputation. As a routine part of his planning, Tony had catalogued all the important political players, including lobbyists and large donors. Based on a few stray comments from various people, he chose not to list Aberson as a potential ally. He had always known he would have to deal with him at some point, but Aberson's invitation for drinks at the Summit Club caught him by surprise.

After stepping off the elevator into the dramatic white marble halls of the Summit Club on the fiftieth floor of the Bank of America Tower, the maitre d' led Tony through the huge, carved wooden doors into the main dining room to a table by the windows, where Aberson waited. Aberson was obviously in his element as he waved and nodded to several distinguished patrons.

When Tony approached, the lobbyist struggled to his feet to greet him warmly. "Tony, it's good to see you again!" Pug smiled broadly as he firmly gripped Tony's hand. "It's been way too long. And thank you for meeting me on such short notice. I know you're busy and I appreciate you taking the time."

"It's my pleasure, Pug. Thanks for inviting me. I've been meaning to call you since the election, but you know how it is, too many irons in the fire. I'm glad you took the initiative. What can I do for you?"

Accustomed to the endless palaver typical of the good old boys network, Tony's directness took Aberson a little by surprise. "Well, Tony," he replied with an obsequious smile, "I just thought we should get to know each other a little bit. If you have the time, I'll buy you a steak dinner, or we can just share a drink and talk about affairs of state. I'd like to learn your thoughts on some of the current issues before the commission."

"Gee, Pug, I have dinner plans for tonight, but I suppose a drink would be fine."

Aberson had already waved to the waiter, who appeared with two whiskeys on the rocks. "I hope you're happy with the best single malt," Pug said, raising his glass for a toast. "And now," he continued with a flourish, "here's to the Great State of Oklahoma and its newest public utility commissioner. May his first term be pleasurable, productive and profitable!"

"I'll drink to that," Tony replied, raising the crystal highball glass and taking a sip of the golden liquid. Setting his glass on the table, he leaned back and smiled, knowing better than to get too cozy.

"Tony, you're a bright young man," Aberson continued earnestly. "Your campaign was brilliant. You have a future in this state. You have progressive ideas and you're good with people. I just want to do whatever I can to help you because I know that you're going to be very good for Oklahoma. I fully expect that you'll be Governor some day."

Tony laughed. "Gee, I love that kind of talk, Pug. You keep that up and I'll have no choice but to appoint you to my kitchen cabinet!"

Pug smiled and nodded amicably. "No, seriously, Tony, you're going places. Maybe straight to the top. But you can't forget the first rule of politics. You gotta help those who can help themselves."

Tony gave him a quizzical look. "Now…what rule was that?"

"You gotta help those who can help themselves." Pug nodded slowly and seriously, looking Tony in the eyes. "You know, Tony, there are forces in every state who can accomplish their purposes with or without you. They can help themselves. They're the ones who you *have* to help, Tony, or they'll help themselves anyway. And that would be bad for you." Aberson glanced out the window and took a long, slow sip of his drink.

"Pug, what are you talking about?"

"You know, Tony, the ones that matter. The ones you can't do without— the power players. They'll see you to the Governor's office or see that you never amount to a hill of beans." Pug took another swallow of his drink and motioned for the waiter, raising his glass.

Tony warily waited.

"You're pretty new at this game, and I've been in it for about a thousand years. Let me help you understand something. Things can go smoothly, or things can get rough. Your work at the commission can be easy, productive, and profitable, or it can be unpleasant and unproductive. A handful of people will make the difference. You need to know who they are and you need to give them what they want, when they ask for it. If you do, you'll be a hero. The public will love you. They'll make sure of that. But if you don't help them, Tony, you'll regret it. It's been that way for fifty years, and it's not about to change." Pug leaned forward, placing an arthritic hand on Tony's arm as he continued, "I just want to help you understand what your job is, so that you'll become the great success that we all know you *can* be."

Tony had been watching Aberson intently. His gaze strayed out the window to the dramatic golden sunset reflected on the Arkansas River. He could see for at least twenty miles down the river to the west and north, all the way to the green rolling hills of Osage County. "Oh, my. Look at that sunset, Pug."

He turned to look. A minute passed in silence. Tony took a sip of his drink. Aberson shifted in his chair and searched for the waiter with his second drink.

Still taking in the fiftieth floor view, Tony said quietly, "Pug, I think you came here to tell me something. What is it?"

"Tony," Pug said earnestly, "you know there's money to be made in your new job. You can make a lot of money at the commission. You worked hard for it, son. Law school is no picnic. I know that the campaign trail was grueling, with all of the speeches and glad-handing. And the risk! All of that effort with no guarantee of success. You're set to live off the fat of the land now, *if you don't forget who your friends are.*" Pug scratched the back of his hand. Tiny beads of perspiration were beginning to appear on his pink forehead.

Although Pug could not tell from his calm appearance, Tony was quickly considering his options. There was no time to plan a response to Aberson's obvious and unanticipated overture, but he knew he had to confirm his suspicions.

"Let's drop the platitudes, Pug, and stop shadowboxing. Speak your mind. This doesn't happen to have anything to do with the Greanleaf Project, does it?"

Suddenly, Pug was all business. "Okay, Tony, I'll be straight with you. Some people want that project to happen. They're people you should want to please. If you help them, they'll help you. Over time, you'll find yourself in a very favorable position, both politically and financially. I am in a position to make that assurance."

The message was loud and clear. Although he knew what was about to happen, he wasn't sure how to respond. He needed to buy some time, to end the conversation before too much was said. Taking a deep breath, he sat up straight in his chair and stated, "Pug, I appreciate your advice. It's nice to know that I can count on your support. And don't you worry, I do know who my friends are."

Pug was anxious. Frustration pinched his round, pink face. He had hoped to close the deal in one meeting. In the past, commissioners, state senators, judges, even a congressman or two, had known the score and been waiting with both hands out. This new generation had too damn many idealistic college kids and not enough old-fashioned, homegrown politicians.

Tony stood, and Aberson rose to shake his hand, knowing that the meeting was over. A sudden smile swept away Pug's nervousness and he was again the consummate politician. "Tony, we need to talk again real soon. I want you to get off on the right foot. You go think about what I said, and I know that you'll do the right thing. 'Cause Tony, *there's nothing else* to *do*," he whispered with a wink.

* * * * *

At half past twelve the following day, Tony picked up the telephone in his office and dialed a familiar number. After two rings, a young woman's voice answered. "Law offices, may I help you?"

"Natalie, this is Tony Angelletti."

"Oh hey, where have you been? I haven't seen you in months!"

"I'm still pursuing that fruitless but faithful quest for an available young lady who can match your peerless beauty and grace, love."

"You *are* a sweet talker, aren't you? You already have more ladies than you can count! What would you do with another one?"

"Just leave that to me, love. When the time comes, I'm sure we'll think of something."

"Oh, I'm *sure* you will!"

He chuckled, easily envisioning the sweet young receptionist blushing. "I really do need to talk with Sam today. Do you know where I can reach him?"

"He's out to lunch right now. If you're downtown, I bet you could catch him at Louie's on the square."

"Thanks, Natalie. You know that I love you."

"Yeah, me and all the other girls west of the Mississippi. So, when are you coming to see us?"

Tony laughed. "I'd come right now, sweetie, but I'd have to take a ticket and wait in line behind all your other love interests."

"Yeah, yeah, you're all talk but no game," she playfully challenged.

"I'll see you soon, I promise. Bye for now." Cradling the receiver, he headed for the door.

* * * * *

Sam Littlehawk leaned his wooden chair against the ancient brick wall of Louie's and gazed out the window. Although he enjoyed Louie's pub atmosphere, hot pasta, and cold beer, the real attraction of the place was the front window's view of the city's street life. Strategically located on Main Mall, Louie's was at the center of downtown. During the noon hour, virtually everyone who worked downtown passed by Louie's. Sam browsed the newspaper and watched the parade of sun dresses on the mall, while nibbling on a sandwich. He was scanning the sports page when Tony dragged up a chair across from him and plopped down.

"Well, there you are," Sam said, straight-faced. "I've been expecting you for about three months now."

Something between a grin and a grimace spread across Tony's face. "Sambo, I knew you'd be here when I needed you. And here you are! Sorry I haven't caught up with you sooner, man, but it's been pretty crazy lately."

Sam wasn't going to let him off quite so easily. "Yeah, between that new commissioner job and all the highfalutin' ladies, I bet you're burning the candle at both ends again, just like in the old days," he said with a wry smile.

"Well, I guess things don't change all that much," Tony smirked. "But I've sure had some fascinating new experiences since I last saw you." With a glance around the room, he dropped the bantering tone a notch. "Sam, can we talk? I think I need a quarter's worth of your sage legal advice."

Sam squinted at his friend, the politician. "Are you serious? You mean you'd pay two bits for the same gibberish that you've been getting free for twenty years? Praise the Lord, it's finally come! Time to cash in!"

"Now let's not get carried away there, buddy," Tony retorted. "I might pay two bits for some good *legal* advice, as opposed to your usual *illegal* advice. And it's gotta be *good* advice, none of that hogwash you sell your clients every day for five bucks a minute. You *are* still a lawyer, aren't you? Or are you really an ancient Aztec warrior, reincarnated and dumped here for the purpose of chasing ambulances, saving wayward kids, and defending little old ladies against evil bill collectors?"

"Is that a yes or no question?" Sam asked innocently.

Tony rolled his eyes and shook his head. "Actually, believe it or not, Sambo, I am quite serious. I'm here seeking your counsel and advice in a matter of great importance, both to me personally and to everyone in Oklahoma—a matter of such vast magnitude and portent that it may escape even your quite considerable comprehension. Nevertheless, I humbly seek your guidance, counsel, and advice," he added, sitting up a little straighter.

Sam smiled wickedly. "In that case, my friend, it'll cost you big time. Ten dollars cash, no credit, no wampum, no tomatoes from Grandma Leone's garden, no patronage position as your campaign treasurer. Cold, hard cash. Pay me tomorrow. Now how can I help you?"

Tony laughed aloud, then took a deep breath and shifted gears, still smiling, but dropping his joking tone entirely. "Seriously, Sam, as my lawyer, I want to tell you something that's very sensitive. Anything I say is confidential and privileged and I am instructing you not to repeat it to anyone for any reason, unless you obtain permission from me first. Is that agreed?"

Sam nodded his assent, fully aware of the implications. "Don't worry, Tony," Sam said quietly, "your secret's safe with me."

Tony glanced around the dining room. The lunch hour was winding down and most of the tables were empty.

"You are not going to *believe* this." He leaned forward, softly recounting the details of his meetings with Tom Huntington and Pug Aberson.

Across the mall, a tall man in a light grey jacket sat on a park bench reading a newspaper. Occasionally, he glanced over the paper at the front window of Louie's.

Chapter 2

Sam and Tony walked the block and a half north on Main Mall to Sam's office in the Old Union Station. The broad windows of his second floor suite afforded an excellent view across the fountains and arbors of Liberty Square. The ornate gothic decoration and cut stone arches in the old building suited Sam, as did the mix of small businesses and artists who had found a home amid its asymmetric interior spaces and studios. Once a bustling center of rail transportation and commerce, it had long ago been abandoned by the railroads. Bordered on the south by the city's downtown business district and on the north by the nouveau art district with its tangle of restaurants, studios, galleries and clubs, it provided an intriguing blend of history, culture, business and the arts.

After three years at the Station, Sam had developed a strong bond with several other tenants. He enjoyed the boisterous good humor of Mel Feather, whose Native American Art Gallery filled a vast room that had once housed porters and luggage bound for Chicago, Phoenix, and other distant points. Across the cavernous tiled lobby were the offices of the Hispanic American Society and Gina's Language Center, which provided translation and interpretive services in several languages for the city's international business community. Near the revolving brass doors, Camille's Café offered sandwiches, gourmet coffees, and fresh pastries to the diverse crowd.

The second floor housed an international trading company that sold oil field pipe and supplies to the Middle East, and the offices of several independent attorneys. Sam's office was the largest single office space on the second floor, with an excellent southern exposure and a window that caught the faint aroma of Camille's delicious coffees wafting up from below.

Tony sat on the worn leather couch in Sam's office and sipped from a cardboard cup of Camille's Kona blend. His voice was tinged with bitterness as he summarized, "So that's it, Sam. Sell out to vested interests or get out of politics. It's as clear as the nose on your face. I never thought it would come to this—at least not in such a big way—and so fast. I haven't even been in office for three months!"

Sam leaned back in his antique oak desk chair, leather boots on his desk, hands cupped behind his head, deep in thought. His familiarity with the Huntington bunch stretched back to the summer after his second year of law school. At the time, it had been an honor to be selected for a clerkship from a field of a hundred prime candidates. A Native American with tribal standing and top grades in law school, Sam could have been an asset to Huntington, Bandini & Fane. His primary project as a summer clerk had been to assist in the ongoing public utility rate making process for the firm's key client, Southwest Energy Company. During long lunches at the Petroleum Club and the Summit, Sam had caught a glimpse of the good old boys network, the political maneuvering and the outright horse-trading that was involved. He had kept quiet, done his work, and learned all that he could.

Despite his youth, or perhaps because of it, some senior staffers were drawn to Sam's easy, quiet manner. During his short stay, they had confided in him and he had learned about personal alliances and the income levels of various members of the firm. Gossip among the disillusioned staff soon led Sam to realize that most of the firm's lawyers were driven by greed and intimidation. Sinister undercurrents permeated the place and it quickly became clear that honesty was not a virtue that led to success. While some of his classmates were lured by the posh surroundings and the power wielded by the partners, others were simply attracted by the promise of easy money. Sam wasn't attracted by either. He soon grew disgusted by what he considered to be an abomination of the guiding principles of the law.

Huntington demanded loyalty, but most of all, he demanded billings. A bright and capable young lawyer might be an asset to the firm, but a lawyer who could spend six hours at the golf course, take a middle manager of Southwest Energy out for drinks and dinner, and still find a way to bill the company fourteen hours a day would be a surefire success. No other firm in town paid better for lawyers and staff alike, but none demanded more. Huntington's strict policies of loyalty and obedience were routinely ignored, however, and certain senior staff seemed to thrive on secretly breaching his unyielding code of silence. The restrooms and break rooms buzzed with stories of ruthlessness and treachery.

The utility company's legal bills, of course, were part of the rate base and were routinely passed through to the company's customers by a compliant Public Utility Commission. For many years, the commissioners had simply accepted that legal fees and expenses were a necessary cost of doing business, and the bills were never questioned. If a few entertainment expenses for the executives found their way into the legal bills, classified under deposition costs or library additions, who was to question it? Likewise, no one questioned the thousands of hours of attorney time it took every month just to keep the utility company in business. The law firm's bills were paid within hours of their submission to management, all of which took place on the twelfth floor of Southwest Plaza, an immense marble edifice that was home to both the Huntington firm and the utility company that supported it.

As executives of the company and the firm's lawyers advanced to higher positions in the organization, alliances were forged. They realized that their futures were secure as long as Huntington and Pug Aberson maintained their influence, and the cycle continued. What was good for the company was good for the firm, and vice versa. Huntington and his allies in senior management rewarded the executives of the company and the commissioners, and the ratepayers footed the bill. After all, what was a measly five bucks a month on a million different electric bills?

Sam had known little of this twelve years before, when he had been called into Huntington's office for a personal exit interview at the end of his summer clerkship. At that time, he had seen only the general contours of the relationship between Southwest Energy and the Huntington firm. But he had known enough to realize that he could never fit the Huntington mold. He had declined their offer of a full time position after law school, letting Huntington know that he had several offers from regional law firms, but he was considering a job with a senator in Washington, or possibly running for the tribal council. In the years that followed, however, Sam had continued to watch and listen and had learned more about the company and its cadre of lawyers.

"Earth to Sam, earth to Sam, come in Sam," Tony said as he swigged the last of his coffee.

Sam shook his head and blinked. "Sorry, I was just thinking back on that summer I spent with Huntington."

"With Huntington? Am I in the right camp here? Has my white knight been bedding down with the enemy?"

Ignoring him, Sam replied, "From what you say, Huntington and his cohorts have taken their petty graft to a new dimension."

Tony grimaced. "This Greenleaf Project is beyond belief. It's ludicrous to think that we need another five hundred megawatts of power generating capacity. We have thirty percent more capacity than we need right now, and more under construction. Even assuming substantial growth and sales on the western grid, we're good for at least ten more years. The ratepayers don't need to spend half a billion dollars, especially on another coal plant. Then there are the environmental issues that haven't been adequately addressed. There is no way that much coal power could be needed in our lifetimes, Sambo, and I plan to live a long time."

Sam's brow furrowed. "Something ain't right here, hombre. Huntington and his buddies have been siphoning money here and there for decades, but they've never tried anything this big. Why are they so greedy all of a sudden? Aside from the usual rake-off, where will the money go?"

"Bet you a dollar to a donut it won't go to the Widows and Orphans Home."

Sam spun his swivel chair to face the computer on his credenza and selected the Internet icon. "The information in your project report is pretty sketchy, but with a little imagination, maybe we can learn a thing or two about this deal."

Half an hour later, Sam hit the print button and disconnected from the net. "It's not much, but it's a start," he said. "An address in New York City for Midwest Holdings, Ltd., the parent company of Greenleaf Project Partners, and an address in Oklahoma City for Development Properties, Inc., the record owner of the project site."

Tony shrugged as he stared out the window. "I know what this is, Sammy. I can smell it. I don't need public records to tell me. This project is designed to line the pockets of the senior executives of the company and the firm and to provide a capstone for Huntington's long career of embezzling public funds. How they actually accomplish it is immaterial."

"You may be right," Sam replied. "That may be all there is to it. A few family members own the land, an uncle owns a construction company, some kickbacks from key suppliers, they manage to rake off thirty or forty million bucks, and the state ends up with a white elephant that will drain the ratepayers' pockets for decades. But then again, there could be more to it than that. Something tells me that Huntington and his cronies didn't cook up this scheme alone. It's too big for them. I think I may need to go visit the Big Apple."

Tony turned toward his friend. "Well, I managed to kill your whole afternoon, Sam. The least I can do is buy you a beer. Let's talk about this again tomorrow. Meanwhile, it's time to clear our heads. And there's someone I want you to meet."

Sam closed the project report and dropped it on the desk with a thud. "Now you're talking! Your account stands at three longnecks, *and* five pounds of Grandma Leone's tomatoes, payable on demand. Time to pay up! Let's go!"

* * * * *

The Full Moon Café was in the afternoon lull as Meg, the bartender, polished the long mahogany bar to prepare for Friday's typical happy hour rush. Two green and brown neon palm trees framed a large mirror behind the bar and a white full moon hovered in the expanse between them.

At 4:35, Katrina Petrovna settled on a high stool at a table near the bar. Just a few months out of Moscow, she had recently completed her first semester at the University of Tulsa. Like many of the students and faculty, Katrina found the restaurant's casual, friendly atmosphere perfectly suited to her temperament.

As a young ballerina in the Russian National Ballet, Katrina had jumped at the opportunity to further her education by accepting a teaching fellowship in the United States. The international exchange program between the Universities of Tulsa and Zelenograd offered new contacts and a chance for international exposure for the beautiful, talented young dancer. Although Tulsa hosted an excellent professional ballet troupe in which she played a key role, at the moment, her career was the farthest thing from her mind.

From a distance, Katrina's lithe figure seemed to bear the weight of the world. Her lovely, full lips showed no hint of a smile and her brow was creased as she thought of the two men wreaking havoc in her life. She stared at her long, slender fingers, wondering what to do.

Katrina's trance was broken when Tony lifted her hand and placed it in his. Sliding onto the stool across from her, he smiled and gently squeezed her fingers. "For a beautiful ballerina who has just received rave reviews from every critic in Dallas, you look pretty glum."

She managed a half-smile. "Tony, you compliment me and torment me."

"A little pain and pleasure mixed together can be a fun thing," he replied, his eyes twinkling. "You should give it a chance. But in the meantime, I have a surprise for you."

Tony glanced at Sam, who was approaching the table. "I brought a friend to meet you. Kate, this is Sam Littlehawk. I've known Sam since we were kids. Sam, meet the most beautiful ballerina in the entire world."

Sam smiled, extending his hand. His dark brown eyes revealed that he agreed with Tony's assessment.

Katrina looked into Sam's eyes and felt her pulse quicken. In a less than a second, she took in his tall, muscular form, strikingly handsome features, piercing eyes and smooth, tanned complexion. Something in his bearing reminded her of Baryshnikov, only darker and more powerful. Taking his outstretched hand, she felt the strength in his grip and his hard, calloused palm, and a slight tremor coursed through her body.

"It's a pleasure to meet you, Katrina. Your beauty and grace are legendary." Sam bowed slightly without breaking eye contact. He held her hand for a second longer, then released it. "Congratulations on your success in Dallas."

Katrina smiled and modestly looked down for a moment. "Thank you for your kind words. But I only danced. It was not even a full ballet…"

Sam chuckled. "From the reviews, Katrina, it seems that when you dance, the world stops turning."

Though she was accustomed to lavish praise, Katrina blushed.

Tony gave Sam a sidelong glance.

Sam smiled at his old friend. "Tony, you have always been the luckiest man on earth, and your luck is still holding. Katrina, you'd better be careful with this Italian stallion. Your beauty and his luck could make for a dangerous combination." He caught and held Katrina's eyes for a few more seconds, then glanced up at the large, illuminated clock on the wall behind the bar. With a little gasp, he added, "Oh, geez, Tony, I almost forgot! I've got to be somewhere soon. I promised to referee at the Big Brothers basketball game tonight. I'd sure like to stay longer, but I have to run. Nice to meet you, Katrina. I'll see you kids later." Without waiting for a reply, he turned and walked out the door.

Alone together, Tony leaned close to Katrina. In the few short weeks they had known each other, they had developed a strong bond. He was attracted to Katrina for all of the obvious reasons, and was somewhat relieved that their extensive professional involvements kept thoughts of a serious relationship at bay. "So what is it, princess, why the long face?" he asked.

"Oh Tony," she sighed. "You remember me telling you about Anatoly Karmakov—the man who was obsessed with me in Moscow. He's here now. He found me at the University and says he wants to marry me and take me to Europe."

"Might be a good catch, Kate. A brilliant musician like Karmakov, professor, composer, world class pianist, matched with an internationally acclaimed ballerina—you would have the world by the tail!"

"Shhh! Don't say such a thing, Tony! Anatoly is not a bad man, I think. He was good to me at first, but he is so intense, so harsh, so driven. And there is no, how do you say, 'chemistry' between us? Is that the word you used?"

Tony smiled wanly. He took a deep breath and thought for a moment about his many experiences with the eternal triangle before responding, "Yes, Kate, there's definitely chemistry between you and me."

For nearly two decades, Tony had been a dance-away lover. Using his powerful charisma and strong animal magnetism, which he directed both consciously and unconsciously toward every attractive woman he met, the chase was always the game. But when the object of his desire fell prey to his beguiling charm, he invariably lost interest and moved on.

"Can I get you something?" The waitress smiled at Tony, who glanced at Katrina. "Friday night, Kate. How about a margarita?"

"Thank you, but I dance tomorrow."

"Just give us a minute to think about it, okay?" he asked the waitress. With a smile and a nod, she left.

Katrina's dark eyes were still troubled. "Tony, I must tell you one thing more. Anatoly is quite angry. He thinks you are taking me away from him. But I was never his—we only dated casually for a few months. I tried to tell him that you are just a friend. But there is talk about us at the University and he is so passionate and so angry. Tony, you must be careful!"

Tony pondered her words for a moment. He had encountered more than his share of jealous suitors in the past. But in a moment, his perplexed look was replaced with a smile. Always more comfortable with the direct approach to every problem, he asked, "Where is Anatoly tonight, Kate? We'll just go set this thing straight right now. This is nothing but a little misunderstanding. I'm sure we can talk it out." Before the words were out of his mouth, Tony was moving with Katrina in tow.

A few seconds later, a man at the bar casually tossed down a twenty dollar bill and followed them out the door.

* * * * *

Two miles away, dusk was falling in the canyons between the tall buildings downtown. Main Mall was deserted except for a flurry of activity in front of the lone convenience store on the distant south end. The doors of Old Union Station were already locked.

A tall man in a grey jacket briskly approached the Station's entrance from the mall. After flashing a plastic identification card in front of the security device at the front door, he entered the lobby then quickly ascended the stairs to the second floor. Without any difficulty, he located the Law Offices of Sam Littlehawk, P.C., and manipulated the door's lock. Entering the foyer, he proceeded to the inner office. Placing a tiny device inside the receiver of the phone, he used a white handkerchief to carefully wipe it clean, before planting a device the size of a dime in a niche in the scroll work on the front of the large antique desk.

In less than five minutes, the silent intruder slipped back down the stairs and out of the building.

* * * * *

At nine the next morning, Tony let himself in the front door of Sam's office. He found Sam enjoying a steaming cappuccino while sitting in an easy chair with his feet propped up on the low marble window sill. Tony closed the door, crossed the room, and eased into Sam's desk chair. The two knew each other so well that there was no need for small talk. A comfortable silence spanned a few minutes.

Finally, Tony spoke. "Sam, I've been thinking."

"Uh oh, now we're in trouble."

"Well, this is a really crazy idea. I know it's crazy. Actually, it's totally insane."

Sam gave Tony a deadpan stare. "I guess that means you haven't changed your ways."

Tony rolled his eyes. "You know, I've thought about this ever since law school, even before law school. I think anyone who goes into politics has to face it some day. And it's not pretty. Apparently, there are two ways to get to the Governor's office. I could let those creeps bully and buy me, then they'd own me for the rest of my life—I'd be their pawn. Or, I can face them, clean out the rat's nest right now, and ride to the Governor's office on a wave of popular support. *Which is me, Sam? Which is me?* Remember Professor Deakins' class back in college, PoliSci 201? Remember the *real* leaders who have stood firm against overwhelming odds and won? Remember King? Ghandi? Kennedy? Remember the way it's *supposed* to work? Government *for* the people..."

Sam nodded. "And how many of those great leaders lived long enough to write their autobiographies?"

"What choice do I have, Sam? Cave in and be their shill, their lackey for life? Resign from office and leave the territory for good with my tail between my legs? Give up? What would Momma Leone think? That ain't me, Sam. Besides, I never could stand the thought of skunks in the henhouse." Tony wrinkled his nose for emphasis.

Sam thought about all the Friday nights when he had handed off the football to Tony and watched as his friend, known to the local high school football announcer as the "Italian Stallion," charge headlong with total abandon into a solid wall of defenders. Never a moment's hesitation—no matter how uneven the odds—just total dedication to the cause. Then he remembered their late night political discussions in college and later in law school, and their mutual commitment to ethics and the rule of law. Sam knew Tony too well to think that he would back away from this challenge, even though the enemy this time was formidable, ruthless, and possibly deadly.

He looked at Tony for a long minute. "Nothing I could say would change your mind, would it?"

"Nope."

"So what's your idea?" Sam ventured.

Tony bounced up, flashing a winning grin at his friend. "Yes! Sam, you da man! I can carry the ball anywhere, if you'll just quarterback! It'll be just like old times!" His childlike enthusiasm was comic as he danced a little jig around Sam's desk. After a brief celebration, he calmed down a bit and asked, "Didn't you once mention that you have a good friend in the FBI? I think it's time we give him a call."

* * * * *

Sunday morning, Pug Aberson rolled out of bed late, a little fuzzy-headed from the night before. He had spent much of Saturday afternoon at the horse races, then whiled away a long evening sipping single malts, smoking cigars and swapping lies at the jockey club, just like the good old days. It was great to have money to spend again. But it did seem to be getting harder and harder to shake off the effects the next morning.

After two cups of strong coffee, Pug showered and dressed casually, ready for the golf course. He had been greatly relieved when Angelletti called early Saturday afternoon to ask for a meeting. It was a positive sign. Angelletti's jovial tone implied that the boy had finally come to his senses. His suggestion of Sunday brunch at the country club had sounded good to Aberson. Pug had felt positively smug as he drove to the track and even better when he collected eight to one on a hundred dollar bet and bought a round for the entire sky box. He didn't feel quite so good now, though, driving to the country club with half a pot of strong coffee and the remains of several whiskeys churning in his round belly.

Tony had arrived at the club early. The morning was pleasantly warm and sunny, promising another hot afternoon to come. He secured a secluded table on the veranda, where they could enjoy the morning breeze and where Aberson would feel comfortable talking.

At Aberson's suggestion, they ordered a "bracing" Irish coffee "to get the day started right," and the two men swapped small talk and ate for three-quarters of an hour. They had finished their eggs Benedict and were still nibbling at an array of fresh fruits and sweetbreads when Aberson finally got to the point.

"So Tony, have you thought about our talk?"

"I have thought about it, Pug."

"So, what do you think?"

"Well, Pug, I think it's quite clear that we both want what's best for the State of Oklahoma."

"That's my boy!" Aberson exclaimed, "That's the ticket!"

"We just have to decide what's best for the state, Pug. What do our friends want me to do?" Tony shifted in his seat and leaned forward a little.

"You know what they want, Tony. They want your vote, that's all."

"And they're willing to pay for it?"

Aberson's joyful demeanor began to melt. He eyed Tony through watery, bloodshot eyes. He had made hundreds of deals before, even on this very veranda, but it had rarely been necessary to talk about it so much. The first payoff was always the most difficult. After that, the marks got more cooperative. They had no choice. What was the problem with this kid, anyway?

Pug reached into a satchel and pulled out an envelope. Without saying a word, he placed it on the table in front of Tony.

Tony glanced at the waiter, who was at the far end of the veranda attending the only other occupied table, but made no move for the envelope.

"I don't want to open that right now, Pug. Not here. Maybe you can just tell me what's in it."

Pug cringed. His head hurt, his stomach was queasy, and this brat sure wasn't making his job any easier. What was so hard about taking a small token of appreciation from friends anyway? What was so damned hard about putting an envelope in your pocket? Pug had a moment of self-doubt—maybe he wasn't as smooth and persuasive as he used to be. Maybe he was just getting too old for this job. He wished he could go back to the high rolling days of the oil boom when everyone was on the take and the only question was how much. He'd just have to lay the cards on the table.

"Come on, Tony, it's payday. Ten big ones. One hundred crisp, new hundred dollar bills. I told you that your friends would take care of you. There's more where that came from and it's yours. Take it."

Tony leaned forward in a confidential pose to say, "Pug, I'd like to know who my friends are, so I can send them a thank you note."

"No thanks necessary, Tony, just vote right."

"Pug, I have to know. Is it Huntington? Which of the kind folks at Southwest Energy are my friends?"

"For God's sake, *everyone* is your friend!" Pug was beginning to sweat more profusely and his stomach was churning. Maybe that second Irish coffee wasn't such a good idea. The sun felt hot and his vision was starting to blur.

Tony pressed again. "Tom Huntington met me here last week to ask for my vote on the Greenleaf Project. Is that what this is about? Let's quit beating around the bush. Is Huntington offering me ten thousand dollars to vote for the project?"

Pug was feeling faint and desperately needed to go to the men's room. "Take it as you will, Tony, but just take it."

Tony stepped in for the knockout. "Pug, is this the company's money? Do I have friends in Southwest Energy?"

Pug paled, fighting back another wave of queasiness. Although he didn't mean to answer, the words leaped out, "You don't think Huntington got so filthy rich by giving away his *own* money, do you?" Pug's eyes widened as he realized what he had said.

Tony rose and slipped the envelope back into Aberson's satchel. Patting his arm, he said, "This meeting has been a great help to me Pug. Let me think about it just a little more. I'll get back to you in a day or two. That's a promise."

As Tony walked briskly down the stairs of the veranda, Pug rose stiffly from his chair, wondering if he would make it to the men's room in time.

* * * * *

Sam shook off a sweaty leather work glove and reached across the front seat of the Jeep to answer his cell phone. Braking to a stop at the top of a rise in the pasture, he glanced at the caller ID and said, "Hi, Tony. How did it go?"

Tony was ecstatic. "You won't believe it, Sam. Wait until you hear it. Aberson was classic. If this isn't enough to bring in the feds, I don't know what is! Haul your butt into town so we can get to work!"

"Hold your horses there, cowboy. I got a lost mama cow and calf to find. And you aren't going to call in the cavalry on Sunday afternoon. The bad guys will still be there in the morning, as long as you don't tell 'em we're coming. Meet me at the Station at nine tonight and we'll lay a plan."

"Perfect," Tony said with satisfaction. "And Tonto," he added, "Catch me a rattlesnake while you're out there in the canebrakes and canyons."

"Sounds like you already caught one, city boy. And you'd better hold it good and tight by the neck, or it'll sure enough swing around and bite you."

Chapter 3

Sam rolled his Jeep over a curb in front of the Station seconds before Tony eased his Austin Healey into a slot across the street. Sam's dark hair was still damp from a quick shower, and he wore clean blue jeans and a white cotton tee shirt that revealed a sinuous body strong from constant ranch work. The two men lost no time making their way to Sam's office.

Once inside, Tony handed a microcassette to Sam, who stopped in the reception area at Natalie's desk. He dropped the tape into the Dictaphone next to the computer and hit the play button. After listening for several minutes, Sam stopped the tape and asked, "Has anyone else heard this?"

"No."

"Good. Let's keep it that way for now."

"Do you think we have what we need? Can we nail 'em with this?"

"Depends. It would create a hell of a scandal, but proof beyond a reasonable doubt of a felony? I doubt it. And who have we got? Who are your "friends" in the company? Who is involved in this besides Huntington and Aberson? If the story broke, I doubt Aberson would be anywhere he could be found for a very long time. He might not live long enough to give testimony. And Huntington would deny knowledge of any meeting between you and Aberson. He'd say it was a set up. It's all circumstantial, except for this tape."

Crestfallen, Tony groaned. "So what are you saying? We still need more proof?"

Sam nodded. "Remember—we've got to get 'em good and tight around the neck or they'll swing around and bite us."

Standing, he opened the door to his office. Tony followed him inside and sat on the wide marble windowsill, while Sam eased into his leather easy chair and propped his feet on the sill.

"So where do we go from here, Sam? You're calling the plays."

Through the broad window, Sam could see the top of the twenty-two story building that housed the headquarters of Southwest Energy. Somewhere on the top floor of the grey marble edifice was a conference room where Huntington and his protégées plotted strategies to lighten the load of the average ratepayer and fill the executives' personal coffers. And now they were planning a colossal waste of public funds that would be a financial burden on the unsuspecting public, especially those living on fixed incomes, for decades to come. Sam took no pleasure in the thought of foiling their plans for the Greanleaf Project. It was just something that had to be done, like pulling a fat tick off a dog's back.

As Sam stared at the dark monolith a few blocks away, an idea began to take shape. "I think I've been hanging around with crazy Italians too much. Now *I'm* having crazy ideas. This one's a doozy. Totally insane."

Tony beamed. "That's my man."

"Somewhere in that building over there," Sam motioned toward the edifice, "is the information we need. All we have to do is go and get it."

"Oh, now you really *are* talking crazy. That place is guarded like Fort Knox. And I don't think the information you want is going to be filed in the public archives."

"No, but I've got a pretty good idea where to look," Sam said with a glint in his eye.

"If you're thinking what I think you're thinking, it probably involves about a dozen felonies. There would be no more law or politics for two tired old jailbirds released after an eon or two in the slammer."

"Forget that, Tony. If we got caught, we probably wouldn't live long enough to be prosecuted."

"What about our oath to uphold the law?"

"And to do justice, Tony. Don't forget the part about 'upholding the principles of justice.' Sometimes, upholding the principles of justice is just not as easy as blind obedience to a statute book. Sometimes, we have to weigh difficult choices and choose the lesser evil. Now that you've really got me thinking about it, we can't just sit back and let this travesty go forward. It's a major public rip off and they're trying to effectuate it through bribery of public officials, specifically, you. It stinks. And I have no doubt that it goes a lot deeper than we know."

"So you're saying we have to charge the citadel?"

"Not a frontal assault, just a short visit to help an old friend with some filing. Besides, when I left the firm after my clerkship twelve years ago, Huntington did say to 'stop by anytime!'"

Sam looked at Tony with the same cracked grin that Tony had seen when they were both climbing on saddle broncos at the Willow Springs rodeo the summer after their senior year of high school.

"And you call us Italians crazy," Tony said, shaking his head is disbelief.

"So you're in?" Sam asked, still grinning.

"Do I look like a lily-livered bench warmer, coach?"

"Okay, let me think about this. Tomorrow, we'll talk time, place, and means."

* * * * *

At ten minutes past eight on Monday morning, Dave Sanders walked through the doorway of the state headquarters of the FBI and poured the first of ten cups of coffee he would consume before noon. He settled in his aging desk chair to begin reviewing seven thick files that comprised only a tiny fraction of the documentation of a new electronic bank fraud investigation he had been assigned. Ten minutes later, he was noting with interest that his own small retirement account was on deposit in one of the target banks, when the telephone rang. He reached for the receiver, knocking over his half-full styrofoam cup of coffee in the process. Another Monday.

"Sanders," he said gruffly as he grabbed a wad of napkins to sop up the spill.

"Dave, this is Sam Littlehawk. You got a few minutes this morning?"

Sanders stopped mopping. "Is this the same Sam Littlehawk who wanted to borrow a few little trinkets on Saturday afternoon?"

"Is this the same Dave Sanders who can eat an entire lemon meringue pie without lifting a fork?" Sam shot back, recalling Sanders' selfless participation in a recent charity pie eating contest.

"You got me there, buddy. What is it now, still trying to figure out which button on that contraption is *Play?*"

"Can you meet me in ten minutes at Camille's? If you do, there'll be a double latté and a chocolate éclair waiting for you," Sam offered.

"Man, you don't play fair. You know all my weaknesses."

By eight-thirty, the two men were head to head in a corner booth in the back of Camille's. A few patrons were coming in for shots of espresso or Danishes, but the main dining area in the rear of the shop was virtually empty.

"What's so important that you're willing to spring for breakfast on Monday morning?" Sanders asked between enormous bites of pastry.

Sam stirred his mocha. "I need a little more help, Dave."

"Didn't the wire work?"

"You won't believe it when you hear it. It's good, Dave. But we need more. And there's no way we can hit the same target again, at least not now. We have to try another route and I'll need your help." He looked intently at his friend, who knew more than anyone else in the state about covert information gathering.

Sanders hedged. "It would really help, buddy, I mean *really* help me a lot, if I knew what this was all about. I can bend the rules a *leetle* bit for you, but there are limits. I'm way out of bounds already. When are you going to return the wire?"

Sam ignored the question and feigned a hurt look. "I just thought you could help me with a few questions about penetration, a subject on which I'm sure you have a great deal of expertise."

Sanders grinned and swallowed Sam's diversion. "After twenty years as a bachelor cop, I've learned a thing or two about penetration. What do you want to penetrate?"

"Got any gadgets that would help get me through surveillance cameras, security guards, and locked doors with hard-wired alarms? No need to worry about the safe though, I think I've got that figured out already."

Sanders' smile froze and then cracked like plaster falling off a wall. "What the hell are you doing, Sam, going shopping at Fort Knox? Sounds to me like you're getting in way over your head!"

Sam shifted in his seat, still smiling confidently, but for a fleeting moment wondering if his friend were right. Was he in too deep? The thought left his mind as quickly as it had appeared. "Dave, you know I'll dump this entire mess in your lap just as soon as I can. There's nothing I'd like better than to call in the troops before I get scalped. But it's not time yet."

Sanders grimaced as Sam continued, "We don't have enough evidence to hang the rascals yet. There are people in high places, including the fourth floor of the federal building, who would put the skids on any investigation that you might try to initiate. And that's not all they might do. This isn't a friendly bunch, and they're well-connected. We don't know how high their tentacles go. We've got to have enough evidence to bring down the lot of them before they suspect anything."

After a quarter century in law enforcement, Sanders knew Sam was right. If things were half as bad he suspected, if there really was an extensive criminal conspiracy, building an airtight case in complete secrecy was absolutely essential. Still, he couldn't help but wonder if Sam Littlehawk was the right person to lay the groundwork.

Four years earlier, Sam had helped him stop organized crime from infiltrating the Indian bingo halls in the southeast corner of the state known as "Little Dixie." Sam's knowledge of the tribes, intelligence, and resourcefulness had been key factors in their success. Plus, Sam had an incredible mind for both detail and strategy. As an experienced trial lawyer, he knew how to build a case. But Sanders still had his professional ethics to consider.

As though reading his mind, Sam said, "Dave, if there was any other way, you know I would do it. If I brought you in now, you'd have to file a report, inform your superiors, and the word would be out. We'd be shut down. If you didn't file the report, you'd risk your pension."

"I'm risking my pension right now."

"Trust me, Dave. One more time. There's no other way."

Sanders rolled his eyes and muttered, "I hope you know what you're doing, Sam. And I hope you're the *only* one who does."

* * * * *

Pug Aberson dutifully called Huntington first thing Monday morning. After a brief conversation, a meeting was set for ten o'clock. Aberson arrived promptly and Huntington's private secretary immediately waived him into the inner sanctum. The minute he walked through the door, Huntington closed it behind him and turned, glowering.

"What do you mean, he turned down the money? *Again.*"

Aberson nervously blinked as a small smile curled the corners of his pink lips. From Huntington's demeanor, he knew that it wasn't the time to deliver bad news. "Everything's fine, Tom. He's coming around, he's just a little nervous. He didn't want to take the money at the club. We were in plain view of a lot of people. Someone might have been watching." Aberson attempted to look and sound positive. "He'll come around soon. He said he will get back to me in a day or two."

Huntington glared at Aberson. He had no tolerance for failure in his organization. "Aberson, you make this work. You have until Friday. If it isn't done by then, return the money. *All* of it. If you can't do the job, I know someone who can. Wrap this up fast or get out of the way."

Aberson tried to swallow, but his throat was too dry. He was thinking about the cash that he had used to pay a few old debts and the down payment he had made on the new BMW. He stood, projecting as much confidence as he could muster. "You know me, Tom, I'll get the job done. I always do, don't I?"

"Do it *now*, Pug," Huntington growled, "or face the consequences." Turning his back, he picked up the telephone. Aberson eased out the door and past the executive secretary, who glanced up with a cool smile and a knowing look in her eyes.

* * * * *

Fifteen minutes later, Wilbur Olsen, Huntington's nephew, chauffeur and general lackey, nudged open the door to the executive suite. Although he had worked at the firm for eight years and was heavily involved in most of its secret deals, the young man still addressed his uncle as "Mr. Huntington," as did everyone else in the firm except Bandini.

"Mr. Huntington?" Wilbur said, then waited to be acknowledged.

Huntington continued to look at the papers on his desk for another thirty seconds for the sole purpose of making his minion wait. He finally looked up and growled, "What is it?"

Wilber entered the office, followed by Bandini and Gus Barton, the head of Security for Southwest Energy. He closed the door as Huntington rose from his massive desk and moved to a group of chairs surrounding a coffee table. Motioning for the men to be seated, he settled into a large arm chair and asked, "I assume that there is a purpose for this visit?"

Barton nodded. "We have something, sir, that we think you will find interesting." Without another word, he pulled a small handheld tape recorder from his pocket and pressed the play button. The tape hissed for five seconds, followed by the distinct sound of a door opening and closing. Then a voice could be heard, distant and hollow, but still audible.

> *"So where do we go from here, Sam? You're calling the plays."*
> *"Tony, I think I've been hanging around with crazy Italians too much. Now I'm having crazy ideas. This one's a doozy. Totally insane."*
> *"Somewhere in that building over there is the information we need. All we have to do is go get it."*
> *"Oh, now you really are talking crazy. That place is guarded..."*
> *"...I've got a pretty good idea where to look."*

When Barton pushed the stop button, Huntington looked from him to Olsen and back. "Is that *it*?"

"That's all that can be understood," Barton replied. "One of them must've leaned against the desk or somehow blocked the bug. We need to make some technical adjustments. But it's enough. We know their next move."

Huntington eyed him cynically. "What the hell do you know, Barton? You know that a two-bit street lawyer and a green politician are having crazy ideas.

So what else is new?"

Measuring his words carefully, Barton said, "I think they're planning an offensive on this office, sir." He swallowed, clearly abashed, expecting a violent response.

Huntington did not erupt. Although he could hardly believe that Angelletti and Littlehawk would have the nerve for a frontal assault on the company or the firm, he was intrigued by the possibility of catching them in the act. He savored the thought of having the young rebel's arm twisted up behind his back, under Huntington's complete and unrelenting control. There was no doubt he could humiliate Angelletti before forcing him into strict obedience. But he would save his most creative and vindictive retribution for Littlehawk, who deserved no less for his ingratitude.

"What makes you think Angelletti and Littlehawk are stupid enough to try to breach our security?" Huntington asked.

Bandini finally spoke. "What else could you conclude from that tape, Tom? Angelletti is playing games with Aberson. He told you himself that he wouldn't support the project. Now he's huddling with his lawyer buddy and they're talking about entering a guarded building to get the information they need. It's as plain as day. I told you this town turns out a fool a minute."

"Then we'll be waiting for them," Huntington replied with a note of grim satisfaction. "Barton, you keep close tabs on those two and find a way to let them know that the security system will be down this Saturday evening for repairs. And put a bug on Aberson. I want to know what's *really* being said, not what he reports."

Bandini laughed. "Time to play rope a dope, huh, Tom?"

Huntington's eyes held a sadistic gleam. He could already see Angelletti and Littlehawk in handcuffs, downcast and waiting for him to decide their fate. It would be a fun Saturday night.

* * * * *

The county courthouse was only half the size of the imposing federal courthouse across the street, but it was more than twice as busy. Its hallways were perpetually crowded with all echelons of humanity. Top litigators from silk stocking law firms, judges, local politicians, bureaucrats and law enforcement officials were familiar faces in the hallowed halls of justice. But the majority of those milling around were down and out, for one reason or another. From morning until late afternoon, the courtrooms handled divorce trials, child custody battles, evictions, petty criminal offenses, debt collection actions, and civil cases of all stripes.

The downtrodden generally are not in a good mood when forced to confront reality and authority in the courthouse. The mood becomes even more somber two or three times a day, when gangs of handcuffed prisoners, chained together at the waist and clad in jailhouse orange jumpers, are escorted by armed deputies into courtrooms for arraignments. Emotionally wrenching scenes occur regularly when relatives of convicted felons attend sentencing hearings, and cries of anguish are heard. The dismal mood is frequently broken, however, by lawyers in jovial spirits on important missions for clients, saluting judges and gossiping with colleagues as they pass in the halls.

Tony was waiting in the hall when Sam walked out of a courtroom after a Tuesday afternoon docket call. Tony was obviously excited.

"You won't believe what happened! I tracked you down just to tell you." He looked both ways to ensure that he would not be overheard, then dropped his voice. "Believe it or not, the security at Southwest Plaza will be down this Saturday night for repairs. No one will be in the building, except in the first floor security office. We can get in, find what we need, and get out in time for last call at the Full Moon!"

Sam looked at Tony in disbelief. "How on earth did you discover this useful bit of information?"

"I know you won't believe it, but it fell right into my lap! I was talking to Bob Gannon, a constituent of mine who owns Bankers Security Group, the company that provides security equipment to Southwest Energy. I happened to ask him if he had a big weekend planned, and he said that he has to install some new equipment at Southwest Energy. I couldn't believe it!"

"And I'm sure that having great presence of mind, you immediately asked him when the systems would be down, which systems, and for how long?"

Tony grinned. "I may be slow, Sammy, but I'm not stupid. After all, I do have supervisory responsibility over Southwest Energy. Being the concerned public utility commissioner that I am, I just asked him whether the work would pose any security risks for the company, and he told me not to worry, the security will only be down between nine and twelve on Saturday night, the building will be empty and secure at that time, and all of the work will be done in the first floor security office. Voila! Ask and ye shall receive!"

"And so you think this is our big break?" Sam asked with a thoughtful expression.

"Sure. Why not?"

"Doesn't it seem a little too convenient that you happened upon your friendly constituent at this particular time, and he just happened to drop this information? Where did you meet him?"

Tony's excitement began to fade. "I bumped into him while I was having lunch at Hideaway Pizza. He was alone and stopped for a minute to talk…" A frown creased Tony's brow. "You don't think this is a set up, do you?"

"Do you?" Sam's deadpan expression answered the question.

"But how could they have known that we were even considering…"

Sam eyed the busy hallway of the courthouse. "Let's get out of here. We need to go somewhere we can talk." He looked at his watch. "Meet me at Camille's in an hour."

As the two entered the elevator, a tall man who had been loitering in the courthouse hallway headed down the stairwell at the end of the hall.

* * * * *

"I had a hunch," Sam said, as he dropped into the booth across from Tony. "They must know what we've been planning. It was too much of a coincidence that you *just happened* to bump into Gannon and he *just happened* to mention that the security systems at Southwest Energy would be down this weekend. And there's only one way that they could have known."

"There's *no way* they could have known, Sam. The only time we discussed it was in your office…" Tony's words trailed off as his eyes widened.

"I found this." Sam laid a small metal disk on the table. "It was in the handset of my telephone. Small, but effective."

"A bug?" Tony whispered incredulously.

Sam nodded with a wry smile. "They know we were planning to pay them a visit, but they don't know when. Now they're trying to set us up, to make it easy to catch us red-handed. Wouldn't that make an interesting headline? *Public Utility Commissioner and Lawyer Burglarize Power Company.* I'm sure Huntington, Bandini and friends have already concocted a great story about what we were attempting to steal."

"These guys are ruthless. They bugged your office."

"I guess turnabout is fair play. We use a wire against Aberson, and they bug my office. *Everyone* loves the wonders of technology!" Sam laughed. "It's all part of the game in this electronic age."

"So I guess the attack on the citadel is off," Tony said. "We can't go in there when they know we're coming."

Sam's smile broadened and his eyes gleamed. Tony felt a familiar pulse of excitement that he had experienced many times in the presence of his careful, but sometimes daring, friend. "I don't like that look in your eye, Sammy boy. It can only spell trouble."

"What did we do, Tony, when we found out that the Broken Arrow Tigers had our new play book right before the state championship game? We turned it around on them and won the game. They knew what to expect, but we gave them something else. Cheaters never prosper, Tony. This is actually the best thing that could have happened!"

Tony looked at his friend with a mixture of doubt, respect, and awe. "You don't mean that you intend to walk into their trap?"

Sam grinned. "Not the way they expect it. Now let's go—we've got work to do."

Chapter 4

The main auditorium of the Performing Arts Center was empty late Tuesday afternoon when Tony slipped in the side door. Only the stage lights illuminated the gargantuan, plush theater. Designed with flawless acoustics and excellent visibility from every seat in the house, it was the perfect venue for a performance by a world class prima ballerina. He took a seat far to the left in the third row of the orchestra section.

Tony watched silently as Katrina practiced a few graceful movements. She was poised, balanced, and elegant. Confidence born from many years of hard work was evident in her smooth execution of every movement. Her strong, supple arms were bare and her platinum blonde hair was pulled back in a loose ponytail. Clad in a white gossamer knee-length dress that floated with every movement, she was breathtaking. *No wonder critics worldwide give her such high acclaim*, he thought. *She deserves it.*

As Katrina completed the practice session, the lone stagehand manning the control booth brought the lights down. No longer blinded by footlights, Katrina could see the auditorium. Tony stood and moved toward the stage, clapping. "Bravo, bravo! A magnificent performance by the most incredible ballerina alive!" He trotted up the wing stairs onto the stage.

Katrina crossed the stage to meet him, her smile revealing perfect white teeth. "Tony, I am so glad you came," she said warmly. "I am just trying to polish a few movements for my next performance."

"You're perfect already," Tony said as he brushed her cheek with a kiss. "I'm sure you'll be stunning on opening night. But I don't want to interrupt your practice. Are you ready for a break?"

"I'm finished," Katrina said as she pushed a lock of loose hair away from her face. "After I change we can talk."

Five minutes later, Katrina opened the door to the dressing room and Tony entered. In jeans, a baggy cotton shirt and white tennis shoes, she was as appealing in casual clothes as she had been on stage. She pulled up a chair for Tony, then sat on a wooden bench against the wall.

Tony could see that she was very troubled. "I came as soon as I got your message."

Her deep sigh ended with a small shudder. "Tony, I do not know what to do. Anatoly is calling me two or three times every day. I cannot concentrate on my work. I have told him that I am happy here, that I want to stay here for now, that this is what I need to do and want to do, but he tells me that my career is in Europe and he will not see me waste my life. He says we must leave together for Paris."

"Why don't you just tell him to bug off and leave you alone, Kate? Just explain that you don't want him in your life and he should go back to Russia where he belongs."

"You don't understand, Tony. You are an American, not Russian, and you have not met him. When we were together last Friday, I hoped that we would find him, so that you would understand. He is not normal, Tony. He has changed since we met a year ago. I do not know what he will do if I tell him that I will not go to Europe."

"If he gets violent, Kate, we'll just put him away. He'll be picked up and deported so fast it'll make your head spin."

"But he could cause much trouble for me in Russia, Tony. We share many friends and colleagues at the University there and he has contacts in the government. He is a passionate Russian artist who is obsessed with me and very jealous of you. In this condition, I do not know what he could do. He could become violent. He could certainly damage my career and my future in Russia."

"Maybe your future is not in Russia, Kate," Tony quickly replied. Then he paused, considering for a moment the gravity with which she spoke and the unintended implications of his comment. "What do you want me to do, Katrina? I would still be happy to talk to him."

"Would you, Tony? That would be wonderful! If he could somehow release his jealousy, we might be able to talk rationally about my future. But I think it would be best to meet him in a public place. Possibly Friday afternoon at the Full Moon? I could invite him to meet us there about four. If things go well, perhaps we could all have dinner?" she suggested.

"Whatever works for you, Princess. Your wish is my command."

Katrina rose from the bench and Tony met her. She embraced him tightly for a moment, then released him and stepped back, taking his hands in hers. "You have been such a good friend, Tony, I knew you would help me with Anatoly. I cannot thank you enough."

Tony inwardly cringed. This relationship was not going exactly as planned. Dealing with a busy, career-oriented prima ballerina was trouble enough without adding an angry, jealous suitor. Yet Katrina's friendship was worth the effort, even if friends were all they ever would be. And now, the three of them were going to have dinner. Cozy. Perfect. He made a mental note to kick himself hard at the first opportunity.

With a weak smile, he said, "So, four o'clock Friday at the Full Moon. I'll be there with bells on!"

* * * * *

After saying goodbye to Pauline Kingsley, Sam stood in the foyer of Old Union Station and watched the venerable widow wave and wink as the elevator door slid closed. He nodded and smiled. Clients like Mrs. Kingsley made Sam love his work. At seventy-four, she was charming, intelligent, witty, and now rich. Thanks to an unexpected inheritance, she would soon be realizing her lifelong dream—photographing African wildlife—and Sam would be helping her make generous donations to several children's charities. Practicing law did sometimes have its rewards.

Sam was still smiling and pondering the mysteries of good fortune when the second elevator door opened and Tony stepped out. "Uh oh, here comes trouble!" Sam exclaimed loud enough for Tony to hear, as he turned and strode back into his office.

Practically on his heels, Tony followed him inside, saying, "Not so fast, cowboy, I've got business with you." Clearing the door, he noticed Natalie at her desk. "Oh, hi, gorgeous! If Sam's too busy for me, maybe I could do some business with *you* today!"

Natalie blushed and tried unsuccessfully to hide a self-conscious smile. "I don't think Sam's too busy for you today, Tony. Maybe another time."

"You have the most beautiful eyes," he replied, tossing a wink over his shoulder before closing the door to Sam's office.

"Always the ladies' man," Sam commented, sinking into his easy chair and motioning Tony toward the couch.

"Every woman deserves to be noticed. It's a philosophy of life. No, actually, it's a way of life. But on to the business at hand. Are we still on for Saturday night?" He shot Sam a knowing look.

"I'm in if you are. It was lucky that Gannon told you that the security would be down this Saturday. I'm sure the records we need are in the real estate department on the fourth floor, east end. All we have to do is slip in the Fifth Street emergency exit with this electronic key card," Sam held up two fingers with nothing between them, "then go up the east elevators and help ourselves to the files. In and out in a flash. The security guards will be busy with the system upgrade, and any unusual activity will either be ignored or blamed on them. Should be a piece of cake."

"So it's all set then?"

"I'll bring a couple of pairs of surgical gloves to avoid leaving fingerprints. We'll walk from here so we won't need a car. I think that's everything." Sam winked.

"I'm glad that's settled. So until Saturday, okay?"

"Good, Tony. I'll walk you out."

They left the office without saying a word, strode past Natalie, out the door and past the bank of elevators, then entered the wide staircase. "Do you think it worked?" Tony asked.

"Other than sounding a little bit like the three stooges planning a heist, I thought we were pretty convincing," Sam replied.

"It was classic to replace their bug and use it to confirm our Saturday night appearance," Tony said. "But then, I never underestimate the conniving powers of lawyers, especially this one. I hope you've devised an equally brilliant way to protect our ethical backsides."

Sam winced. "Don't remind me. You understand, of course, that we just intentionally created incriminating evidence of our own future burglary. It's a good thing their bug is illegal and their recordings can't be used against us in court. Unless, of course, Huntington's federal connections somehow find a new way to legitimize burglary and wiretapping. But we'd best not underestimate our adversaries."

"Seems to me that our taped evidence is as illegal as theirs and couldn't be used in court either. But then, I'm relying on you, Sammy boy, as I always have. Guess it doesn't really matter anyway, because as you correctly pointed out, we probably won't live long enough to worry about the inevitable prosecution."

* * * * *

Two hours later, Bandini entered Huntington's office followed by Wilbur Olsen and Gus Barton. Huntington was standing by the large, curving window that overlooked the expanse of the Arkansas River. He turned and regarded the men as a drill sergeant would view a group of new recruits. "So, what is it?"

Barton replied, "They took the bait, sir—hook, line, and sinker. Mr. Bandini's idea to use Gannon as a decoy worked like a charm. We confirmed by the wire that they're planning to enter the building on Saturday night. They were even talking about going to the fourth floor to look in the real estate files. What they think they'll find there, God only knows, but we'll be waiting for them."

"Damn right we'll be waiting," Huntington said indignantly. "You and a few armed security guards should be more than enough to nab these two-bit burglars. And a photographer. Don't forget to bring a photographer. I want some good pictures of those two renegades in handcuffs. Then bring them to my office and I'll have a little talk with them. After that, I'll decide whether they'll be prosecuted or released. Bandini, I want you to personally oversee this operation. Find a good reason to be downtown on Saturday night, then when you receive the call from Barton and Gannon, call me at the club."

"I'll be there," Bandini acceded. "Just don't count on total capitulation. Angelletti, maybe. But Littlehawk? I doubt it. He's quiet, but I'll bet he has a stubborn streak a mile long. Maybe it's the Indian blood—but the look in his eye tells me that he's not gonna bend easy. It'll take more than fear of embarrassment to change that boy's mind."

Huntington scowled at Bandini, who simply shrugged.

"They were sure the team to beat in high school!" Olsen declared. "They set some running and passing records that still haven't been beat." A second later, Olsen blanched as he became the target of Huntington's withering glare. "Well, I guess they weren't that good, really," he muttered, staring at the floor.

"Bandini, you tell Aberson to call it off," Huntington said. "He's finished with this job. And tell him I want all of the money back tomorrow. No point wasting it on the other commissioners. When I'm done with Angelletti, they won't need any more convincing."

With that, Huntington stood, making it clear the meeting was over.

* * * * *

"You aren't getting cold feet, are you?" Sam asked Tony, as they sat astride their dirt bikes on top of a hill on a deserted oil lease in Osage County. After an hour of bouncing along narrow dirt trails, they were both dusty and sweaty. In spite of the hot, humid weather, trail riding was one of their favorite ways to relieve stress in the summer.

"Cold feet? How could I get cold feet in these leather boots when it's about a hundred and twenty degrees outside? I'd love to get cold feet right now—in an icy Rocky Mountain trout stream," Tony replied.

"Trade that dirt bike for a road cruiser and we'll head for Gunnison tomorrow. I'm sure Natalie could handle things for a few days."

"I'm sure Natalie can handle anything you throw at her," Tony countered with a smirk. "Colorado sounds great, but I sure wouldn't want to miss the fun we've got planned for this weekend."

Sam cast him an inquiring glance. "No second thoughts? Seriously?"

Tony shrugged. "Well, you know, now that you mention it, Aberson was undoubtedly right. I do deserve to cash in. Law school was hard for me, not being a brilliant scholar like you. Then there was the campaign and all that sucking up to a lot of creepy old toads. I took a substantial risk, throwing my hat in the ring, and I won. That's not to mention my natural entitlement to unimaginable wealth. Considering everything, and since I'm destined to be the Governor anyway, why not get there the easy way? All I have to do is sit back and let Huntington and his crew shovel money my way!"

"Why you lowdown, lying, worthless sack of rotten fish guts! If Huntington doesn't nail your lousy hide to the barn door, I will! You're dead meat," Sam said convincingly.

"Well, if my days are numbered anyway, there's no point in worrying about the consequences. May as well throw caution to the wind and blast ahead like *the charge of the light brigade!*" Tony ended with a shout as he kicked the starter pedal of his bike and grabbed the handlebars with sweat-stained work gloves. "Bet you two long necks you can't beat me to the highway!"

In a flash, Sam gunned his engine and the two bikes burst forward in a cloud of red dust. They were neck and neck as they cleared the farthest hill.

* * * * *

Tony strolled into the Full Moon at quarter to four on Friday afternoon. He knew that the happy hour crowd inside would be too boisterous to conduct any serious conversation, so he asked the hostess for one of the tables near the outdoor bar, which enjoyed the shade of a huge live oak tree.

It was hot outside, but not oppressive, and there was a light breeze. Dressed casually in blue jeans and a polo shirt, Tony thought the weather was pleasant for an August afternoon in Oklahoma. After ordering a beer, he sat back to watch the varied crowd drifting into the popular nightspot.

Five minutes later, the hostess escorted Katrina to the table. With her hair pulled into a ponytail and wearing a short sleeve leotard and skirt, she looked far younger and more vulnerable than she had while performing in front of the footlights. With a brotherly hug, Tony said, "I'm here, for whatever it's worth."

She embraced him and briefly laid her head on his shoulder, as though he were a pillar of strength in her tumultuous life. "It is worth a lot to me if you can make Anatoly be reasonable. He must understand that he cannot dictate how I will live my life. And I *will not* go to Europe with him or marry him. I cannot."

Tony's stomach knotted as he contemplated the coming showdown. He could not fathom how he got himself into these situations. Shaking his head in disgust, he motioned to the bartender and turned to Katrina. "The usual Perrier with cranberry juice, milady?"

"I think this is the time for that margarita," she replied, then suddenly grabbed Tony's forearm and whispered, "He's here! But he has two men with him. I don't know who they are, but I can tell from their clothes that they are Russian. Look, they're talking to the hostess." Tony followed Katrina's gaze through the open French doors.

Tony spotted the three Russians, easily recognizing Anatoly Karmakov. His intense dark eyes burned with sullen anger. High cheek bones and a prominent nose hinted of his Middle Eastern heritage, and his dark complexion seemed to emphasize the furrow in his brow. His black jacket and pleated white shirt were noticeably out of place in the casual summer atmosphere on the deck. Their eyes met, and held. From Karmakov's defiant stare, Tony guessed that the chances of a calm, intelligent conversation without a confrontation was completely out of the question.

Tony knew that Katrina's heart was racing. His own pulse skipped a beat when he first saw the three Russians, but he knew that it was his job to be the anchor in the tempest. He took a deep breath and smiled at Katrina as Karmakov and his companions cleared the open door twenty feet away. "Don't you fret, Kate, I'm sure that this Anatoly is a reasonable guy. We just need to set a few things straight."

The two henchmen stopped just outside the door, taking positions on each side of the deck, while Karmakov continued toward Tony and Katrina. Tony took a step to meet the advancing Russian and extended his hand with a smile. Karmakov stopped five feet short, clasping his hands behind his back with an angry stare.

"So you are the famous Anthony Angelletti," Karmakov said in a derisive tone. "I have heard far too much about you."

The arrogance of the man was palpable, with a dangerous, barbed edge. Tony dropped his outstretched hand, which Karmakov had ignored. "And you must be the great Anatoly Karmakov. I've heard a little about you, too. It's a pleasure to finally meet you." Tony smiled and looked for a way to break the ice. He had to try to placate the man if they were to have any semblance of a productive conversation. "I've heard that you're an excellent musician. I hope to hear you play some day."

"You may attend one of my concerts," Karmakov replied stiffly, "if you are in Paris or Vienna. That is where Katrina and I will be performing soon."

"That's not how I understand it," Tony said, breaking eye contact to glance at Katrina, who had quietly moved to the bar in order to give the two men privacy. Her liquid brown eyes urged Tony to push forward. "Anatoly, Katrina has a plan for her life and it may not include you. This might come as a shock, since you came all the way from Russia to take her back, but believe it or not, she has some say in this matter, and she tells me that she doesn't want to go."

Karmakov took a quick, menacing step forward and hissed, "Katrina is not the problem, Angelletti, *you* are the problem. *You* have convinced her that she should stay in this wretched wasteland, far from civilization. *You* have convinced her that she is better served wasting her life here, rather than dancing with the greatest ballet companies in Europe. *You* are the thorn which I must remove from her life…"

"Wait a minute now, slick, you don't know what she…"

"*Silence!*" Karmakov's command was so loud and abrupt that heads turned at the far end of the deck. Twenty feet away, Katrina winced. Karmakov lowered his voice a little, but not its intensity. "I did not come here to negotiate with you, Angelletti. I did not come here to listen to you tell me what is good for Katrina. I came because Katrina asked me to meet with you."

"*And* I came to tell you that if you do not stop interfering with my plans, you will be removed." Karmakov turned his eyes toward his two henchmen who were still standing near the door, staring intently at Tony. One of the two opened his jacket briefly, revealing a handgun in a shoulder holster.

"So I guess this means that we're not having dinner together after all?" Tony quipped with a winning smile. His coolness raised the suppressed fury in the Russian another notch.

"You ignorant cretin!" he seethed. "You are not worthy even to lay your eyes on Katrina. You will certainly never lay your hands on her again. You will *not* interfere with my plans for her future. You will tell Katrina that she must go to Europe with me, or you will exit this life permanently."

Tony's smile froze. Then with equal intensity, he demanded, "Now *you* listen to *me*, Karmakov. I will not exit this life, but *you* will exit this country permanently, as soon as I have a talk with the U.S. immigration service. *You* will *not* interfere with Katrina's life and she *will* make her own decisions. And I have no fear of your hulking goons with guns. Your intimidation techniques are straight out of a third rate gangster movie. I really expected more creativity from a person who purports to be a world class artist. I guess this just proves that *you* are the only cretin here."

Karmakov bristled at the insult, barely holding his anger in check. "If you disregard my advice," he threatened, "you will suffer the consequences."

There was a moment of hesitation as Tony considered a hot retort, but Karmakov abruptly turned and walked to the bar. Tony watched as he spoke a few words to Katrina, then firmly gripped her wrist and began leading her toward the door.

Within a few steps, Katrina wrenched free from his grasp and uttered an audible, "No!"

Karmakov paused for a moment, looking over his shoulder at her with a withering stare. Then he walked quickly out the door and his gunmen followed.

As soon as they were out of sight, Katrina was in Tony's arms, trembling. He held her for a moment, then said brightly, "Well, that went well! Delightful fellow. Sorry he had to leave so soon. So, what's for dinner?"

Katrina rolled her eyes and wiped her tears, releasing a small, nervous laugh. Although Tony's composure and good spirits were contagious, she was still filled with dread. "He wants me to go with him now, Tony, without delay. He said that he will not wait any longer and that I have no choice, I must go. He thinks that once we are in Europe together, I will learn to love him. But that could never happen."

"That man is evil, Kate. You have to stay away from him."

"But I'm afraid of him and his bodyguards. Did they threaten you?"

"No, not really. They're no threat," Tony said, not feeling nearly as confident as he sounded.

"Above all, Tony, I do not want you to be hurt. You have been such a good friend to me since I arrived here. I do not understand why he is so filled with anger and jealousy. I would feel horrible if anything happened to you because of me."

"Hey, kid, forget it! Good guy runs off bad guy and wins beautiful lady! It's part of the script. Without a bad guy, how could I impress the princess and win her affections?"

Katrina laughed as she sniffed back her tears. "Tony, you are a true friend. I do not know how I can thank you enough for helping me."

"I'm sure that with a little imagination, we could think of something," Tony said with a smile. "But first, can we have dinner? I'm starved!"

Chapter 5

Two hours later, the summer sun was setting over the Arkansas River as Tony and Katrina strolled across the ancient iron railroad bridge that had been converted for foot traffic. The pedestrian bridge's heavy timber frame and meticulous landscaping provided the perfect backdrop for an evening stroll. Couples enjoyed the fountains and benches strategically placed along the bank's footpaths and along the bridge. A few fishermen tended their lines from their favorite outposts. The slow moving waters of the river reflected the brilliant gold and orange hues of the setting sun, as Tony and Katrina leaned on the railing and watched a line of white summer clouds slowly turn pink over the skyline.

"I don't know, Tony, for as long as I can remember dancing has been the most important thing in my life. I was just seven years old when I started and soon I was dancing at least three hours every day. When I left my family to dance in Moscow, I was only twelve. I have not seen them much since then. My life is the ballet. I was happy here at the University, polishing my skills, learning more about my art, until Anatoly came. Yes, I would like to go to Europe and dance with the greatest companies at some point, but this is not the right time. And even when that time comes, I do not want to go anywhere with Anatoly Karmakov. He scares me. I could never be the wife of a man who is so cold, so…"

"Ruthless?"

"Heartless. How can a man who is a world famous artist, a musician of such high acclaim, have such little regard for the feelings of others? He is so totally obsessed with his career, his performance, his image, his grandiose plans for the future, that he completely disregards my feelings and desires."

"It's simple, Kate. He's a narcissistic egomaniac with a double dose of vanity. He doesn't care about you as a person. He just wants to possess you and be seen with the most beautiful and popular ballerina in the world."

"Oh, Tony, what am I going to do?"

He looked at his watch. The sun had set and the color in the clouds was fading from rose to deep violet. It was nearly time to meet Sam.

"The first thing you're going to do is go home and lock the door. Make sure that your neighbors know that you're home and make sure someone is nearby. Tomorrow morning, we'll call a friend of mine who used to work at Immigration in Washington. He'll know who to talk to about getting Anatoly deported and out of your life for good. By next week, Anatoly Karmakov will be nothing but a bad memory."

"Thank you," she said with gratitude. "Thank you for being such a good friend."

"For now," he replied with a wink, "I guess I'll just have to be content with that."

* * * * *

"You're late," Sam said to Tony as he closed the ancient six-panel walnut door of his residence in the Greenwood District. Just a few blocks from the Station, Sam's home was built into a space that half a century earlier had been the second floor living quarters of an old firehouse. Sam had managed to obtain a long-term lease with options and had remodeled the building to his specifications, including a large garage on the ground floor accessible by way of the original brass fireman's pole. Windows lined the south and east walls of the spacious living area, giving an impressive view of Tulsa's skyline. The brick west wall was covered with original artwork—paintings and sculptures of animals. The antique oak furniture rested on oriental carpets, while overhead two ornate brass ceiling fans that appeared to be as old as the building slowly turned. Sam's family and friends simply called his unique living space the "Firehouse."

Opening a cabinet, Sam pulled out a large pad of drawing paper and colored markers, then sat at the table. "I don't have a blueprint, but I do have a pretty decent memory," he said as he began drawing the floor plan of the twelfth floor of Southwest Plaza. "The building layout is simple and should present no problems, if we can get past the security without tripping an alarm. As far as I know, there are no alarms in the offices, only locks. I guess they figure that the armed guards at the front door twenty-four hours a day and the security cameras in the main hallways will be enough to deter most folks."

"Yeah, most folks probably wouldn't want to waltz through Huntington's office at midnight anyway. I can think of a million better places to be."

Sam sketched the basic floor plan of the building and the parking garage across the street. "There may be some executive summaries in Huntington's office, or in any of the offices, for that matter. We don't know who besides Huntington and Bandini have worked on the project. Disclosure of sensitive information is on a 'need to know' basis at the firm. Any really incriminating files will be in the safe room." He tapped a finger on the drawing as he explained, "There's a large room of archived dead files across the hall from Huntington's office, here. In a wall in the back of the archives is a heavy steel door with an old safe-type cylinder lock. That's where they keep incriminating information—like compromising pictures of half the politicians in the state."

Tony grinned. "Man, this could be fun! Did you pack your digital camera and pocket scanner with lots of memory cards?"

Sam patted the small backpack on the chair next to him. "Those, plus a few other tools of the trade that I borrowed from a friend. We should have no trouble fooling the security cameras for an hour or so with the gadgets I borrowed that will replace real time video of the hallways with a static image. The guards will never know the difference, since there's no activity in the halls at night anyway. Ain't technology great?"

"What if the guards decide to check the halls?"

"Not likely. Once they know the building is secure, they won't be expecting anything. If they check the monitors, they'll see an empty hallway. The chances of a guard checking the safe room are slim, since Huntington doesn't advertise its existence. I doubt if they even know it's there."

Tony was nodding as he watched his friend draw. "Sammy, how do you know that everything is the same as it was several years ago, when you were there? Lots could have changed."

"Remember Jenna? We went out together a few times when I worked there. She's a secretary for Joshua Pointer, one of the partners. We've stayed in touch on and off over the years, so I called her for lunch this week and we had a little talk. Secretaries know much more than their bosses like to think they know. They could bring down the world if they ever got organized. Anyway, Jenna still thinks of me as an insider. Even as a summer associate, I learned about the safe room from the professional staff. We didn't know what was in it, of course, but it's pretty hard to hide a steel door with such a big lock."

"So she filled you in on the current state of affairs?"

"Well, we joked a little, like most secretaries at the firm do, about what must be behind that locked door. Lots of skeletons in the closet and all that. She said it's still there just like it was ten years ago. Nothing's changed. The only ones with access are Huntington and Bandini and their personal assistants. Still has the same old cylinder lock, like the door of an old safe."

"So what are we waiting for? Let's get this done!"

* * * * *

"We'll walk from here," Sam said as he pulled his Jeep into a deserted lot behind a cathedral on Eighth Street. Parking in an area hidden from view behind the large church, Sam handed Tony a small pack and picked up his own. "This should be a piece of cake."

"Won't Huntington and his crew be surprised when they learn that we beat 'em to the punch?" Tony chortled as they walked quickly toward the Southwest Energy parking garage. "They'll be looking for us tomorrow—a day late and a dollar short!"

"With luck," Sam countered, "they'll never know we were here. When we don't show up tomorrow night, they'll think we got spooked and called it off. Let's cut the chat and stay focused. Follow me."

The two men slipped over an open half wall into the parking garage. The only security in the garage was the gated auto entrance. They moved quickly to the lowest level of the garage, where there was an entry door to the tunnel under Seventh Street. Sam produced a key card, and in an instant, they were inside the tunnel leading from the parking garage to the basement of Southwest Plaza.

Sam knew from his recent reconnaissance that just inside the doors at the far end of the tunnel was a wall-mounted security camera that monitored the inner hallway. But just below it to the right was the door that accessed the cavernous basement storage area known as "the catacombs." As long as they stayed beneath the security camera, they could edge their way around the wall and through the door without being detected.

While Tony held a small flashlight, Sam pulled a stainless steel tool from his pack and quickly picked the lock on the double doors. "Looks like you've done this before," Tony whispered.

"Shhhh! This is where it starts to get sticky," Sam replied. "Move carefully and follow me." They slipped through the door, then edged around the wall under the security camera until they reached the next door. Sam easily picked the lock and they slipped noiselessly into the catacombs. He checked for more security cameras, but found none. The two men moved silently to a utility installation enclosed in a heavy wire cage near the back of the catacombs. Once again, Sam picked the lock in less than a minute.

"I want one of those little gadgets," Tony said as they eased into the cage.

Sam soon found what he was looking for—a wiring chase large enough for human access that ran from the basement's main power supply to the utility control room on the first floor. "Okay, this is it," he whispered. "So far, so good. You stay here while I go do a little rewiring. I'll be back in five minutes."

"What's the contingency plan if you're not?"

"Don't worry, I will be."

Entering the chase, he crawled a hundred feet to a vertical shaft where steel rungs on the wall provided access up the twenty foot shaft. Sam climbed to the top in seconds, crossed the short horizontal shaft that ended at the building's main utility control room, then stopped at an access cover that was screwed to a metal frame set in the block wall.

Once again, he pulled a tool from his pouch. With a special ratchet-pliers combination, he managed to back out the screws and set the cover aside. "Gotta buy Dave a case of beer," he muttered as he slid through the opening.

Attached to the back wall of the control room was a large, steel grey electrical box with an impressive exterior panel of colored lights. Opening it, Sam quickly found the video cables he needed and used alligator clips to attached a small jamming device that would loop the security system's video signals.

Retracing his route, he was back at Tony's side in seven minutes flat. "Let's go," he whispered as he brushed dust and cobwebs out of his hair.

The two crossed back through the catacombs into the basement hallway, past the deactivated security monitor, and around the corner to the lone freight elevator. It was empty, and a minute later, they stepped onto the twelfth floor of Southwest Plaza within a few feet of Huntington, Bandini & Fane's double glass doors. Sam immediately began to examine the lock.

"Hey, Sam," Tony whispered a moment later from down the hallway. "Look at this!" He twisted a doorknob and pushed open an unmarked wooden door that directly accessed an inner office.

"Good security," Sam muttered as he pocketed his tools and followed Tony into the dark hallway of the firm. "They must have been expecting us."

Within seconds, they were at the safe room's door. "This always works in the movies," Sam said, taking out an old-fashioned doctor's stethoscope. As he carefully turned the dial, he listened for the tumblers to fall.

"You would think that they'd upgrade their security system," Tony whispered. "That lock looks like it could be fifty years old."

"It's worked for thirty years already, why rock the boat?" Sam responded. "Besides, this lock is really just to deter curious employees of the firm. I'm sure they'd never expect anyone to be crazy enough to do what we're doing."

A few more turns of the dial and the lever on the door fell under Sam's grip with a satisfying clunk. Once inside the windowless safe room, Sam flipped on an overhead light.

"Okay, mastermind, what now?" Tony asked as they considered the ten large lateral file cabinets lining the walls of the small room.

"There's got to be some organization to these files. Start with the obvious. Look for files on the Greenleaf Project, Pug Aberson, or anything else that looks suspicious."

"Everything in here is suspicious!" Tony countered.

"Whatever you do, do it fast," Sam said. "We don't have much time. No telling how long it will be until they realize that the hall security monitors aren't working. When and if that happens, I don't want to be here. I'm going to Huntington's office to see if I can find anything that will give us a clue what to look for."

Sam left the safe room and made his way in the dark to Huntington's office across the hall from the archives. With his small flashlight, he scanned the desk top, where four light green files were stacked in a neat pile. Sam quickly flipped through the files, finding nothing of interest. He was beginning to look through a stack of telephone messages, when a small notepad by the telephone caught his eye. Scratched on a corner of the pad was the word "Greenleaf" and next to it the words "Karmakov" and "August 10."

Seeing nothing else of interest, Sam walked back to the safe room, where he found Tony rapidly scanning a pile of documents. "Sam, grab your camera and get busy!" Tony said. "I hit paydirt! Look at this!"

Sam took a quick look at the files that lay open on a small table across from the filing cabinets. The top file contained a detailed financial analysis and other information about the Greenleaf Project.

"This is great!" Sam said. "Keep copying!"

"Did you find anything?"

"Not much. Does the name 'Karmakov' mean anything to you?"

Tony looked up, perplexed. "Karmakov? What has he got to do with this? We've got to keep our minds on business and get out of here, Sam!"

"Okay, let's just get the copying done and get out of here. I'll explain later."

* * * * *

Twenty minutes later, a relief guard stepped through the door of the security control room on the first floor of Southwest Plaza. The guard at the console of video monitors jumped as if he had been shocked. "How the devil did you get in here?" he demanded.

"I climbed down the chimney with Old St. Nick," the relief guard shot back. "How do you *think* I got in here? I walked in the front door, as always."

"How come I didn't see you on the monitors?"

"You were asleep as usual, I suppose."

"I was *not* asleep," the guard growled. "I've been sitting here scanning the monitors for the last ten minutes. Why don't you step back out into the hallway? Maybe there's something wrong with the monitor." The relief guard complied, and in a few seconds returned to the control room. The guard at the monitors was tapping one of the screens and playing with the controls.

"We've got a problem, Les. This monitor doesn't work. Why don't you go around front. Let's see if those cameras are working."

In a minute, he was back again. The guard seated in front of the bank of monitors shook his head. "Nothing. What the heck is going on? Something strange must be happening with the system. Why don't you go on up to twelve and twenty-two and let's check to see if the cameras up there are working."

The relief guard headed for the elevators.

* * * * *

Sam and Tony were stepping back onto the freight elevator, packs in hand, when they heard a whir coming from the bank of elevators across the hall. Sam quickly hit the button for the basement. "Not a minute too soon," he whispered to Tony as the freight elevator door closed.

Ten seconds later, the relief guard stepped from the elevator onto the twelfth floor. Keying his two way radio, he asked, "Anything?"

The guard at the console in the control booth responded, "Nothing. We definitely have a problem. You aren't showing up on the twelfth floor monitor either." At that moment, the relief guard heard the whirring of the freight elevator.

"Who's using the freight elevator right now?" he barked into his radio, suspicion rising in his voice. "It's past midnight. Who's in the building?"

"No one has signed in," the control room guard responded. "There's no one in the building but us, or at least there shouldn't be."

"Someone is in here, or that freight elevator has taken on a life of its own! Meet me in the basement, quick!"

Sam and Tony stepped off the freight elevator and into the basement hallway a minute ahead of the security guards and sprinted down the hall to the tunnel doors. Just as Tony pushed the tunnel door open, Sam remembered the jamming equipment he had left clipped into the wiring of the control panel. He grabbed Tony's arm. "Tony, I've got to go back into the catacombs! If I leave that jammer, they'll eventually find it and trace it to Dave. I can't leave him hanging out. Just go out the way we came in and do it fast! I'll meet you back at my place."

"Sam, are you crazy?" Tony panted. "You can't stay in here!"

"No time to talk. Go now, and don't worry about me. I'll see you in a few minutes." With that, Sam darted back through the door into the catacombs.

The tunnel door was swinging shut when the guards rounded the corner at the other end of the hall. They ran the hundred feet to the tunnel doors and burst through them, then sprinted down the tunnel and through the doors into the parking garage. In the dim light, they saw a dark figure hurdle the half-wall at the other end of the garage. The guards dashed to the wall to look for the intruder, but all they found was a dark street. He could have gone in any direction, so further pursuit was pointless.

"Did you get a good look at him?" the breathless relief guard panted.

"No, he was already over the wall. Jesus, I can't believe this! Twelve years I've been here and there's never been a breach of security. Not once!" He shook his head in disgust. "We'd better check the building, then call the boss."

Five minutes later, standing at the console in the control room, the lead guard watched a monitor in disbelief as the relief guard appeared on it, walking though the hallway toward the elevator. The guard shook his head as though to clear it, then keyed his two way radio. "You may as well come back, Les. I don't know what happened, but the system is on line again. We had better think this thing through before we call Mr. Gannon. You know how he hates false alarms."

At that moment, Sam slipped under the tunnel's reactivated security camera in the basement. A minute later, he slid over the half-wall of the parking garage and disappeared into the night.

By two-thirty a.m., Tony and Sam were back in the Firehouse, studying their spoils. After downloading the digital photographs and files, they began to organize the mass of data. In an hour, they were convinced that they had enough information to hang Huntington and a half dozen others involved in the project, if there were an honest prosecution. Of course, that was another issue entirely.

Finally, Tony stopped reading and leaned back in his chair, blinking his tired eyes. "Just curious—why did you ask me about Karmakov when we were in the heat of battle? That was pretty surreal, at the time."

Sam looked up from a pile of papers. "On Huntington's desk I saw a notepad that had the word 'Greenleaf' written on it, and right next to it were the words, 'Karmakov' and 'August 10.' Any ideas?"

"Couldn't be the same man. Not possible..." Tony said thoughtfully.

"What's not possible? Anything's possible..."

"Are you sure that the notepad said 'Karmakov'? I've never met anyone else with that name, but I don't see how he could be involved with Huntington. It doesn't make any sense. On the other hand, birds of a feather..."

"If you would kindly tell me who Karmakov is, perhaps I could help you make some sense of it," Sam said.

Tony scowled. He had not shared with Sam the melodrama of Katrina's life, and he hated to admit to his friend that once again, he was involved in a three-cornered romance that was bound to have a tragic ending, as so many others had in the past. "Karmakov is the name of one bad Russian dude who I hope I never see again."

"That helps a lot." Sam stared at Tony, waiting, his eyes narrowed with a look of grim determination.

"You really don't want to know."

"Know what?" Sam asked as he picked up an orange from the table and began to peel it, clearly intending to force the issue.

Tony knew that there was no way to avoid telling his friend the sad tale, so he quickly outlined the recent events in Katrina's life, closing with the previous afternoon's confrontation with Karmakov and his henchmen. Sam listened intently until Tony finished his story, only reacting with a visible glimmer of anger when Tony described the Russian's harsh treatment of Katrina.

"Is Katrina safe?" Sam asked when Tony finally finished.

"I think so. She has double locks on her doors and friends living in the apartment next door. I told her not to open her door for anyone tonight and I would speak with her first thing in the morning. We may be able to protect her for a day or two, but our first priority must be to get that Russian menace out of town, preferably deported."

"Good thing we haven't got anything else going on right now," Sam retorted wryly. "Here we have a big pot of political scandal at a full boil and you season the stew with a double handful of murderous Russians."

"But how could there be any connection between Huntington and Karmakov? They're from opposite sides of the globe, both literally and figuratively. What could Karmakov possibly have to do with the Greenleaf Project?" Tony was totally nonplussed.

"From your description of Karmakov, he and Huntington have at least one thing in common," Sam managed to say through a mouthful of juicy orange. "They're both arrogant megalomaniacs with a penchant for ordering people around and no interest in anything but their own vain desires. It would be interesting to see how they would work together, from a strictly academic viewpoint, of course."

"But that still doesn't explain how Karmakov could be involved in this scam. Maybe there's no connection at all. Maybe Huntington's planning to go to a Karmakov concert or something."

"Possible, but I think it would be interesting to know where Mr. Karmakov plans to be on August 10th."

"And how, pray tell, do you intend to find that out?" Tony queried.

"I thought maybe I'd just ask him," Sam answered innocently. "Why should you have all the fun, rescuing the damsel in distress and chasing away the fire-breathing dragon? Maybe I'll just invite our esteemed Russian visitor for coffee in the morning. But right now, it's well past my bedtime. If we're going to look and feel our best tomorrow, it's time for some shut-eye. You're welcome to use the guest bedroom, if you like."

"Thanks, I'm dead on my feet."

"Let's hope not."

* * * * *

At ten o'clock on Saturday morning, Sam dialed the number for the Adams Mark Hotel, the only five star accommodation downtown, located just a few blocks from the Station and less than a mile from the Firehouse. The switchboard operator quickly put the call through to Karmakov's room.

A male voice with a heavy Russian accent answered. "Mr. Karmakov is busy now. Who is calling." The words were a demand, not a question. Sam could imagine the rumpled brown tweed suit worn by the heavyset gangster that Tony had described.

"Tell Mr. Karmakov that I am a friend of Tony Angelletti and Katrina. Tell him that I am a lawyer with a strong interest in his U.S. activities. Tell him that I want to meet with him to talk about our mutual interests." There was another pause on the other end of the line. Sam winked at Tony, who was sitting on the couch in his jeans and tee shirt, sipping a cup of steaming coffee.

"Yes," Sam continued, "please tell Mr. Karmakov that I've talked with Mr. Angelletti and I think we can work things out to your mutual satisfaction. I will be in the hotel lobby in one hour." After another brief pause, Sam placed the telephone back in its cradle. "Well, nothing ventured, nothing gained," he said with a smile.

"You are entirely too chipper this morning," Tony muttered sleepily. "Don't you go get yourself shot up by the Russian Mafia just because you're in such a damn good mood."

* * * * *

"Those lowlife sons-of-bitches!" Huntington ranted to his captive audience. Barton sat quietly, leaning forward on the arms of his chair and staring at the floor, while Wilbur Olsen cowered next to the bookcases against the wall. Bob Gannon, chief of the security company that guarded Southwest Plaza, paced the floor and shook his head in disbelief.

"Mr. Huntington," Barton began, "we really don't know anything yet. It might not have been them. We can't confirm that it was Angelletti and Littlehawk..."

"And whose fault is that?" Huntington thundered. "*You* can't confirm squat! Who else do you think it *could* have been? There hasn't been a security breach in decades! And you think that this was some vagrant who got past the security cameras and onto the twelfth floor? Maybe into this very office?" Huntington was livid. "There's no *question* what has happened here. They beat us to the punch. But why last night? *You* said they were coming tonight!" Huntington glowered first at Barton then at Gannon in turn, his face dark red with anger.

"You don't think they could've known we were laying a trap for 'em, do you?" Wilbur volunteered, trying hard to rise to the occasion.

Huntington shot him a look that would wither a cactus. "Of course they knew, you moron, which means they found the bug in Littlehawk's office. They played us for fools." He raised his voice an octave to imitate Barton. "'They swallowed the bait, hook, line and sinker,' you said. *Idiots!* Get the hell out of my office so I can think. And get Bandini down here *now!*"

* * * * *

Sam strode into the cavernous lobby of the Adams Mark at precisely eleven o'clock. Several white marble tables, each surrounded by three or four arm chairs, were scattered around the lobby. After Sam had seated himself at a table near a bubbling fountain, a waiter offered him coffee and the morning newspaper. He was scanning the headlines when three men stepped off the elevator and headed in his direction.

There was no mistaking Karmakov. Sporting black silk pants, a white linen shirt with billowing sleeves, and long, dark hair, he perfectly fit the part, as did his henchmen.

As the three approached, Sam stood and extended his hand to Karmakov. In his most formal tone, he said, "Mr. Karmakov, I presume. I am Sam Littlehawk. It is a pleasure to meet you."

"I am Karmakov, world renowned concert pianist," the Russian responded formally, nodding slightly without taking Sam's hand. "And you are an American lawyer in a small Midwestern state. Earlier, you referred to our mutual interests. What interests could we possibly have in common?"

"Please sit down," Sam motioned to the arm chairs. "Will you have coffee?"

"No coffee," the Russian said as he sat on the edge of a chair across from Sam, while his companions moved to discreet positions some distance away. "You asked me to meet you. I am here. What interest do you have in me and my business?"

Sam sensed that Karmakov was curious, but any false step at this point would end the interview as abruptly as it had begun. "Tony tells me that you have big plans for Katrina in Europe," he ventured.

"Katrina is a superb artist with immense potential. Her talents must not be wasted. She must go with me to Europe, where together we will achieve a level of acclaim that she could never find in this country."

"Obviously, you have made this decision for her."

"Soon enough, she will thank me for placing her feet on the path to immortality."

"And you plan for her to be your wife?"

"In time, she will understand that this is best for her. She is a great Russian ballerina, and she will soon eclipse all who have come before her. She will be immortal and her talents will be remembered and celebrated for centuries. I am a great Russian pianist. We were meant to be together. Russian women sometimes require persuasion. I will soon persuade her that this is the right path."

Sam leaned back and absentmindedly scratched his jaw. "Huh," he said, "I must have been mistaken. For years I've thought that since perestroika, Russian women have been free to make their own decisions, without interference from the government, much less interference from casual acquaintances."

Karmakov's face darkened and he leaned forward as if preparing to pounce. "I will not debate this issue with you, now or ever. Decisions have been made. Katrina will leave with me within one week. Any interference from you or anyone else, including your comrade Angelletti, will be dealt with swiftly and harshly. Interference will not be tolerated."

Karmakov glanced across the nearly empty lobby toward his bodyguards loitering by the coffee bar like well-trained dogs. His habitual anger was boiling just below the surface, but he managed to maintain control.

"Leaving within the week," Sam echoed, as if he were carefully turning that thought over in his mind. Then abruptly, he declared, "But that would be before your August 10th meeting with Huntington."

Karmakov instantly tensed. Suddenly, the Russian was on his feet, agitated, unable to sit still any longer. "What do you know of Huntington?" he demanded.

"I know that you're involved in the Greenleaf Project," Sam shot back, hoping to push him to reveal more than he intended. "I know that you're planning to meet with Huntington on August 10th," Sam stated. "I know that this alliance will mean nothing but trouble for you in the future. Is your meeting here or in New York?"

Karmakov's fists were clenched. Long, tangled strands of dark hair partially hid the malevolent look in his eyes. He stepped closer to Sam and hissed, "Whatever you think you know, my American friend, *forget it now*, if you value your life. Huntington is a mere puppet, a pawn in a much larger game. You believe you are a match for Huntington, but to the players in this game, you are *nothing*. Believe it. *Nothing!*" Karmakov uttered the last word with such vehemence that it hung in the air like a foul odor. Turning, he stalked toward the elevator, followed by his faithful hounds.

Sam glanced at his watch and sipped his coffee. Less than twelve hours had elapsed since their covert visit to Southwest Plaza. They had learned a good deal in a short time.

* * * * *

Bandini was lounging in an arm chair in Huntington's office, thinking about the stinging rebuke that Huntington had dealt to the security people an hour earlier, when the phone rang. Huntington, who was seated at his desk, answered it and listened for a minute. His face first reflected surprise, then confusion. "How could he know? He's guessing. He's baiting you. He knows nothing." Huntington listened for another minute, then returned the phone to its cradle and turned to Bandini. He was assessing his options, and it seemed to him that he did not have many.

"That was Karmakov," Huntington said in a tone filled with frustration and distress. "Littlehawk and Angelletti know about the Russians *and* about the meeting in New York. How much more do they know? Their invasion of this office last night is a disaster! Littlehawk just met with Karmakov and asked him about the New York meeting. These bastards have gone too far, Bandini! They're more than just a nuisance now. They're a serious threat to the entire project, even to the company. They know too much, and it's clear they intend to use it. They've got to go! Today! Before this virus spreads." The senior partner's voice held a small but uncharacteristic element of dejection.

Bandini rose and began to pace. His smooth brow wrinkled into a frown. "It's risky, Tom," he muttered. "They're both prominent people. Whatever happens to them, there will be lots of questions. Hard to take them both out at once. Maybe a car wreck. No, too obvious…" Suddenly a glint lit Bandini's eyes and a smile spread across his thin lips. "Yeah! What an idea!"

Huntington looked at Bandini with skepticism, but also with a degree of admiration. More than once Bandini's scheming had brought them through difficult times. "If anyone is devious enough to solve this one, Bandini, it's you."

"Thanks for the vote of confidence, boss."

* * * * *

After Karmakov's dramatic exit from the hotel lobby, Sam walked the eight blocks from the Adams Mark back to the Firehouse. Pondering the complex situation, he considered the curious implications of Karmakov's words. There were many issues to consider, but the fundamental question was, to what length would Huntington go to save this project and the empire that he had spent his life building? Sam knew Huntington too well to underestimate him. This was certainly a time for extreme caution.

Yet Huntington might be the least of their worries. He was a cold-blooded, calculating, Machiavellian type, who would use all of his powers against them, but at least he was a known quantity who could be predicted. Karmakov, on the other hand, was clearly a loose cannon—a highly emotional, impulsive egomaniac with two gunmen for companions. He was also a foreigner who could commit crimes of any magnitude, including murder, with impunity and be out of the country before the blood was dry on the bodies. Even with the cooperation of international law enforcement, it would be unlikely that he could ever be brought to justice once he crossed the border. He thought he was above the law, and in a sense, he was.

Then there was the dark horse to consider. Karmakov had referred to other *players* in the project who made Huntington look like a pussycat. Who were they? What was their game? What threat did they pose? Or were these *players* just a ruse by Karmakov to try to intimidate them? Sam didn't think Karmakov was fast enough on his feet to lie so convincingly. Someone had definitely introduced Karmakov to Huntington. Clearly, there was an unknown connection.

Sam ran up the Firehouse stairs three at a time and found Tony poring over the documents. Tony flinched, then gasped, "Sam! It's only you."

"A little jumpy there, *amigo?*" Sam asked as he pulled a chair up to the table.

"What happened? Did you meet Karmakov?"

"He and his Russian wolfhounds. You described them well. He sure is a testy sort. He was positively perturbed when I asked him about his upcoming meeting with Huntington. I hit a live wire there."

"You didn't."

"Sure I did. It's clear now that the note on Huntington's desk was no coincidence. Karmakov obviously knows Huntington. Somehow, they're in this together. But the million dollar question is, who else is in it with them?" Sam related the details of the brief meeting and Karmakov's vague reference to other players.

"Is that all you could get out of him?" Tony asked.

"Talking with Karmakov is kind of like hand feeding rats to a cobra. I thought I did pretty well, considering I walked out with all my fingers and toes."

"So what do we do now? Dump all the information on the FBI and go for a long vacation on an uncharted tropical island?"

"Not so fast, champ. When we finally get to that point, *if* we do get there, I'm sure that you'll be needed here to testify. The beach will have to wait until this is over. And there is no way we can give this to the FBI. How much do you think would ever get before the grand jury? Remember how we got this stuff? Then there's Huntington's friends on the judiciary to consider. This would all be suppressed, even if we were able to get an honest prosecution going in this town. No, we have to use what we've learned to build an airtight case before we hand it over directly to the Justice Department in Washington."

Tony looked glum. "Sam, how in the world are we going to do that?"

A grim smile slowly crept across Sam's face. "That's not the hard part, Tony. The hard part is staying alive while we do it."

Chapter 6

"So who's their main target, you or me?" Tony asked.

"I'm sure they'd like to hang both our hides on the barn door," Sam answered. "But they can't just come in with guns blazing and hit both of us at the same time. That would certainly prompt a major investigation, and there would be lots of unanswered questions. It would also result in a search of our personal effects, and they don't know where the evidence is hidden, or who we've told about it."

"So what do you think they'll do?"

"Try to stage some kind of an accident. Get us both at once. And somehow, they'll try to retrieve or destroy the evidence that we have. They know they'll have to be mighty clever. And they'll need to work fast, before we have time to act on what we know."

Tony swallowed hard. "You know, Sammy, this all sounded like a pretty good idea a few days ago, but I think reality is starting to set in. What do we do now?"

"We have to separate and lie low while I digest what we've learned and lay a plan for how to present it to the proper authorities. We're at greater risk when we're together. Also, we have to protect Katrina. Karmakov will try to grab her and disappear. Whatever her thoughts are now, they could be a lot different after a month or so of 'persuasion' by Karmakov. She's no safer at this point than you or me, maybe less so."

"We need a game plan, Sam, one with a surprise in the fourth quarter."

"Didn't you say that Katrina is dancing tonight at the Performing Arts Center?"

"Yeah, it's an exhibition for Friends of the Ballet, followed by a reception. She asked if I would be her escort."

"Good. Karmakov wouldn't dare try to snatch her just a few hours before a public performance and right after our talk this morning. He knows we're watching and the bloodhounds would be after him in minutes. He's smart enough to wait until he can get at least a few hours head start before he makes his move. It will probably be tomorrow or later. But after the reception tonight, Katrina won't be anywhere that Karmakov and his gangsters can put their hands on her. You and Katrina will disappear until I contact you. Remember the old line shack on the north side of the ranch, down the Jeep trail by the creek? It's isolated and stocked with provisions for at least two weeks."

Tony grinned as the plan began to unfold. "Hmmm, yes. That's it! A long vacation in an isolated cabin with Katrina? I'm starting to feel better already! Sam, you are blessed with so many really great ideas. You do the heavy lifting here and I'll ride back into town in a week or two on a white stallion and take a seat in the witness stand, to bring truth, honor and justice back to our state. Great, let's do it!"

"You better go home and pack a bag, hombre, you're about to disappear—just not the way Huntington has in mind."

* * * * *

A full hour before the scheduled performance, Sam parked his midnight blue BMW roadster on Second Street, just half a block east of the Performing Arts Center, where it would be easily accessible. Since Karmakov would certainly be at the performance and there was a chance they would see Huntington or some of his crew there, he and Tony had agreed that they both should attend. They felt there was little risk of violence in a public place, and Katrina needed as much protection as possible. After the reception, Tony and Katrina would discreetly slip out through a tunnel exit near her dressing room, which would lead them to Tony's car. Undoubtedly, Karmakov's men would be shadowing Katrina, so Sam laid out a circuitous route to be certain that they were not being followed before heading to the ranch.

Sam reviewed their escape routes as he walked through the halls of the nearly empty building that would soon be bustling with patrons. Satisfied with his plan, he lingered in the mezzanine to watch the guests arrive.

Twenty minutes before curtain time, Tony joined Sam in the foyer. Both men were dressed in black tuxedos, white pleated shirts, and bow ties suitable for the occasion. Tony had chosen a maroon cummerbund and black studs, while Sam wore jade cuff links and studs with a black brocade vest.

After easing away from the milling crowd just inside the main entrance, the two began quietly discussing their escape routes and the plan for eluding Karmakov's followers. As Sam detailed the plan, Tony listened, while making frequent, furtive glances in the direction of the growing crowd. Sam recognized Tony's agitation and knew his cool veneer was wearing thin. Finishing his explanation Sam asked, "Is Katrina on board with the plan?"

"I explained everything. She's terrified of Karmakov and his goons. She'll do just about anything to get away from them."

"For good reason. He's a maniac," Sam said. "Her best bet is to get as far away from him as possible. The only question is how to do it. There's no point in taking any more chances than absolutely necessary. The instant the performance is over, you go to her dressing room and guard the door. There should be some security guards around, too. As soon as Katrina is dressed, you two make a brief appearance at the reception, then excuse yourselves. I'll be watching your back until you're gone, and it will be hard for anyone to follow you on the route we've chosen. Is your car in place?"

"Yes. And Sam, *you've* got to get out of here, too, and *fast*!"

"Don't worry, I will. But first I've got to have one more little talk with Karmakov. Then I'll meet you at the ranch."

"No, Sam! You can't do that! It's way too risky! And once we're gone from here, you've got to *stay away* from Katrina and me," Tony said, a little too loudly. Several heads in the crowd turned their way.

"Keep your voice down! And relax. We can do this."

Tony took a deep breath and lowered his voice. "Sorry, man. I guess I'm a little tense. I just don't want you taking unnecessary chances meeting with Karmakov alone. And I'd hate for any of those creeps to follow you to our hiding place. We've got to be *really* careful."

"Don't worry," Sam said with a casual smile. "My skin is one of my favorite things. I've grown pretty attached to it and I don't plan to lose it anytime soon. Nor would I do anything that would put you or Katrina in danger."

Relaxing a little, Tony cracked a familiar smile and squeezed Sam's shoulder. "Okay, pal, your game plans have worked for the past twenty years. Why lose faith now?" Then rising on his toes to see over the crowd, he added, "Don't look now, *amigo*, but our favorite Russian organ grinder and his two trained monkeys just walked in. Shall we greet them?"

"But of course," Sam replied in a tone that was at once both gracious and dangerous. "I certainly want to welcome our esteemed international visitors."

Sam and Tony moved through the bustling foyer, passing throngs of people dressed in black formal attire and sparkling party dresses, drinking champagne and awaiting the performance. They were still several yards from the Russians when Karmakov saw them coming.

"My American friends," Karmakov said with a slight nod that faintly resembled a bow. "Your presence shows that you at least have some appreciation for the fine arts. Or perhaps you just have an appreciation for the finest woman in the world. It is truly unfortunate for you that she will soon be leaving with me, removing the only point of light in this dark, desolate corner of the world."

Tony bristled and began to respond, but Sam put a restraining hand on his arm and calmly said, "Wishful thinking, Karmakov. She won't be leaving with you. Actually, she abhors you. To her, you are an abomination. Wasted talent."

Karmakov's eyes flared, but he maintained his composure. "Gentlemen, this will all be over very soon. Katrina and I will depart for Europe. I will win. You will die. We must discuss this fascinating subject further after the ballet." Without waiting for a reply, Karmakov brushed past Sam and Tony and into the performance hall, followed by his two henchmen.

"Well, I guess I'll just have to take him up on that invitation," Sam said with a smile as he followed Karmakov toward the entrance. "The more he talks, the more we learn. I want just one more chance after the show to pump him for information. He has a loose tongue when he's angry. In the meantime, let's enjoy the performance."

Sam and Tony moved with the crowd into the main hall. Tony found his seat on the left aisle in the tenth row of the orchestra section, an excellent vantage point from which he could clearly see the stage and make a quick exit to the backstage area. Sam stationed himself in an empty seat several rows further back, where he could keep a close eye on the three Russians seated at the opposite end of Tony's row. Sam had a clear view of any possible action. As the lights dimmed, he saw an usher handing Tony a note, which Tony folded and slipped into his jacket pocket.

For the evening's short program, the orchestra had been limited to twenty pieces, but its performance was superb. Clear, exuberant sounds filled the theater, enhanced by the perfect acoustics of the immense chamber. As the music began to build, a group of eight dancers clad in sheer, black bodysuits took the stage in a series of fast acrobatic movements that set the tone of the dance. A minute later, a ninth dancer entered, spinning and turning, her snow white satin costume flashing in stark contrast with the rest of the troupe. Instantly, Sam recognized Katrina as the lead. Her perfect form was unmistakable and was exquisitely elegant in a floating, knee-length skirt that accentuated her lithe form. He quickly settled in to enjoy the performance.

The three compositions on the program were all original with both musical scores and choreography composed by members of the Fine Arts Department of the University. Katrina had played a major role in every facet of the production, which was designed to highlight her strengths. As usual, her execution was flawless.

The graceful movements of the dancers soon fused with the music, giving visual expression to haunting melodies and eliciting a strong visceral response from the audience. Sam was entranced. Never before had a performance so touched his soul—he was captivated by Katrina. At the conclusion of the first composition, he joined the audience's standing ovation with enthusiastic applause.

The second composition was a rhythmic celebration of Latin origins. Fifteen dancers including Katrina were clad in elaborate costumes suitable for *carneval* in Rio de Janeiro. The festive frolicking engendered contagious excitement, and before the end of the dance, the audience was on its feet again, moving with the music. The second dance ended with a roaring tribute to Cuban salsa that was comic in the outrageous movements of the six male dancers.

The third and final dance had a more pensive quality, not quite melancholy, but touching and meditative. Katrina again performed the lead, backed by five other dancers. Her classical ballet experience was evident in the slow, graceful movements that bespoke deep and powerful emotions. Sam understood why the critics had marveled at her seemingly effortless ability and perfect balance. But more than that, he connected with the deep emotions that she expressed so eloquently, without a spoken word. The third dance ended quietly, with stage lights dimming to blackness and a long, reverent silence before the applause began.

As the lights came up and the performers filed onto the stage for a curtain call, Sam awakened from the trance that had overtaken him during the last dance. He glanced toward the Russians, noting that Karmakov was still in his seat applauding, but his two henchmen were gone! He turned quickly to look for Tony, but his seat was empty, too. Sam was stunned to realize that Tony had already gone backstage where he was to meet Katrina in her dressing room immediately after the performance.

As the audience rose for a standing ovation, Sam left his seat and walked quickly toward the back door of the performance hall. People standing in the aisle slowed his progress, but in a moment, he was out the back door, around the corner, and racing down the outside corridor toward the stage area.

In less than a minute, he found the stage door. From the corridor, he heard the muted sound of the continuing applause in the auditorium, as the dancers and orchestra took another bow. Sam threw open the door and rushed into the backstage area, unnoticed by the stagehands standing in the wings, applauding. Although he had never been backstage in the theater before, he had no trouble locating the hallway to the dressing rooms. Every sense was on edge as he peered down the hall, expecting the Russian gunmen to appear. Surely, in the five minutes since the performance had ended, nothing could have happened.

Seeing no one, Sam found his way to Katrina's dressing room, the last door on the right. Standing with his back against the wall next to the door, Sam looked quickly in both directions, then put his hand on the doorknob and pushed the door open. Leaning forward, he peered into the room. Sam felt his heart miss a beat when he saw Tony sprawled on the floor, face down in a dark pool of blood, a gaping wound behind his left ear. Suddenly, Sam's heart was pounding.

In an instant, he was kneeling at Tony's side, pressing his fingers against his friend's carotid artery. No pulse! A tremor of panic gripped him as he looked frantically for a telephone to call for emergency services. He spotted a phone mounted on the wall ten feet away. Leaping to his feet, Sam jumped over Tony's inert body, but found himself upended and falling when his foot rolled on something cylindrical on the floor. Sam hit hard on his back in the pool of blood next to Tony, atop the object that had caused his fall. Excruciating pain shot through his back as he groaned and rolled to his side. Standing, he picked up a heavy, magnum champagne bottle covered with blood. Holding it by the neck, he realized that this was the weapon that had bludgeoned his fallen friend.

Suddenly, Sam heard a woman's shrill scream. He looked up to see Katrina and two other dancers at the dressing room door. Before he had a second to think or speak, Katrina was kneeling at Tony's side. "He's not breathing!" she cried. "Somebody call an ambulance!"

As one of the dancers rushed to the telephone, more dancers and stagehands flooded into the dressing room. Pandemonium broke lose while Katrina tried to revive Tony with CPR. A very young ballerina hovering nearby looked at Sam in disbelief. "You killed him! He's dead!"

Sam suddenly noticed the heavy champagne bottle still hanging in his hand and his blood-soaked clothing. Involuntarily, his fingers released the neck of the bottle and it fell from his hand, making a loud clunk as it hit the floor.

Katrina's eyes searched his. "Sam, you could not have done this. He was your best friend."

"I didn't do it, Katrina. It was Karmakov's thugs. It must have been. I found him this way seconds before you got here." Their gaze held for a moment, and then she nodded, looking down again at Tony as she pressed her white, gauzy skirt against the deep gash in the side of his head. An approaching siren announced an ambulance was nearby.

"There he is! He did it!" The young dancer pointed a trembling finger at Sam, directing an armed security guard and an usher. The usher, an older man in a red jacket, eyed Sam warily, then looked at Tony's inert body still lying on the floor. "I saw those two arguing in the foyer before the performance," he said to the guard. "The one on the floor was telling that guy over there to keep away from him."

The guard looked at Sam, moved his hand to his holster, and gently released the leather strap. Sam leaned over, whispering to Katrina, "This looks bad, Katrina, really bad. I've got to get out of here, and *fast*. I can't do anything for Tony now, and I can't do anything for any of us if I'm locked up in jail, or dead. I'll explain everything to you as soon as I can. Don't worry. I'll find you."

At that moment, two things happened—the emergency exit door on the outside wall of the dressing room burst open as the response team rushed in, and Karmakov entered from the opposite hallway. As one of the medics deftly pulled Katrina away from Tony, another pushed Sam toward the emergency exit. Recognizing an opportunity, he headed for the open outside door, then hesitated and turned, unwilling to leave Katrina in Karmakov's hands.

Looking directly at Karmakov, Sam noticed a sinister gleam in his eyes. Obviously enjoying the trap that he had laid for the two Americans, he nudged the security guard and snapped, "Quickly! Your murderer is getting away!"

Sam knew he had no choice. As he turned again to dash out the open door, he caught a glimpse of Katrina standing in her once white costume, now covered with blood. Through the tears in her eyes, he could see fear and trepidation, like the eyes of a gazelle that had lost the chase and was about to be devoured by the lion.

Before the security guard could negotiate his way through the crowded room to the emergency door where Sam had disappeared, he was around the corner of the building and running the few short steps to his roadster.

* * * * *

The smaller of the Russian bodyguards pushed Katrina into the back of the limousine and entered after her, sandwiching her between himself and his larger counterpart. Karmakov sat facing her with a broad smile on his face. Katrina was dressed in sandals and a simple cotton shift that she had pulled on in place of the blood-soaked costume.

"Don't worry about your clothes, my dear, we have a new wardrobe waiting for you on the plane. I am sure that you won't be missed for a while, in the chaos of the moment." Karmakov paused to light a cigarette, then continued his soliloquy. "Quite shocking that your American friends are so murderous. It is best that we get you as far away from this hostile place as possible."

Katrina glared at the smug gangster, finally recognizing him for what he was. "Sam did not kill Tony, I am certain of that," she said with conviction.

Karmakov raised one finger. "But how can you be so sure? How well did you know this killer? How many times had you even met him? Once or twice? You heard the usher say they argued before the performance. How can you be so sure?" Karmakov lost no time beginning the re-education of Katrina. He took another drag on his cigarette, then opened the limousine's small bar and pulled out a bottle of vodka. "Perhaps a drink would calm your nerves and prepare you for the flight."

"I am not going anywhere with you," Katrina said in a tone that left no doubt as to her intentions and her resolve.

Again, Karmakov smiled magnanimously. "Some day you will thank me for taking you away from this dangerous place, Katrina. You must know that I am only thinking of you and your future…our future."

Katrina cursed him silently and turned to look out the window. They were obviously bound for the airport. She wondered how her circumstances could have changed so quickly. Just half an hour earlier, she had thought that at this moment, she would be escaping to safety with Tony. As she pondered her predicament, something caught her attention. A blue BMW roadster appeared in the outside lane of the five lane expressway. It quickly pulled up parallel with the limo, then just as quickly, it slowed and moved to the left lane. The car's unusual movement drew her attention, and she watched it suddenly accelerate, then exit onto another expressway.

"You will find the flight quite pleasant, I am sure," Karmakov said as he stubbed out his cigarette. "My friends have loaned us a Learjet that will fly us non-stop to Florida. We will rest there briefly before we go on to Moscow, where we will spend a few weeks. Soon you'll begin your professional career in Europe. Nothing could be better for the world's finest ballerina."

Repulsed by Karmakov's attempt to charm her, Katrina remained silent, knowing from experience that any attempt to dissuade him would be futile and any criticism she might voice would likely be dealt with harshly.

Darkness was falling when the limousine pulled through a gate in the perimeter fence of the airport and drove toward a large hanger surrounded by business aircraft of various sizes and types. Eight gleaming business jets were inside the hangar, while another five were parked on the adjacent tarmac. Directly in front of the open hangar stood a small Learjet with its passenger door open. Through the cockpit window, it appeared that the pilot was preparing for flight. The limo driver pulled onto the tarmac, driving toward the Learjet. Katrina's breath caught when she noticed a blue BMW roadster parked next to a twin engine plane a short distance from the waiting jet.

Obviously, Karmakov's departure plans included no delays. The limousine stopped twenty feet from the Learjet. The four passengers quickly exited the limo and crossed to the jet, with Karmakov in the lead and Katrina between the two gunmen close behind.

Karmakov ascended the short stairway to the door of the jet and was about to step in, when a figure suddenly appeared in the open doorway. Karmakov, who had been issuing instructions over his shoulder as he climbed the stairs, was taken by surprise. As he turned to enter the door, the figure he found blocking the entrance spun to the left and planted a heel squarely in Karmakov's chest, landing a mule kick that sent Karmakov tumbling backward into the others on the stairs behind him. Like four dominoes in a line, Karmakov, his henchmen and Katrina tumbled down into a heap on the tarmac.

In an instant, Sam leaped from the plane and was on the first bodyguard, who was on top of the pile trying to get to his feet. A quick, hard kick to the solar plexus doubled the guard over in pain and he fell to the ground, gasping for breath. Just a step away, the second guard was trying to roll out from under Karmakov while groping inside his jacket for his gun. With a goal line leap, Sam cleared Karmakov and Katrina and slammed his fist squarely into the middle of the second guard's forehead. The guard slumped to the ground as Karmakov struggled to drag the gun from the shoulder holster of the first guard, who was still on his hands and knees, gasping for breath.

Just as the weapon slipped free, Sam's iron fist grasped Karmakov's wrist and twisted it hard. The pistol clattered on the tarmac as Sam ducked under Karmakov's arm and then jerked it down, flipping Karmakov head over heels. The Russian landed flat on his back on the pavement. He tried to rise, but Sam was on him again, this time slamming a heavy fist into the bridge of his nose. "That was for Tony," Sam said with satisfaction as Karmakov's skull bounced on the pavement.

Sam's actions were quick and effective, but he was outnumbered. Although he had subdued Karmakov in just a few seconds, when he turned, he was face to face with the first guard, who had managed to get to his feet and recover his weapon. Sam froze, eying the business end of a loaded Uzi in the unsteady hands of the angry guard, who was still breathless from Sam's well-placed kick.

"Shoot the bastard!" Karmakov yelled in Russian as he struggled to rise from the ground, obviously in pain, blood streaming from his broken nose. "Shoot the damned American dog!" The guard raised his gun to fire.

"*Niet!*" Katrina shouted from five feet to the left of the guard threatening Sam. She raised the pistol she had taken from the other guard, who remained prostrate on the ground. The hair-triggered automatic weapon was less than three feet from the guard's left ear. There was a moment of hesitation as Karmakov, Sam, Katrina and the bodyguard each assessed the situation.

Katrina spoke first, in Russian. "Put the gun down, you fool! Are you ready to *die today* for your master, *Karmakov*?" She spat out the last word as though it left a vile taste in her mouth. Her tone of voice left little doubt that she was prepared to pull the trigger if necessary. Slowly, the guard bent as if to lay the gun on the ground. Then, quick as a striking viper, he ducked and spun, slapping the gun from Katrina's hand. Instantly, Sam lunged with a full body block to the armed guard's exposed ribs, knocking him to the ground. At the same time, Sam grabbed for the gun. A long burst of automatic weapon fire ricocheted off the tarmac as Sam struggled with the guard.

"Run, Katrina, get the car!" Sam yelled as he tried to wrench the weapon from the guard's hand. Katrina sprinted the twenty yards to the roadster and hurdled into the driver's seat.

Calling upon years of self-defense training, Sam disabled the guard with a sharp knuckle blow to the hand that gripped the gun, followed quickly by a back fist to the temple that rattled the guard's senses. He dislodged the Uzi from the guard's numb fingers just as Karmakov picked up the automatic pistol Katrina had dropped. Sam and Karmakov swung into firing positions at virtually the same instant.

"You're a bloody mess, Karmakov, but not nearly as *dead* as you'll be if I pull this trigger," Sam said, holding the dazed bodyguard in front of him as a shield, the Uzi leveled at Karmakov, who was partially shielded by the aircraft's landing gear.

Karmakov slowly waved the barrel of his weapon as he stared at Sam through glittering, hate-filled eyes. "Perhaps I will send you both to hell right now," he said slowly, blood dripping from his nose and chin. "Or, perhaps I will let you live, so that we may fight another day."

"I hope that day comes real soon," Sam replied coldly.

At that moment, the roadster skidded to a stop just behind Sam, engine racing. Keeping his eyes and weapon trained on Karmakov, Sam propelled the dazed guard toward the Russian gangster, then leaped into the car. As Katrina spun the tires on the tarmac and accelerated toward the open gate by the hangar, Sam turned to see Karmakov holding his bleeding nose and climbing the stairs of the jet, followed by the two limping and bruised bodyguards.

As the blue roadster sped down the access road and turned onto the freeway entry ramp, three police cars with sirens blaring were exiting on the other side. A few minutes later, from their vantage point on the freeway, Sam and Katrina watched a white Learjet rocket off the runway.

Karmakov may have escaped, Sam thought, *but Katrina is safe, at least for now.*

* * * * *

As soon as Sam felt certain they had not been followed, he asked Katrina to pull over and they traded places. Settling into the driver's seat that fit him like a glove, he deftly pushed the high performance sports car through its paces, heading downtown.

"You are bleeding," Katrina said, noticing a cut on Sam's cheekbone and another on his chin. "I don't even have a tissue. When Anatoly and his men forced me to go with them, I was not even allowed to get my purse." An involuntary shudder shook Katrina's shoulders as a fresh wave of terror surged through her.

Sam absentmindedly wiped the blood off his cheek and onto his pant leg. The small cuts on his face did not hurt half as much as his smashed, cut knuckles. For a moment, he remembered with satisfaction the look on Karmakov's face as his head thumped the pavement, but that thought quickly brought to mind the horrific head injury Tony had suffered. "I hope that murderous bastard Karmakov has a headache for a month," Sam exclaimed through gritted teeth. "He will pay for what he did to Tony."

Katrina leaned forward and put her face in her hands. They drove in silence for a few minutes, until she took a deep breath and slowly released it. In the dim yellow light of the streetlamps flashing by, Sam noticed Katrina's tear-stained cheeks. "Did you love him?" he asked quietly, stealing a sideways glance at Katrina, whose eyes were fixed on the road ahead, her face tense with emotion.

She shook her head almost imperceptibly. "Tony was a good friend to me, Sam, and such a fun person to be with. He cared for me and he made me laugh. He made me feel welcome here. I do not know what I felt. Maybe I did love him, in a way. But could he ever have truly loved me back?"

Sam drove on without responding. His mind filled with a tumultuous collage of images of his best friend—high school football star, prom queen escort, irrepressible college Romeo, bright and promising young law student, and finally, savvy politician. Tony always loved people, and people loved him. But lucky in love he was not. Sam silently mourned the loss of his friend as they drove the remaining distance to downtown.

Believing his home could be under surveillance, Sam parked two blocks away and they walked down a dark alley to the back entrance. Seeing nothing suspicious, Sam opened the door and they climbed the stairs to his flat. Inside, he found what he had feared. The files he and Tony had left on the table were gone, as well as the CPU of his computer, which contained the evidence they had compiled. Huntington had undoubtedly coordinated both the attack at the theater and the burglary of the Firehouse. There was no doubt they had declared war.

"Do you think that it is safe to be here?" Katrina asked as Sam made a quick reconnaissance of the building.

"Safe is something we won't be for a while. But there are some things that I need here, and you're probably safer with me than you would be on the streets. This won't take long."

He opened a small drawer in a roll-top desk and removed a key, which he used to unlock a door hidden in the side of a teakwood coffee table. He removed an automatic pistol and an unmarked CD and stuffed them both in his jacket pocket. "I'll explain later. Now let's get out of here before we have more company."

Sam and Katrina left the same way they had entered and hurried down the dark alley to Sam's car. He unlocked the door, then paused. "They'll be looking for this car. It's pretty obvious. Since we seemed to be alone, let's make a switch."

As he wheeled the roadster slowly down the alley to the Firehouse, Sam touched a button on the dash of the car that opened an overhead door.

"Well, at least they weren't into grand theft auto," Sam said, relieved to see his Jeep was still there. "They'll probably be on the lookout for the Jeep, too, but we may need four-wheel drive where we're going." He helped Katrina in and they drove out into the night, the overhead door closing behind them.

Half a block south of the Firehouse and across the street, a man in a parked car picked up a cell phone.

Chapter 7

W hat do you mean, he's not dead!" Huntington thundered, slamming his highball glass down on the table so hard that the premium whiskey inside sloshed onto the table. It was past midnight on Saturday night and Huntington had been drinking for several hours, which had not improved his disposition.

Barton stood at attention in the living room of Huntington's penthouse as he reported to Huntington and Bandini. "I just received word from one of my men at the hospital. Tony Angelletti is in the intensive care unit with a severe concussion and serious loss of blood. Apparently, the blow to his head fractured his skull and the trauma to the brain sent his heart into fibrillation, but the emergency medical team managed to bring him back from the brink. He would have been a goner, if they had been just a few minutes later."

"Just our luck," Bandini muttered, slouching deeper on the couch.

"He's not out of the woods yet," Barton replied. "The doctors said he may be slipping into a coma and the skull fracture could be enough to kill him. We'll know more in the morning. In the meantime, he won't be doing any talking."

"Where's Karmakov?" Huntington growled, still fuming.

"He kept to the plan. He and his men took the Learjet and headed for Nevada." Barton paused and swallowed. "But there was a little complication at the airport. It seems that there was an altercation. That Russian girl he took with him got away."

"What do you mean, an altercation?"

"We're not real clear on that just yet, sir, but the hangar security guard said the pilot was just calling in his flight plan from the hangar office when they heard a burst of automatic weapon fire. The security guard and pilot both ran outside just in time to see a woman burning rubber out of there in a BMW roadster. Someone jumped in the car with her, but the guard barely got a glimpse of him. No one had been shot, but Karmakov and his two bodyguards were pretty bloody and beat up. The hangar guard only had a few seconds to talk with them before Karmakov hustled the pilot onto the plane and they took off. Apparently, they figured they'd better get out of there before the cops arrived. Anyway, it must have been a tough outfit that jumped them. Karmakov's two bodyguards were both armed. The bottom line is, the girl got away and we don't know where she is."

Huntington grimaced. "I should have known better than to trust that operation to that idiot Russian and his two moron sidekicks. Should never have let him take that girl. She's got nothing to do with our business. She's just a liability." He paused for a long moment for the whiskey haze to clear a little, then focused an evil glare on Bandini. "It was your idea to let Karmakov handle this. What are we going to do now, Einstein?"

Bandini was cool, as always. He rose from the couch and paced the length of the spacious living room with his hands in his pockets. "Minor adjustments to the plan, that's all, Tom. Angelletti is not likely to make it through the night. If he does start to come around, he's going to have a serious relapse; we can make sure of that. Littlehawk's on the run. He's the obvious suspect in the killing of Angelletti. He was identified at the scene of the crime holding the murder weapon, and then ran when he was confronted. Karmakov had plenty of time to scatter a few little souvenirs around to make the case against Littlehawk even stronger. We've also recovered the stolen data from Littlehawk's apartment. Add a few twists and turns to cover our tracks, and *Voila!* Problem solved." Bandini had fabricated a plan to meet every contingency.

Huntington poured another double shot of whiskey into his glass, set the bottle down on the table, and looked squarely at him. "We've got to get this done *now*, Bandini. Don't screw it up, or we'll *all* be in the soup."

"You worry too much, Tom," Bandini responded with a thin smile, as he stopped in front of the bar and reached for a highball glass. "Trust me. Everything's under control."

* * * * *

Special Agent Dave Sanders pulled his pillow over his head for the third time, but it was no use. Sleep had evaporated, and with it, the sweet dream of tropical palm trees and beautiful Polynesian women serving him cold beers, massaging his shoulders and hinting of a promiscuous evening in paradise. Sanders clung to the dream images as long as possible. As the last vestiges of tropical beaches slipped from his mind, he realized that it was Sunday. He could relax. With the warm summer sun streaming through the window, he began to look forward to his Sunday morning routine—fresh ground coffee on his balcony overlooking Riverside Park, scrambled eggs and bacon, toast and marmalade, a new jazz CD and an uninterrupted hour to read the newspaper—a leisurely chance to recharge his batteries for another week.

Yawning and stretching, Sanders walked to the front door and opened it. He inhaled deeply and smelled the fresh scent of newly mown grass in the park across the street. Picking up the paper, he headed back to the kitchen, where the pungent aroma of fresh ground coffee beans filled the air. Sitting at the kitchen table, he unfolded the newspaper and his eyes were drawn to a bold headline on the lower half of the front page: *Ballet Shocked by Attempted Murder*. As Sanders scanned the article, his jaw dropped and he drew in a quick breath.

Public Utility Commissioner Anthony Angelletti is listed in critical condition at St. John Hospital after being brutally attacked while back stage at the Performing Arts Center after last night's ballet performance. The popular commissioner was struck in the head and suffered a severe concussion and other serious injuries. An investigation is in progress. The attacker is still at large. A local attorney, Sam Littlehawk, was seen fleeing the scene. He has been identified as a prime suspect and is wanted for questioning.

The harsh impact of the news kicked Sanders' sleepy brain into gear and he stood up so fast that he knocked over his chair. As he reached for the phone, he exclaimed, "Holy shit, Sam, what have you got yourself into?"

* * * * *

Detective Jason Walker reached across his cluttered desk and grabbed the receiver of the buzzing telephone. "Homicide, Walker," he said without expression.

"Morning, Detective Walker, this is Dave Sanders."

"Yeah, Sanders. FBI, right? What do you need?" Walker curtly asked.

"Have you read the paper this morning?"

"Nothin' in there I don't already know. What's your point?"

Sanders recognized Walker's brusque attitude as that of a detective who had been awake all night working a crime scene and was seeing Sunday morning through tired, jaded eyes. Having been there too many times himself, he knew Walker was probably floating a couple of donuts on a dozen cups of coffee, with a creeping headache and dry eyes. "You working the ballet case that hit the front page this morning?" he asked.

"Just spent all night at the Performing Arts Center. Why?"

"This could be FBI jurisdiction," Sanders replied. "It's a federal crime to attack public officials. I thought it would be a good idea to get an early start, just in case."

"Well, we've got an assault and battery and attempted homicide. From what I hear, it might turn out to be a homicide. Last word is that the commissioner is in a coma and might not make it. Someone whacked him pretty good on the noggin with a champagne bottle. Lot's of blood, cracked skull, quite a mess."

"So who do you suspect?" Sander asked nonchalantly.

"Thought you said you read the paper. Eye witnesses said a local lawyer, Sam Littlehawk, did it. They walked into the room and found him standing over the victim with the alleged assault weapon in his hand. When a security guard tried to take him into custody for questioning, he ran."

"Sounds bad. Any other evidence implicating this lawyer...who did you say? Littlehawk?"

"Yeah, another witness saw him arguing with the victim before the show. And we recovered a note in the victim's jacket pocket from the lead ballerina. The note's pretty incriminating. Seems that there was some kind of a love triangle going on with her in the middle. Looks like she was trying to keep these two from killing each other and not doing a very good job of it. It's pretty strong evidence.

But you know what will happen. If the victim lives, some cocky defense lawyer will say it was a crime of passion or maybe self-defense and the guy will walk. Victim dies, he might get two years. Makes me sick."

Sanders knew that eight hours of sleep would make Walker feel better about a lot of things. Late night crime scenes, hysterical witnesses, sleep deprivation, and too much lousy coffee tend to generate a cynical attitude.

"So, any idea where to find this Littlehawk?" Sanders asked, knowing that there were probably already several members of the city's homicide unit on his trail.

"We've got some ideas. But don't you worry about it, we got this under control. It's not a federal investigation, not yet. It's not even a homicide. If it turns into a homicide or the city calls in the feds, I'll let you know. Meanwhile, enjoy your day off."

"Yeah, thanks. Go get yourself some sleep."

Sanders hung up, certain that a good deal more was going on than Walker would admit. A high profile victim with a possible violent killer on the loose meant the media was already on the case. The city's homicide unit would be working around the clock to find Sam. He had to find Sam first, and fast. But where to begin?

Sanders poured a cup of coffee and thought long and hard. Although he and Sam had been acquainted professionally for years and were friends, he knew little about his personal life, other than the fact that he spent much of his free time on his family's ranch in Osage County, where his mother lived. Finally, for lack of any better ideas, Sanders decided to question a few of Sam's friends—maybe someone had heard from him or would know how to contact him.

As he drove downtown, he considered the situation. Discretion was essential. He was not willing to reveal his personal interest in the case to Walker and the city homicide crowd, much less to the FBI, since his friendship with Sam could disqualify him from working on the case. His recent meeting with Sam was still fresh in his mind. Sam's secret investigation was obviously connected to the attack on Angelletti. "Damn his hide!" he muttered, wishing he'd forced Sam to disclose more before equipping him with the FBI's high tech equipment. As his stomach started to churn at the prospect of the city homicide investigators finding FBI equipment in Sam's possession, Dave pushed a little harder on the gas pedal.

Although Camille's was a popular breakfast spot on Sunday morning, it was still early, so he easily found space to park in front of the Station. Camille greeted him as he stepped inside. "Morning, sir, table for one?" she asked, wiping her hands on the front of her white apron.

"Hi, Camille. Call me Dave. Remember me? I've been in a few times with Sam Littlehawk for your famous chocolate éclairs."

Recognition dawned on her face. "Oh yes, Dave, I remember. Glad to have you back again. Are you meeting Sam here this morning?"

Apparently Camille hadn't read the morning paper. "Not today. Actually, I'm looking for Sam. I need to talk with him about some business. You don't happen to know where he is, do you?"

"No, I haven't seen him today."

"Any idea where I might find him?"

"Well, if he's not at the Firehouse, you might try his mother's place. I think he usually spends Sundays on the family ranch. You know they have a place off Highway 20, out west of Skiatook. Sam's told me about it many times. They have a couple of thousand acres that borders on Skiatook Lake. Betcha he's out there."

Sanders nodded. *It's as good a place to start as any*, he thought. Maybe Sam's family would have some idea where he would go. His mother would need to be informed of the circumstances. In any event, it was a nice morning for a drive in the country.

"Thanks, Camille. You've been a great help." Sanders shook her hand.

"No problem. No breakfast this morning?"

Sanders looked toward the pastry case and sniffed. "Those fresh cheese Danish sure smell good. You couldn't put a couple of them in a bag to go, could you? With a tall cinnamon latté?"

"Oooh, they are irresistible, aren't they?" Camille said with a wink and a smile.

"The best!"

As Camille set a small sack and a steaming cup on the counter, Sanders counted out his change. "If you do see Sam, tell him to call me, will you please? Here's my cell phone number." He handed her his card.

"Sure thing, sweetie. And come back when you can stay for a real breakfast," Camille said with a smile.

* * * * *

North of Tulsa on Interstate 75, the terrain quickly changes from wooded lowlands to the vast, rolling grasslands that were once the boundless tallgrass prairie. On both sides of the divided interstate, herds of cattle graze belly deep in grassy fields that undulate in the wind like ocean waves. Once past the edge of suburban development, only creek beds, scattered stands of cedar and persimmon trees, and occasional ranch houses, break the rolling grasslands. For the most part, the land has remained unchanged for thousands of years, except cattle have replaced the buffalo and the vast acreage is divided periodically by barbed wire cross-fencing.

The small town of Skiatook, home of several rodeo heroes and one drive-in theater, lies about 20 miles northwest of Tulsa. Located on lands somewhat lower than the surrounding prairie, Skiatook is an oasis of pecan groves, truck farms, and small ranches. Further north and west in Osage County, the ranches are larger and the country is wilder. In northwestern Osage County, near the county seat of Pawhuska, many ranches are measured in sections rather than acres. On the expanses of prairie, broken by occasional creeks and canyons, the timber wolf still howls and sightings of cougar and bear are sometimes reported. The Tallgrass Prairie Preserve, more than eighty square miles of grassland that has never seen a plow, boasts a herd of well over a thousand buffalo that roam free, nurturing the land in the endless cycle of prairie life.

West of Skiatook, rougher terrain is broken by forested areas, rocky outcroppings and deeper canyons. Rolling grasslands still dominate the high terrain, but the grassy swells are punctuated by hidden valleys that are overgrown with oak, cottonwood, willow, and cedar, with clear streams that provide cover from winter's blizzards and the blazing summer sun, for both the grazing livestock and the abundant wildlife.

The land comprising Eagle Rock Ranch had been the home of the Littlehawk family for as long as anyone could remember. Long before Oklahoma was designated as Indian Territory, Sam's ancestors walked these same lands, which had provided year round sustenance for their horses and an excellent base of operations for hunting. When the Five Civilized Tribes had been compelled to move to Oklahoma in the forced migration that came to be known as the Trail of Tears, the Littlehawk clan and their Osage Tribe, which had been in the region for centuries, remained relatively undisturbed. Even when federal authorities instituted Indian land allotments generations later, the Littlehawks had banded together to maintain their claim on their ancestral lands. At the turn of the Millennium, Sam's family still owned nearly three thousand acres of prime grazing land.

Faye Littlehawk was a strong woman who had lived and worked on the land all of her life. At sixty, she still worked alongside her ranch hands, Red McGivern and Danny Roper, during busy times. On a weekly basis, she still rode her grey Arabian mare from one end of the ranch to the other. Widowed when Sam was in high school, Faye had managed the ranch without a husband for nearly two decades because she loved every aspect of ranching.

Tall and slender, with wavy auburn hair showing streaks of grey, Faye favored her Scottish father more than her Osage mother. Orin McNabb had abandoned Scotland to come to Oklahoma in 1938, looking for opportunity in the oil patch. He found both the opportunity he was looking for and an irresistible Indian princess. In a year, Faye was born, followed quickly by a brother and a sister. Twenty-three years later, Faye married Ben Littlehawk, a third generation Osage rancher and a leading citizen of Osage County.

Faye had been exceedingly proud when Sam excelled in college and then decided to go to law school. Although she would have gladly turned over the ranch to him at any time, she did not regret his decision to practice law. His legal training and experience gave him a depth of understanding and sound judgment that few could match. The Littlehawk clan needed a strong leader and Sam had proven to be wise and capable beyond his years, farsighted and conservative in his actions. At least most of the time.

But Faye was frightened. At five in the morning, as the first hint of dawn grayed the sky in the east, Sam had aroused her with a shocking story of murder and political intrigue, kidnapping, and international gangsters. Although the details were vague, it was clear that Sam had somehow become involved in a very dangerous situation. Accused of serious crimes, he was hiding from the authorities. She would do whatever she could to protect her family, but exactly what that might be was uncertain. Sam's instructions were sketchy at best. He had told her not to tell anyone he'd been there, not to repeat anything he'd said, and that he would contact her as soon as possible.

Sick at heart about Tony, Faye cleared the dishes from a late breakfast as she worried about Sam and pondered what she should do. A car driving down the long gravel driveway to the ranch house caught her attention, and she stopped working and watched as a man dressed in khaki slacks and a polo shirt park and approach the front door. Faye opened the door before he had a chance to knock.

"Good morning, ma'am. My name is Dave Sanders. Are you Mrs. Littlehawk? I'm a friend of Sam's. Could I talk with you for a minute?"

Faye hesitated, wondering for a moment whether the man was indeed a friend, or a foe. Unaccustomed to thinking in such terms, for a moment she froze before her innate hospitality took over. Inviting him inside, she replied, "Why certainly, Mr. Sanders, any friend of Sam's is a friend of mine. Please come in. Could I offer you a cup of coffee?"

"No thank you, ma'am," Sanders said as he stepped through the open door into the spacious, rustic living room. "I just had a cup on the way from the city. But thanks, anyway." Sanders waited a polite moment, then continued. "Mrs. Littlehawk, I came because I thought you might know where I could find your son. Actually, I was hoping that he would be here. There's some very important business we need to discuss."

"No, I haven't seen Sam this weekend," she lied unconvincingly, feeling quite awkward. "I don't know where he is. Have you tried calling his place in town?"

"Yes ma'am. He's not there." Sanders paused, waiting for a further response. When she did not volunteer any more information, he pressed on. "Ma'am, I hate to be the bearer of bad news, but Sam is in some serious trouble and I want to help him. That's why I'm here."

Faye hesitated, wondering what to say, then abruptly dropped her facade. "I saw the news this morning, Mr. Sanders. I know what they're saying about Sam. I also know that Tony Angelletti is Sam's best friend and Sam would never hurt him. Anyone who knew them would tell you that. They've been best friends since childhood. Tony's been like my own son."

"Yes ma'am, I know Sam is innocent and he would never hurt Tony. But there are those who would like to blame this crime on him. I just want to help, which I think I can do, but only if I can find him."

"If I hear from Sam, I'll let him know that you want to talk with him," Faye said quietly, but firmly. From her tone, it was clear that she was not going to cooperate further.

Sanders reached in his pocket and pulled out a business card. "Mrs. Littlehawk, here's my cell phone number. Please have Sam call me, if you see him." He turned to go, then seeing Faye looking at the card, he paused. "Yes, I am with the FBI, ma'am, but I'm not here on official business today. I'm here as Sam's friend. Really. Please, have him call me."

As Faye watched the Ford sedan ease down the road in a cloud of dust, she picked up the keys to Sam's Jeep, which were lying on a side table by the front door. The Jeep was in the barn where Sam had hidden it. Faye desperately wanted to warn Sam about the FBI agent and let him know that Tony was still clinging to life in the hospital. But could she risk a trip to the cabin? Sam had said her house was probably being watched. Faye paused with her hand on the doorknob, gripped by indecision, then slowly dropped the keys in a small Navajo clay pot sitting on the table by the door. No, she must keep to Sam's plan. He would come back after dark, as promised. That would have to be soon enough.

* * * * *

Hours later, Faye was still pondering her decision when she heard light footsteps padding down the sweeping wood staircase at the other end of the lodge room. She turned to see her nine-year-old granddaughter, a lovely child with long, honey-brown hair tousled from sleep, coming down the stairs with a cowboy boot in each hand and a big grin on her face. "Hi, Grandma. Is today the day I get to ride Jessie?"

Faye smiled and relaxed at the sight of Sam's tomboy daughter, Emily, who had spent more of her life on the ranch with Faye and the animals than she had spent in the city. "I thought you were going to sleep away this whole day, child!' she replied. "That was a good afternoon nap. Now you'd best get a move on if you want to try out Jessie before it's time to feed the cows. But first you need to fill up on some of this lunch I made for you."

Emily sat at the table and began to pull on her boots, while Faye uncovered a sandwich and sliced apple. As Faye set the plate on the table with a glass of milk, Emily suddenly looked up with a frown. "Grandma, is Daddy here? He was supposed to be here last night. He said he'd help me ride Jessie today."

Faye hated misleading her granddaughter, but she had no choice. "He had an emergency come up, child, and he had to stay in town. Said he'd be here later this evening. But he did say that you could ride Jessie, if I stay right with you."

That satisfied Emily. The prospect of riding the newest horse on the ranch, a beautiful dapple grey Arabian gelding, was enough to wipe out any concerns she might have had about the whereabouts of her father. To Emily, Sam was omnipotent and omniscient. He was her father, but he was also her best friend and companion. Since he had never wavered in his love for her, her confidence in him was boundless. Emily had relied doubly on Sam since the loss of her mother and Sam's beloved wife, Sarah, who had died six years before, when Emily was only three. The tragic and premature death of Sarah in an automobile accident drew Sam and Emily even closer together.

"Finish your sandwich, Emmie, and we'll head down to the barn. Danny left Jessie in the corral last night, so we won't even have to catch him." Faye picked up her hat, wondering what she would say if Emmie noticed the Jeep in the barn.

* * * * *

Nearly three hours later, Faye was loosening the girth on the new grey gelding and listening to Emmie's excited chatter, when she heard the familiar creak of the barn door opening. Slipping the girth strap through the cinch ring, she turned around, half expecting to see one of her two hired hands, although it was their custom not to come to the ranch on Sunday. Instead, she found two men in dark suits. They looked completely out of place in the dusty barn full of animals and farm equipment.

"Mrs. Littlehawk?" inquired the taller of the two men, whose grey moustache matched the short grey hair that stood up stiffly on his squarish head.

"That's my name. Who're you?" she asked bluntly.

"FBI, ma'am. Agents Wilkerson and Southerd," the tall man replied, flipping out a badge in a small leather billfold and holding it open for only a second at a distance too far away for Faye to read the credentials. "We need to know where your son is."

Faye looked from one man to the other and shook her head. "You're too late, boys, the FBI has already been here. Why don't you tell me who you really are?" She turned back to her saddling, keeping the two men visible in her peripheral vision.

The tall, grey-haired man stood his ground while the younger man with the curly brown hair and weak chin began to move slowly around the large barn, looking at the farm implements and other gear.

"This may come as a shock to you, ma'am, but your son is wanted for attempted murder. We are here to take him in peacefully. We have reason to believe that he's here on your ranch and we intend to find him and take him. It would be safer for both you and your son if you cooperate and *tell us where he is.*" The last few words were said in a tone that left no doubt that it was an order.

"You are not the FBI, sonny, and you have no right to be on this ranch," Faye said with equal vehemence. "Where's your warrant?" She lifted the saddle off the horse with arms and shoulders that were strong from lifting feed sacks, carrying buckets of water and performing a myriad of other farm chores. "Don't have one, do you? You don't come here and threaten me or my family." She took a step away from the horse, dropped the saddle, and picked up a pitchfork. "Now I think it's time you leave before you wear out your welcome."

The taller man was opening his mouth to reply when his curly-haired sidekick spoke from the far end of the barn, where he had raised the corner of a tarp. "Hey Barton, look what I found! A red Jeep!"

"Get the hell off my property!" Faye shouted in frustration as she raised the pitchfork menacingly.

The man swiftly reached into his jacket and produced an automatic pistol, which he pointed at Faye. "Put that pitchfork down, lady. I'm not here to hurt you, but if you get in the way, it might happen. Now back off with that pitchfork!"

Hearing the threats, his partner dropped the corner of the tarp and dashed forward, stumbling over the tongue of a wagon blocking his way, then slipping on an empty feed sack on the floor. Drawing his gun with some difficulty as he tried to regain his balance, he stopped ten feet from Faye, dusty and disheveled.

Faye couldn't help but laugh. "You two are a sight. Two grown men with guns standing off one little old lady with a pitchfork. Put those peashooters away and vamoose from my ranch before I lose my temper. And I guarantee you wouldn't want that to happen. It would be an ugly sight."

Her humor was lost on them. While the younger man loosely held his pistol and brushed hay and dust from his suit, the other flushed with anger. Stepping toward her, he seethed, "You'll tell me where your son is *now*, lady, if you value your life."

Faye stepped back a pace, glancing up as she moved. She had glimpsed movement in the hayloft, the edge of which was directly over the heads of the two men. As she glanced up through the open loft door, she saw Emmie's boots sticking out from behind several bales of hay that had been carelessly stacked at the very edge of the loft. The boots disappeared for a second and then reappeared with the soles planted flat against the side of the bottom bale. Emmie's back was braced against a large stack of bales a few feet further from the edge.

"Take another step toward me, you mangy coyotes, and you'll be eating dust," Faye scoffed sarcastically.

The two gunmen couldn't resist responding to the taunt. They stepped forward with obvious evil intent, but before they reached Faye, there was a scraping noise directly overhead. As they looked up, half a dozen bales of hay tumbled down on them, knocking them to the ground and leaving a cloud of loose hay and dust hanging in the air.

The bales of hay muffled the sound of a single gunshot as the two men sprawled in the dirt on the barn floor.

Chapter 8

Dr. Weaver checked his patient's vital signs for the third time in half an hour and shook his head in disbelief. Just twelve hours earlier, this patient had been near death, in a coma from a severe concussion and the ensuing shock. Besides the apparent neurological damage from the skull fracture, he had nearly bled to death.

Amazingly, though, the patient was showing signs of rapid improvement. Although he had not regained consciousness, the light sedation that had been administered during emergency surgery to repair the fracture was wearing off and the EEG monitors indicated a return to normal brain activity. While his breathing and heart rate were not quite normal, they were at least regular.

During his years in the intensive care unit, Dr. Weaver had seen incredible recoveries, some that he would even call miraculous, but none more so than this one. He would like to have attributed his patient's rapid improvement to some new breakthrough in medical science or his own skill, but he could not. His treatment could have been administered in any hospital in the country—even the skull fracture surgery had been relatively routine. Dr. Weaver could only attribute the patient's quick rebound to a healthy constitution, the first aid administered by the paramedics, and perhaps an uncommonly strong will to live. Looking once again at the monitors, it seemed to Dr. Weaver as though his patient was simply willing his body back to life.

As the doctor rested the palm of his hand lightly on Tony's bandaged forehead and lifted an eyelid, a nurse appeared in the open doorway of the glass-walled cubicle.

"Hello, you must be Dr. Weaver," the nurse said quickly. "I'm Jane Sellers, a relief nurse. I'm here to round out the team today. One of the regular nurses asked for the day off, it being Sunday and all. I was sent here…uh, I mean, the hospital's regular staffing sent me. I always wanted to work in the intensive care unit." The fast-talking nurse stammered to a stop.

Dr. Weaver glanced at the nurse. She was about thirty-five years old, short and blocky, with a round face and an unruly mop of curly brown hair. Her heavily muscled arms would not have looked out of place in a championship wrestling ring. He had not seen her before, but in a large hospital, meeting new staff was routine.

"Welcome aboard, Nurse Sellers," he said with a tone of authority. "I was just getting ready to go off duty. Dr. Scott will be taking my place soon."

"I'll be pleased to work with Dr. Scott, sir. I hear he's a great physician. But before you go, Dr. Weaver, could you take just a minute to fill me in on the condition of the patients in the ICU?"

"Of course, nurse. You didn't think that I would leave without briefing the duty nurses, did you?" Dr. Weaver asked loftily.

Nurse Sellers took a short step back and dipped her head. "Oh no, of course not, doctor. I just want to make sure that I do my best work and follow the book on my first day here in the ICU. I've never worked in the ICU before. Did I tell you that already?"

As Dr. Weaver turned back to the patient, he rolled his eyes and said a silent prayer for patience. "We'll discuss this patient in depth in the briefing. When he does awaken, *if* he awakens, you need to advise the police officer in the hallway outside the ICU. Mr. Angelletti was the victim of an attempted homicide and there are several people who will want to talk with him as soon as he is able."

"A *homicide?*" the nurse exclaimed.

"Yes, a *homicide,* Dr. Weaver mimicked with a hint of sarcasm in his voice. That's police talk for murder. How long have you been a nurse, anyway?" Dr. Weaver asked irritably as he turned to leave the cubicle. It had been a long shift, with two code blues and five new patients. Twelve hours was just too long a stretch to work in ICU. He knew his effectiveness was impaired, which always made him irritable. And how many times had he told the hospital's personnel director not to send rookie nurses to the ICU?

Dr. Weaver stepped out the door of the glass cubicle, then turned back to Nurse Sellers, who was examining the patient's electronic IV controls. "Do you plan to join everyone for the shift change briefing, nurse?"

She turned abruptly. "Sure thing, doctor, I was just checking to make sure the IV was working properly."

* * * * *

Huntington leaned back in an overstuffed maroon leather chair and put his feet on the heavy glass-topped coffee table. Dressed in a light green polo shirt, tan slacks and saddle shoes, he stared out the broad window overlooking the river. Bandini, also dressed for a Sunday golf game, was pacing the length of the lush living room of the penthouse.

"No, he has not regained consciousness, and no, he never will," Bandini said, only partially masking the exasperation in his voice. He made an about-face and continued to pace. "That's being handled. There are operatives at the hospital right now."

"Quit pacing. You're going to make a permanent track in my carpet," Huntington growled. "Still no word from Barton?"

"He hasn't checked in since he was on his way to Littlehawk's ranch a few hours ago. Said he was pretty sure that's where Littlehawk and the girl are. If they're there, he can find them."

"He'd better, and fast," Huntington muttered. "Your frame job could fall to pieces pretty damned fast if Littlehawk and that girl ever get to the right authorities. They've got to be found and silenced."

Bandini dropped into an armchair opposite Huntington. "Listen, Tom," he said earnestly, "we've got to stick to the game plan. The frame job is solid. The eye witnesses were a stroke of luck, but they make it so believable. Littlehawk is toast. He'll take the fall for the death of Angelletti. But even if he somehow manages to slip the noose, no one could connect the attack on Angelletti to us. Karmakov and his men are long gone and we recovered all the stuff on the Greenleaf Project from Littlehawk's apartment. We're clean. On the other hand, if Littlehawk turns up dead right now, no one will believe that he's the one who killed Angelletti. The whole plan starts to unravel."

Huntington shot him a withering stare. "That's the main problem with you, Bandini, you're gutless. *No loose ends.* You know the rule. Littlehawk knows far too much, and so does the girl. And he's too damned smart. He'll figure out a way to hang us, if he lives long enough. He and the girl are together now and they have to be found. They need to have an accident. Soon. Tonight at the latest."

Leaning forward, he hoisted himself from the chair. He took three steps to the window and looked west across the river, toward Nevada. "I expect that right about now, Karmakov is sharing the news with our partners in Vegas. We'll be getting a call soon, and we'd better have some answers. We wouldn't want them to start thinking of *us* as loose ends, now would we?"

* * * * *

Nurse Casey Sellers was uncomfortable in her stiff, white nurse's uniform. She had been a nurse for exactly four hours, and she did not like it. Although she'd done a lot of gigs in her life, she'd never seen herself as an angel of mercy. It really didn't fit her personality. Dealing cards may have been the best fit—it had certainly been easier and healthier than her first gig in Vegas. At seventeen, she had enjoyed the excitement and danger of prostitution. The money had been good, but she hated the pimps and finally tired of the party scene.

Dealing blackjack had been better. Certainly safer, and she did not have to worry if she gained a few pounds, or quite a few, which she had done without remorse. The problem was that after a few years of dealing, she was bored to tears. After so many years in Vegas, it had been easy to start selling crack to the tourists and occasionally rolling a drunken winner—more lucrative trades that brought a little excitement back to her dull life.

From the first, she had naturally gravitated to an easy buck. And the longer she lived, the less she cared how she got it. Sure, people got hurt. Everyone gets hurt. She had been hurt all of her life, first by her mother and the many men that they had lived with during her childhood, and then by the pimps and the tricks in Vegas. Nearly every day of her life had been marred with pain. Why should she care, if she caused pain to others? Caring was not her strong suit.

It was the drug dealers who had introduced her to the hit business. After all, what was the difference between hitting a drunk in the head and taking his money, and doing the same thing for hire?

That had been three years ago. Although far from being a seasoned professional, her success had merited a referral to the Russians. At first, she had been wary of them, but they had turned out to be more businesslike than the drug dealers she had worked for in the past, who were the most unpredictable and dangerous people of all. A fatalist, she believed that when your number comes up, it comes up, that's all.

She had been a little surprised when she got the call directing her urgently to take the first available flight and advising her that all she would need for the job would be waiting for her at the destination. The Russians obviously planned better than the drug dealers, who usually just gave her a name and address and left the rest to her. As promised, someone had met her at the airport with a bag full of tricks to make the job easy.

"Nurse, would you come here please?" Casey heard Dr. Scott call from down the hall. She had managed to dodge him for most of his first hour on the floor, but if they spent much time together, he would surely know that she was no nurse. She was trying to be as inconspicuous as possible, until she could get two minutes alone with the target. The past hour had been very frustrating, with one interruption after another preventing her from completing her assignment. Already, she had received several long looks from other nurses and even an orderly. She had to get the job done and get out quick, before she blew her cover.

"Yes, doctor, how can I help you?" she asked in the most prim and proper voice she could muster.

"How's our miracle boy in three coming along? Still holding?" he asked as he adjusted the dials on some kind of a monitor.

"He seems to be doing better, doctor, but I think I should go check him again. It's just about time to change his IV."

"Good idea, nurse, just let me know if there is any change in his vitals." Dr. Scott was obviously preoccupied with what he was doing.

Great, Casey thought. *Time to get the job done and get gone.* She walked into the target's cubicle. He was still unconscious, but breathing regularly. Quickly, she unbuttoned the top two buttons of her nurse's uniform and withdrew a small plastic tube the size of a cigarette. Buttoning her uniform again, she removed from the plastic tube a tiny syringe. A quick look over her shoulder verified that she was still alone, although the high level of activity in the ICU guaranteed that she had no more than a minute or two, possibly just seconds, to complete her work.

With the tiny syringe in hand, she turned her attention to the plastic bag of IV solution that she had brought with her to the cubicle. The needle of the syringe was so small and sharp that it pierced the tough plastic IV bag easily. Injecting the clear contents of the syringe into the bag, she quickly removed the syringe and dropped it into a refuse container. She exchanged the IV bag on the machine next to the bed for the new one, then took one final look at the patient. *Too bad*, she thought. *You're not a bad looking dude, even with half your head wrapped in bandages. Bet you're a lady killer, too.* She turned the IV control up a notch.

Casey had been told that if the poison in the syringe was injected directly into the patient, he would die within fifteen seconds. That left no time to escape and it could leave signs of poisoning that might be revealed by an autopsy. Diluted in the IV solution, the poison would take a little longer to reach a lethal dosage, but it would still be fairly quick. She needed to be out of the ICU in five minutes and clear of the hospital in ten. When the Code Blue sounded, she'd be halfway to the airport.

She relished the thought of walking away from the ICU without so much as a word to the good Dr. Scott and the other nurses who had treated her so rudely. It was obvious to Casey that they were a conceited bunch who thought they knew everything. But they would never figure out who she was, why she had been there, or what she had done. The patient would die of natural causes, Casey would collect her fifty grand, and the medical establishment would be none the wiser.

The thrill of victory was almost like the feeling she'd had five years earlier when she'd rolled a drunk and walked away with nearly thirty thousand in cash. Luck had been with her. But the thrill of winning was short-lived. Minutes later, as she stepped into a waiting car parked a block from the hospital, the gray haze of depression descended on her once again. The success or failure of her assignment did not matter. She couldn't care less whether the man she had just sentenced to death lived or died. Nothing mattered. For a second, Casey wondered why she had not simply injected herself with the syringe.

* * * * *

Sam and Katrina sat on a limestone ledge overlooking a small, clear creek a mile from the ranch house. The ledge was in a draw that was hidden from view by surrounding trees, but the opening over the creek gave a splendid view of the sky to the south and west. Sunset was less than an hour away and the towering cumulus clouds were already taking on shades of pink and orange, while the high cirrus clouds maintained their wispy whiteness. Sam felt safe and comfortable, as he had always felt on the ranch, despite the fact that he was undoubtedly the target of intense searches by both legal and illegal forces. In another hour, he would deal with reality. In the meantime, it was enough to absorb the beauty of the land and the sunset in the company of a lovely woman.

"This is a most beautiful place," Katrina said. "I do not remember ever seeing such a sunset before."

Sam smiled. "Last week Tony and I watched a sunset just like this one from a hilltop right over there," Sam said, nodding toward the southwest. He took a deep breath and slowly released it. He still could not believe that his friend was gone.

"You and Tony have been friends for a very long time, haven't you?" Katrina asked quietly.

"Most of our lives," Sam replied.

"He was a fine man," Katrina started, then catching herself, she said, "He is a fine man."

Sam turned to look at her and said, "It's all right, Katrina. We have to face the facts. It's as bad for you as it is for me. I think you loved him, too."

Katrina frowned. "Yes, I think I did love him, in one way, but not in the way that he wanted. He was a wonderful friend to me. I kept telling him that he was like a brother to me, but he laughed when I said it, or he acted as if he was hurt. He wanted something more from me." As Katrina spoke, she became more and more animated. "I enjoyed his company and he enjoyed my company, too. I cannot believe that I brought him to meet Karmakov. I was so stupid! But…I can't talk about this now!" Katrina's face clouded and she shook with emotion, holding back tears. Finally, she drew in a deep breath and exhaled the words, "I'm so sorry, Sam."

"You've been through a lot these last few days, Katrina," Sam replied. "You have a right to be tense."

Minutes passed as the two sat in silence, wrapped in their own thoughts, letting raw emotions mend as the dying sun slowly fell below the horizon. A crow cawed somewhere down the valley. A hawk circled overhead. Sam thought of the times that he and Tony had speculated about what it would be like to be reincarnated as a hawk, floating on summer breezes, with a perfect view of the sunset. Perhaps that was Tony circling overhead now. They could still watch sunsets together. As the sky before them deepened into spectacular shades of red and gold, Sam thought that this was a sunset that Tony would truly appreciate.

Finally, Katrina spoke. "I never thanked you for saving me from Karmakov," she said. "You were incredibly brave to attack Karmakov and his men alone."

"Incredibly foolish, you mean," Sam responded. "We could have both been killed. There were surely better ways to handle that situation. I just couldn't think of any at the time."

"I would rather be dead than go through the brainwashing that Karmakov had in mind for me. He has friends who were KGB. Now they work for the Mafia in Russia. I know what would have happened to me. I know Russia and I know Karmakov, perhaps too well. I am nothing but a toy for him."

"Well, you're far more than that to me," Sam said impulsively. Then realizing the import of his words, he quickly continued, "I mean, you are…a great artist. You deserve to be…you deserve to be treated with respect." Sam felt his face flush. "Besides, Karmakov is an animal."

Katrina looked at Sam for a moment, beginning to understand him—bold to the point of recklessness, yet genuine, loyal and caring. She rested her hand on his forearm and felt his muscles tense. "Whatever happens," she said, "I want you to know that I appreciate all that you have done for me. Your strength has given me hope."

Sam gazed at the billowing clouds that were changing from deep rose and purple to dark blue. Stars were beginning to pop out overhead as the last dying embers of the sunset faded on the horizon. Finally, Sam rose to his feet and extended a hand to help Katrina stand. Although she took his outstretched hand, she rose in one smooth, effortless movement. Instantly, she was on her feet, standing only inches from Sam, her hand still clasped in his. Their eyes met. No words were spoken, no conscious choices were made, but they shared something at that moment that has passed between men and women for a thousand generations—a force as old as mankind.

For several seconds they stood together, but Sam could not ignore their tenuous situation. Finally, he broke the spell. "I'd love to stay and enjoy this beautiful evening with you, Katrina, but there's work I must do. We may be safe here for a little while, but Huntington and Karmakov won't leave us alone for long, nor will the police, if I am indicted for murder, which is obviously their plan. I have to organize the evidence and deliver it to the right people, before it's too late. If I'm ever arrested, Huntington has the power to make sure I never tell the story. But I would bet that he doesn't plan for the police to find me alive."

"And what do you think they plan for me?" Katrina said, realizing the danger that they both faced. The grim look on Sam's face answered her question.

"Karmakov might convince them to spare you," he said, "if he can persuade them that he will effectively erase your memory and take you away permanently. More than likely, though, they wouldn't be convinced."

The two walked the short path back in silence. Entering the log cabin, Sam lit a kerosene lamp and opened the cupboard. "There's plenty to eat. I think you'll be safe until morning. Only a few of our close friends and the ranch hands know this cabin exists, and it would be nearly impossible to follow the trail in the dark. Even in the daylight, it can be hard to find this place in the dense cedars. With luck, I'll be back no later than noon tomorrow. If I'm not, you can follow the trail back to the ranch house. My mother will be expecting you."

Katrina smiled. She was no stranger to adversity. "Be safe, Sam," she said.

Sam grinned. "Danger is my middle name." And with that, he was out the door and down the trail.

He moved quickly and silently in the dark. Having walked the trail from the ranch house to the cabin a thousand times, every dip and turn was familiar and easily traversed in the dim moonlight. Ten minutes later, he was on the last stretch of path when he sensed that something was wrong. It wasn't late, but no lights burned in the house. He glanced toward the barn where a light shined from the open stalls on the south end of the building. With every sense on edge, Sam crept silently through the darkness toward the light.

Chapter 9

By the time the last bale of hay rolled to a stop, Faye was standing over the fallen men with the business end of a pitchfork hovering four inches above one of their noses. "You move a muscle and I'll shove this pitchfork right down your throat!" she said in a tone that left no doubt of her ability to carry out the threat. Slowly, she sat on the bale of hay that lay lengthwise across the younger man's belly, adding her weight to the bale. On the ground, he gasped for air and coughed on the alfalfa dust that filled the barn. "You wouldn't be the first sidewinder that's been skewered on this pitchfork," she added, as she moved the tines of the pitchfork an inch closer to his nose.

A few feet away, his partner rolled out from under a bale of hay and sat up, blinking the dust from his eyes. In the tumble, his gun had discharged harmlessly into the ground. Pointing it at Faye, he slowly got to his feet.

"I suggest that you put that thing down, lady, and move away from him before someone gets hurt."

"Someone's going to get hurt alright," Faye replied, not budging. "I don't like snakes in my barn and they always seem to come in pairs. There's the last pair that I caught in here," she said, cocking her head toward to two diamondback rattlesnake skins tacked to the barn wall. "I'll hang your sorry hides right next to theirs."

"I'm afraid that won't be possible, ma'am," The tall, greying man said as he took two steps back, craning his neck to get a better view of the hayloft. "Now why don't you tell your friend to come down before I have to go up there."

"You're not going anywhere if you value your partner here," Faye snapped, pushing the pitchfork so close that the younger man's nose was centered between the tines.

"Lady, you'd better think twice," he said, squeezing the trigger. The deafening report caused Faye to leap involuntarily to her feet as the bullet buried itself harmlessly in a bale of hay. "You better think about whether you want any stray bullets flying around in that hay loft," he continued, raising his pistol and waving it toward the loft.

Faye hesitated for a moment, then stepped away and leaned the pitchfork against the barn wall, knowing that her bluff had been called. With a grunt, the younger man shoved the heavy bale off his chest and struggled to his feet, shaking hay from his clothes and wiping his eyes.

"Now, tell your friend to come down here," the tall man barked, again pointing the gun in Faye's direction. Faye called to Emily and light footsteps trod across the wooden floor of the loft. Emily slowly climbed down the ladder and stood next to her grandmother. The man scowled when he saw that the accomplice in the hayloft was a small girl, but he maintained his cool. "Now, you two ladies take a seat on that bale of hay," he said, handing his weapon to his partner, who had been looking for his own gun in the scattered bales of hay. "I don't think my associate is too happy right now, and he's a little tense. So don't do anything stupid."

The man pulled a cell phone from his jacket pocket and blew the dust off of it, then moved away from the three toward the other end of the barn and punched in a number. Faye watched the man scowl as he talked, obviously reporting to his superiors. It was clear that there was a bitter disagreement over the situation and the man wanted vengeance, but she could tell from the little she could hear that his superiors were more interested in Sam's whereabouts than anything else.

After pocketing his cell phone, the man turned to Faye again. "You can save us both a lot of trouble, lady, if you'll just tell us where your son is." Faye glowered at him, but remained silent. Without another word, the man reached in his pocket and pulled out a lighter. Making sure that Faye was watching, he flicked the lighter a couple of times, picked up a handful of loose hay, then lit it. Dropping it on a small pile of loose hay on the floor, he smiled sadistically as the acrid smell began to fill the barn. Turning to his partner, he said, "Put them in that tack room and bar the door. Then get the car ready. This place will go up fast."

"Even you two aren't stupid enough to do that," Faye said, as Emily gripped her arm in a paroxysm of fear. "Murdering us won't get Sam for you. It'll just make you both murderers."

"I might just be crazy enough to do it," he replied sharply. "There'll be nothing here but a pile of ashes in an hour. You'll be gone without a trace. No evidence of a crime at all. Just another tragic accident." As the smoke in the barn got thicker, he spoke harshly. "Last chance, lady. Where's Sam Littlehawk?"

* * * * *

"I'm right here," Sam called from the shadows of the horse stalls in the back of the barn. "And I've got you in the sights of a twelve gauge shotgun. If I squeeze the trigger, your guts will make such a mess it'll take us a week to clean this place up. And then I'd be forced to shoot your buddy too and burn the barn down with both of *you* in it. Like you said, in an hour there'll be nothing here but a pile of ashes." Sam paused as if in thought. "In fact, the more I think about it, the better it sounds. We've been needing a new barn. This one's a real firetrap. There's nothing I'd like better than to exterminate a couple of polecats and get a new fireproof barn to boot. And I might just be crazy enough to do it."

There was silence while the men considered their predicament. Then Sam continued, "Mom, would you relieve those gentlemen of any weapons and cell phones they might have?" She quickly did as he asked, then led Emily to a safe distance. "And would you now please escort the two gentlemen into the tack room and bar the door behind them?"

"Now just wait a minute, Littlehawk," the tall man said as he took a step toward the back of the barn where Sam was hidden. "You can't just lock us up and…"

"Oh can't I?" Sam interrupted. There was an earsplitting roar and a board five feet above Barton's head splintered, showering him with dust and debris.

The men jumped like they'd been shot, then stood and looked at one another, bewildered by the rapid turn of events. They didn't have long to consider their options before the next shotgun blast hit the floor in front of them, pelting them with dirt. "Get in the damn tack room, *now*!" Sam snarled, and this time the two men moved fast. Faye quickly dropped the bar across the tack room door behind them.

Sam stepped out of the stall where he had been hiding, found a hose, and immediately began spraying the smoldering hay. Luckily, it had only been a small pile of loose hay, which was quickly extinguished. Trembling, Emily ran to Sam and wrapped her arms around his waist, sobbing with relief. Faye walked over and embraced them, obviously shaken but resolute.

"Now what are you going to do with them, big chief?" Faye asked Sam as she snuffed out the remains of the smoldering hay with the toe of her boot.

"Call Jake Fielding," Sam said. "I'm sure the Osage County jail will have room for these two buzzards. Trespass and assault with a deadly weapon are serious offenses. Judge Herd will set a hefty bail when he hears what they did. I'll bet Sheriff Fielding would be willing to send out a deputy to keep an eye on the place. Meanwhile, these guys can regret their mistakes with the mice in the tack room." Sam hit the light switch on the outside wall of the tack room. "It's pitch black in there at night, and that room is pretty tight. I don't think they're going to get into too much trouble."

"But Sam, if Sheriff Fielding hears the whole story, he'll know you were here. What if the *real* FBI comes looking for you again?"

"*Real* FBI? *Again*? What are you talking about?"

Faye related the story of Sanders' visit earlier in the day and the fact that their two prisoners had claimed to be FBI agents as well. Sam shook his head in disbelief at the stupidity of Huntington's men. "Impersonating the FBI? That must have been pure inspiration on their part," he said. "Huntington does have friends in high places, but the federal authorities take a dim view of people who impersonate the FBI, not to mention arson and death threats against innocent women and children. I seriously doubt that Huntington ordered these guys to pose as FBI agents or to burn down the barn with you and Emily in it."

"There's something else you don't know," Faye said suddenly, realizing that she hadn't seen Sam since before dawn. "Tony is alive! It was on the news this morning, and I called the hospital when I heard it. They wouldn't tell me much, but I did learn that he's in the ICU at St. John Medical Center. At the time I called, he was still unconscious, but he's stable and they think that he's going to pull through."

A thrill of surprise surged through Sam, followed by a wave of relief. He felt as if a heavy burden had been lifted from his shoulders. "Thank God! Is it true? He's really alive? Last night I thought he was a goner. He had no pulse and it looked like he'd lost a gallon of blood. It's amazing that they were able to save him. Thank God he's alive!"

"I don't think he's out of the woods yet," Faye responded. "He may still be in danger from the head wound. He had a severe concussion and a skull fracture."

"He's in more danger than that," Sam said grimly. "Tony knows as much as I do about Huntington's plot. They don't want either one of us to live long enough to talk. They're already after me, and they'll go for Tony, too." Sam's entire body tensed again as the gravity and urgency of the situation hit him. "We've got to do something fast. Tony won't last long unless he's protected. There's no way the police could keep Huntington from terminating him, even if they knew he was still in danger."

"Why don't you just call the authorities and tell them the whole story, Sam? Then they could put Tony under protection at the hospital."

"They'd trace my call, for starters. For now, I'm a wanted man. Murdering a sitting politician is a capital crime. Attempted murder is just about as bad, and they think I did it. I don't recall the police being anxious to take advice from murder suspects before they lock them up. Second, they wouldn't believe me if I did tell them the whole story. It's too incredible. And even if they did give me the benefit of the doubt and provided protection for Tony, it would be too easy for Huntington's forces to get through and finish him. Tony's in fragile condition and probably unconscious. It wouldn't take much to do him in."

Faye nodded. "I see your point. But how can you get real protection for Tony? And what can I do to help?"

"You can stay here and keep Emmie and Katrina safe. Obviously, all three of you are in danger. They may try again to get to me through you. But with Sheriff Fielding on call and his deputy here at the ranch, you should be safe enough. You have a gun and you know how to use it. Just be ready."

"And what are *you* going to do, Sam?" Faye asked, with the concern of a mother for her son.

"I'm going to arrange the best protection I can for Tony, then I'll blow the whistle on Huntington's whole scam just as fast as I can. Now let's go up to the house and call Sheriff Fielding. We need those two hombres in jail and protection for you. But first, there's something I want to do."

Sam took the cell phone from Faye and hit the redial key. The phone rang twice and then, just as Sam had suspected, Bandini answered. "Barton, what the hell is going on out there? Why haven't you called us sooner? Have we got Littlehawk?"

"Yeah, Bandini, you've got Littlehawk all right. Now what are you going to do with him?" Sam asked.

There was a pause on the other end of the line, then Bandini queried, "Barton?"

"You'll find Barton with Huntington's worthless nephew in the Osage County jail, charged with trespassing, assault with a deadly weapon, and attempted murder. And I'm really looking forward to seeing you up on the same charges, Bandini. Are you the one who told Barton to burn down the barn with my mother and daughter locked inside?"

A few seconds passed while Bandini assimilated the information and calculated a response. "You wouldn't be talking to me if the barn had burned, now would you Sam? Give it up, son. Angelletti won't make it through the night. If you turn yourself in, I'm sure that Mr. Huntington could prevail upon the authorities to go easy on you. There's no hard proof that you did it, and even if you did, you obviously didn't intend to kill him. Crime of passion and all that. Huntington will buy you a top criminal defense lawyer and you might even walk without doing any time at all. The charges might be dropped. You could still get with the winning team. If you do, I promise, you'll come out smelling like a rose."

As Bandini spoke, they both knew that he was wasting his words. The die was cast. Sam had no doubt that they had done an excellent job of framing him, and he knew that they expected to finish Tony off that night. If anything, Huntington's influence would be used to convict Sam, not to exonerate him. But Sam also knew that if he turned himself in, it was extremely unlikely that he would live long enough to go to trial. "You're dreaming, Bandini. Tell Huntington to save his money for his own criminal defense. You're both going to need it. And don't bother to send anyone else to the ranch. We won't be here."

Sam snapped the cell phone shut, dropped it in his pocket, and turned to Faye and Emmie, who were listening with wide eyes. "Let's go call Sheriff Fielding," he said. "We don't want to leave those two yahoos locked in the tack room for too long. And I need to get moving, pronto."

Ten minutes later, Sam hung up the phone and turned to Faye and Emily, who were sitting at the kitchen table. "Okay, Sheriff Fielding said he will come down himself to pick up those two hoodlums in the barn, just as soon as he can break away. In the meantime, a deputy is on the way. He should be here any minute. You can also call Danny and Red."

Sam looked at his mother, who was shaken, but stoic, and his daughter, whose eyes were pleading for him to stay. Although it touched his heart, he knew that every moment of delay was a further threat to Tony's life. He had to go, and as soon as possible. Taking Emily's hands in his, he smiled, then knelt to give her a hug. "I'm sorry, peanut, but I've got to go help Tony. He's in danger, and needs me right now. I'll be home just as soon as I can. I love you more than anything. Now you take care of your Grandma until I get back."

Neither Faye nor Emily could see the mist in Sam's eyes as he turned quickly and headed out the door.

* * * * *

At first, there was no pain, only a vague sense of existence. It was a dreaming state, short of consciousness, yet not totally oblivious. Floating in a black void, unknowing, shapeless, and without identity, thought or feeling. Only pure awareness. In this province, between the realms of the mind and soul, time and space were meaningless. There was no form or substance. When awareness finally achieved thought, the first impulse was to remain in this perfect state, unburdened by conscious judgments or feelings.

Then suddenly, there was pain. Nothing but clear consciousness of intense pain. Incredibly excruciating pain that seemed to sear every cell in his body, every aspect of his being. There was no perception of the passage of time, and it seemed as though the pain was all that had ever existed. Little by little, as awareness of his physical body returned, the pain became more intense, but also more localized. It felt as though the inside of his skull was being roasted with a welding torch, while the outside was being squeezed in a vice. The agonizing pain left no room for thought, only room for feeling more pain.

Yet as the waves of pain poured over him like molten metal, he began to feel another angry, burning sensation, as though a spike was being driven into the back of his hand and up the veins of his arm. Creeping up his arm, the new pain was becoming sharper moment by moment, demanding attention, even overshadowing the shooting pains in his head. It would be easier to float back into the original state of awareness, leaving the torturous pain behind. But the increasing intensity of the creeping pain in his forearm demanded nothing less than his full attention.

He tried to open his eyes and met with an entirely new pain as bright light confronted inflamed retinas. His eyes quickly closed, but then opened again as the pain in his arm reached a new level. It felt as though his entire arm were being attacked by a swarm of angry killer bees. Forcing his eyes open, He found the root of the pain in the back of his hand. He did not question why a needle and plastic tube were there—he simply pulled them out. The needle and tube dropped to the floor and he fell back onto the hospital bed, barely conscious.

But the pain did not go away. It seemed to be radiating from his arm throughout his body. Something was seriously wrong. With intense effort, he managed to sit up and swing his legs out of the hospital bed, before crashing to the hard tile floor. Monitor cables popped off and warning buzzers sounded as equipment tumbled in his wake. In a matter of seconds, a doctor and two nurses were lifting him back into the hospital bed. Mercifully, the black void returned.

When Tony regained consciousness, the throbbing in his head was still extremely intense, but bearable. The pain in his arm was negligible compared to the other pains throughout his body. He was able to open his eyes, as long as he closed them every ten seconds to gather more strength. Slowly, Tony realized that he was in a hospital room, but he had no idea what had happened or how he had gotten there. For a while, he focused on the surges of pain, and when they subsided, he tried to remember what had happened, to sort things out, but it was too difficult to think.

Tony was feeling slightly better two hours later when a man in a white lab coat with a smile as sterile as his clothing walked into the room. "Hello, Mr. Angelletti. I am your physician, Dr. Weaver," he said. "Do you know why you're here?"

That's a stupid question, Tony thought peevishly, but then he realized that he had no idea why he was in the hospital, other than the fact that he had a pounding pain in his head and serious doubts about his ability to stand up.

"You took a very serious blow to the head, son. For a while there, we thought we might lose you." The doctor's words rang in Tony's ears, as though he were speaking at close range through a megaphone.

"Could you speak a little softer, Doc, I've got a hell of a headache," Tony managed to whisper, as pains shot through his head like Roman candles.

"You have a severe concussion from a blow to the head just behind your left ear. Your skull was cracked and you lost nearly two quarts of blood. It's a miracle you're alive. It's even more amazing that you're conscious right now."

"Right now I wish I weren't," Tony responded weakly.

"No, it's better that you're awake," the doctor continued. "We don't need another scene like we had in the ICU."

Tony had a foggy recollection of being attacked by a swarm of angry bees and crashing to the floor, followed by a great commotion. "What happened, Doc?"

"You apparently thought you were good to go. You ripped the IV out of your hand and tried to walk out of here."

As Tony tried to think, bit by bit, memories began to take shape. "I hit the floor, didn't I?" he asked.

"You did a lot more than that. You destroyed a brand new computerized IV unit and sent the entire ICU into pandemonium," the doctor said. "After that, we moved you to this private room and replaced your IV with a more traditional model." Tony noticed that an IV was attached to his left hand, but there was no swarm of killer bees attacking his arm.

"Now we're going to remove the IV. We've loaded you up with whole blood, plasma, and medications. You'll need to remain under observation for a few days. But the main things you need now are rest and time to heal." He checked Tony's pulse and looked into his eyes with a tiny flashlight. "You seem to be dong fine, considering the circumstances. We have extra security on this floor now, so you can relax and recover. I'll check back later."

"Thanks, Doc," Tony nodded. "Thanks for your help."

A few minutes passed, then Tony heard the door open again. This time it was the security guard looking in on him. A burly fellow with short blond hair and blue eyes, the guard wore a tan uniform shirt with dark brown trousers. When he saw that Tony was awake, he spoke in a gruff voice. "Sorry to disturb you, sir, I was just checking to make sure everything is all right in here."

"Everything's peachy, if you're into near death experiences," Tony replied.

"Just checking, sir." The guard turned to go, and Tony noticed a familiar patch on the shoulder of the guard's uniform. Gannon Security. He had also noticed a name patch on the uniform above the guard's breast pocket. The guard's name was Jerry. Tony had a sudden inspiration and called to the guard.

"Hey, Jerry, how's Jed? Jed Gannon?"

The guard stopped in his tracks, hesitated, then turned. "Mr. Gannon's fine, sir, as far as I know."

"Did you know his name is Jedediah?"

"No sir," the guard said, somewhat perplexed.

"Names can be real interesting, Jerry," Tony said. "What's your last name?"

The guard was caught unaware. He hesitated, then quickly looked down at the patch on his uniform, then looked up with uncertainty in his eyes. There was no last name on the uniform.

"It's, uh, Summers, sir, Jerry Summers."

Tony's suspicion was confirmed. He would probably never know the man's last name, but it was a cinch that it wasn't Summers.

"Well, Jerry, I'm sure glad to have you guarding me. You never know when someone will take a pot shot at you these days. Guess I proved that. Thanks for your good work. I'll make sure that Mr. Gannon knows you did a good job."

"Oh, he knows I'll do a good job all right," the guard said ominously, then he turned on his heel and exited.

Tony closed his eyes and breathed deep, letting the pain in his head subside for a minute before reaching for the telephone.

* * * * *

Sam steadied the steering wheel of the '66 Ford pickup with his knee, pulled the cell phone from his pocket, and answered it on the third ring. He was shocked to hear Tony's voice. "Tony, where are you? I thought you were out cold in the ICU."

"I escaped from the ICU. There wasn't a single nurse there worth hanging around for," Tony said, making a weak attempt at humor. "Actually, I'm in a private room now, but I haven't escaped. That's where you come in. Right now, I'm being guarded by a beefcake wearing a Gannon Security uniform. But I don't think he's really a security guard."

"Uh oh."

"Yeah, I know."

"Do you have any idea what happened to you last night?" Sam asked.

"Judging from how I feel, I figure I either drank a gallon of tequila and ate the worm, or I was hit and dragged a couple of miles by a train, or maybe both."

"Seriously, Tony, did you see who or what hit you?"

"Haven't really thought about it, Sam. My thinkin's kind of spotty right now. I guess it must've been one of those bad guys, whoever they are. All I can remember is going to Katrina's dressing room after the show, and…then the lights went out. Hey, what about Katrina? Is she okay?"

"Don't worry, she's okay. We've got a lot to talk about, but first we've got to get you out of there. Not to worry you, buddy, but I'm sure that they plan to finish you off tonight. Don't eat anything, and don't take any medication. Keep the doctors and nurses close and try not to fall asleep. We'll get you out of there tonight. In the meantime, don't mention to anyone that you talked to me."

"So I guess you're still *persona non gratis*?"

"Better than that," Sam said. "They've framed me for your murder. The only hitch in their plan is—you're not dead yet."

"And I don't plan to be any time soon!" Tony replied in a more spirited tone. "I may *wish* I were dead, but I'm not gonna *be* dead, not if it would give Huntington and his crew any satisfaction. I want to be around to watch them hang."

"Sit tight and be on your guard, *amigo*. The cavalry's on the way."

Sam snapped the cell phone shut just as he approached the Utica Street exit on the expressway. Now if he just had a plan for pulling the rabbit out of the hat.

Chapter 10

The halls of St. John Medical Center were nearly empty by the time Sam arrived at midnight. It was Sunday night, which was usually a slow night at the hospital, and this was no exception. Always a believer in a straightforward approach, Sam went directly to the main reception desk and asked the all night attendant for Commissioner Angelletti's room number. The middle-aged woman, whose graying hair was more starched than her uniform, responded with a cold stare. "Visiting hours were over at nine o'clock, sir. You may wish to return tomorrow morning." She turned back to her computer screen, dismissing Sam with a sniff.

"With all due respect, ma'am, this can't wait until tomorrow morning. It's very important that I see Commissioner Angelletti immediately. This is official state business. I'm his attorney and I have some urgent information for him."

"I'm sure that whatever you have to say to him can wait until morning," the attendant said, still looking at her computer screen. "I can see right here that visitors are restricted for this patient. Obviously, the doctors don't want him to be disturbed."

"But this is a life and death matter, ma'am," Sam said with all of the urgency he could muster. "It is critically important that I see Commissioner Angelletti now, not tomorrow."

"And hospital policy is hospital policy," the attendant intoned with a nasal twang. "I don't make the policies, sir, I just enforce them."

Sam could see that the conversation was going nowhere. He would have to try another tack. He glanced around and noticed a picture of a young woman with a baby on the counter behind the reception desk. "That wouldn't be your grandbaby in that picture, would it?" he asked, pointing at the picture.

"Why yes, it is," she said, turning to admire it.

"What a fine looking child," Sam commented, as he leaned over the counter and peered at the computer screen. "That child has the brightest blue eyes!" The attendant studied the picture, her demeanor softening. "Those blue eyes must come from your side of the family," Sam continued, viewing the screen from an oblique angle while the attendant admired her grandchild. At the top of the computer screen, Sam could see the patient names in alphabetical order, with Anthony Angelletti at the top.

"Oh my, yes!" she exclaimed. "You should have seen my husband's eyes. They were so blue, and he gave them to all three of our daughters. I think those eyes are carrying right on through to the grandchildren. This one's such a darling. Looks just like her mother. That's her mother there in the picture with her." The attendant had completely forgotten about hospital policy.

"You're a very lucky lady," Sam said with feeling, as he noted the room number and its location on the computer screen, Seventh Floor West, Room 732.

"Yes, I guess I am," she beamed, looking at Sam.

"Well, I'll be seeing you tomorrow, then," he said with a broad smile. He turned and headed for the hospital exit.

"That will be just fine, sir," the attendant responded happily.

* * * * *

Once outside, Sam silently paced the length of the hospital courtyard a dozen times, thinking hard and fast. Finally, he stopped and looked up. "It'll be a miracle if this works," he said aloud. "And if it doesn't? Well, we'll just have to improvise."

With that, he pulled his cell phone from his pocket and dialed a familiar number. A youthful voice answered, "Hideaway Pizza, how may I help you?"

"Are you still delivering pizzas at this hour?" Sam asked.

"If you get your order in right now, we can still get you one out. We don't close until one."

"I'd like a large Mexican pizza with extra hot peppers delivered to St. John Hospital. Can do that?" Sam asked.

"Sure thing, mister, we deliver anywhere! Do you need any drinks with that?"

"No, but do you still have those scorching hot habeñero peppers? I like my pizza really, really piping hot."

"Those peppers'll roast your gizzard, mister. But if you want 'em, we got 'em."

"Great. Load 'em up. Put plenty of cayenne pepper on it, too. And one last thing. Could you have the delivery guy meet me at the north entrance of the hospital, under the big arches?"

"You got it. Twenty-five minutes at most."

"Great. I'll be waiting."

So far, so good, Sam thought. Twenty minutes should be just enough time for phase two of his plan. He dialed the hospital's main number. "Would you connect me with room 732 please?" he asked the hospital operator.

"I'm sorry sir, but we do not ring patient rooms after eleven o'clock. Hospital policy, sir. If you would like, sir, I can ring the nurses' station on that wing."

"Yes, please do that," Sam said. After waiting what seemed like an eternity, a voice came on the line. "Seven West, Nurse Pickens, may I help you?"

"Yes ma'am, could you connect me with room 732?"

"I'm sorry sir, but that patient is resting now. The doctor left strict orders that he is not to be disturbed tonight."

"I don't suppose it would make any difference if I told you that this is a life or death situation?" Sam asked hopefully.

"I'm sorry, sir. I have to follow the doctor's orders."

"All right, thank you," Sam said as he disconnected. So much for filling Tony in on the plan, he thought. Oh well, Tony's always been pretty good at rolling with the punches. He'll just have to improvise too. Provided he's conscious. And alive. Sam put the grim possibilities out of his mind and focused on executing his plan.

Precious minutes had been wasted on the call to the nurse on Seven West, and Sam hurried from the courtyard around the outside of the hospital to the emergency entrance. He walked quickly through the vestibule and double doors. Without pausing in the admissions area, he entered the main treatment area of the quiet emergency room. There was some activity in one curtained cubicle, but the hallway was empty.

Having made several trips to the emergency room in the past, Sam was familiar with the layout of the area, and he soon found the changing room for hospital personnel. Quickly, he donned a set of hospital green scrubs over his jeans and cotton shirt. For good measure, he added a matching green paper cap and stuffed a pair of flimsy paper shoe covers in his back pocket. A look in the mirror confirmed that he could pass for a doctor, if no one looked too closely. He was only missing a hospital ID, a stethoscope, and a medical education.

Without further delay, Sam left the changing room and walked out of the emergency treatment area into the main corridor of the hospital. He made his way to the north entrance to the hospital, arriving just seconds before a Hideaway delivery car pulled into the circle drive and parked. He met the delivery man at the door of the hospital.

"Hi. Got a pizza delivery there?" Sam asked.

"Sure do," the delivery man replied. "You the guy who ordered it?"

"Yep," Sam said, pulling out a twenty dollar bill. "But I've got an emergency I have to deal with right now. Could you go ahead and deliver it upstairs to the waiting room on the seventh floor, west wing? You can keep the change," Sam said, handing the delivery man the bill.

"Sure thing, doc," the delivery man replied.

"Will you do me a favor?" Sam asked. "This is for the two Gannon Security guards who are hanging around Room 732. When you deliver it to them, will you tell them it's compliments of Mr. Gannon?"

"No problem," the delivery man said as he pocketed the bill and headed in the door of the hospital.

With his improvised plan on schedule, Sam returned to the emergency area, where he had noticed a blank physician's order pad abandoned on a windowsill. The pad was still there, and Sam ripped off two sheets, tucking them under his green smock. He slipped into a private restroom in the emergency area and quickly scribbled a medical directive on one of the sheets, signing it with an illegible flourish typical of doctors everywhere.

Sam left the emergency area again and walked the short distance to the snack bar on the first floor. Just as he had hoped, he found four young orderlies at a table, drinking coffee and eating donuts. He walked briskly up to their table and assuming his most dignified air, he cleared his throat to address the group as if he were a colonel addressing a group of new recruits on their first day in boot camp.

"Gentlemen, if your coffee break is about over, there are patients in this hospital who are in need of your services." The four young men snapped to attention, one of them dropping his donut in mid-bite. The orderlies were not accustomed to being addressed directly by doctors, which was fairly unusual in the hierarchy of the hospital, but Sam's hospital greens and air of authority were sufficiently convincing.

Sam selected a fresh-faced young man with thick brown hair who looked eager and, Sam hoped, trusting. He thrust the directive he had written at the orderly and said, "Please bring this patient from his room down to Emergency X-ray. You'll need a wheel chair. And don't delay. We have a radiologist standing by to read the x-rays as soon as they're done. I'll be waiting for you there."

The orderly nodded as he squinted at the paper and said, "Right away, doctor, uh, doctor…"

"Hawk," Sam interrupted. "Tell the patient that Dr. Samuel Hawk ordered the x-rays. Make sure to mention my name. And by the way, there's no need to stop at the nurses' station. I just came from there. The patient is already cleared to go."

"Sure thing, Dr. Hawk," the orderly replied. He nodded again, looking at the written order, and headed toward the elevators.

Sam followed the orderly down the main corridor at a discreet distance, then turned down another corridor to a bank of elevators in the east wing. He ascended to the seventh floor and cautiously made his way down the quiet halls toward Seven West, praying that the timing would be right. Nearing the Seven West waiting room, he took a position in a small alcove that commanded a view of the entire central area. In seconds, Sam's prayers were answered when he heard the animated voices of the two guards in the waiting room. He realized then that his Trojan horse had made it through the city gates. The pizza had already arrived! And as expected, they had started to devour the treat without delay.

"Oh my God," one of the guards exclaimed as he chewed. "This is one hot pizza."

"Getting hotter by the minute, too," the burly blonde guard muttered through a mouthful. A few seconds passed, then Sam heard one of the men blowing air rapidly through his pursed lips and the other gasping as he held his mouth wide open. "Is there anything to drink around here?"

"Wow, man, this thing is burning hot!" the first guard said with a note of panic in his voice. "Nothing to drink here. Gotta get a soda fast!"

"Me too! I'm with you! Where's the pop machine?" Sam heard the clatter of plastic furniture as the men bolted for the vending machines around the corner and down the hall. They would be out of sight for at least a few minutes.

As if on cue, the orderly from the snack bar appeared, coming down the hall from the elevators, pushing an empty wheel chair bound for Room 732. Sam willed the orderly to move faster and prayed that Tony would be awake and cooperative. He knew that they had only a couple of minutes to get Tony on the elevator before the two guards would return.

Seconds seemed like hours to Sam as he feverishly thought through several options, improvising as needed. He had to distract the two nurses on duty, but without drawing attention to his presence on the floor. Engaging them in conversation was not an option and there was no more time to think about it. The orderly had entered Tony's room and in the quiet of the hallway, Sam could hear the guards dropping change in the vending machines. He had to act! He quickly slipped the green smock off over his head, taking the paper cap with it. Hopping on one foot, he managed to slip off the pants as well. He stepped out of the alcove and took five steps to the nurses' station with the hospital clothes in hand, having no idea what he would say or do. In an instant of divine inspiration, Sam saw his opportunity and he took it.

A custodian had been mopping the floor and a mop bucket was sitting just in front of the nurses' station. As Sam approached the counter, he kicked the bucket over, spilling its sudsy contents on the floor and feigning a fall. Sprawling his arms across the counter to catch himself, Sam managed to knock a large stack of files onto the desk below and into the lap of the duty nurse, who was filling out forms. She was taken completely by surprise, as files and papers scattered in all directions.

"Oh, I'm *so* sorry!" Sam exclaimed. "I slipped on the wet floor. Let me help you pick up those files." He started around the counter, then stopped. "Or maybe I should get a janitor," he said. "That wet floor is dangerous."

The nurse looked at the mess in dismay, then glanced up at Sam. "No, no, that's all right, sir, the custodian is just around the corner. He was right in the middle of mopping the floor when he got called down to Seven East to clean up a spill." The nurse called to her assistant, "Sarah, would you help me with these files? But first, will you step down to Seven East and get the custodian to come finish the floor? We've got a mess here." Sarah nodded and stepped out of the nurses' station.

Sam slipped around the counter and knelt to help pick up files. The duty nurse also began gathering loose papers. "I just came over from Seven East myself," Sam said. "I wanted a drink from the vending machine, but I couldn't get the machine to work. Then these two security guards came in and started making a lot of racket. Didn't you hear them?" he asked. "I was just coming to tell you about them. They were really loud and obnoxious. You ought to go check on them while I pick up these papers. I'll try not to mess anything up," Sam said resolutely.

Sam rose with a large handful of files and banged his elbow on the counter, scattering the files again at the nurse's feet. The nurse gasped with frustration. "Sir, would you *please* just step *out* of the nurses' station, or preferably go back to Seven East, or wherever you came from. I will take care of these files."

As the nurse bent again to pick up the scattered files, Sam looked out the door and saw the orderly pushing Tony down the hall toward them. He stepped across the nurses' station and turned in the doorway, momentarily blocking the view of the hall. "I'm awfully sorry, ma'am. Are you sure I can't help you with that? I could sure sort those files out for you. I'm a real good sorter."

"We will handle this," the nurse said through gritted teeth, as she squatted to pick up the papers that covered the floor. "You better just go on back to Seven East." The nurse kept her eyes on the floor and her back to Sam.

"Yes ma'am," Sam said as he turned to go. "But if you want help, call me. I'll be down the hall and I would sure like to help." Sam discreetly picked up the hospital uniform that he had dropped on the chair by the door and stepped out into the hallway, just as the elevator doors closed behind the orderly.

After ducking in the alcove to don his hospital garb again, he took the elevator to the first floor and hurried to Emergency X-ray.

Sam turned the corner at the east end of the hallway just as the orderly was pushing Tony down the hallway from the west. Sam was astonished when he caught his first glimpse of Tony. A large gauze bandage completely covered the top of his head and his left ear. Tony's left eye was blood red and there was a black and blue bruise on his right cheekbone where he had hit the floor. His skin was pallid and he looked very weak. If Tony recognized Sam, he did not give it away.

"Thank you for your prompt assistance, young man. I will take the patient from here," Sam said, dismissing the orderly, who promptly headed back to the snack bar where his friends and donuts were waiting.

In a moment, the hallway was again clear. Without a word, Sam pushed the wheelchair past the doors marked "Emergency X-Ray" and through another set of double doors into the main treatment area of the emergency room. A doctor who was talking to a nurse at the end of the hall turned his head toward them momentarily, then resumed his conversation.

Sam knew there was no time for small talk. "Tony, we've got to get out of here, before the guards or the nurses on the seventh floor discover you're missing," he said urgently. "Can you walk?"

"Since I was two," Tony answered jovially. "That's more'n thirty years ago. Why, I was on my feet just yesterday and my legs worked fine."

He must have taken some pain killers, Sam thought. "Okay, wise guy, but can you walk out of this place right now?"

"With vicious assassins on my trail, or without?"

"With," Sam said, looking back down the hall over his shoulder.

"No problem, man, just let me get up…" Tony made an effort to rise, but Sam put his hands lightly on Tony's shoulders.

"Sorry, champ, but you can't go walking out of here in that hospital gown. Someone might object to you mooning the whole waiting room. We've got to make a quick change."

As unobtrusively as possible, Sam pushed the wheelchair into one of the empty examination rooms and drew the curtain. He slipped out of the hospital greens again and helped Tony slide the smock over his bandaged head. Sitting on the examination table, Tony was able to get into the pants, and Sam helped him arrange the cap so that it partially covered the bandage on his head. Tony stood, and Sam examined their handiwork.

"Uh oh," Sam said, looking down. "Not many doctors in this hospital practice medicine with bandages on their heads. But I don't think *any* of them work barefooted. Better try these." He reached in his back pocket and pulled out the pair of paper shoe covers that matched the green scrubs. "I almost forgot I picked them up."

Tony sat back down on the examination table and managed to slip the shoe covers over his bare feet. He stood up again, swaying unsteadily. "Okay, Cap'n, we're good to go," he said as he took a long, lurching step toward the curtain.

"Whoa there, buddy," Sam whispered, holding back his friend. "Just wait a second while I make sure the coast is clear." Sam pulled the curtain over a few inches and peered into the corridor. They were in the last of four examination rooms, closest to the exit and farthest from the nurses' station, where only one nurse was visible. A few feet further down the hall, the doctor who had looked at them moments earlier was now on the telephone, facing the other direction.

"Now's as good a time as any," Sam said. He drew back the curtain and took Tony's arm. "Let's just hope that nobody takes a good look at you."

"Well you wouldn't be winning any beauty contests either, bozo, if you'd just had your noggin cracked open like a watermelon," Tony chided, glaring at Sam from one bloodshot eye.

"Shut up and get moving," Sam ordered as he eased Tony into the hallway and toward the double exit doors. The automatic doors swung open and they were out of the main emergency treatment area and into a large vestibule which served both as admissions office and waiting room. The room was virtually empty, but for a few sleepy friends and relatives waiting for patients to be released.

Tony and Sam were fifteen feet from the double glass doors and freedom when they heard a female voice addressing them loudly from behind the intake counter. "Excuse me, gentlemen, but have you completed your paperwork for dismissal?"

Sam swallowed hard and gambled. "Yes ma'am," he said without turning. "We left it with the other lady."

"Sir, there *is* no other lady. I'm the only attendant on duty tonight. And you have not checked out with me. We have to process the dismissal records before you can leave the medical center. It's hospital policy."

Sam hesitated, his mind whirring. How could he explain? A seriously injured, barefoot doctor wearing hospital greens and nothing else, releasing his perfectly fit patient and walking him to the car? No way. Perhaps Sam was a doctor in street clothes releasing his drugged patient in hospital garb? With no records of either the doctor or the patient in this hospital? Forget it. And to make matters worse, Tony could not stay vertical for another five minutes.

"Shit," Sam whispered to Tony. "Can you run?"

"Run? Can I run? Just point me toward the goal line, Cap'n!" Tony was virtually reeling as he lurched sideways and bumped the wall.

Without looking back, Sam propelled Tony forward into a stumbling trot. As they passed through the automatic outside doors and out of the foyer, the attendant shouted, "Hey, stop! You can't leave! Come back here!"

The two escapees took a quick right and stumbled down the concrete entry ramp of the emergency room toward the parking lot. Halfway down the ramp,

Sam heard the attendant, who had followed them out the doors, shouting in frustration, "Come back here right now or I'll call security!"

"Lord a' mercy, my head hurts," Tony muttered as Sam fumbled with his keys and unlocked the door to the truck. He helped Tony into the passenger seat and jumped into the driver's seat just as the two Gannon guards and two hospital security guards raced out the door. Sam fired up the engine. As he spun the truck out of the parking lot and into the street, he looked in the rearview mirror. One of the Gannon guards and a city cop were jumping into a patrol car that had been parked on the ramp. *Uh oh*, Sam thought. *Now we're in for it.*

* * * * *

Sam gunned the engine of the old truck and it lurched forward, slowly picking up speed. He shifted into second gear, then third, and the truck was doing fifty miles an hour before they had covered three blocks. Just as the police cruiser turned off of the hospital ramp and into the street four blocks behind, Sam took a quick left turn and swung the truck onto Swan Lake Drive. They had passed seven large homes on Swan Lake Drive when Sam suddenly braked and whipped the truck into the walled courtyard of a large Spanish style house. He immediately turned off the lights, cut the engine, and let the truck coast to a stop behind the courtyard wall, out of view from the street. The two sat silently in the truck as the police cruiser rolled slowly past the driveway and on around the lake. When the cruiser was finally out of sight, Sam breathed a sigh of relief.

"Rough ride," Tony grumbled. "When can I get off this roller coaster and throw up? I don't feel so good."

"We're there now," Sam replied in a low voice. "I hate to wake anyone up at this time of night, but there's no choice. You wait here while I go arrange some accommodations."

"Don't worry, I'm completely entertained by the light show in my head."

"Just wait until the drugs wear off," Sam muttered.

Sam stepped out of the truck and around to a side door of the house. He rang the bell twice and waited. First a light came on upstairs, then one suddenly illuminated the porch. A wizen old face with a week's worth of rough grey whiskers peered out the window next to the door, and then the door opened.

"Is that you, Sam Littlehawk? What in the world are you doing at my door in the middle of the night? I haven't seen you in ages. You're too busy being a big time lawyer to visit your old friends." The old man at the door was bent over and his long, tousled grey hair flew in all directions. He was wrapped in a blue terrycloth bathrobe and balanced himself on a cane.

"I'm really sorry to awaken you at this hour, Doc, but this is an emergency and we need your help. I have a seriously injured man out in the truck and for reasons that I'll explain later, I can't take him to the hospital. Could we come in?"

"Why sure, Sam, why didn't you say so," the old doctor said, blowing long mustache whiskers out of his mouth as he talked. "I don't know what an old coot like me can do to help, but I'm always willing to help another human being in need." He pushed open the screen door for Sam and turned back through the tiny entryway and into the kitchen, turning on lights and talking as he went. "I don't know much about this newfangled medicine, with all the computers and machines and such, but I sewed up a few in my day. Why, your Daddy could'a told you lots of stories 'bout what we did fifty years ago. Did'ja know we were in the big war together? Did'ja want a cup of coffee? How's yer mom?"

Sam smiled at the familiar banter of their old family friend. Even though they only saw one another on rare occasion, Sam knew that he could always count on Doc Robins. Interrupting, he said, "I'll get my friend now, Doc. And maybe we shouldn't turn on all the lights in the house. No point wasting electricity," he said, switching off the porch light.

"Well, that's real smart thinking, sonny," the old man said, reaching for the coffee pot. "These electric companies are 'bout to steal us old folks blind. Sure costs a lot these days to keep a light bulb burnin'—and the coolin' bills in the summer? Whew! Three hundred dollars for this old house last month! I don't know what they could do with all that money. But it's real good to be economy-minded these days…"

Sam was already out the door. He roused Tony, who was napping in the truck, and led him through the dark to a seat at the kitchen table.

"Doc Robins, this is my friend, Tony Angelletti," Sam said formally. "I hope that you will consider letting Tony be your house guest for the next few days. He's been seriously injured and needs medical care, but we can't take him to the hospital."

"Looks to me like he's already been to the hospital, sonny," the old doctor quipped, eyeing the green smock and trousers that Tony still wore. "They run y'all off?"

"In a manner of speaking," Sam said. "The hospital is not a safe place for him right now."

"Didn't I see somethin' 'bout you on the news last night?" the doctor asked Tony.

Tony looked at Sam, then turned to the doctor with a droll expression. "Beats me, Doc, but whatever they said about me, it ain't true." He laughed at his own joke, just before his eyes rolled up in his head.

"We need to get him to bed, Doc," Sam said. "He's had a pretty rough time."

"I can see that," the doctor answered seriously. "Let's take him upstairs. The guest room's all made up. I can sit with him 'til morning. I don't sleep much anymore anyway. Maybe we can have a cup of coffee together in the morning."

As Sam helped Tony upstairs, he gave the doctor a brief explanation of Tony's injuries and his quick recovery. Without elaboration, he explained the need for complete secrecy.

"Oh, don't you worry 'bout that, sonny. It's the physician's oath, ya know. Never catch me talkin' 'bout a patient. Why, I remember treating some fellas back in the sixties that were in trouble with the law…"

Sam interrupted. "Gotta go, Doc, but just remember, keep him in bed until I get back, and mum's the word, okay? I'll just let myself out."

"Don't you worry, sonny, your man's in good hands."

"I have no doubt of that," Sam said confidently as he trotted down the stairs.

* * * * *

Sam tiptoed to the courtyard gate and peered outside. All was quiet on Swan Lake Drive. The sky was clear overhead and a silvery half moon reflected on the calm waters across the street. Doc's house was opposite the fountain in the middle of the lake, which was quiet now, and Sam could see snow white swans and a few wood ducks asleep on the boulders surrounding the fountain. The world was at peace. Sam thought for a moment about the many happy hours that he and his family had spent during his childhood feeding the ducks and swans and having picnics in the small park at the end of the lake. The cool night air, the familiar smell of the lake, and the sight of the moonlight on the water calmed and rejuvenated his spirits. He leaned against the high masonry wall, letting the ambiance of the moment sink in and savoring the fact that Tony was alive and recovering, safe in the hands of a trusted friend. So far, so good.

He suddenly shook his head as he realized he was beginning to doze off standing up. No time for that yet. He quickly backed the truck up and pulled out with the lights off. After circling the lake in the dark, he accelerated and switched on the lights as he headed downtown.

At three o'clock on Monday morning, downtown was as quiet as a cemetery. After parking the farm truck where he had left the roadster scarcely thirty hours earlier, Sam slipped down the dark alley and into the Firehouse through the back door. Without turning on any lights, he climbed the stairs and moved to his desk, where he withdrew a small flashlight from a drawer. Opening an address book by the telephone, he found Dave Sanders' unlisted home phone number and wrote it down. On second thought, he pocketed the entire address book and the flashlight. Grabbing an apple and a banana off the counter, Sam headed downstairs. Firing up the BMW roadster, he drove into the night.

Chapter 11

Surfacing slowly from a deep sleep, Dave Sanders knocked the telephone off the bedside table as he reached for it in the dark. Eyes closed, he fished around on the floor until he found the buzzing receiver and raised it to his head.

"Yeah," he muttered thickly.

"Hey, Dave," Sam said cheerfully, "It's time to get up and go to work."

Sanders yawned and blinked, trying to focus on his bedside clock. Slowly, he made sense of the hour and minute hands. "Sam, it's three in the morning," he groaned.

"Since when have you kept banker's hours?"

After ten seconds of silence, he finally replied, "Okay. Okay...yeah. Uh, it's three in the morning. So, what's the plan?"

"We need to get together right away," Sam said. "In about four or five hours, things are going to get pretty crazy around here. I'll fill you in when we're together. I don't trust this cell phone. Anyone could be listening."

"Okay," Sanders said, starting to bring the circumstances into focus. "I'm glad you called. No doubt the hounds are hot on your trail. First thing in the morning, I'm sure they'll have an indictment. Then the fun will really begin."

"Right. That's why we've got to get together *now*."

"You just say where and when," Sanders responded. "Oh, by the way, Sam," he continued in a softer tone, "I guess you've heard that Tony survived the attack? But I was told that they don't expect him to make it until morning. I'm sorry."

Sam responded brightly, "Don't you worry about Tony, Dave. He's going to be all right after all. And he's out of danger now. I'm sure of that."

There was a pause on the other end of the line. Sam could almost see the light dawning on Sanders face. "Don't tell me, Sam, that you've been taking some kind of an active role in Tony's recovery?"

"Let's put it this way. I made sure that whoever took the first shot at him doesn't get a second chance. He's in good hands now, safe from harm."

"I should've known you wouldn't leave anything to chance," Sanders said. "So where do you want to meet?"

"You know that new internet café on Cherry Street in Lincoln Plaza? It's open 24/7. Meet me there as soon as you can."

"I can be there in fifteen minutes, if I don't brush my teeth."

"In that case, make it twenty."

* * * * *

Sam strolled into the Cherry Street Connection at half past three and ordered a double cappuccino from the lone employee manning the coffee bar. It would take at least a couple of hours to bring Sanders up to speed, and he needed some fortitude. He found a computer near the back of the café that looked like it would do the job. Pulling a CD from his pocket, he popped it into the drive. In seconds, he saw familiar data on the screen. He began to scroll through the documents that he and Tony had been organizing on his computer in the Firehouse. Although it had only been forty-eight hours since then, it seemed like it had been weeks.

He continued to scroll though documents, organizing and making mental notes for another ten minutes while sipping his cappuccino. He had little concern for privacy, since he was the only customer there. Finally, Dave Sanders walked in the front door, looking fairly disheveled and wearing only blue jeans, a tee shirt and sneakers. He walked through the deserted café and pulled up a chair next to Sam, motioning to the waiter for coffee. "I hope this is worth losing sleep over," Sanders said. "This is the second night in a row I've been dragged against my will from an incredible tropical paradise filled with the women of my dreams, back to the local crime scene with you and Tony Angelletti in the center ring."

"You can't spend you entire *life* dreaming of buxom beauties strutting around on tropical beaches, Dave," Sam said in a patronizing tone. Then squinting one eye, he scrutinized Sanders for a moment and said, "But then again, maybe you could."

"And why not? Can you think of anything better to dream about? Besides, I don't think the women of my dreams are any of your damn business!"

"I'd like to meet the women of your dreams some time, Bucko. But right now, I want to introduce you to a few other characters."

"Are any of them belly dancers?"

"More like international gangsters," Sam answered apologetically. "But then, you always liked chasing the bad guys."

Sanders sighed. "So it's back to the salt mine for me. No rest for the weary. Okay, Sam, you got me here. It's three in the morning, but here I am, ready to work. So why don't you start by telling me where you've been since yesterday morning, when your mother wouldn't tell me where you were?"

"Let's go back just a little further," Sam countered. "Let's start with a meeting Tony had last Friday afternoon with a man named Karmakov."

For the next ten minutes, Sam rapidly summarized most of the events of the past three days, omitting just a few small details that he thought best to ignore. Sanders interrupted only twice, to ask about the aircraft Karmakov used to escape and the two men who were in the Osage County Jail.

"What do you bet we got a major turf war brewing?" Sanders asked.

"Tomorrow will undoubtedly be an interesting day," Sam responded. "Sorry I'll miss all the fun at the courthouse."

Sanders looked sternly at Sam. "You know that you have to turn yourself in now, don't you, Sam? I mean, you can't keep running from the law. They'll find you. It's a risk for me even to meet you here. The Bureau would consider it a major breach of etiquette, considering you're wanted for attempted murder, not to mention the burglary of Huntington's offices and a few other high crimes and misdemeanors."

"That's why we've got to work fast," Sam said, turning back to the computer. "When you see what we have here, you'll understand why turning myself in would be suicide. Look at this."

Sam led Sanders through a series of documents on the computer that he and Tony had scanned, photographed and organized. As Sam explained the significance of each document, the story of the perversion of the Greenleaf Project began to unfold. Sanders watched intently, beginning to comprehend the magnitude of the scheme that Sam and Tony had uncovered.

"So let me get this straight," Sanders finally offered. "By bribing politicians, Southwest Energy plans to build a big, expensive power plant that we don't need, at an exorbitant cost to the ratepayers, and the top executives and their lawyers will profit big time from their ownership of everything from the land where the plant will be built to the construction company that will build it. That about it?"

"You have an amazing facility for understatement," Sam said dryly. "That's the background. Then to protect their scheme, these boys have engaged in a little, shall we say, unsavory behavior? Putting it in lingo an FBI agent can understand, you have abuse of the public trust, illegal wiretaps, bribery, extortion, kickbacks, kidnapping and attempted murder, for starters. And that's just what we know about. We've only scratched the surface. I still have more to sort and analyze."

Sanders rubbed his unshaven chin thoughtfully. "Sure looks like a mountain of evidence to me. Do they know that you have all of this information?"

"They should know by now. They grabbed my computer from the Firehouse while I was at the performance on Saturday night. The files were password protected, but I'm sure that they'll get into it, with enough persistence. They may not know that I made a backup disk, but they'd be stupid to assume otherwise."

"Well, even without the documents, you obviously know a lot about their dealings. They can't afford to have you walking the streets. That's why you're such a hot property right now."

Sam looked furtively at the broad windows at the front of the store, then at his watch. "We don't have much time. There are a few more things we need to do with this disk." He tapped some keys, then squinted at the screen as a list of the hundreds of files scrolled past. "Ah, there it is!" The document he found contained nothing but a list of websites and alpha numeric codes.

Utilizing the high-speed internet connection, he scanned the websites on the list, while Sanders unsuccessfully tried to suppress a yawn. Suddenly, Sanders leaned forward and touched Sam's arm. "Hey, I've seen that website before."

Sam looked at the glitzy homepage video of Las Vegas hotels and casinos. There was an advertisement for stage shows, with miniature dancing girls high-kicking across a window on the computer screen. Below the window, a series of digital buttons on the screen allowed the viewer to make reservations for rooms, rental cars, shows, and other types of entertainment. As Sam watched, Sanders reached for the mouse and said, "Look at this." He scrolled to the bottom of the screen, placed the cursor on a small logo in the credits, and then typed a twelve character password. Another screen appeared, this one with a dark blue background and small green letters requesting another password. Sanders typed again, and the screen sprang to life, this time displaying a blackjack table complete with dealer's hands, playing cards, and money.

"Don't tell me you're hooked on gambling," Sam said, watching the screen.

"Can't afford to gamble, with my addiction to women," Sanders chuckled. "Besides, my whole life is a gamble." He continued to key the computer, his eyes glued to the screen. "This website is the jewel we were looking into last week at the office. Glad to see that our computer nerds in blue haven't taken it down yet. Seems that illicit gambling over the Internet is generating big bucks these days. Worst part is, they're cutting Uncle Sam out of his share. The IRS is getting really fussy about it. They've called in the Bureau."

"So this site is under surveillance?" Sam asked.

"These things pop up for a few days and then disappear, like cockfights. Mostly word of mouth promotion, or I should say, e-mail promotion. People who gamble seriously usually know a few other gamblers, and word travels fast. We got the codes from one of our undercover agents in Vegas. Problem is, it's damned hard to stop people from logging on anywhere in the country, and the sites come and go fast. The numbers are overwhelming. We can't hope to prosecute or even investigate them all. We can only try to bust a few of the most insidious ones and make an example of them, in hopes of deterring others. The Bureau really wants to get the guys who put up this site. Watch this."

Sanders drew the cursor to the tool bar at the bottom of the screen, placed it on a pair of smiling red lips, and clicked the mouse. The screen displayed eight windows, each containing an active video of a smiling, nude woman in a provocative pose. At the bottom of the each window was a price. Across the bottom of the screen was a banner, "A nighttime of entertainment for your next trip to Vegas."

"Bet this one goes over big when the biker studs come to town," Sam said.

"It gets better, or worse, depending on your point of view," Sanders said, clicking the mouse at an accelerating pace. "Check this out." He placed the cursor over a tiny pair of handcuffs on the tool bar and typed in another password. A linked website opened, displaying a similar group of windows containing eight scantily clad girls who appeared to be young teens, mainly of Asian and Latin American origin. The prices displayed at the bottom of each window were much higher, and the banner read, "A lifetime of entertainment wherever you are."

Sam's eyes widened in amazement. "Slavery?"

"That's why the Bureau is so interested in this site. Judging from the website links, this is a very serious bunch. That innocent little row of icons on the toolbar, with the right passwords, will get you all kinds of illegal drugs, serious weapons— just about anything the well-rounded misfit might want to buy. Slavery just happens to be one of the more disgusting aspects of their criminal trade. They're also into crimes that are more sophisticated. Look at this one." Sanders tapped a few more keys and a screen opened that appeared to be a homepage for an investment company. "Y'know Sam, securities fraud ain't what is used to be. The big boys are still into drugs, sex, gambling, weapons, all the traditional stuff, of course. But they've also started to understand that there's no need to get your hands dirty when you can prey on people's greed and just talk them out of their money over the internet. The ways to take money are virtually endless for the criminal mind."

The website on the screen offered a variety of real estate and commodities deals, promising phenomenal returns on investments with unbelievably short terms. Sam shook his head in disbelief. "It's amazing that people buy into this stuff. How can they possibly believe that it's real? Double your money in ninety days? I was always told that if it looks too good to be true, it is."

"They *want* to believe, Sam. It's the greed factor. Some people want so badly to be rich that they'll risk everything, take a blind leap of faith and give their money to strangers on the naked promise of a quick buck. Unfortunately, it's usually those who can least afford to lose their money. Too often it's the gullible little old ladies and retirees living on fixed incomes who fall prey to these fraudulent deals."

"And then it turns out that the things they think they're investing in don't even exist."

"Actually, most of the time they do exist. Some of the most deceptive scams are based on actual investments. The real estate or commodities offered for sale exist and are owned by the promoters. But the promoters oversell the properties or misrepresent what people are buying. Promise impossible returns that never materialize, sell the same property several times, that sort of thing. By the time the investors realize they've been bilked and the authorities sort it out, the promoters and the money are long gone." Sanders continued punching keys and scanning screens.

Sam looked at his watch again. Coming up on five o'clock. "Listen, Dave, we've got to get moving. It's going to be daylight soon. We need to…" Sam's words trailed off in mid-sentence as looked at the screen. "Hold it, Dave, stop! Wait…go back to that last screen. What the…That's the Greenleaf Project!"

"I don't see the word 'Greenleaf' anywhere."

"It doesn't say it on the screen, but that's it! I've seen those elevations before. The layout of the plant there is exactly the same." Sam pointed to a diagram on the screen. "See the name of the owner, Midwest Utilities Development, Inc.? That's the name of one of the companies we found in the files that we, uh, borrowed. This page describes an investment in a power plant to be built and sold to Western Utilities Holdings, Inc. Look at that…'Guaranteed fifty percent annual return for a limited number of qualified investors,'" Sam read aloud.

"What do you want to bet that when the investors in this deal try to collect their profits, they'll find that the holding company holds nothing but thin air? There *is* no holding company."

"I won't take that bet, but I *will* bet that there's something pretty strange going on with this computer right now," Sander said as he double-clicked the mouse and tried again to exit the web page. "Seems like we're stuck at this website. Something's preventing me from breaking the connection. It's like, holding the line open. Very strange." He hit the icon marked "hang up now" with no result.

"Let me see that thing for a minute," Sam said, repositioning the keyboard and mouse. He typed in several diagnostic commands. "Nothing seems to be amiss on this end. The connection is being held open from the other end somehow. We may have a live monitor."

"That's not too surprising," Sanders replied. "They probably have a program to automatically check and catalogue the use of their websites. We've made a lot of links and used a couple of secret codes in the past half hour. It may be that our activity triggered a monitoring program. They may have the capability to identify the caller by tracing the telephone number. They might have red-flagged all calls from this area code. There's a lot that they could do from the other end."

"They wouldn't need to hold the line open to know where the hit came from. They had that information when the call connected," Sam reasoned. "But they could be tracing the call, or uploading information from this computer, or downloading into it." Sam noticed the small green light on the CD drive was flashing, indicating it was in use, although *they* weren't using it. He quickly pulled the CPU away from the wall and disconnected the DSL cable. The light on the CD drive went dark.

Sam and Dave looked at one another. "These guys are really good," Sam said, raising his eyebrows. "Let's see what they did to the disk."

"Okay, but whatever you do, you'd better do it fast. They may have already pinpointed the location of this computer from the phone number. No telling where their server is located, but with the miracles of modern telecommunications, it's pretty likely that your trigger-happy friends in town will be getting a message any minute telling them to head for this location."

"Oh, man," Sam gulped. "Back on the run again. But I've got to know if they damaged the backup disk."

"Okay, but then we gotta beat feet."

Sam quickly scrolled through the list of documents again. "I can't really tell, but it looks like it's all still there. They must have been scanning it online when we disconnected. I imagine that it must have looked suspicious to them when they hacked into a computer accessing their websites and found nothing but operating systems, but no data files, only an active CD drive. For whatever reason, they targeted us. I wonder how much of the information on the CD they saw before we cut the connection."

Sam punched the disk out of the drive, slipped it into a cover and handed it to Sanders. "Here. Get this to your friends at FBI headquarters in Washington, as high up the food chain as possible. I don't trust anyone around here. No telling how far this conspiracy reaches. We'll help them analyze this stuff at length when things are a little safer."

"So you're finally ready to leave this up to us pros?" Sanders asked nonchalantly.

Sam grinned. "I hand you baked salmon on a silver platter, and you complain that I wouldn't let you in the kitchen. Wait until I tell Tony about your ingratitude. He'll probably tell me just to drop the whole thing."

"Right now, Count Dracula, you'd better get back to your casket before the sun rises. Daylight is almost here," Sanders replied, noting the graying sky through the windows of the café.

"I think it might be wise to avoid the front entrance at this point," Sam said, looking toward the back door of the café, which opened onto an alley. "Thanks for coming, Dave. I'll give you a call at work later."

"You wouldn't want to come on down to the office with me now, would you? Turn yourself in, make a full report, all that jazz? We could give you full protection as a witness." Sanders knew Sam's answer before he asked the question, but he felt duty bound to ask anyway.

At that moment, headlights from a car parking in front of the building suddenly illuminated the dimly lit back wall of the café.

"Gotta go, Dave," Sam said, gripping his friend's shoulder. "That may be the bad guys now. Don't worry about me. I'll be in touch soon enough." Sam turned and in an instant, he was out the back door.

"Don't worry about the tab…" Sanders started to say, once again marveling at the audacity of his friend, as the door slammed shut.

* * * * *

Sam crept around the building as dawn began to streak the sky in the east with orange and gold ribbons. Sunrise was just a few minutes away. He found his BMW parked in the alley where he had left it two hours earlier, knowing that he'd best keep the conspicuous sports car out of sight. At this point, however, he had no choice but to drive it, even though he would be recognized in an instant. Pausing for a moment, he unlatched the convertible top and hit the button that lowered it. As long as he was that obvious, there was no point in trying to hide. He might as well enjoy the drive.

The sun was rising and Sam easily shook off the slightly dazed feeling he had endured during the last two hours at the computer terminal. He had pulled all-nighters before. No problem. Just like the first day of trial. The adrenaline level was certainly high. Many times, Sam had been up at dawn after a sleepless night, practicing the opening statement or closing argument he would present to a jury in a few hours. Sleeplessness was just one of the hazards of his profession, like many others. Sam laughed to himself, knowing that he could and often did push himself far beyond the normal limits of endurance. Secretly, he enjoyed challenging himself and feeling the exuberance of testing his stamina, both physically and mentally.

There was a cool edge to the early morning air that blew through Sam's hair as the midnight blue sports car hummed along the nearly vacant freeway. Sam marveled at the beauty of the magnificent cumulus clouds that shone pink and blue overhead, much like the sunset he had watched with Katrina. He thought what an incredible sunset it had been, somehow more beautiful than any he had seen in a long time.

Sam circled the downtown area at a sedate speed and then eased the needle of the speedometer just past eighty as he launched the sports car onto the interstate heading north. Twenty-five minutes and he would be back on the path to the cabin. Ten more minutes, and he would see Katrina again. Sam felt a surge of energy at the thought of telling her about saving Tony from certain death. Reflecting on the situation, he was filled with joy and thankfulness for Tony's extraordinary recovery. As the brilliant hues of the sunrise continued to play on the clouds overhead, Sam could think of nothing but sharing his incredible feelings with Katrina. She would be thrilled to know that Tony was no longer in danger from either the head wound or the threat of further violence from those who were pursuing them. He wanted Katrina to feel as good as he did at this moment.

He pushed the speedometer needle to one hundred ten in a vacant stretch of divided highway, just to be certain he was not being followed. Turning off the main road a mile early, Sam wound his way through a few miles of unmarked country roads, watching the rearview mirror carefully, before approaching the ranch. He turned off the road, then pulled into a clearing in a grove of persimmon trees half a mile from the ranch, certain that he had not been followed. Climbing out of the sports car, he jogged to a path that intersected the one to the cabin.

Trotting through the early morning air on a forest path that he had known since childhood, Sam felt a strong sense of kinship with his surroundings. Twittering birds and blooming wildflowers, rugged oak and hickory forest and tall grasses all sang to him and made him feel totally alive. Sam enjoyed his life in the city and the challenges he faced there, but he really lived for the long walks and horseback rides through the beautiful lands of his ancestors. When the stresses of the civilized world became overwhelming, a solitary walk on the ranch always gave him balance, a new perspective. Early morning walks were the best for nourishing the spirit and viewing wildlife.

Sam paused when he saw a grey fox trot across the trail a dozen yards ahead with a small cottontail rabbit in its mouth. Suddenly, a hawk swooped down from its perch on a dead tree, screaming at the fox, talons bared. It struck the fox on its back, and the fox dropped the rabbit and ran for cover, looking back just once to see if it was being pursued. In an instant, the hawk wheeled and plucked the rabbit from the ground, returning to its perch in the tree. The theft of the rabbit took less than five seconds, then all was quiet again. *Ah,* Sam thought, *a very propitious sign. This will certainly be a good day!*

Leaving the hawk to its feast and the fox to hunt again, Sam continued at a brisk walk down the trail toward the cabin. Following the creek and then skirting the large pasture for two hundred yards, he entered the trees again and was soon nearing the cabin's sheltering grove of cedars. It was six-thirty in the morning, and he expected to find Katrina asleep. He thought it would be fun to awaken her with the good news, then share coffee and make breakfast together while planning their next move. With Tony in good care and the evidence in the hands of the FBI, their only job would be to lie low until the smoke cleared and indictments were issued. Sam could think of worse things than spending a week or two lying low with Katrina.

Appealing mental images propelled him forward, but as he neared the cabin, he instinctively slowed his pace and listened. He heard nothing more than the wind in the cedars and the distant cawing of crows. Leaving the trail and slipping quietly through the dense woods, Sam approached from the side, just in case. Hearing nothing, he rounded the corner of the cabin and saw the front door standing wide open. He could see the glow of a kerosene lantern still burning on the table beside the door. Suddenly, his eagerness was replaced by a cold, sinking feeling in the pit of his stomach. He bolted the few steps to the front door, threw it back and stepped into the one room cabin.

The cabin had been ransacked and Katrina was gone. A large bone-handled hunting knife that he kept in the cabin was planted in the wooden table, pinning down a handwritten note: YOUR SILENCE FOR HER LIFE.

Sam yanked the heavy knife from the table top and picked up the note. Looking at it carefully, his mind whirled with questions. How had they found the cabin? How could they have known where to look? Did Katrina put up a fight? Was she hurt? How long had they been gone? Where would they take her? He had no answers, but was certain of one thing. If Karmakov's men had returned and seized her, they would take her out of the country as quickly as possible. On the other hand, the kidnappers could be more phony FBI agents or security guards hired by Huntington. It probably didn't matter, since the two factions were obviously working together. In either case, he had to act fast!

The fact that the kidnappers had not staked out the cabin and waited for his return suggested that there was only one or two of them, or perhaps that Katrina had convinced them that he would not return any time soon. Sam suddenly thought of his mother and daughter in the ranch house only half a mile away. Had they also been kidnapped or mistreated? How had the kidnappers gotten past the deputy sheriff who had been sent to protect his family? How had they known of the cabin?

Questions and fears haunted him as he flew back over the trail toward the ranch house. Looking down as he ran, he could not believe that on his walk to the cabin, he had missed the obvious signs on the trail. The flat, rounds soles of the kidnappers' shoes left clear tracks in the soft earth, and he should have easily recognized Katrina's tracks heading away from the cabin. Normally, he watched for animal tracks on the trail to know what animals were prowling the ranch, but this time his head had been in the clouds, dreaming of a lovely morning with Katrina. Damn! He could have saved nearly half an hour if he had just stayed focused.

As Sam approached the ranch house, he stopped in the trees a hundred yards away to consider his options. He realized that he could be walking into a trap. As anxious as he was to know the fate of Faye and Emmie, he knew that it would do none of them any good if he was picked off by a sniper's bullet. Sam slowly moved forward through the open forest, watching the house and listening. In the quiet of the early morning, sound traveled well, and as he neared the buildings, he heard a muffled banging coming from the barn. Bending low, Sam skirted the corrals and entered the barn, as he had the evening before, through the stalls. The banging was coming from inside the tack room where Sam had confined Barton and Olsen. The bar was still over the door. It had been nearly twelve hours since Sheriff Fielding had promised to come to the ranch immediately and assign a deputy to guard the family. Sam had complete faith in Sheriff Fielding, and he had assumed that shortly after he had left the ranch, Barton and Olsen had been taken into custody. Could they still be in the tack room where he'd left them?

As Sam crept silently toward the tack room door, he heard voices inside, but they were all too familiar. He quickly opened the door to find Faye and Emmie peering from the dark tack room into the morning light.

"Sam!" Faye cried with relief, as Emmie ran to her father and wrapped her arms around his waist. "Thank God you're back!"

Sam gave his mother a hug over Emmie's head and asked, "Are you all right?"

"Oh, we're fine, considering we've been locked up in there most of the night."

"What happened? I thought Sheriff Fielding was on his way out here when I left. And where's the deputy he promised? He said that the deputy was less than ten minutes away!"

"The Sheriff came alright, and he took those two mangy coyotes to jail up in Pawhuska. And the deputy showed up and stayed quite awhile. I stayed up with him, too. I was way too wound up to go to sleep. Then about three a.m., the deputy got a call to go check on some ruckus down by the lake. Said he'd be right back, but he never showed up. I guess he thought we were safe enough, since they'd put those two weasels in jail."

"Apparently, you weren't."

"Wasn't twenty minutes after the deputy left that two *more* buzzards busted in here and started threatening again, just like the first two. I think the second bunch must've talked to those first two yahoos, 'cause they seemed to know everything that happened here last night."

Sam nodded. "Barton probably made some calls from the Pawhuska jail. The jailers up there are way too easy about letting prisoners use the phone. The second two could have been the security guards from the hospital. Once I lost them in town, they probably assumed I brought Tony here."

"Well, whoever they were, they made me get Emmie up and they threatened to fillet us with a butcher knife, if I didn't tell 'em where you and Tony were. They were real nasty to us. I didn't *know* where you were and I told 'em so. Then I told 'em Tony was in the hospital and that really seemed to get their goat."

Sam chuckled. "Tony's out of their reach now, Mom. I took him to stay with Doc Robins."

"Oh good! Then he must be doing better?"

"He's got one helluva headache, but he'll live."

"That's great news," Faye said with a smile. But her smile quickly faded and a frown creased her forehead as she continued her story. "When we couldn't tell them anything about you and Tony, they started asking about Katrina. You know I've never been a good liar, Sam. They could tell that I knew where she was, and they were threatening to do all kinds of wicked things to Emmie and me, if I didn't tell 'em where she was. I don't even want to say what they threatened to do to us." Faye's earlier fear showed in her eyes and her shoulders began to quake. "I'm sorry, Sam, but I had to tell 'em where Katrina was. I just couldn't let them hurt Emmie."

Sam felt a surge of savage anger. Until that moment, he'd maintained a calm veneer and a calculating mind, even when Tony's life hung by a thread and Katrina had been kidnapped by Karmakov. He'd managed to keep a cool head during his confrontation in the barn with Barton and Olsen and throughout his raid on the hospital. But the thought of his mother and child being threatened with brutality pushed him beyond the limit. Sam's eyes blazed as he gripped the hunting knife he had carried with him from the cabin. "They have Katrina and she's in danger," he said in a voice tight with anger. "I have to go get her."

Faye eyes were pleading. "Sam, don't you think you should let the police handle this now? Those slimy snakes mean business. You could get hurt, or worse, God forbid. Emmie and I couldn't get along without you."

As she spoke, Faye knew from the steely glint in his eyes that her son would follow this fight through to the end, whatever the cost. It was his nature. It was the blood that ran in his veins and the veins of his ancestors for a hundred generations. Faye had known all of her life that the blood of the plains Indians and the Scottish highlanders was a dangerous mix. Sam wore the trappings of civilization well, but underneath was the fierce independence, fearlessness, and tenacity of the long line of tribal warriors that preceded him. Sam carried the genes of men and women who for centuries had fought to the death, if necessary, to defend their families and tribes. He had no more choice than a wild mustang defending his herd from a pack of wolves. Instinctively, he would attack and fight, oblivious to pain and personal risk.

Sam loosened Emmie's grip on his waist and slipped the bone-handled knife under his belt. "There's no time to wait for the authorities, Mom. If I did try to explain this whole mess to them, the first thing they'd do is arrest me. They still think I killed Tony. In the meantime, we'd lose Katrina. No telling what they'd do with her. No, I've got to follow this through myself, and fast." Emmie began to whimper as she realized that her father was going to leave them again. Sam squeezed her shoulders with both hands, then hugged her tight. "I hate to go, but there's really no choice. Let's get up to the house and call Sheriff Fielding. This time, we'll make sure that the deputy stays put."

As they walked from the barn toward the house, an old green Ford pickup turned off the road and started up the long driveway. "Great," Sam said. "It's Red and Danny. They'll protect you while I'm gone. Mom, you and Emmie just stay here on the ranch with Red and Danny. Those two could stand off the entire Mexican army for a week, if need be. Tell them everything you know and then be prepared for anything. Keep the shotguns loaded. I'll stay in touch."

Sam gave his mother a hug and then knelt to hug Emmie, who was still clinging tightly to him. Wiping the tears from her eyes, he whispered, "You take care of your Grandma now, munchkin. I'll be back as soon as I can. You know I love you more than anything in the world." He held his daughter tight to his chest for a few seconds and then quickly stood, and without another word, he trotted across the pasture toward the grove of persimmon trees half a mile to the west.

Chapter 12

Somewhere in the back of his mind, Sam knew that the midnight blue BMW roadster was a dead giveaway, yet he was so obsessed with finding Katrina that he did not take time to consider the dangers he would encounter in a head on confrontation with her kidnappers. His sole mission was to find her and stop her captors from spiriting her out of the country.

Finding a straightaway of more than a mile on the winding country road, Sam simultaneously pressed the accelerator and reached for the cell phone on the passenger seat. As the needle nudged a hundred, Sam pressed the send button while watching fence posts flash by in his peripheral vision. He held the telephone in one hand, the other hand gripping the steering wheel like a bull rider grips the rawhide strap that holds a ton of explosive energy and raw muscle. Where would they have taken her? What was their plan? Sam took the most obvious course first, straight back to the airport. He didn't know where else to go.

"Sanders…" a sleepy voice answered on the other end of the line.

"Dave? This is Sam. Where are you?"

"Where do you think? Where any decent human being would be at this hour. Uh, what time is it, anyway?"

"It's nearly eight in the morning," Sam said dryly, as he slowed to pass a farm tractor pulling a wagon. "What did you do, go back to bed?"

"Well, after you abandoned me on Cherry Street, I stopped by my place to get ready for work, and I guess I did doze off on the couch for a few minutes. I mean, you kept me up half the night. I just wanted to catch a couple of winks…" he trailed off weakly.

"Haul your butt out of bed and get moving!" Sam shouted into the telephone as he accelerated around the tractor. "They grabbed Katrina again. I'm headed for the airport. I'll need your help."

Sanders jumped to his feet, wide awake. "Well, why didn't you say so? I'm on my way!"

"Better call in some reinforcements," Sam said, weighing the risk of being arrested against the urgency of saving Katrina. "Another FBI agent or two would be welcome. And I'm sure that Immigration would be very interested."

"Any doubt that they're headed for the airport?"

"We'd better hope so. Otherwise, I have no idea where to look. Meet me at the Millionaire hangar as soon as you can." Sam snapped the phone shut, knowing that it would take Sanders half an hour to get to the airport, longer if he waited for reinforcements. Sam was only twenty minutes away, fifteen at the speed he was traveling.

As he pressed the accelerator to the floor, he considered the immense risk of the course of action he was about to take. In the span of a few minutes, he thoroughly evaluated the dangers ahead and laid a tentative plan. The odds of success were minimal, yet he flew on without hesitation, thinking to himself, *"Damn the torpedoes, full speed ahead."*

* * * * *

Chief District Judge Hans Mickelson's grizzled, grey beard hid a double chin that matched his rotund belly, which was straining to pop the buttons off an extra-large grey pin-striped vest. Entering his office by a side door, he hung his worn jacket on a hook in the corner where it had hung for most of the past eleven years, and dropped heavily into his swivel chair. "Coffee, Lena," he said, loud enough to be heard in the outer office. He slowly surveyed the piles of files on his desk and then swiveled his chair to look out the window and across the square toward City Hall. *Eighteen more months*, he thought. *Eighteen months and I'm out of here.*

Moments later, a tall, slender woman with short blond hair, ruby lipstick, and matching dagger fingernails floated into the room with a steaming mug of coffee. "Here you are Judge," she said with a warm smile. "Did you know you already have visitors waiting?"

"What? I don't have any appointments this morning," the Judge said, clearing his throat loudly. "Who is it and what do they want?" For the past several years he had done a pretty fair job of delegating to the younger judges and court administrators. Occasionally, he got caught in his office by a prominent lawyer or a political patron looking for a favor, but not usually this early on a Monday morning, unless he had scheduled it himself. He had just opened his newspaper and did not want to be disturbed, at least not until after his second cup of coffee.

"It's Mr. Bandini, Judge, and Tom Wallace. They want to see you as soon as possible," Lena said, her voice pregnant with unspoken meaning. "They didn't say why they're here, but they seem real serious."

Great, Judge Mickelson thought, Wallace and Bandini on serious business first thing on Monday morning. This could *not* be good. He thought for a moment about delaying or attempting an exit through a side door, but there was no point. "Well, bring 'em in, then," he muttered with a scowl as he folded his newspaper closed and reached for his mug of coffee.

Half a minute later, Bandini and Tom Wallace, the County's District Attorney, walked into Judge Mickelson's office. Both men reached forward over the Judge's desk to shake his hand and Bandini's notorious grin shined forth for the obvious purpose of putting the Judge at ease. Instead, it made him all the more wary. The Judge leaned forward to shake hands with the two men, but remained seated.

"It's good to see you, Judge," Bandini said. "We'd like to have a few words with you, if you could spare the time."

The Judge sensed trouble, but he had no choice but to invite the two men to be seated. Political courtesy dictated that he give the District Attorney an occasional audience when it was requested, on rare occasion. And the Huntington firm had heavily supported his re-election campaigns for practically his entire career. These were some of the most powerful players in the state. He knew that Huntington's firm had a close relationship with the office of the District Attorney. If he valued his retirement, he would treat these lawyers with kid gloves. Any reasonable request would not be refused. He knew it and they knew it. Unreasonable requests would have to be at least, well, considered. He prayed to God that their request would not be too far out of bounds.

"Sit down, gentlemen, please," the Judge intoned in a deep baritone. "What brings you two down here so early this morning?"

Tom Wallace, a tall, thin man with a beak for a nose and a wreath of curly dark brown hair replied, "It's an urgent law enforcement matter, Judge. We need both search and arrest warrants immediately in connection with the attempted murder and kidnapping of Commissioner Tony Angelletti. You may have read about it in the paper yesterday."

"Would have been hard to miss," the Judge said, taking a sip of coffee. "Front page spread with a picture. Angelletti still with us, then?"

"Yes and no, Judge. He was at the hospital in the ICU until late last night, when he was kidnapped by the same person who tried to kill him. All of the evidence points to Sam Littlehawk as both the assailant and the kidnapper."

A flicker of surprise showed through the Judge's normally deadpan expression. "Littlehawk? Kill Angelletti? That's nonsense. I've known both those boys since they were in high school. Teammates on the football team, if I'm not mistaken, and best friends as well. They went to law school together. Why in God's name would Littlehawk want to kill Angelletti?"

"A woman, Judge," Bandini said with studied seriousness. "Jealousy is a wicked mistress. Those two were fighting over a woman and it looks like Littlehawk just lost it and did in his best friend in a fit of anger. Stranger things have happened." Bandini shook his head sadly, as though the very thought of such a vicious act pained him.

Wallace was nodding his head vigorously, his wire-rimmed glasses slipping up and down on his beak nose. "Yes, Judge, and we have evidence. Eye witnesses to both the attempted murder and the kidnapping, and a note found in Angelletti's pocket proves the motive. It's really pretty clean, Judge. Littlehawk did it. We just need to pick him up before he decides to hightail it out of the country. We think he's still in town, but he could decide to bolt at any time." Wallace pulled some papers from his satchel and slipped them across the desk toward the Judge. "If you'll sign these papers, Judge, we'll just be on our way and let you finish your coffee."

Judge Mickelson pursed his lips and stared for a moment at one man and then the other, then glanced over the papers on his desk. Leaning back in his swivel chair, he slowly stroked his beard. He knew that he would sign the warrants, but he also knew that it was important to emphasize who held the power here. He was the Chief Judge, not some stooge they could call upon at any time of the day or night to do their bidding. It was important that he carefully consider all aspects of the matter before giving them what they wanted.

"Have you talked to the eye witnesses, Tom?"

"Well, not personally, not yet, sir, but Mr. Bandini here has spoken with one of them and the police have spoken with the other."

"Was Littlehawk positively identified?"

"He was seen by a whole crowd of people at the scene of the attempted murder. The first witnesses there saw Littlehawk standing over Angelletti's body with the murder weapon in his hand."

The Judge peered from under his bushy eyebrows at Wallace. "Murder weapon? I thought you said Angelletti wasn't dead yet?"

"Well," Wallace said, acknowledging his overstatement, "I guess it's really not a murder weapon yet, but I'm sure it soon will be. Angelletti was just about dead when he was kidnapped from the hospital. He wasn't expected to survive the night."

"That's the part that I don't understand," Judge Mickelson countered. "If this was a crime of passion committed in a fit of jealousy, why would the attacker go to the hospital several hours later to kidnap the victim, who's almost dead already? Doesn't make any sense to me. It's not easy to kidnap an unconscious person from a hospital room. And it would be too easy to get caught, especially if everyone and their dog had seen the assailant and could identify him. Besides, why not just finish him off then and there?"

"People do strange things under stress, Judge," Bandini said. "Maybe he thought it would be harder to make a murder charge stick without a body."

"Well, something about all this just doesn't add up," Mickelson said as he reached across the desk for the papers and picked up a pen. "But I guess it won't hurt anything to get Littlehawk in here for questioning. Maybe he's got a perfectly good explanation for everything." Bandini visibly relaxed as Judge Mickelson penned his signature on several copies of the warrants and shoved the papers back in Wallace's direction.

"Thank you, Judge," both men said almost simultaneously, as Wallace picked up the papers and they rose to go.

"You know, Littlehawk's a pretty cool character," the Judge said, stroking his beard. "He tried a tough case in my courtroom last spring, and I was impressed. He definitely has a good head on his shoulders. You may have your hands full with this one, Tom."

"Thanks, Judge, I'll keep that in mind."

As the two men left the outer office, Judge Mickelson sipped from his mug of coffee. They had been right about one thing. Stranger things had happened. In twenty-eight years on the bench, he had seen a lot of bizarre human behavior. Violence was often directed against friends, lovers, and family. Still, something about this case troubled him. Littlehawk was not the personality type to commit a crime of passion, certainly not murder. And even if he had done it, he was far too smart to get caught. The kidnapping was inexplicable. None of it made any sense.

And why was Bandini involved? Judge Mickelson had refrained from asking Bandini what interest he had in the case, and Bandini had not volunteered anything. It was not unusual for Bandini to be in the thick of things, but what connection could he have to this murder investigation? As attorney for Southwest Power, Bandini did have a professional relationship with the commissioner, but Bandini had no other obvious ties to the investigation. It seemed unlikely that he would take such a strong interest in this case, unless there was some other motive.

Of one thing, Judge Mickelson was certain. This was *not* a simple crime of passion, committed by one friend against another, both respected members of the bar. There was a lot more here than met the eye. But Mickelson was also satisfied that he had done the right thing, indeed, he had done what he had to do—their request had not been too far out of bounds. What harm could it do under the circumstances to bring Littlehawk in for questioning?

* * * * *

Just outside the boundary of the airport, two security guards with badly blistered tongues and bad attitudes sat in their car, awaiting further instructions. They had been hoodwinked by the enemy, lost their target at the hospital, and spent most of the night looking for an elusive farm truck. Plus, they were in serious hot water with their boss and would doubtless be on duty non-stop until they found their target again or nailed the guy in the blue roadster, who was probably half way to Canada already. To make matters worse, they were both sleepy, but their mouths were too burned and blistered to drink coffee. Out of sheer boredom, the guard in the uniform bearing the name "Jerry" adjusted the police scanner for the twentieth time.

"Unit 78. Blue BMW roadster eastbound on I-244 traveling at a high rate of speed, officers request assistance…"

Both heads snapped up, as if an electric shock had passed through the car seat, jerking the guards from their torpor. "That's got to be him!" Jerry shouted as he turned the key and slammed the car into gear. "He's coming back to the airport. We'll nail him before he gets close!" Tires spun as the heavy Chrysler fishtailed forward. "Fast as he's going, he'll be here in two minutes."

The security guards were only a mile from the airport when they saw the speeding blue sports car approaching on the opposite side of the expressway. As the two cars drew closer, the Chrysler suddenly braked, spun across the wide grass median, then swerved onto the highway just ahead of the speeding roadster. The BMW barely slowed, then deftly dodged the Chrysler and hurtled ahead.

"Jesus, what are you trying to do, kill us all?" the guard in the passenger seat shouted at the driver as he clung to the handgrip above the door. "He could've hit us and blown us all to hell!"

"Just trying to get close enough for you to get off a shot, deadeye," the driver replied as he pressed the accelerator to the floor again in pursuit of the blue bullet. "Now why don't you do something constructive like shoot out his tires? We gotta catch this guy or our goose is cooked."

The guard in the passenger seat was leaning out the window with pistol in hand when he caught a glimpse in the side view mirror of flashing red lights behind them. "Don't look now, Jerry, but the posse is on the way. What do we do?"

"Stick with him. Maybe we can get some of the credit for nailing the sucker."

The dispatcher's voice crackled over the police scanner. "Unit 78, we are advised that a blue roadster may be heading for the Millionaire hanger at the airport. Officers are already in position. Suspect may be armed and dangerous. Repeat, armed and dangerous. Proceed to follow suspect at a distance, but do not attempt to apprehend."

"Well, I'll be damned. Sounds like they're expecting him. They've already set up a welcoming party," Jerry said, as he slowed the car down to seventy and let the police cruiser pass. "Let's just follow along here and see what happens."

* * * * *

Gunning the car through the hangar gate, Sam raced onto the tarmac to a line of parked jets and skidded to a stop. Five hundred yards down the taxiway, a white Learjet was taxiing for takeoff. Sam could not see the markings on the plane, but its shape was familiar and he knew in his heart the Katrina and Karmakov were on it. Could it be stopped? How? What could he do?

Suddenly, a booming voice on a police megaphone broke his intense concentration. "You in the blue BMW, exit your vehicle with your hands up. You are under arrest. Repeat. You are under arrest. Exit your vehicle with your hands up."

Sam glanced toward the hangar and saw two police cars and uniformed officers with weapons drawn kneeling behind open car doors. His only thought was, how could they have anticipated where he was going and gotten here ahead of him? Then he realized their source—Bandini.

Without thinking, Sam downshifted and floored the accelerator, sending the sports car flying down the taxiway after the Learjet, which was just turning from the taxiway onto the runway nearly a thousand yards away. Sam speed-shifted through the gears and in seconds was approaching at a hundred miles per hour. At the same time, the Learjet began to accelerate down the parallel runway toward him. Sam jerked the speeding car across the smooth grass median separating the runway and taxiway, hoping to intersect the path of the aircraft before it could leave the ground. If he could somehow force the pilot to abort the takeoff, he would have just a chance of saving Katrina. The move was bold and reckless, but desperate times call for desperate measures.

Less than one hundred yards separated the car and the aircraft when the jet reached rotation velocity and suddenly rose from the runway. A second later, the rising plane flashed by the roadster with a deafening roar and Sam caught a glimpse of the gloating face of Karmakov at a port window. With a wrenching feeling, Sam knew that Katrina was also on the plane. He was too late! The BMW skidded to a stop in a hot cloud of jet fuel exhaust.

Sam had little time to ponder the magnitude of their misfortune. As the jet roared into the distance, the sound of sirens became audible. Four police cruisers with flashing lights were speeding down the taxiway. Now what? Slamming the accelerator to the floor, he shot across the taxiway and the tarmac heading toward a private gated airport entrance. With luck, the gates might be open and Sam could lose the heat in the adjacent industrial areas.

No such luck. As Sam rounded the American Airlines building, the gate was manned and closed. Another police cruiser was parked outside the gate and the four patrol cars were closing fast. Sam swallowed hard and grimaced. It had been a foolhardy effort, but he had *almost* made it! He pulled the roadster in front of the guard shack and turned off the engine. Vaulting out of the car, he tossed his keys to the guard who had stepped out of the shack and was eyeing him quizzically. "Would you mind looking after this for me for a few hours?" he said coolly to the guard. "You can drive it, but don't let anyone else. I'll be back soon to pick it up."

With that, Sam walked calmly through the gate to meet the waiting police officers.

Chapter 13

Sam stood at the center of a vortex of nearly a dozen uniformed police officers. The extended high speed chase had clearly raised the tension level of the group. Three of the officers had drawn their weapons and it was clear to Sam that he would be best served by demonstrating a cooperative attitude. He held his hands up, palms forward, at chest level. At the order of one of the officers, Sam laid his hands on the roof of a police car and stood passively while another officer frisked him and checked his pockets.

"You are under arrest," the officer muttered in a robotic voice as he patted Sam's legs one at a time. "Anything you say can and will be used against you in a court of law. You have the right to remain silent…"

Suddenly, one of the state police officers in the group, an older man in a tan uniform, stepped forward and slammed a long black nightstick hard across the middle of Sam's back. As the heavy nightstick connected with rib bones a loud *crack!* broke the relative quiet. Sam was knocked forward against the car, incapacitated by the unexpected blow. Then, before he could crumple to the ground, the officer swung the nightstick again with both hands, this time planting a vicious blow across the back of Sam's knees. The reflex action from the second blow left Sam lying dazed on the pavement, intense pains shooting through his back and legs, lights flashing in his head. Through a haze of pain, Sam could see the attacking officer's grim face. It was a mask of anger and fury. "That'll teach you to run from the cops, you murdering scum! I'll make damn sure you fry in hell before you ever run from me again!"

None of the other officers in the group moved or spoke. Slowly, the officer bending over Sam stood, then he drew back his foot and swiftly kicked Sam's face three times with a heavy black boot. Sam's world spun out of control as new pains shot through his head. Most of the officers in the group looked away in disgust, but one short, thick-bodied officer stepped forward, putting his hand on the forearm of Sam's attacker.

"Aw, Marty, wha'd you have to go and do that for? You know you could get into serious trouble for beatin' on prisoners."

The older officer's ruddy face was still flushed with emotion and his breath was short, but he had released most of his fury on Sam and he was no longer clinching the nightstick like a major league batter. "I didn't hurt 'em that bad, Buzz, and this is prob'ly the only chance we'll get to teach this dirt bag a lesson. He'll just get some high dollar lawyer and be out defyin' the law again next week. You can bet on it." The officer slapped the nightstick repeatedly against the palm of his hand as though waiting for his next victim.

"Maybe, but you know it's wrong to beat on the prisoners. You just can't do that anymore—there's too many hidden cameras these days. You better remember what the Chief said."

"Don't matter what the Chief said, Buzz. This scum ain't gonna prove nothin' by none of these boys, now is he?" The red-faced officer looked slowly around the group of younger officers, who alternately looked at the ground or into the distance. The violent acts of the older officer had put them all in a difficult position, but no one spoke.

"See, Buzz, like I said, it don't matter at all. These boys'll all just forget about this." He turned to two of the young officers standing nearby. "Now why don't you two get this scum behind bars down at the city jail where he belongs? I got to get back to the highway." Without turning to look again at the group of police officers, Marty and Buzz walked to their state police cars, leaving the city police to clean up the mess.

Lying on the ground, head pounding, Sam hoped that he would survive long enough to see the city jail. He knew that many a suspect had been shot dead during the arrest, or between the arrest and the booking room. Huntington wanted him dead, and Huntington's reach undoubtedly extended to the city police force. After the beating he had taken, Sam calculated his odds of reaching the lock-up were less than fifty-fifty. Lying face down on the ground, he ran his tongue over his teeth to verify that they were all still in place and wondered what manner of execution was planned for him.

Two officers were lifting Sam to his feet when a Ford sedan slid to a stop near the group of police cars. Through blurry eyes, Sam saw two men in casual clothes step from the car and walk briskly toward the group of officers. By the time the newcomers reached him, Sam was leaning against the police car with an officer holding each arm, blood dripping from a deep crease in his forehead left by a steel-toed boot. "Too bad you couldn't have gotten here five minutes sooner," Sam said as he spat blood from his bleeding lips and gums. "That state trooper wasn't too friendly."

Dave Sanders noted the bruises and cuts that Sam had suffered at the hands of the trooper, but he kept a poker face. He knew it would not serve any purpose to disclose his concern for Sam. He drew his ID from his pocket and showed it to the arresting officers. "Agent Sanders, FBI," he said officially, and nodding at his partner, he added, "and Agent Whittaker. This is a federal investigation now. We'll take this prisoner off your hands. We need to take him in for questioning."

"Not so fast." A plainclothes detective who had been standing behind the uniformed officers stepped forward. A pink golf shirt was stretched tight over his barrel chest and tucked carelessly into tan trousers. His casual dress looked out of place among the green and grey uniforms, but his thick, tattooed arms and his calm air of authority suggested that he was a veteran who had collared many a lawbreaker during his years on the force. "Who says this is a federal investigation? You can't just waltz in here and take this prisoner without some authority. We have a warrant for this man. I was told that the D.A. wants him real bad. What do you have that gives you the right to take him?" The detective stood between the FBI agents and Sam, as solid as a naval blockade.

"If you've read the warrant, you know that the victim was an elected official," Sanders countered. "That makes his attempted murder and kidnapping a federal crime. It's our job to take this prisoner into custody."

"What difference does it make who takes him in?" the detective responded. "He's going to end up in the same jail anyway."

"I just want to make sure he gets there," Sanders replied. "Seems that there are people who would just as soon see him dropped while trying to escape."

"Not on my watch," the detective growled, taking a pair of handcuffs from one of the officers. "This one is special delivery to the D.A. I'm taking him there myself and in twenty years, I've never lost one yet. You boys want to trail along with us, that's okay by me, but I'm taking him straight to the office of the Chief Judge, where the D.A. will be waiting."

Sanders decided he had carried his bluff far enough. "No problem, friend, we'll just follow you on down to the Judge's office and let the prosecutors figure out who gets to fry this guy first," Sanders said, looking at Sam with a grim expression. Sam glared back at him, knowing that Sanders was taking some perverse pleasure from his predicament. "He must have put up a fight I guess," Sanders continued, surveying the blood on Sam's face and clothes.

"Resisted arrest," the detective responded curtly, as he snapped the handcuffs on Sam. "These guys just never learn."

"Yeah, I know the type," Sanders added, staring at Sam and shaking his head. "Incredibly stupid to try to run from half the city's police force. He could just as easily be dead. But then, if he had half a brain, he wouldn't be here, would he?" Sanders turned back to the detective. "You might want to clean him up before you get to the Judge's office. Judges don't like their offices messed up by bloody prisoners. We'll just follow you in."

* * * * *

Sam limped off the elevator and into the hall outside Judge Mickelson's chambers and was immediately blinded by half a dozen flashbulbs. A news camera was filming. Apparently, the press had been tuned to the police band and knew that he would be appearing immediately before Judge Mickelson. Sam smiled confidently at the cameras, showing a bruised and scraped cheekbone, cut forehead and swollen lower lip. He wondered what Faye and Emmie would think when they saw him on the evening news.

He was ushered into the Judge's office by the two officers who had driven him to the courthouse, as well as the pink-shirted Detective Michaels. Sam, whose hands were cuffed in front of him, was directed to sit in a wooden chair across from the Judge. The two uniformed officers stood behind him, one with a heavy hand tightly gripping Sam's shoulder. Sam scowled over his shoulder at the officer and squirmed under his grip, wrenching his shoulder free. The officer relented and stood at ease behind Sam's chair. Wallace sat in a chair beside the Judge's desk, his gold-rimmed glasses bouncing on his beak-like nose as he nervously shuffled papers and sniffed from chronic allergies.

"Hi, Tom," Sam said, addressing Wallace. "What brings you down here so early on a Monday? I haven't seen you since the election. Bandini still chairing your campaign committee?" His voice was superficially cordial, but carried a biting undertone reflecting his edgy state of mind and contempt for the prosecutor.

"I don't believe that Mr. Bandini's political affiliations are at issue here," Wallace sniffed, leaning his head back to peer through the glasses that had slid down his nose. "This interrogation concerns your continuing criminal activities."

"Interrogation, is it?" Sam replied. "What a surprise. I thought that we were all gathering here this morning for a nice cup of coffee and a discussion of state politics. You know, there are some very intriguing political issues being discussed on the street, like what major public project is being blocked at the Corporation Commission, and who would want a certain commissioner *dead*."

"This is not a tea party, Littlehawk," Wallace said coolly. "If it were up to me, you'd be in the city jail right now, making friends with some of the bad boys down there until your arraignment in a couple of months. It's only Judge Mickelson's professional courtesy, or perhaps his curiosity, that brought you here."

Judge Mickelson, who had been leaning far back in his swivel chair, loudly cleared his throat, getting the attention of everyone in the room. He let his chair tip forward and leveled his best judicial stare at Sam. "I just want to know, Littlehawk," he said slowly, "what you have to say about these eye witnesses who say they saw you standing over the victim with a weapon in your hand and later saw you kidnapping the commissioner from the hospital. For now, I guess we'll forget about you driving a hundred and fifty miles an hour on the freeway, eluding the police, trespassing on airport property and reckless endangerment. But tell me about the eye witnesses."

Wallace did not give Sam a chance to answer. "Your Honor, this really isn't at all necessary," he said quickly. "This suspect has all of the safeguards of the criminal justice system at his disposal and as a practicing attorney, he is as familiar with them as you and I are. He will have ample opportunity to make his defense in due time, in the proper forum, with counsel of his choosing. Right now, we have sworn statements of at least four eye witnesses that cannot be negated by anything he might say here. He *must* be bound over for trial, without bail."

Ignoring Wallace's interruption, Judge Mickelson continued to stare at Sam with a deadpan expression and uttered one word. "Well?"

"I don't suppose you'd believe me if I told you that we've uncovered a high level criminal conspiracy involving bribery of state officials and..." Sam paused. Whatever he said would immediately be relayed to Bandini, and he still needed to keep them guessing as to how much he knew.

"What about the eye witnesses?" the Judge asked pointedly, not to be deterred by either Wallace *or* Sam.

"They saw what they saw, your Honor," Sam said, looking the Judge squarely in the eyes. "But I can tell you that I never hurt Tony Angelletti and I certainly didn't kidnap him. And *you* know that under these circumstances, I can't risk waiving my Fifth Amendment rights by discussing this any further at this time."

"See Judge, he has *nothing…*" Wallace injected acidly.

Judge Mickelson interrupted Wallace with a glare, and in a loud, authoritative voice, his eyes still locked with Sam's steady gaze, he asked, "And what evidence do you have of this…conspiracy?"

"There's a mountain of evidence, your Honor, and it's already in the hands of…" Sam stopped in mid-sentence, knowing that he could not divulge who had custody of the evidence yet. It was clear that the conspirators would stop at nothing to protect themselves, and he had no desire to put Dave Sanders in danger. He was also relatively sure that Huntington and his cronies had the power to derail any FBI investigation, if they knew of its existence. Without the evidence Sanders possessed, the investigation would grind to a halt. It was not time to tell all that he knew, even at the risk of being jailed.

"Cat got your tongue?" Wallace asked in a sarcastic tone, obviously enjoying Sam's predicament. "Who has this evidence, Littlehawk? What is it?"

Sam leaned back and breathed deeply. "You will see all of it in due time, your Honor," he said quietly, still looking at the Judge.

"Like I said, Judge, he has *nothing,*" Wallace crowed. "It's time for this little charade to end. You have no choice but to bind him over for trial."

"We'll see about that at the arraignment tomorrow," the Judge growled. "But right now, Littlehawk, you have not given me any good reason to turn you loose, while the D.A. has given me lots of good reasons to keep you in custody." Without waiting for a reply, Judge Mickelson looked straight at Detective Michaels. "Book him," he said flatly. "We'll hold him, at least until his memory gets better."

The two officers standing behind Sam lifted him from his chair by his biceps and quickly escorted him out of the Judge's chambers. He was led the few steps to the elevators and one of the officers pushed the down button. A few seconds later, a smiling Tom Wallace strolled out of the Judge's chambers. As he passed the men waiting for the elevator, he paused and stared sadistically at Sam for a moment. "See you in court, sucker," he said.

"I hope so," Sam shot back. "I'll enjoy witnessing one of your last acts as D.A. And by the way, you and Bandini might want to review your campaign finance reports. Seems that they don't quite agree with some information that's about to be posted on the Internet. Bye now!" Stepping onto the elevator, Sam turned and grinned at Wallace, who stood stock still with a perplexed look on his face, his mouth gaping open.

Chapter 14

The elevator descended to the basement of the courthouse where there was a holding area for prisoners in transit between the courts and the jail. The jail was eight blocks from the courthouse and shuttle buses with armed guards routinely transferred prisoners between the courthouse and jail. The transfer schedule often required prisoners to wait for several hours in the basement holding area.

The jail was relatively new, a fifty million dollar investment by the taxpayers to serve the city through the next century. Designed by a blue ribbon team of architects and consultants and operated by a private security firm under a long-term management contract, the facility was state-of-the-art. In spite of the many political headaches the privatization of the jail had caused, including displacement of many long-term public employees, it remained the pride of the city's administration. Even though Sam was a prisoner, he was curious to see whether the string of problems that had initially plagued the facility and its management had been resolved.

Detective Michaels led the way from the elevator to the basement holding area, with Sam and the two uniformed officers following. When they arrived at the intake desk, they were met by a young guard wearing one of the brown and tan uniforms that identified him as an employee of CMI, the private security company that ran the jail. He was tall and lanky, with coarse blonde hair cut in a flat top, a pale complexion, and a moderate case of acne. Two years earlier, he might have been a high school basketball star, or a high school dropout. The jailer slapped a plastic clipboard on the counter as Detective Michaels removed Sam's handcuffs.

"Fill out the forms, please," the jailer said in a flat tone as he dropped back into his swivel chair and turned up the volume on the six-inch television he was watching. From the tinny speaker of the television, Sam could hear the *Wheel of Fortune* turning and outbursts of the studio audience, punctuated by the jailer's loud bubble gum popping.

"*You* fill out the freakin' forms," the burly Detective Michaels said in disgust, shoving the clipboard back across the counter toward the jailer, whose eyes never left the television screen. "You want the freakin' forms filled out, you can do it yourself."

"New policy," the jailer said, pausing to pop a large bubble. "You cops got to fill out all the intake forms. Supposedly y'all know more about the prisoners than we do, even though we spend all day with 'em and y'all just smack 'em in the head a coupl'a times and bring 'em in here to bleed." The jailer never took his eyes off *Wheel of Fortune.*

"Bullshit!" Detective Michaels said with anger fueled in part by his disgust with the CMI privatization and the new standards it imposed. "I've never filled out a damn jailer's form in twenty years and I'm not about to start now. I don't give a damn about your new policy. I caught him and I got him down here. He's yours now. That's the way it's always been. If you lose him, it's your hide, not mine."

The jailer reluctantly looked up from the television. "Sorry, buddy, but I can't fill out the forms no more," he said, picking stray scraps of bubble gum from his pimply chin. "Company policy. You gotta fill out the forms."

"I'll be *damned* if I'll fill out your stinkin' forms!" Michaels shouted furiously. It was easy to see that the cool composure with which he handled challenging and dangerous situations in the field did not extend to office paperwork and dealings with ignorant teenage jailers.

"Maybe I could help," Sam volunteered, stepping forward while continuing to rub his wrists, which were chafed from the handcuffs. "I think I know just as much about me as either of you do. I'm a lawyer and I'm used to filling out forms. These don't look too tough to me." Sam reached for the clipboard and picked up the pen.

"I don't give a rat's ass who fills out the damn forms," Detective Michaels declared belligerently, addressing the room at large. "I collared him and I delivered him. He's your responsibility now." Ignoring the minimum wage jailer who had returned his full attention to the television, Detective Michaels spun on his heel and headed back toward the elevator, followed by the two uniformed officers who were awed by his command of the situation and his bold and dramatic treatment of the jailer.

As the three police officers disappeared around the corner, Sam stood at the counter and continued to look thoughtfully at the forms. Thirty seconds later, the jailer glanced up from the television for a moment with a blank stare, saw Sam filling out the forms, and then returned his full attention to *Wheel of Fortune.*

Sam completed the forms, removed them from the clipboard, and peered over the counter at the piles of white, yellow, and pink forms stacked in metal baskets on the counter next to the small television. He carefully separated the forms, dropping the originals and the pink and yellow copies in the appropriate baskets. The young jailer glanced up momentarily and noticed Sam placing the forms in the baskets. He blew a large bubble, popped it between his teeth, then cocked his head toward an armed guard across the room who was reading a newspaper. "Go with that guard," the jailer said, "he'll show ya' to yer room."

The jailer smiled broadly at his attempt at humor, revealing yellow buck teeth and a huge wad of bubble gum, then turned his attention back to *Wheel of Fortune.*

Sam heard the quiet thud of the steel door close behind him as he stepped into the holding cell. Unlike jail cells of the past, this room was large and open, with plenty of light from thick glass windows located at the top of fifteen foot high walls. The room resembled a waiting room in a bus or train station, but with stainless steel benches bolted to the walls and little else in the room. An unarmed guard sat in a contoured steel chair near the door. Video cameras were mounted on each wall just below the windows, well out of reach. Six prisoners sat or lay silently on the wide steel benches, pondering their sins, or perhaps considering the impossibility of escape, each unwilling to converse with the other prisoners. Sam was thankful that all of the prisoners in the holding cell were returning from their court proceedings and had been in custody long enough to be sober. He stretched out on a steel bench and promptly fell asleep.

Some time later, Sam's eyes popped open as the toe of a black boot bumped his leg. Before he fully regained consciousness, a large hand grabbed the collar of his bloodstained shirt and hoisted him to a sitting position. Sam had been roused from a deep sleep. He shook his head and tasted the sourness in his mouth. He was not sure how long he had slept, but the stiffness in his back suggested that it had been a few hours. He glanced at the windows overhead and noticed that the light came from a different angle.

A tall, stout guard stood in front of him. "Hey, are you Madison? Wake up. It's time to go."

Sam sat still for a moment, his body still heavy with sleep, but his mind took quick focus. "Yeah," he muttered sleepily, "I'm John Madison. Where we going?"

"Upstairs. You get to go see the Judge, if you're sober enough."

Sam slowly stood and smoothed his clothes as best he could. The guard waited while he tucked in his shirttail and combed back his longish dark hair. Sam took a deep breath and smiled at the guard. "After that nap, I feel like a million bucks! I can't wait to go see the Judge!"

"Well, I don't think she'll be so anxious to see you. She hates dealing with drunks. You'll be lucky if she doesn't send you over to the slammer for a few days to dry out. Now get a move on."

Sam walked across the cell, out the door and through the corridor, followed by the hefty guard. As they passed the intake desk, the guard with Sam picked up a blue copy of the form that Sam had filled out hours earlier. "Takin' this one up to the Judge," he said to the gum-popping jailer, who was at that moment totally entranced in a *Gilligan's Island* rerun. "Prob'ly won't be back," the guard continued when there was no response from the jailer. Sam hoped and prayed that the guard was right.

"Huh? What? Yeah, okay, just leave the forms in the basket," the young jailer said absentmindedly as Sam and the guard headed down the corridor to the elevator.

* * * * *

The elevator doors opened on the third floor of the courthouse and Sam and the guard stepped off. They turned to the right and walked a few steps down a dark marble corridor to the double walnut doors of the small courtroom used by Special Associate District Judge Janice Bowling. Entering the courtroom, Sam saw two other prisoners in street clothes seated in the jury box, overseen by a bailiff and a uniformed police officer. Sam walked toward the front of the courtroom followed by the guard.

"Here's another add-on to the misdemeanor docket, Bob," the guard said to the bailiff as he handed off the blue form. "Take a seat there with the others," the guard said to Sam, nodding at the jury box before he turned to leave.

Five minutes later, the bailiff positioned near the Judge's bench said, "All rise," and the three men in the jury box stood. A small blonde woman in a large black robe entered the courtroom and took the bench. She sat down and briefly studied the three blue forms on her desk, then looked at the three men. Sam looked down and cringed, saying a small prayer that she wouldn't recognize him. His breathing nearly stopped as the young Judge surveyed them with a critical eye.

"Bailiff, please bring the prisoners forward," the Judge announced with an affected air of authority. The three men were escorted forward and took their places in a line in front of the raised bench. The Judge read each of the three blue papers in front of her, then assumed a serious demeanor.

Sam knew that Special Judge Janice Bowling had been out of law school for a little more than four years and had held a position on the bench for only three months. She was obviously experimenting with her new power and trying to develop effective means of using it. Handling petty criminal matters was an important part of a new judge's training. In misdemeanor court, she could learn to wear the mantle of authority and exercise judicial powers without risking a serious mistake, leaving life and death decisions and touchy political situations to more experienced and savvy jurists.

"Mr. Barnes, would you step forward, please?" The broad-shouldered man in dirty work clothes standing next to Sam took one step toward the bench.

"What do you have to say for yourself, Mr. Barnes?" the Judge continued, fixing the prisoner with a most stern look from her pretty, perfect blue eyes.

"Well ma'am, I mean yer Honor, I jest drank a little too much beer last night and got in a little fight in a bar. I didn't start it and I didn't hurt no one, 'cept that one guy that hit me over the head with the pool cue, and he was askin' for it. He was nothin' but trouble anyway."

"I understand you destroyed some property in the bar, is that right?" the Judge responded sternly.

"We broke a couple of chairs, and I guess the light over the pool table."

"And you understand you will be responsible for the damage?"

"Yes ma'am, I mean yer Honor, I got the money to pay. I'm gonna go pay the bartender soon as I get out of here. I got me a good job in the oil fields."

"Well, I understand that the man you attacked is not going to file any charges."

"No ma'am. I'm sure he don't want to have nothin' to do with no cops or no courthouse or nothin'."

"Mr. Barnes," the Judge continued seriously, "You are a lucky man, this time. But I don't want to see you here again. If we do see you here again, we will have no choice but to lock you up for not less than thirty days. Do you understand?"

"Oh, yes ma'am, I mean yer Honor," the prisoner said, ducking his head several times. "I'm goin' back to Texas jest as soon as I pay the bartender."

"Well, I recommend that you stay there," Judge Bowling added. "You are free to go now, Mr. Barnes." The Judge banged her gavel on the bench with vigor.

"Mr. Madison?" the Judge called and Sam took one step forward, his heart pounding. Would Janice Bowling remember shaking hands with him three months before, at the reception for the three new special judges? He had only spoken with her for half a minute and she had met a lot of lawyers and judges that day. Had she seen him on the television news or in the newspaper yesterday? Sam could only pray and trust luck that she would not recognize him in this context.

"Have I seen you before, Mr. Madison?" Judge Bowling looked at him critically, trying to make the connection. "You look familiar."

"No ma'am," Sam said, affecting a bit of Mr. Barnes' heavy Texas accent. "But I work at a convenience store down on the south side. Maybe you've seen me there. Lots of people think they know me and they've just seen me in the store." Sam kept his head tilted slightly down, so the Judge would not have a clear view of his face.

"Well, Mr. Madison, public drunk is a serious offense," the Judge said, looking back at the blue form in front of her. "That seems to be the only charge here. I see that you've been in the holding cell since about four o'clock this morning and it appears that the arresting officer recommended you for release when sober. It's now past four in the afternoon. Are you sober enough to conduct yourself properly?"

"Yes ma'am," Sam nodded, still facing downward. "I've been thinking about going into a treatment program right away. Maybe even today."

"That's a good thing, Mr. Madison. You should do that. But right now, I'm going to have to fine you $50 and impose court costs of $20, which you can pay to the court clerk within the next ten days. If you don't pay it, I'll be seeing you back here again, which would not be good for you." The Judge made a note on the blue form, then looked up. "You are free to go now, Mr. Madison." The Judge again banged her gavel loudly, then called for the remaining prisoner, "Mr. Thompson?"

Sam turned and quickly walked to the door of the courtroom, catching a glimpse over his shoulder of the comely Judge Bowling, whose attention was focused entirely on her next charge. It had worked like a charm. So far.

* * * * *

Sam stepped out of the courtroom and into the dimly lit empty hall of the third floor of the courthouse. He moved quickly to the broad marble stairs at the end of the hallway and cautiously proceeded down two flights. He was about to step off the stairs at the second floor level when he heard a familiar voice in the hall. Abruptly stopping on the last step, he peeked around the corner and instantly jerked his head back. Tom Wallace was standing near the courtroom doors, not more than fifteen feet away, conferring with an assistant. Sam overheard Wallace's nasal whine critically addressing the young assistant D.A.

"What do you mean, he hasn't been booked yet? Judge Mickelson sent him down for booking six hours ago! I need to know exactly where he is, his conditions of confinement, when the arraignment is set, everything! And I need it *now*! You *did* file the charges, didn't you?"

The assistant respond so quietly that Sam couldn't make out the words. Then Wallace continued in a demanding tone, "Well then get back down there and *stay* until you *find out* why he hasn't been booked yet. Is that so difficult? *Do it!*"

Sam heard the assistant's "yes sir" and then footsteps, which could only be the assistant heading toward the stairwell where Sam was hiding. At that same moment, Sam also heard footsteps trotting up the marble stairway from the first floor. A sudden surge of adrenaline made his heart skip a beat. Looking down the stairwell, he saw the green and grey uniform of a city police officer on the next flight. Did he dare continue down the stairs at the risk of being recognized? He was a scant fifty feet from the outside door of the courthouse and freedom. Could he stay ahead of Wallace's assistant and slip by the police officer without being recognized? There was no time to think, only to act. In the space of five seconds, Sam was again on the third floor, silently listening and cursing his ill fortune as he peered over the railing of the stairwell to the floor below.

The officer nearly knocked over Wallace's assistant as they both rounded the corner of the stairwell from opposite directions, the officer with some momentum from trotting up the stairs. The officer instantly recognized the young assistant D.A., as he caught him by both arms to keep him from falling.

"Oh, sorry, Mr. Jackson, I didn't mean to bowl you over. I was just in a hurry to get up here to let you know that they still haven't found your prisoner. They just can't figure it out over there at the jail. I'm sure he's in the system, they just can't find him right now. We've got a call in to Detective Michaels, but he's on a drug bust this afternoon and he may be out of touch for a few hours. We've got two men backtracking every foot of the way from Judge Mickelson's office to the jail. Don't you worry. We'll have him located in a jiffy!"

The assistant D.A. stared at the officer, his eyes wide, as Wallace slowly walked up beside him, a blank expression of total disbelief on his face. "You don't mean to tell me that you still can't find Littlehawk?"

"Oh no, sir, don't you worry, we'll find him. We've got a pretty good record on keeping track of prisoners. I'm sure this one will turn up," the officer said cordially. "But if anyone did lose him," the officer added, "I'm sure that it *wasn't* the city police."

"You tell Detective Michaels and Chief Welleston that they had better get every damn man they've got out after this Littlehawk, before he gets clean away. And you'd better move damn fast. Littlehawk is as slick and clever as they come. If he escapes, there will be hell to pay."

Sam snickered silently as he heard Wallace fuming, not twelve feet away. Wallace was right. There would be hell to pay. Without a sound, Sam slipped back into the shadow of a coat rack that stood in the third floor hallway. He slowly counted to five hundred, then, without hesitation, he walked back to the stairwell and down the stairs. No one was on the second floor. He continued to the first floor. As he crossed the hall toward the outside door, his confident stride did not attract the attention of the few people who still lingered in the building, preoccupied with their own legal problems.

Stepping into the hot afternoon sun, Sam squinted at the clock on the bank across the square. Quarter to five. Monday. Still Monday. Just twelve hours earlier, Sam had been with Sanders at the Cherry Street Connection. The few hours of sleep in the jail had helped, but it wasn't enough. It was time to find a safe place to hide and regroup. But how? He was on foot.

Sam quickly inventoried the contents of his pockets. Luckily, the guards at the holding cell had only searched him and had not taken his personal effects. That would have occurred later at the jail. He still had a few resources at his disposal. But no wheels. He would have to walk through downtown.

Just a few steps away, on a bench at a bus stop, sat two vagrants. Despite the summer temperature, one of the bums was wearing a trench coat and a stocking cap with long, greasy grey hair streaming out below. The other was a slim young man in a torn tee shirt and dirty blue jeans. From their appearance, he concluded that both men had been living on the street for a long time. An idea struck him and he crossed to the bus stop where he'd be out of view of the courthouse.

"You boys need some cash?" Sam asked, as he approached. Both men eyed him suspiciously, but neither spoke. His question was incongruous; certainly not something they expected to hear on the street. They both surveyed Sam, as if to determine whether he was a mirage or a miracle.

Finally, the grey-haired tramp in the trench coat harshly replied, "No, man, we don't *need* no cash. We both millionaires. We *loaded*, can't ya' see? You *blind*, man? We *loaded*!" The aging derelict broke into a loud, hoarse laugh that turned into a rasping cough.

The younger bum looked at his companion, then back at Sam. "We got no cash, man, and we could sure use some. I got to catch a bus to Ohio tonight and five bucks would sure help. You gonna give me some help?"

The man in the trench coat recovered from his coughing fit and was wiping his mouth and looking at Sam with interest. "I don't need no bus ticket, man, I need a drink and I need it real bad. I'm not lying about no bus ticket. I need a drink. Five bucks would sure make my day."

"I'll give you ten bucks for that trench coat and cap," Sam said, producing two bills from his pocket. "And I'll give your buddy another ten for his bus ticket. You just give me the coat and cap and forget you ever saw me."

The grey-haired bum paused and looked at Sam, his bleary eyes narrowing. "What you gonna do with a coat and a cap in August, man? It's way hot outside. Besides, I'm pretty attached to this old rag." The derelict looked down at the worn and dirty grey overcoat. "This thing got me through the winter under the twenty-third street bridge, ya' know. I don't think I could part with it for less than twenty bucks." He looked up at Sam expectantly, breathing heavily.

The young bum stared at his companion in disbelief. "Are you out of your freakin' mind?" he shouted as he grabbed the filthy coat by the shoulders and began to drag it off its owner. "This man has cash! You can pick up another coat at the mission. It's too hot for that damn thing anyway. Don't ask stupid questions, for God's sake. Just give him the damn coat, fool!"

"And the stocking cap," Sam added, as the two vagrants scuffled, the grey-haired fellow putting up token resistance. In a moment, Sam was pulling the foul smelling cap over his hair and slipping into the dirty trench coat, while the grey-haired bum stood before him, with his white, saggy skin showing through holes in a dirty T-shirt.

"Here's an extra ten bucks for your trouble," Sam said, handing the two the cash he had promised and another bill. "Make it Cuervo Gold tonight."

"Why wait 'til t'night, man, the liquor store's right down the street!" The two men wasted no time snatching the bills from Sam's hand and walking quickly away from the bus stop. Half a block away, the younger bum turned and called out, "Hey, thanks, man," and then they were gone.

Sam bent over, and assuming an unbalanced posture and affecting a limp, he slowly hobbled away from the bus stop in the opposite direction. With his face to the ground and the stocking cap pulled low over his brow, he bore no resemblance to the confident, athletic, neatly dressed lawyer who was known in the city. Sam hoped that his disguise would be sufficient to prevent recognition as he walked several blocks across downtown.

Moving slowly but steadily and taking alleys whenever possible, Sam made his way without incident to a hotel parking garage two blocks from the Performing Arts Center. He hobbled through the open door of the parking garage and found it nearly empty, with no attendant on duty. The gate to the garage was open, as it usually was after five o'clock. Casting a furtive glance over his shoulder, he walked to the far end of the garage, where there was a metal door with a sign indicating the stairs to the skyway above. Near the door to the stairwell was Tony's Austin Healy, where Tony had left it three days earlier.

Sam felt a wave of relief as he shrugged off the overcoat and pulled the stocking cap from his head, then tossed them in the open trash receptacle near the door to the stairwell. He moved quickly to the sports car and reached under the fender, removing a magnetic hidden key box. Moments later, Sam was in the car turning the key in the ignition, when he noticed a security guard in grey slacks and a white short sleeve shirt walking toward the car. The guard was too close to ignore. The gate to the garage was still open, but Sam had no desire to engage in another car chase with the police. Bolting would only be a last resort. Sam grimaced, put the car in gear, rolled down the window and waited with his foot on the brake. He hoped that his disheveled appearance would be offset by the fact that he was driving a fine British sports car.

The guard approached the open window and looked inside the car and at Sam.

"Did you see a bum in a trench coat follow you in here?" the guard queried.

"I saw him from the hotel window. He came in here about a minute ago."

"Yes sir, he went through that door over there," Sam replied, pointing toward the door to the stairwell. "I saw him drop his coat in that trash can."

"But that door is supposed to be locked," the guard responded suspiciously. "That's an 'exit only' door to the skyway. You can't get in it from this side."

Sam smiled and shrugged his shoulders as the guard frowned and turned to walk toward the door, scratching his head. Releasing the brake, Sam called, "Hope you catch him!" The last thing Sam saw as the Austin Healy slipped through the garage exit was the security guard rattling the knob on the stairwell door, while looking quizzically from Sam to the overcoat in the trash receptacle.

Sam gunned the engine and hit second gear as he turned into the street. The less time he spent in the area the better, at least until he had a change of clothes and a solid plan of action. It would not do to be picked up again, after adding escape to his growing list of charges. He had slipped the noose once, but there would be no escaping a second time. And there was undoubtedly a dragnet of police combing the city for him. Keeping to the back streets, he considered his next move.

Chapter 15

"What do you mean, he's under arrest? He's supposed to be dead!" an angry and belligerent Huntington bellowed at Bandini as soon as he closed the heavy oak door of his office. "Can't you get anything right?"

Bandini was more annoyed than unnerved by Huntington's overt hostility, but he had a healthy respect for the man's impulsiveness and his tendency toward violent outbursts when stressed. Bandini selected his words carefully. "It would've been dangerous and messy, Tom, if he had not made it to the courthouse, and would undoubtedly have resulted in an inquiry. No telling where that could have led. It's much better to let Littlehawk become a victim of jailhouse violence. That'll be easy to arrange and much cleaner."

"And what if he talks first, before you can stifle him?" Huntington's jaw was set as he turned to glare at Bandini.

"Not a chance. We have good friends at the jail and I'm sure that your orders are already being carried out," Bandini responded coolly. "Besides, use of the police for this kind of operation should be a last resort. It's too risky."

"This whole situation is getting out of hand, Bandini," Huntington said. "Quick and decisive action wins the war. Dragging this out with Littlehawk is going to backfire on us. And what about Angelletti? He has to be found, and fast. I have no interest in explaining this situation to Svetlanikoff. No telling what he'll do if he finds out."

Huntington turned and looked out the bank of windows behind his desk. The late afternoon sun made a gold reflecting pool of the Arkansas River, as it wandered through the green rolling hills beyond. "I've built an empire with bold, decisive actions. That's the only way you can stay ahead of the pack. You should've learned that by now."

"Don't worry, Tom, this operation is still under control," Bandini responded in a tone calculated to soothe the savage beast. "Our empire...*your* empire is as secure as ever."

Huntington turned to face his partner. "We need a plan to dispose of Littlehawk and Angelletti, and we need it now. You claim to be the master strategist. Make a plan and make it happen *now*, or *we may not need you anymore*." Huntington's quiet words were far more unnerving than his shouting, and the look in his grey eyes sent a chill down Bandini's spine. He knew Huntington to be as cold-blooded as a pit viper. Bandini's cleverness and political savvy had been useful to Huntington for many years, but he also knew that personal loyalty was not a part of Huntington's business philosophy.

A cell phone buzzed and Bandini drew it from the inside pocket of his suit jacket. "Bandini," he said in a terse monotone. There was a pause as his eyes widened and his face blanched. He quickly stepped toward the door of the office. "What? No...no...Yes, he's here, but...okay, we'll talk about that when I get there."

Bandini snapped the phone shut and headed quickly for the door. Huntington called out, "What was that about?"

"Nothing," he shot back a little too quickly. "Everything's still on track. I have to go get this straightened out. Don't worry." Bandini was out the door and down the hall before Huntington had time to respond.

Seconds later, Bandini shut and locked the door to his own office, popped open the cell phone and hit redial. In two rings, Wallace answered. "What the hell happened?" Bandini demanded. "How could he have gotten away? He was in the custody of three cops in the Judge's office."

"As of this moment, we don't know. He was supposed to have been booked as soon as he arrived at the jail. We filed the charges this morning, but when we went to the jail to verify the booking, he was nowhere to be found. The police took him to the holding cell for transportation to the jail, but apparently, he never got on the bus. There's no paperwork on him anywhere."

"Have you talked with that detective who arrested him? Michaels? You know, the guy with the pink shirt and hams for biceps. He was the one who took him to the holding cell, wasn't he?" Bandini asked anxiously.

"Detective Michaels is incommunicado right now, out on a drug bust. We'll talk with him just as soon as he can be reached, but it probably won't be until sometime tomorrow. What is this guy to you, anyway, Bandini? Why is it so important to Huntington that we catch him? You're both treating him like public enemy number one."

"Littlehawk's a violent criminal who tried to kill one of our commissioners. That's reason enough. Besides, he's a desperate escaped felon, probably armed and dangerous, and I doubt he'll be taken alive. I suggest that you call your friends on the force and advise them to use all necessary force to apprehend him."

"What is it, Bandini? What's he got on you?" Wallace asked skeptically.

Bandini paused, then continued in a lower tone of voice. "You do your job, Tom, and I'll do mine. Do yours well and you'll be rewarded. Same goes for your friends on the force. We want Littlehawk out of the picture, and I know you'll see that Huntington's orders are carried out. If it doesn't happen, you won't like the results." Bandini hung up without waiting for a reply.

Walking across the spacious office to his desk, Bandini opened his cell phone again and hit a speed dial button. He thumbed nervously through some papers, not focusing on what he saw, until there was an answer on the other end of the line.

"Gannon? Bandini. Bad news. Littlehawk escaped and is back on the street. Yeah, they had him, but somehow he got away. Now I'm telling you that he's armed and dangerous. I want all of your men on the street looking for him, and if they find him, tell 'em to shoot on sight. He's too smart and too dangerous to take any chances. Of course, if there is an investigation, we'll provide the best legal defense money can buy, but trust me, there won't be any investigation."

Bandini closed the cell phone, leaned back in his chair and took a deep breath. His immediate problem was how to prevent Huntington from learning of the escape until Littlehawk was just a bad memory, soon to be forgotten.

* * * * *

Sam pulled the Austin Healy into a parking space at the Riverview Apartments and walked to the door numbered 105. It was past six o'clock and Sam could hear the evening news on the television through the window. He knocked, and moments later, the door opened to reveal a very surprised Dave Sanders. Without a word, Sanders grabbed Sam by the front of his blood-stained shirt, dragged him inside, and slammed the door.

"What the hell are you *doing* here, Sam? Did you know that there's a police dragnet looking for you? If they find you here, I'll be in the slammer with you! Why did you have to go and escape, anyway? We'd have sprung you soon enough." Sanders looked like he'd just swallowed a bad oyster.

Sam grinned at his friend. "Shucks, Dave, I didn't escape at all. Judge Janice Bowling turned me loose. Told me I was free to go. There is a slight possibility that she had me mixed up with someone else," he said with a wink, "but I really think that she was just taken with my devilish good looks."

"Probably couldn't stand the thought of you showing all the other prisoners how to walk out of jail without a trace," Sanders retorted, "so she threw out the rotten apple to avoid spoiling the whole bunch."

"Speaking of apples, you got any food?" Sam asked, looking toward the small galley kitchen. "I'm starved. It's hungry work, sawing through steel bars with a fingernail file. I think the last time I ate anything was yesterday morning."

Sanders could see that it was no use trying to talk sense to a hungry man, so he opened the refrigerator and made two sandwiches. "Food first, then talk," he said as he sat down across from Sam.

After a few minutes of feasting on cold turkey sandwiches and chips, Sam leaned back and smiled. "I knew I could count on you, Dave. When this is all over, I'm going to buy you a whole dozen chocolate éclairs."

"Don't spoil me, Sam. Just eat and tell me how we're going to save your sorry hide. Looks like everyone in town is after it right now."

"Okay then, on to the business at hand," Sam said, popping the last bite into his mouth. "I'm not concerned about the escape. I walked away clean. It would be very hard for them to track me and they won't conduct a door to door search of the entire city. That would be impossible. As long as I stay out of sight and don't take any chances, I think we're pretty safe."

"So you say," Sanders said skeptically. "Since you don't know squat about law enforcement technology, I'm assuming that your risk analysis is based on your most recent palm reading. Or was it tarot cards?"

"You worry too much. My real concerns are finding Katrina, if she can be found, and getting the evidence against Huntington's bunch to the right people, so we can nail these dirt bags."

"Well, I can give you some help on the first score," Dave said with a degree of self-satisfaction. "While you were busy hoodwinking Judge Bowling, I was in touch with my friends at the FAA. Luckily, this wasn't the first aircraft I've had to track. It was easy, once the air traffic controllers understood that I was after that little white Learjet that had the blue sports car and the fleet of police cruisers chasing it down the runway. Now that's something they don't see everyday," Sanders said with a droll expression.

"So you know where Karmakov took Katrina?" Sam asked impatiently.

"Your damsel in distress is presently in Miami, Florida, or at least the plane she left on is still there."

"Guess you knew that she would be on my mind," Sam said, almost apologetically.

"Hey, this has got nothing to do with you, buddy. I always do my best to find kidnap victims at the first opportunity. Especially if they're beautiful women or small children. It's a personal thing."

"Thanks, Dave. Any idea what they're doing there or what their itinerary is? Is she still with Karmakov?"

"That's asking a little too much, son. They've only been in Miami for about four hours. But I've got a friend in the Bureau there and I've asked him to take a look around for me. I'll know in a few minutes whether a new flight plan has been filed. I just wish like hell we could call in the troops at the Bureau and round up the whole bunch of them right now," Sanders said with frustration. "But at this moment, thanks to you, we don't even have a case file open."

"We've talked about that, Dave. An hour after you open an FBI file on this, Huntington will have its contents on his desk. The federal building is not immune from his influence. He has eyes everywhere. No, I've got to put this together myself. By the way, where's the CD that I gave you this morning when we were leaving Cherry Street?"

Sanders looked perplexed and rubbed his chin slowly between his thumb and forefinger. His eyes were fixed on a point midway across the table. "Well, Sam," he said, "After your little escapade at the airport this morning, I went to my office to have another look at the evidence. I was scanning the CD at my computer when I got up to get a cup of coffee. I wasn't gone for five minutes, but when I came back, it was gone. Someone took it out of the drive."

"That isn't funny, Dave. Tell me you're kidding."

"I think it must have been Smithson who picked it up," Sanders continued. "He uses my computer sometimes and he could have pulled the disk out and done something with it. He was gone when I got back with my coffee."

"Have you tried to reach him?"

"Yeah, but no luck. Surely you have a backup?"

"That *was* the backup," Sam said grimly.

"Oh, geez, Sam, that's not good. But surely it'll turn up. Besides, we know their scheme now and we know where the original information is hidden. We'll just go get a subpoena and storm the place with a boatload of FBI agents," Sanders said, trying to make the best of the situation.

"Correction, we know where the evidence *was* hidden. Once Huntington realized that we had found his cache of incriminating information, I'm sure he moved or destroyed it all. He's nobody's fool."

"Well, at least the Bureau already has an eye on those websites—that's something. Don't worry, Sam, that disk will turn up somewhere in my office. Smithson probably just put it in the wrong cover. I'm sure that this is just a simple mistake."

"Yeah, maybe. Or maybe that disk is already in Huntington's hands," Sam fumed. Suddenly he slammed his palm down hard on the table. "*Damn* it! We took one helluva risk for that information, and we had 'em…" Sam stopped in mid-sentence, his frustration melting into a thoughtful expression. "Maybe there's still a way…" Then just as abruptly, Sam jumped to his feet. "But now, it's time to get moving! First things first. We've got to get Katrina back before Karmakov takes her out of the country. When's the next plane to Miami?"

"You're not going to Miami without me!" Sanders exclaimed avidly. "You're gonna need some backup. Besides, there are some Latin ladies down there in South Beach to die for! Figuratively speaking, of course. Besides, I need to practice my tango." Sanders began to high step around the room, leaning back dramatically and swaying in a curiously awkward way while humming a Latin rhythm.

Sam shook his head in disbelief. "You're a piece of work, Dave. You mean you'd forsake all of your imaginary Polynesian sweethearts at the drop of a hat for one hot Latin lady?"

Sanders was gazing into space with stars in his eyes. "White sandy beaches, ice cold cervezas, sweet little Cubanas catering to my every whim…This is gonna be sweet! When do we leave?"

Sam considered resisting his impetuous friend, but then he thought of the vast knowledge and experience in covert actions that Sanders possessed and he decided that he could not hope for a better partner. Still, he did not want to risk his friend's career and reputation. "What if we both get picked up by the authorities?" he asked. "As you are so quick to point out, I am a wanted man."

"Who better to arrest you than yours truly?" Sanders said beaming. "If we get caught, you'll already be in my custody! I'll get the credit for catching you and I can stay right with you till…uh, let's cross that bridge when we come to it."

"Well, I guess that's a pretty solid plan under the circumstances," Sam said with a wry look. "Let's move. With luck, we can be in Miami by midnight."

* * * * *

Five hours later, the two men stepped out of a borrowed Cessna Citation onto wet tarmac and walked a short distance to a private hangar at Miami International Airport. A tropical storm had swept through less than an hour before and gusty winds were still rattling the palm trees beyond the airport's perimeter fence. Thunder rolled in the distance and occasional lightning lit the night sky. The storm had cooled the air considerably from the oppressive heat and humidity that had prevailed earlier in the day. As the two walked from the plane to the hangar, Sam felt his pulse quicken from the stormy weather and the building anticipation of unknown dangers to come.

"Good thing you had a friend with a fast airplane, or we'd still be eating peanuts in coach somewhere between here and Atlanta," Sanders said. "Make sure to thank the tribe for me."

"When you manage operations of the magnitude of the Cherokee tribe, you need a few good aircraft," Sam replied. "It's a big business. Bingo alone nets the tribe about fifty million a year. But it was just pure luck that I was able to get us a ride on such short notice."

"It took more than luck, buddy, to get a ride like that with no questions asked," Sanders said with a knowing look. "You called in some favors, big time. But I don't care how you did it. We're here. Let's go get a beer in South Beach where they party all night long! The night is still young!"

"Hold your horses, Romeo, did you forget something? Remember the beautiful lady we're here to save? Remember the bad guys we gotta catch? We've got work to do. Party later."

"Oh yeah," Sanders said sheepishly. "Nearly forgot. I guess South Beach will have to wait." He hung his head in mock despair.

"Buck up, Dave," Sam said. "When this is over, I'll buy you a whole case of your favorite Mexican beer."

Sanders instantly perked up. "Wow, a case of Mexican beer and a dozen chocolate éclairs! Throw in a box of premium Cuban cigars and I'll go out and nail all of the bad guys single-handed! Now where is that Learjet we were looking for, anyway?"

"I think it's right over there." Sam pointed to a group of about twenty sleek business jets a few hundred yards away, lined up in two rows in front of a commercial hangar bearing the name "Tropic Air" in large turquoise letters. The apron in front of the hangar was well lit, making it easy to survey the array of planes from all over the globe. A new Gulfstream bearing Arabic letters on its fuselage first caught their eye, followed by a variety of Learjets and Cessna Citations, a few KingAirs and a couple of new canard wing business jets. The heavy metal arrayed on the tarmac represented an awesome display of the best of private aviation.

"Based on the information you received while we were in flight, one of those Lears has got to be it."

Sanders scanned the planes through a tiny pair of binoculars he produced from his pocket and finally exclaimed, "There she is! Small white Lear bearing 'N' number N6602."

"Bravo," Sam exclaimed. "That was about as hard as finding your thumb in the dark. Question is, now that we've found the aircraft, how do we find its occupants?"

"Just leave that to me. Like I told you, this is my business. Do I ask how you go about proving that your obviously guilty client is perfectly innocent so he can go scot free? *Noooo.* So you just give me a few minutes and let me work my magic."

Sam eyed Sanders skeptically, wondering for a moment whether it would be safe to turn him loose in Miami. "Okay, Sherlock, you go do your thing while I check out the coffee bar. I'll be waiting there."

"No need to be out of touch," Sanders said. "While we're apart, we'll stay in contact with these." He reached into his satchel and produced two wireless communicators with nearly invisible earpieces and handed one to Sam. "I don't go anywhere anymore without a couple of these gizmos. Plug that receiver into your ear. If you need me or you need to change locations, just say so. And drop this in your pocket, too." Sanders handed Sam a small disk the size of a quarter, but thicker. "It's a beeper. Down at the Bureau, we call it a Marco Polo. The tracking device transmits a signal, a 'Marco,' and the beeper answers, 'Polo.' Even lets you know if you're hot or cold, just like the kid's game called Marco Polo. Pretty neat toy, huh?" Sanders grinned like a boy with a new baseball glove. Anyway, gotta go now, see you soon!" He disappeared around the corner of the hangar as Sam studied the communications devices.

Half an hour later, Sanders found Sam sitting in the all night coffee bar staring into space with a large Styrofoam cup of coffee cooling in front of him. The place was empty as a tomb, but for one pilot planning an early departure and a night watchman on his regular circuit around the premises. Sanders pulled up a chair and plopped down, setting a Coke can on the table. "What are you thinking, Sam? Is something going on in there, or are you sleeping with your eyes open?"

"I was just thinking about my mom and Emmie. Mom's got to know by now about the escape and be worried sick. I just wish I could let them know that I'm alright, but I guess it's just too risky to call them."

"Sam, the phone at the ranch could be tapped. In fact, it probably is tapped by now. It would be a mistake to call. They've got confidence in you. They'll worry some, but they'll be alright."

"Then there's Tony," Sam continued, slightly despondent. "I just wish I knew how he was doing."

"There again, Sam, you need to just forget it," Sanders said in the didactic tone of a high school teacher. "Tony's in good hands and as long as they follow your instructions, everything will be fine." He leaned forward with a broad grin and clapped Sam on the shoulder. "Besides, I've got good news!"

Sam perked up a bit. "What news? Why didn't you say so?"

"I've got a good take on Karmakov and his goons. They're on a yacht parked in the inland waterway. Probably headed out to sea in the morning, judging from the provisioning of the yacht during the past few hours. The boat is a hundred and twenty footer called the *Trieste* and it's moored not too far from here."

"Is Katrina with them?" Sam asked.

"Don't know, but our contact said there wasn't a woman with him when he left the airport. He and his goons were picked up by a Mercedes limo that headed toward South Beach."

Sam looked at Sanders skeptically. "What kind of magic did you do, anyway, to get that kind of information?"

"Let's just say that it's good to have friends in the right places, as you well know, Mr. Osage Chief. After twenty years with the Bureau, I've got a few friends, too. Good thing they trust me and don't ask too many embarrassing questions. I called them hours ago and they've been on the job ever since. Oh yeah, I also managed to borrow a car." He pointed out the window of the coffee shop at a new Jeep Cherokee parked outside.

Sam cast a quick glance out the window and grinned back at his friend. "It's a miracle! We've got wheels! What do you do for an encore, walk on water? So what are we waiting for? We can talk in the car."

"That's the spirit!" Sanders said. "Now how about a quick plate of Mexican food in South Beach? It's on the way, and I do hate working on an empty stomach!"

Chapter 16

Sam was finishing off a tasty chile relleño and mopping up frijoles with a thick flour tortilla, when Sanders shoved his plate aside and reached for his satchel. "I threw in a few more gadgets that might be useful," he said as he pulled a small metal cylinder from the bag. "Looks like this one will come in handy. This little jewel will pick up a normal conversation through a glass window at fifty yards. Simple as an automatic camera. Just plug it into this micro-recorder, set it to the frequency of your earpiece, then point and shoot." Sanders fiddled with the gadget, testing it on a couple seated at an outdoor café across the street. A few seconds later his eyes opened wider as he listened with interest.

"What? What is it?" Sam asked.

"Wow, do they have some interesting plans!" Sanders exclaimed. "Sounds like a fun evening ahead for those two. *We* should be having so much fun. But no, we gotta go chasing bad guys all over South Florida and maybe get shot in the bargain. I guess that's just what I get for eavesdropping on late night conversations in South Beach. At least *some* people are having fun tonight," Sanders said, polishing off his second cerveza in one gulp while continuing to stare across the street. "Good thing I'm not a voyeur or this little jewel could be dangerous. South Beach would sure be an interesting place for a full blown test of the old equipment. But I know, I know, gotta keep my mind on the business at hand. No use in getting too involved in the lives of strangers. Besides, I'm saving myself for that one special Latin lady."

Sam reached over and lifted the high-powered listening device from Sanders' hands. "Quit eavesdropping on people, Dave, and *please*, will you quit rattling on like an old woman at quilting bee? We've got serious work to do. Now where did you say the *Trieste* is moored?"

"Just down the street a couple of blocks," Sanders replied, looking hurt. "And I really resent that crack about rattling on like an old woman at a quilting bee. I don't even think old women go to spelling bees, anyway. Besides, I was just trying to say that we ought to have a little fun while we're down here in South Beach. I mean, you only go around once in this life and this is one of the best places to have some fun…" Sanders was still talking and stuffing equipment into his satchel when Sam rolled his eyes and headed for the restaurant door.

Once on the street, the two stopped the small talk and walked briskly through the clamor of South Beach. It was past two in the morning, but bands continued to play Latin rhythms in the courtyards of several clubs, and a riotous crowd milled on the broad sidewalk. Across the street, a huge party was in progress on the white sands of Miami Beach. The revelry was in full swing and would continue until dawn. Sanders vowed to return to the party just as soon as they completed their business.

Parking was at a premium in the densely populated district of high fashion shops, clubs, and restaurants, so they decided to leave the Jeep and walk the four blocks to the pier where the *Trieste* was moored. The earlier storm had blown out to sea, leaving a balmy summer night.

As they approached the pier on the inland waterway, the two men found a sheltered position behind a stone wall in the shadow of a large mango tree and began to study the situation. The *Trieste* was moored at the end of the pier, as anticipated. A locked gate secured the pier, and they could see a dark figure, presumably a guard who appeared to have a weapon slung over his shoulder, on the bow of the yacht. The pier was quiet and there were only a few small launches moored along its length. The yacht was dimly lit inside, while a light on the end of the pier partially illuminated the deck.

"This is where the fun begins," Sanders whispered with eager anticipation. "The boat is a little out of range. I'm going to penetrate the gate and find a safe listening post inside. You stay here for now and keep your ear piece tuned in. You'll be able to hear everything I hear, and we can also communicate between ourselves."

Sanders pulled a small tool from his satchel, similar to the one he had recently loaned Sam. "This will get me in the gate," he whispered. "You keep an eye out with these, and let me know if you see anything suspicious." Handing Sam a miniature set of binoculars, he added, "Digitally enhanced night vision. Very advanced. I have to return those, so take good care of them and whatever you do, *don't* drop 'em in the water." With that, Sanders slipped over the limestone wall into a mangrove thicket, headed for the gate that was fifty feet down the pier.

The distant thump of music emanated from the clubs on the beach side of the narrow barrier island, but the inland waterway was quiet. Using the binoculars, Sam watched Sanders weave though the dense mangrove trees and hoist himself onto the pier just beyond the circle of light cast by the streetlight at the head of the pier. Sanders moved quickly to the gate, then knelt to pick the lock. The old wrought iron gate opened easily. In a moment, he was moving silently toward a large wooden box near one of the launches tied to the pier. He paused in the shadows, scanning the yacht from stem to stern. So far, the guard had not moved and no one else had appeared on deck. Sanders slithered from his position behind the box into a small boat tied to the pier. In a few seconds, Sam could see his head ease up to look over the gunwale of the boat.

"So far, so good," Sam suddenly heard in his ear. It was as though Sanders had invaded his mind, a thought which made him shiver. "Let's see if we can tune to a good station."

There was silence for several minutes as Sanders adjusted his listening device and systematically scanned the yacht, hesitating at every porthole. He detected no sound on the bridge or anywhere aft on the yacht. Sam thought that he heard a faint sound of snoring at one point, but it was not worth mentioning. Then suddenly, there was another voice, a familiar voice, in his ear.

"*She* may die, *mi amor, mi brasileira bonita*. Or perhaps *you* will die. Or you both may live. It is for me to decide, no?"

Sam's blood ran cold at the unmistakable sound of Karmakov's voice, and at his threatening words and malignant tone.

"Gotta love a guy like that," Sanders muttered quietly. "Sure knows how to treat the ladies."

"Shhh!" Sam hushed Sanders. "Listen!" Whatever the reply to Karmakov's words had been, they had missed it.

"Yes," Karmakov continued, "Katrina begins her training tomorrow. My friends in Moscow have provided an instructor who is already with her at the lodge. I am sure that within a few days, she will fully understand that my plan for her life is the best choice that she could make. Just as you have made that same decision, correct Angelica?"

Sam heard a quiet, submissive female voice utter one word, "*Si.*"

"Angelica, you must now prove that you have learned to satisfy my desires. Afterward, I will decide who will live and who will die. So you will make this your best performance, *si*?"

Another minute or two passed and it was clear that the conversation was at least temporarily at an end. The boat was silent. Sam's heart went out to the poor woman who was under Karmakov's control. But she would not be for much longer.

"Man, he is a piece of work," Sanders whispered. "A real creep. No wonder you didn't mind skinning your knuckles on his nose."

For a moment, Sam relished the thought of another shot at Karmakov. It would be a great pleasure to finish the job he had started at the airport, taking the vain prima donna apart one piece at a time. But that would have to wait. The most important thing now was to find Katrina before her "training" began. And that did not give them much time.

Sam scanned the boat again. The guard was slowly pacing the length of the deck at intervals. He had lit a cigar that glowed white in the night vision binoculars as he walked on the dimly lit deck. There was no other sign of activity onboard.

"Dave, I hope you left the gate unlocked because I'm coming in. Something on that boat will tell us where Katrina is being held. If necessary, I'll beat it out of Karmakov."

"Sounds like fun. Can I come too?"

"You stay put. You're in a great back up position and I need you to keep listening and watching my back. Maybe we'll find Katrina before I get a chance to slam Karmakov's head against the wall. Then again, maybe we won't," Sam said with grim satisfaction.

"Did you forget about the dude with the heater pacing the deck? He might not like you dropping in without an invitation."

"That's where you come in. Surely you can manage to create some little diversion off the bow while I slip up the stern gangway?"

"I'm gonna recommend you for a promotion to chief of tactical operations! Now why couldn't I have thunk'a that? But then, I guess that's why they pay you the big bucks, for thinkin' all the time." Sanders felt around the bottom of the small boat in which he was hiding and found a cache of plum-sized lead fishing weights. "I've got just the thing! This should get his attention. Ready to initiate diversion when you are."

Following the path that Sanders had taken, Sam slipped over the stone wall and successfully negotiated his way through the mangroves to the pier, then onto the pier and through the unlocked gate. He stopped in the shadows just inside the gate and waited. On Sam's command, Sanders began to heave fishing weights into the water just off the bow of the yacht. The guard either failed to notice or ignored the splashing, as several of the weights hit the water just past the bow.

"Let's see if I can get this one just a little closer," Sanders muttered. Seconds later, a two pound weight sailed into the air and landed with a loud bang on a metal hatch cover on the yacht's bow. "Eeeeyow, direct hit!" Sanders said, forgetting to whisper.

The guard, who had been quietly smoking on the stern deck of the yacht, ran to the bow to investigate, just as Sanders catapulted another weight toward the ship. It landed with a thud on the deck opposite the guard.

"I said a diversion, not a war!" Sam whispered, as he crept swiftly toward the stern and up the gangway, staying out of the guard's line of sight. "Hold your fire, if you don't want to get nailed."

"You're on your own for now, buddy," Sanders replied, ducking his head below the gunwale of the launch.

Once onboard, Sam silently climbed the ship's ladder to the second deck and followed the rail until he reached the bridge. Slipping in, he found a well equipped command center with large windows on three sides. There was barely enough illumination from the instrument panels to see. He began to search for anything that might reveal the location of the "lodge" that Karmakov had mentioned, determined to find Katrina before Karmakov's underlings could inflict any pain or begin her indoctrination. The insidious means they would use to bend her will were likely to leave permanent emotional scars, if she could be deprogrammed at all. Sam worked grimly but efficiently, searching every nook and cranny of the bridge. After flipping through charts, maps and papers for several minutes, Sam had found nothing that gave any hint as to Katrina's location.

Sam had vowed to force the information from Karmakov if necessary and he was headed for the lower deck to do just that, when Sanders whispered in his earpiece, "Don't look now, *amigo*, but we've got company." Sam's glance out the window confirmed two figures on the pier. They were already in the shadows, beyond reach of the streetlight at the head of the pier, but not yet to the gate.

"Just a guess," Sanders whispered, "but I'd wager that these guys are Karmakov's muscle. Judging from the way they're walking, I'd bet that they spent most of the night drinking margaritas in South Beach. I'm just going to lie real still right here and maybe they won't see me. They look pretty drunk."

One of the Russians fumbled with the gate for a few moments, then threw it open and they continued toward the yacht. Sam's mind raced. He was unwilling to leave without the information he came for, and his escape route was cut off, at least temporarily. He really had no choice but to hide onboard and elude the armed guard on the deck until the two henchmen retired for the night. Then he could resume his search, confront Karmakov, or slip off the boat and lay a new plan for finding Katrina. "I'm going to find a place to lie low for a little while, until these guys pass out in their berths," he whispered. "If you can get out of here, go ahead. I'll meet you back at the car."

"You think I'm leaving you here under fire?" His words were cut short by the approach of the Russians.

There was no suitable hiding place on the bridge and Sam was not inclined to leave the bridge the way he had entered and risk being spotted by the guard on the bow. He passed through a swinging door into a passageway aft of the bridge, hoping to find a storage room or closet. He heard the Russians laughing as they crossed the gangway and he hoped that they would have no reason to come to the second deck. Sam tried the knob of an unmarked door in the passageway. It was locked and there were no other hiding places accessible from his position. He could continue astern, where the passageway entered the main cabin, or return to the bridge.

Footsteps in the main cabin aft of his position made his decision easy. He guessed that the Russians were heading for the bar in the main cabin, which left only a door with a window in it between him and them. A glance by one of the Russians would expose him.

"Sam, if you can talk, what's going on?" Sanders asked. "The Russians are on the boat and near your position. They stopped for a second after crossing the gangway, then headed right for you."

"I'm going back into the bridge," Sam whispered as he placed his palm on the door and paused in the passageway's dim light. "I may need another diversion so I can slip out the side door without being seen. Where's the guard?"

"He's moving aft on the near side of the deck. If you can get out on the seaward side, you ought to be able to make it down the stairs and over the rail, out of his sight. Move quick—they're in the main cabin right behind you."

Sam pushed through the swinging door of the bridge, easing the door closed behind him. When he turned, he found the barrel of an automatic pistol less than three feet from his nose. Behind the gun were the eyes of a malevolent predator on the hunt. A tangle of long, dark hair framed Karmakov's sadistic face. Sam froze as adrenaline flooded his system. Poised on his toes, every muscle was ready for instant action.

"I was just looking for you, Karmakov," Sam growled. "What have you done with Katrina?"

"So you still do not give up this game," he replied in a flat voice, ignoring the reference to Katrina. His mouth slowly curled into a wicked smile. "I am glad you are here. I still have a headache from our last meeting. It is time for me to return the favor. Now *you* will suffer. But I am afraid that you will endure much more than a headache, before you die a *slow and painful death*."

Karmakov uttered the words with a bloodthirsty viciousness that bordered on insanity. His eyes burned with an inhuman light. "Go back the way you came, American dog. My men are waiting in the main cabin." He waved the gun barrel in the direction of the swinging door.

Sam stared at him for a moment, then slowly turned toward the door. As he turned, he abruptly bent forward, shooting his right heel upward in a back thrust kick that connected with Karmakov's chin with a satisfying *crack*. The force of the blow lifted the gangster off the floor and he involuntarily fired a burst of half a dozen shots. A searing pain shot through Sam's upraised leg as a bullet pierced his inner thigh. Karmakov tumbled backward, somehow maintaining his grip on the gun as he fell to the floor, stunned.

Ignoring the pain in his leg, Sam leapt on his dazed opponent, wrenching away the weapon. Grabbing a handful of Karmakov's hair, he dragged him to a sitting position and pressed the barrel of the weapon hard against his forehead. "Now you will tell me, you son-of-a-bitch. *Where is Katrina?*"

At that moment, the two Russian henchmen burst in with guns drawn. Although their reflexes were dulled from an evening of drinking, they quickly assessed the situation and trained their weapons on Sam. Maintaining a firm grip on Karmakov while pressing the gun to his forehead, Sam ordered, "Tell your men to back off, or you'll be shark bait."

"If I die, you die," Karmakov hissed, a baleful look in his eyes. "Kill me and we both go to hell together."

"In that case," Sam replied, "you're coming with me!"

Karmakov grimaced, expecting the end at any second. But instead of pulling the trigger, Sam stood, hauled the gangster to his feet by his hair, then spun him around so that he could grip his throat from behind while holding the gun to his head. Facing the two armed henchmen, he dug the barrel into Karmakov's temple and commanded, "Tell them we're leaving together or we're all dying together. *Tell them now!*"

Karmakov barked a few words in Russian and the two men stared at them, unsure of what to do. "Tell them to drop their weapons. Now!"

Before Karmakov could speak again, the guard who had been patrolling the deck appeared at the bridge's outside door on the pier side, aiming an automatic rifle at Sam and Karmakov. The deck guard's rifle was accurate enough to down Sam without risk to Karmakov, and Sam was in a crossfire. With the deck guard's reinforcement, the two Russians began to move menacingly forward. Sam squeezed Karmakov's throat harder and turned the gun toward the two advancing mobsters, while using Karmakov's body as a shield. He began to inch backward toward the seaward side door of the bridge.

Suddenly, Sanders' voice boomed in Sam's earpiece. "Don't look now, buddy, but I've got a taxi waiting for you just off the bow. Just ease over to the seaward door of the bridge and jump. I'll catch you and we'll scram. Better to live to fight another day."

Out of options, Sam backed toward the seaward door, dragging Karmakov with him. In a second, they were on the deck and he felt the wide mahogany deck rail against his lower back. Raising his injured leg, he placed his foot against Karmakov's back and shoved hard, driving the Russian back through the door and into the advancing gunmen. Karmakov stumbled and fell, choking, just as Sam rolled over the rail with enough momentum to clear the lower deck. The echo of gunfire filled the air.

Sam landed hard on his chest and face on the rear deck of the twenty foot launch idling alongside the *Trieste*. The moment he hit, Sanders jammed the throttle forward and the twin engines roared, propelling the boat forward and raising the bow steeply. The force of acceleration and the tipping deck caused Sam to roll backward and he was barely able to catch himself on the small chrome railing at the stern, just above the churning propellers.

Clinging to the launch, Sam saw one of the Russians on the deck of the yacht, now fifty yards away, aiming a small rocket launcher. Realizing that in a few seconds their boat would be nothing more than a pile of burning debris, he yelled, "Dave, jump! They've got a rocket!" Their eyes met for an instant before they simultaneously leaped from the boat.

A split second after Sam hit the water, a violent explosion erupted ten yards away as the rocket exploded on impact. The deck of the launch was instantly shattered and ablaze, but the hull remained nearly intact and the craft's momentum carried it forward another thirty yards.

From below, Sam watched the orange glow of burning oil and fuel spread quickly on the surface of the water. Finding a dark spot on the surface, he popped his head up to breathe. Unable to find Sanders in the burning debris, he ducked back underwater to avoid the toxic fumes and smoke. Swimming with long, gliding strokes away from the wreck, he resurfaced in the dark more than a hundred feet from the bobbing wreckage.

Sam floated on his back for a few seconds, catching his breath, then resumed his search for Sanders. But before he could find a way to approach the burning launch, he heard an outboard motor from the direction of the *Trieste*. Seconds later, a spotlight on the bow of the yacht began sweeping the wreckage and it became clear from the voices onboard that the *Trieste* was casting off it moorings. Karmakov was preparing to evacuate the area. But first, his search party would make certain there were no survivors.

The searchlight swung in Sam's direction and he quickly ducked underwater and began to swim further away from the wreckage. He continued swimming, surfacing only for quick breaths, for another fifty yards. Still, he was too close. He began a silent breast stroke toward shore as the spotlight swept the area. The skiff bearing the searchers paused in the wreckage and Sam stayed low in the water, swimming silently, barely breathing.

Suddenly, the small craft gunned its engine and quickly returned to the *Trieste*. The unmistakable red and green lights of a harbor patrol boat in the distance explained their quick departure. It had been less than ten minutes since the explosion, but the blast had undoubtedly been reported.

Sam watched the skiff pull alongside the yacht and the search crew scramble aboard. His heart sank when he saw them trying to drag a limp body aboard. It had to be Dave. Sam was sick at the thought of his friend's death, until he noticed that Dave was struggling with his captors. *At least he's alive,* Sam thought. *At least for now.*

A hundred yards from the pier, the flames on the burning launch must have heated the gas tanks to the point of ignition. An enormous blast echoed across the water for miles and a huge cloud of orange flame briefly cast an eerie glow across the dark waterway. Then the launch was gone and only bits of burning debris floated where it had been. Two hundred yards away, the twin screws of the *Trieste* churned the water as the massive yacht gained speed, slowly disappearing into the grey of the predawn night.

Chapter 17

Sam dragged himself into the mangrove trees a hundred feet from the head of the pier just as the harbor patrol boat reached the wreckage. Crawling below the spreading mangrove roots to avoid detection, he assessed his physical condition. Aside from being banged and bruised, his only serious injury was a long, bloody flesh wound on his left inner thigh. The saltwater had stanched the bleeding and although he would limp for awhile, he knew he would survive.

Sam slowly picked his way back through the mangrove thicket to the stone wall that he had slipped over an hour earlier. With the painful wound in his leg, the wall presented a challenge, but he managed to use a nearby tree to make the climb easier. He was soon on the empty street in the grey light of early dawn. Like a thief in the night, he glanced furtively over his shoulder several times as he painfully limped the four blocks to the Cherokee. Thankfully, he still had the keys in his jeans pocket. Once in the car, he breathed a great sigh of relief and pushed back the seat for a few minutes of rest. His eyes closed as total exhaustion overwhelmed every sense.

At the sound of a honking horn, Sam's eyes opened. For a full ten seconds, he did not know where he was or why he was reclining behind the wheel of an unfamiliar car in wet clothes. Then his memory returned in a rush and he realized that falling asleep might have cost him the opportunity to save his friends. *Two* friends in Karmakov's clutches, who seemed to have become Lucifer himself. He cursed under his breath as he slid the key into the ignition. How could he have fallen asleep? The clock on the dash showed that it was nearly eight o'clock—he had slept for more than two hours!

Driving a mile to a swimming area on the beach, Sam parked and changed into fresh, dry clothes in a public bath house. The raw wound on his thigh was painful and oozing some blood, but it appeared to be clean. He bandaged it as best he could with strips torn from a cotton tee shirt. Medical care would have to wait. There was no time to lose.

Since going to the authorities wasn't an option, he would have to find Katrina and Sanders on his own. But how would he ever find the *Trieste* in the hundreds of miles of waterways near Miami? And even worse, how would he find Katrina?

She had not been aboard the *Trieste*, and according to the conversation he had overheard, her "training" was scheduled to begin that morning. Sam cringed at the thought of her suffering, or even facing death, if Karmakov's grandiose and insane threats could be believed. He was galled by the capture of Sanders, who was only in Miami to help him. Although torn with anguish, he knew he had to keep a clear head to function effectively, and he *had* to perform at peak efficiency to rescue Katrina and Dave in time.

Suppressing his raging emotions, he coldly considered his limited resources. While inspecting the contents of the car, he suddenly remembered the small disk that had been in his pocket. Retrieving it from the wet jeans, he turned it over in his fingers. The Marco Polo device! Digging through Sanders' satchel, he retrieved a small electronic unit the size of a Gameboy with a three-inch color screen. He began to experiment with the complicated tracking device that was first cousin to a global positioning system. In a few minutes, he had managed to decipher its controls, open the program, and adjust the screen. Just as he had hoped, the device identified and began to track a target in the vicinity. It had to be Dave!

As Sam adjusted the sophisticated Marco Polo device, he realized its memory included maps of virtually every metropolitan area in the entire country. By combining the South Florida map with the basic tracking program, he discovered that the signal was emanating from Miami International Airport. With dismay, he realized that Sanders and his captors were probably about to board another aircraft. If that occurred, his hopes of rescuing Sanders, and perhaps Katrina, would vanish.

Sam pulled into traffic, following the quickest route to the airport. Keeping an eye on the Marco Polo device, he crossed the bridge over the inland waterway, weaving through traffic at a high rate of speed. In just under fifteen minutes, despite the rush hour traffic, he pulled into the familiar parking lot of the Tropic Air hangar. Driving to a loading area by the hangar, he stopped to study the Marco Polo. The target was still on the screen, apparently in the confines of the airport. But where? Sam grabbed the binoculars and scanned the line of business jets on the other side of the runway. The Learjet bearing the identification number N6602 was still parked and blocked, and didn't appear to be preparing for flight. But strong instincts told him that Karmakov would be on the move.

Although everything in the vicinity seemed stationary, the target on the screen began to move. He blinked and looked again. His first impression had been correct, the target *was* moving. The parked Learjet hadn't budged, nor had any vehicles. The map on the device was not detailed enough to establish the target's exact location, but it had to be nearby. The lingering uncertainty was infuriating. Finally, he spotted a helicopter lifting off. Banking, it was rapidly gaining altitude flying northwest. That had to be it! Sam watched the Marco Polo for several more seconds to confirm that the helicopter and the target shared the same heading. He had no idea where or how far the helicopter would go, but he knew he had little choice but to follow. He turned the Cherokee toward the freeway, realizing that Dave's electronic device was his last hope.

* * * * *

Katrina's eyes fluttered open, but the darkness was so complete that for a few seconds, she was sure that her eyes were still shut. She waited five seconds then opened them again, but it was still pitch black. Touching her face, she made certain she wasn't dreaming. She had no idea where she was or how she had gotten there—and no idea what to do. The thought crossed her mind that this was how it must have been for Jonah in the belly of the whale.

She was lying face down on what felt like a bunk covered by a coarse wool blanket. Reaching out, her fingers grazed a damp wood wall. It was hot and stuffy in the room, the air thick and humid like a tropical jungle. Beads of sweat trickled down her forehead and she felt clammy all over. Again, she tried to remember how she had arrived, but it was as though her short-term memory had been wiped clean. Rolling to a sitting position, her bare feet touched the wood plank floor. She was clothed in a lightweight cotton shift and little else. She could not remember anything that had happened since...when?

Katrina slowly stood and stretched her arms in front of her. Reaching with her foot in the dark, she took a step forward, then another. With the third step, she found another wall like the one next to the bunk. It didn't take long to discover the length and width of her place of confinement. Undoubtedly, there was a door on one of the walls, but Katrina didn't find it.

In the pitch black, in an unknown place, she leaned back on the bunk and closed her eyes. Straining to remember, she seemed unable to focus on the past few days. Her last vague memory was of...a jet taking off. She was staring out a porthole, watching a blue sports car receding in the distance as the jet rocketed off the runway. Katrina puzzled over the image. It seemed odd to see a sports car on an airport runway. It made no sense. Nothing did.

Then another image entered her mind. Karmakov. He was leaning toward her in the aircraft, handing her a glass of water. Anger and revulsion pulsed through her. With the emotional response came a higher degree of mental clarity—she remembered Karmakov's men seizing her at Sam's cabin and dragging her through the woods. Karmakov had kidnapped her, and she was certain that he would stop at nothing to have what he wanted.

Katrina realized then that she had been drugged, probably in the water she had been given on the airplane. Her head throbbed. For some time, she stayed on the bunk, unable even to wonder what would happen next. She did not know how much time passed, nor did she care.

Suddenly, the room was ablaze with blinding white light. Katrina reflexively squinted against the glare. It seemed as though the light was coming from all directions at once. The sudden flash sent pain shooting to the back of her skull, where it seemed to reverberate, echoing through her brain. Clasping her hands over her face, an involuntary moan escaped her lips.

A moment later, intense sound assaulted her senses. A voice projected into the room at such an incredibly high volume that it seemed to penetrate every cell of her body. The voice was not human. It was amplified and mechanical, either computer generated or altered to such a degree that she could not tell whether the voice was male or female.

"You will remove your hands from your face, Katrina. If you do not remove your hands, you will experience this sound until you do."

An incredibly loud, high-pitched screeching and crashing sound, the sound of metal tearing metal, like in quality and volume to a train wreck, flooded the small room. Katrina instantly moved her hands from her eyes to her ears, but the sound was so intense that it caused agonizing pain. Then, as quickly as it had begun, the sound stopped. Katrina sat still. Her ears were ringing and she was shaking from the intense vibration that had rattled her nerves for thirty seconds.

"You will open your eyes and remove your hands from your ears."

Katrina slowly obeyed, first opening her eyes to narrow slits until the light was tolerable, then cautiously lowering her hands. The light was still as bright as an operating room, but not unbearable.

"You will lay your hands in your lap and sit still."

Through squinting eyes, she spotted a door on the wall next to the bunk. She quickly stood and took a step toward the door. Before her bare foot hit the floor a second time, the incredibly intense crashing sound and blinding light made her feel as though she were standing on the face of the sun. The combined assault on her senses renewed the intense pain and totally nullified her equilibrium and muscle control. She crumpled to the floor, striking her elbow sharply and hitting her head on the hard planks. The cacophony and flashing light continued for another minute while Katrina writhed in pain on the floor.

Then the robotic voice was back, speaking to her as if she were a small child. "You disobeyed, Katrina. You must not disobey instructions. If you do so again, it will be necessary to increase your motivation. Do you understand?"

Katrina was lying on her side in a fetal position, wet with sweat. She raised her head long enough to nod weakly, then rolled onto her back to stare vacantly at the ceiling that seemed a hundred feet away. The plank floor felt soft to her touch and she idly mused that her senses were quite distorted. Nothing worked properly. She wasn't sure whether she could actually hear, or not. Trying to think was far too difficult.

"Get up, Katrina, and lie down on the bed." The mechanical voice spoke in a calm voice, encouraging cooperation.

"You will soon be receiving important instructions," the voice continued, as Katrina rose as in a trance and lay flat on the bunk. "You must rest for a little while and consider what you just experienced. You must prepare yourself for receiving instructions that you must never forget. To forget your instructions, or to disobey them, would only result in...this."

Katrina suddenly convulsed in pain as an incredibly loud roar and flashing strobe light filled the room. The throbbing bass sound literally shook the walls and the bunk upon which she lay, terrified and trembling. She instinctively tore the woolen blanket from the bunk and buried her head in it. Thirty seconds later, the sound and light were gone and she was again plunged into total darkness.

"You must remember all that you are told and you must obey your instructions instantly, and without question. Do you understand?" the voice commanded. Katrina lay still on the bunk in a near catatonic state.

"Do you understand?" The same voice spoke, but this time at a volume that shook the walls. Katrina jerked and raised her head to nod.

"Answer audibly!" the voice boomed. Instantly, Katrina bolted upright and shouted, "*Yes, yes, yes, yes, yes…*" before collapsing into unconsciousness on the bunk.

How much time passed before consciousness returned, she did not know. She only knew that her mouth and throat were parched and her ears were ringing. Her head still hurt intensely. At first, upon awakening, she squeezed her eyes shut, willing the pain to go away and unconsciousness to return. When it would not, she slowly opened her eyes and noticed that a small beam of daylight pierced the inky darkness of the room. The door near the head of the bed was open a crack. Slowly, painfully, Katrina rose to a sitting position. She turned toward the door just as it opened wider, framing a familiar silhouette.

"I have water for you, Katrina. Cool, fresh water. You must be quite thirsty and hungry after our long journey." It was Karmakov quietly speaking to her as he placed a glass of cold water in her hand. He also carried a tray with a small loaf of bread and a cup of orange juice.

Katrina accepted the water and drank long and deep. She had never been so grateful for anything in her life. Finally, after draining the large glass, she stopped to breathe. He placed the tray on the bunk next to her. "Please, eat," he said in an ingratiating tone. "I will get you more water."

He was gone for a few minutes, then returned with a small pitcher of water. Katrina was chewing a crust of bread and trying to remember when she had eaten last. As he entered the room again, she looked up at her tormentor. In a part of her mind, she knew that she hated this man, but she was still grateful to him. In a detached way, she understood the enormous, fundamental conflict growing in her mind. But it did not matter. The water was all that mattered at the moment, and escape from the pain.

"Do you have a headache?" he asked innocently. "Here, my love, this will make you feel much better." He handed Katrina two small white pills. "Put them in your mouth and swallow them. You may drink more water if you wish."

Katrina generally avoided taking any form of medication, but she put the two pills in her mouth without thinking and quickly washed them down. As soon as she had swallowed them, she realized that she had no idea what they were. He had drugged her before and would likely do so again. How could she have been so stupid? She could have refused the medication or simply held them under her tongue until he was gone, then spit them out. She felt queasy, wondering what unexpected effect the pills would have.

Then with sudden insight, Katrina realized why she had taken the pills without thinking, without making a conscious decision. It was the voice—Karmakov's voice—that had given her an instruction, and she dare not disobey. There was no voluntary act involved, only blind obedience. It must have been his voice that had commanded her earlier, distorted by a computer, but still recognizable to her subconscious mind. Katrina felt a wave of revulsion at the thought of being subject to such mind control and her hot, clammy skin suddenly chilled.

"As I said, I have a surprise for you, Katrina. I will give you ten minutes to finish your meal and freshen up, then I will teach you another very important lesson about life." Karmakov turned on his heel and left, leaving the door open behind him.

Katrina slumped on the bunk. How could it have happened so fast? Could he have actually taken control of her mind in only a few hours? Had she really wanted to take the pills? Was she only imagining a loss of self-control, due to the unrelenting stress and her weakened physical condition? If she were losing control, would it be temporary? Could she resist in the future? A hundred questions swarmed in her mind as her strength began to return and the pounding migraine subsided. At least she could be thankful, she thought, for the relief from the pain. Then she realized with a start that this was exactly what Karmakov wanted, for her to be grateful to him for giving her relief from the pain that he had inflicted. Another wave of abhorrence spread through her. She swore at that moment that Karmakov would never enjoy her gratitude, for he only merited her scorn.

The door opened wider and Karmakov entered again. He smiled at Katrina with a lustful look in his eye. "And now, you must come with me," he said, and Katrina found herself rising from the bunk and following his dark form out the door. What choice did she have?

Outside, the Florida sun was beating down from directly overhead and the air was muggy and hot. Katrina thought that it must be noon or early afternoon. Squinting against the brightness, she paused to look around. The building in which she had been confined was a tiny cabin situated on what appeared to be a small island in a sea of swamp grass. There were a few shrubs and small trees near the cabin, but the land quickly fell away on three sides and disappeared into black water and masses of lush tropical vegetation. As far as she could see, the island was surrounded by flat, swampy terrain. Katrina realized that they must be deep in the Everglades.

Karmakov was leading the way down a thirty yard long sandy trail to a raised wood plank walkway that traversed the swampland to a somewhat larger island nearby. From a distance, it appeared to be covered entirely with a dense tangle of large trees and vines. Katrina followed, not knowing what else to do and being more than willing to leave the scene of her painful confinement.

The scorching sunlight and tropical heat became somewhat less oppressive as she followed Karmakov into the shadows of the massive trees that covered the larger island. The wooden walkway continued through the trees for another fifty yards, then connected with a large deck made of the same old materials. The deck served as the porch for another rustic wood cabin, this one larger than the one in which Katrina had been confined. Opposite the cabin and across the rough wood deck was a lagoon of deep water, with an outlet to the swamp beyond.

On the far side of the lagoon was a low, muddy bank. Heavy swamp grass grew on the bank in tall, scattered clumps, nearly reaching the water. Katrina caught her breath when she noticed the still form of a huge alligator lying on the bank across the lagoon. There was no railing on the deck, which was only a few feet above the water, and she felt more vulnerable than ever before in her life. Despite the tropical heat, she suddenly shivered and wrapped her arms around herself. Peering into the trees overhead, she wondered what other threats the tropical jungle might hold.

"Welcome to the swamp lodge, Katrina. I hope you will enjoy your short stay here," he said with a smile, as he turned and bowed slightly.

"I do not intend to stay here, nor will I enjoy it," she replied grimly. But as she spoke, she felt a queer sensation throughout her body, followed by a sudden wave of nausea. She choked back the bile that rose in her throat, feeling suddenly out of control, and again knowing that her senses were not entirely trustworthy.

"A very bad attitude for an honored guest. Undoubtedly, a few more lessons will be necessary before you fully understand your obligations. But there will be time enough for that. For now, I have an exciting surprise for you. I will show you what can happen to those who would try to challenge my authority. Come, I have reserved you a front row seat for the entertainment."

Karmakov took Katrina by the arm and guided her to a pair of wooden chairs facing the lagoon near the edge of the deck. Katrina was apprehensive, but had no idea what to expect. As they sat down, Karmakov turned toward the cabin, clapped his hands twice and shouted as though he were a Roman emperor, "Let the games begin!"

Chapter 18

Moments later, the door to the wooden cabin swung open and a man stepped out. Katrina didn't recognize the man whose hand were bound in front of him with rope. His clothes were tattered, his forehead was scraped, and streaks of dried blood ran down his cheeks. In spite of his condition, he walked erect with his head held high, a scornful smile on his face. Behind him, Karmakov's two henchmen followed, along with a short, older man dressed in dirty blue jeans. A sweaty, camouflage-brown tee shirt stretched over his large belly. Short curls of scraggly grey hair hung limply from his round, balding head. A week's growth of grey beard completed the image of a human swamp rat. In one hand, he gripped the top of a large burlap bag that swung at his side.

"Good thang you brought us some fresh meat out here," the swamp rat muttered in a raspy voice, addressing Karmakov. "Them gators is gittin' mighty hungry."

The swamp rat reached into the burlap bag and pulled out the carcass of a large opossum. Its head was split open, cleaved by an ax. At the sight of the bloody animal, Katrina again felt bile rising. "Watch this!" he shouted with eager anticipation, as he swung the carcass back like a bowling ball and tossed it thirty feet into the lagoon. It splashed as it hit the water and in the next few seconds, the tall grass began to rustle as five large alligators slid into the water in a race to the floating treat. A twelve foot alligator with enormous jaws snatched the opossum then dove to swallow its snack in the depths of the lagoon. The four remaining alligators, awakened by the activity, circled in the lagoon, obviously awaiting another handout.

"This here's an old vulture I shot just this mornin'," the swamp rat said, pulling it from the burlap bag as though he were handing out Christmas presents. "Not quite as ripe as that 'possum, but I reckon it's as good as a duck dinner to one of them gators." He tossed it toward the middle of the lagoon. Black feathers splashed and it floated for less than five seconds before a patrolling alligator, driven by the furious serpentine motion of its powerful tail, devoured it. The second alligator was even larger than the first—fourteen feet from snout to tail.

Both were large enough to easily take down a man or a horse.

"I'm gittin' real tired of sittin' out here feedin' nothin' but pig parts and carcasses to these gators," the swamp rat said to Karmakov in a sarcastic drawl. "If yer gonna' feed some fresh meat to them gators, ya' ought'a give it to 'em a little bit at a time, so we kin have us a show. Them gators is gittin' pretty stirred up. They might start fightin' over the big pieces." The swamp rat surveyed the alligators as he tossed the empty burlap bag on the deck. Then he turned to look at the bound man and the two Russian henchmen with a flat stare that made Katrina's skin crawl. With a sinking feeling in the pit of her stomach, Katrina suddenly realized that the fresh meat the swamp rat was referring to was the bound man.

Karmakov turned to Katrina then, and in his eyes she saw a malignant light that she had never seen before. There was something wild there, a cruel and sadistic gleam that was a window on his brutal, twisted mind. At that moment, she realized that Karmakov was consumed with a deadly blood lust that would make him kill and kill again. She understood that he had developed a hidden addiction to torture and cruelty that could only be satiated by the slow and agonizing death of his victims.

"As a part of your training, Katrina, you will now witness the punishment of one who attempted to oppose me. You will soon learn that strict obedience is your only option." Karmakov was becoming excited at the prospect of the bloodletting and enthralled with his own words. He gripped Katrina by both arms and raised her roughly to her feet, his wild, dark eyes boring into hers, filling her with unspeakable fear. "You will learn a lesson today that you will never forget."

"No, *you can't*!" Katrina screamed in Karmakov's face as he held her by the arms. "You have no right to murder this man, whatever he has done to you! You are an animal!" Tears streaked Katrina's face as she broke down into wrenching sobs. Karmakov shook his head in disgust and motioned to one of his henchmen, who shoved her into a chair and held his hands firmly on her shoulders.

Karmakov then barked an order to his other man, who dragged the prisoner to the edge of the deck and began binding his hands to the end of a heavy rope lying on the deck. The rope was strung through a rusty old metal pulley hung in a tree high over the lagoon, and the other end of the rope was in the swamp rat's hands.

"And to think," the swamp rat said, shaking his head, "in New York they bury good carcasses in concrete, or jis' dump 'em in the river. What a waste of good gator chow." He licked tobacco juice from his wet lips and spat a long stream of juice in the general direction of the lagoon. "That riggin' works real good for feedin' gators. When they're done, there won't be a shred a' nothin' left."

"My enemies die by inches," Karmakov boasted, "and this ignorant cretin is no exception. We will lower him slowly into the pit and we will learn which of the beasts in the pool is the strongest as they fight to be the first to tear at his feet, then his legs…"

Dave Sanders had been standing passively while his hands were being tied to the pulley rope, but now he leaned forward to interrupt Karmakov. "Whoa, now, buddy, you wait just a minute and hold it right there. You're getting just a little too graphic for this nice lady. She does not want to hear what those gators would bite next. Can't you just shoot me and be done with it? Then you could cut me up and give each gator his fair share. It'd be more fair for the gators."

Karmakov stared at Sanders in surprise at his flippant remarks, but the swamp rat responded quickly. "Naw, I wanna see how high them gators can jump. Course, we could haul him up there and let 'em jump and then shoot him…"

"Silence!" Karmakov commanded. "You will do as I say…"

"Don't I even get any last requests?" Sanders interrupted again. "I'm really starving for some pizza. Pizza of the Gods with lots of artichoke hearts. It might take a while to get it delivered way out here…"

Karmakov rose from his chair, took three steps forward, and slapped Sanders savagely across the face. Sanders stumbled into the Russian behind him, but did not fall. "I said silence!" Karmakov roared, "Are you deaf?"

"Well, you're going to kill me anyway, so I figured I might as well get in my last request. It's tradition, you know."

Karmakov backhanded Sanders viciously across his other cheek, cutting it with a large diamond and ruby ring he wore. Sanders began to bleed fresh red blood over the crust of dried blood that was already there. He remained standing only because a Russian mobster was holding him. "Time for a miracle," Sanders muttered, looking at Katrina. "You know," he continued, speaking to Karmakov, "if you keep me alive just a little bit longer, we could all go deep sea fishing and you could use me for shark bait. That might be interesting. Sure beats feeding me to a bunch of stupid alligators."

Karmakov turned angrily to the swamp rat and shouted, "Do not waste any more time! He will suffer for his insolence. Do it now!"

The fat swamp rat and one of the Russian henchmen heaved the rope tight as the others watched. Sanders backed away from the edge of the deck, suddenly feeling great trepidation at the prospect of imminent death, but he was pulled forward as the pulley rope tightened. He stumbled toward the edge of the deck.

"*No*," shrieked Katrina, trying to stand, "I cannot bear this! Let him go! Please don't kill him!" The guard shoved her back into the chair, and she buried her face in her hands.

Karmakov grabbed her hair and pulled her head back, gripping her chin hard with his other hand. "You will bear this and much, much more," he said harshly. "Now open your eyes and watch!"

The Russian henchman and the swamp rat heaved, and Sanders was dragged over the edge of the deck and pulled up until he was hanging by his hands, his feet swinging ten feet above the black water and twenty feet from the deck. The two men wrapped the rope around a post on the deck and the swamp rat held it tight, ready to feed it out slowly. Katrina could see the enormous alligators moving in, but there was nothing she could do. Karmakov and his man were both restraining her. "*Oh God, no!*" she cried in anguish. "*Let him go, please, I beg you, let him go!*"

At that moment, the air was rent with the deafening roar of an aircraft engine being revved to full throttle. All heads turned toward the sound at the opening of the lagoon, to see a flat-bottomed swamp buggy picking up speed with Sam at the helm. Keeping one hand on the wheel, he leveled a pistol and fired. The Russian henchman standing next to the swamp rat spun and dropped heavily on the deck with a gaping, bloody hole in his shoulder.

Pandemonium broke loose on the deck. The ungainly swamp rat lurched for cover in the cabin, releasing the rope in the process. The rope slipped, dropping Sanders into the water with a tremendous splash. The second Russian henchman drew a pistol and took two wild shots at the swamp buggy, while Karmakov dragged Katrina toward the cabin.

As the powerful airboat accelerated toward the deck, Sam squeezed off three quick shots at the second Russian, who had dropped to one knee and was trying to take aim. One of Sam's shots connected, and the Russian dropped his weapon as he grabbed his leg in pain. In seconds, the airboat was coasting to a stop in front of the deck and Sam was reaching for Sanders. He smelled the foul reptilian breath of an enormous alligator as it rushed passed the boat, its huge open jaws snapping shut just inches from Sanders' kicking feet, as he tried to wriggle aboard. Grabbing Sanders by the back of his belt, Sam hefted, and with a final tug, Sanders slid over the gunwale and dropped into the bottom of the boat. Sam swung a wooden paddle a few times, slapping at the alligators that were circling the boat until they retreated to the far side of the lagoon to wait for an easier meal.

In the few seconds that passed, the airboat had drifted to within a few feet of the deck. Sam and Dave were on the floor of the flat-bottomed craft below the deck, where they were protected from gunfire from the cabin.

For a brief moment, everything was quiet, except for the slowly idling engine of the airboat, as Sam caught his breath from the exertion of dragging Sanders into the boat. Then in one quick movement, Sam grabbed a hunting knife from a box of tools in the boat and hacked through the rope that bound Sanders' hands. He pulled a pistol from the waistband of his pants and handed it to Sanders, who was more than ready to turn the tables on his tormenters.

"You sure took your sweet time getting here," Sanders said as he checked the load in the pistol. "That was a little too close for comfort. Next time, I think I'll just stay in South Beach."

"Keep the boat here and cover me," Sam said. "I'm going after Katrina."

"Whoa, now, son, let's think about this. They're in there with guns and we're out here with guns. They have Katrina and we want her. It's a Mexican standoff. What would Davy Crockett do? We don't just charge into their guns. We need to do something sneaky to get the upper hand. We need to flush 'em out."

"So what's your idea?" Sam asked.

"Well, when I was tied up behind the cabin this morning, I saw something that might come in handy. Ya' know, they like all kinds of critters around here…"

The two men talked for another minute, then Sanders stepped from the boat into the shallow water by the deck and bending low, waded onto dry land under the deck. Sam watched him make his way under the deck and along the edge of the lagoon until he slipped into the dense tropical foliage on the far side of the walkway and disappeared from view.

For a few minutes, Sam sat in the drifting airboat, contemplating their dire predicament and considering a dozen possible courses of action. The sweltering sun and humidity made it hard to breathe. Dense swarms of mosquitoes hovering over the lagoon were drawn to the smell of blood in the boat. Sam let the swamp buggy continue to idle alongside the deck, the large wooden propeller making a "whup, whup, whup" sound as it turned at 100 rpm. There was no activity or sound from the cabin, where the swamp rat, the two Russian henchmen, Karmakov and Katrina were. Sam checked the ammunition in his handgun and waited.

* * * * *

Inside the cabin, Karmakov stood by the small front window and peered out. The swamp rat stood by the back door with a shotgun in his hands. Katrina sat on a bunk against the side wall beneath an open window, her knees drawn to her chest. The Russian who had been shot in the shoulder lay still on the floor while his partner sat nearby, leaning against the wall and moaning softly, his hand held tightly over a bullet hole in his thigh. It was a scene of quiet desperation.

Suddenly, a window on the back of the cabin shattered as a heavy piece of cypress timber flew through it. A second later, a burlap bag sailed in, landing on the floor nearly at the feet of the swamp rat. Katrina jumped when the timber shattered the window, but she screamed when she saw the top of the bag fall open and several fat timber rattlesnakes wiggle out. With a loud *umph*, the swamp rat tried to jump out of the way just as one of the agitated snakes struck. The snake was quicker, and the swamp rat bellowed with pain as fangs sunk deep in the muscle of his leg. As he snatched the rattler loose, another struck him.

Panic engulfed the room like a bolt of lightning. Karmakov lunged for the front door as his two comrades dragged themselves to their feet and struggled to follow. The limping gunman wasted several rounds of ammunition in a vain effort to kill the advancing snakes, stopping only when the hammer of his gun clicked on an empty chamber. At the same time, the swamp rat fired both barrels of his shotgun in rapid succession, and bits of snake splattered across the room.

Ignoring the chaos, Karmakov paused at the door, looking for a weapon. The boat was still idling by the dock, but Sam was out of sight. Karmakov turned to his companions. One had an empty pistol and the other's gun had been lost when he was hit in the shoulder on the deck. The empty shotgun was lying on the floor within striking distance of two rattlers. Spotting a rusty machete hanging on the wall behind the door, he seized it. Then, with a fiendish gleam in his eyes, Karmakov suddenly threw himself through the door and across the deck toward the airboat.

* * * * *

Katrina was at first paralyzed with fear as the swamp rat staggered forward after being hit by multiple strikes from the rattlers. For a moment, she drew her knees tight against her chest, unable to move. But then she realized that the window behind her was wide open and she was no longer being watched. In one quick movement she leaped out, dropping to the ground just as Sanders ducked around the corner of the cabin.

"Get to the boat, girl, and we're outta here!" Sanders shouted. Katrina needed no encouragement. Together, they headed toward the front deck with Sanders in the lead. They reached it just in time to see Karmakov leap into the airboat on top of Sam, swinging the rusty machete high over his head with a maniacal scream.

* * * * *

Karmakov's frontal attack was both unexpected and sudden. From a sprinter's stance, it had taken him only two seconds to cross the wide deck. Sam's attention had been distracted as he tried to keep the airboat stationary in front of the cabin, and he had but a split second to react. He stepped into the attack and managed to deflect the downward blow of the machete with a forearm block that connected with the handle and sent the blade looping into the lagoon. Both men fell to the floor of the boat in a tangle, with Karmakov's long fingers probing for a grip on Sam's throat. Instead, Sam's knuckles found Karmakov's face and the Russian fell heavily against the gunwale of the boat, blood streaming from his flattened nose.

With a horrific scream, the Russian threw himself at Sam again, but this time Sam was ready for the rush. Planting his feet, he grabbed Karmakov's shirt, thrust one hip forward and twisted, redirecting his attacker's force and launching him into the air. Karmakov twisted like a cat and managed to land on his feet, but he was off balance and stumbling backward toward the idling propeller of the airboat. Too late, Karmakov realized the danger and jerked to his left, toward the prop. The swinging wooden blade caught him under the left arm, cutting it to the bone. The force of the blow tossed him out of the boat like a rag doll.

The Russian splashed into the water, then quickly surfaced ten feet from the boat, a red stain spreading in the water around him. Looking shocked and subdued, Karmakov coughed, spit blood and began to wade toward the shore with his damaged left arm hanging limp at his side. Since he no longer appeared to be a threat, Sam turned his attention back to the controls of the drifting airboat, just as Katrina and Sanders leaped from the deck onto the front of the craft.

"Time to beat feet!" Sanders shouted over the roar of the engine, which Sam was already gunning. "I don't know where those other three goons are! Let's get it moving!"

As the airboat revved and began to pull away from the deck, Sam noticed Katrina staring back at the cabin with a terrified look on her face. He turn and saw the swamp rat staggering wooden-legged across the deck, his face beet red, with a fat rattler grasped behind the head in each hand. He was yelling obscenities as he threw both snakes as far as he could toward the boat, but his words were drowned by the roar of the engine. The snakes fell short, splashing into the water as the swamp rat tottered, then fell forward on the deck, a horrible grimace on his face.

Gaining speed across the lagoon, Sam looked back at Karmakov, who was still nearly waist deep in murky water. His bloodstained clothes and dangling arm were a testament to his pain, but his baleful glare showed only fury and hatred. Behind him, two massive reptilians that had been floating as still as logs in the middle of the lagoon silently disappeared under the water. Sam could trace the course of the monsters moving unseen in the deep, dark water toward their prey. He expected at any moment to see an explosion of energy in the shallows and Karmakov suddenly disappear beneath the surface, but the Russian was still wading toward the deck when the airboat reached the outlet of the lagoon. He had no choice then but to turn his full attention to navigating the swamp buggy.

* * * * *

Once they reached the open water, Sam breathed a sigh of relief and pushed in the throttle, sending the airboat racing across the broad expanse of swamp grass. A few small, scattered islands dotted the vast wilderness of slow-moving water and grasses, and Sam avoided them, holding to an easterly course until he put some distance between them and the horrors they had left behind. After several minutes at high speed, he drew back the throttle to idle and let the boat coast to a stop. Stepping around the central helm of the boat, he took a hard look at Sanders and Katrina, who were both seated in the front of the airboat.

Dave was tired and bedraggled, but his unsinkable attitude was intact. His eyes were clear and he had a smile of triumph on his face, despite the fact that half an hour earlier, he had nearly been the main course at an alligator dinner party. Katrina was not faring so well. She was pale and shivering, in spite of the oppressive heat in the swamp, and her breathing was quick and shallow. Her unblinking eyes were fixed on a point in the distance. The trauma she had undergone had taken a heavy toll. She needed rest and recuperation, but most of all, she needed her confidence restored. It was clear that she was in a highly unstable condition, possibly in shock. Sam's heart went out to her, knowing that she had done nothing to deserve such brutal treatment. At the same time, his searing hatred for Karmakov grew and he fervently hoped that the murderous villain had been divided into equal parts between the monsters floating in the lagoon.

"Dave, can you drive this thing for a while? Just dodge the islands and bear northeast, and we'll be back in sight of the highway in no time."

"No problem, mate, I always wanted to try out one of these contraptions. You say you know the way?"

"We'll just backtrack the way I came this morning. It took four hours in a skiff with a ten horse motor, but with this rig, we ought to be there in half an hour. It was sure lucky they had this thing tied up in the lagoon. I was kind of flying by the seat of my pants on the escape part of the plan."

"So what else is new?" Sanders chuckled as he took the helm.

As Sanders pushed the boat up to fifty miles an hour down an open canal, Sam sat on the bench seat next to Katrina and took her hands in his. She was still staring fixedly at the horizon, as if in a trance. Gently, he placed his fingers on her cheek and turned her face toward his. He placed both hands on her shoulders at the base of her neck and slowly began to massage rock hard muscles. Finally, she blinked several times, her eyes filled with tears, and her entire body began to quake uncontrollably as the shock abated. Sam embraced her, holding her tightly while she sobbed. He could only imagine the agonies and misery she must have suffered at the cruel hands of Karmakov. Sam held her close and prayed silently for her recovery. Finally, he felt her relax. She pushed gently away, wiped her eyes, then embraced Sam again and pressed her damp cheek against his without a word.

The roar of the aircraft engine made talking impossible. Sam leaned back on the bench seat while Katrina rested her head on his shoulder. The breeze cooled them as Sam felt surges of primal emotions that his ancestors, the plains Indians and the highlanders of Scotland, had felt when they had successfully defended their tribes and families against hostile forces in a dangerous and primitive world. He was charged with the thrill of facing danger and surviving victorious, and the grateful satisfaction of having protected loved ones. Sam knew then that Katrina was, and always would be, his to love and protect.

Chapter 19

For thirty years, Everglades Adventures had conducted a good tourist business next to the two lane highway known as Alligator Alley, which connected the dots of islands in the Everglades. The entire resort was actually just one long, low clapboard building that nearly covered a small island in the glades. The building had once been painted bright white, but it had long since aged to a dingy shade of yellow and was badly in need of repair. It housed a diner at one end, a gift shop offering all kinds of alligator memorabilia in the middle, and four small guest rooms on the other end. An old wooden deck typical of the Everglades bordered the entire building. From the deck that ran along the back of the building, two long, parallel piers extended a hundred yards into the glades. Tied to the piers were several small flat-bottomed boats with outboard motors, like the one Sam had rented that morning, and three airboats, including the one that Sam and Dave Sanders had just tied to the pier.

Sam was standing on the pier engaged in an animated conversation with the proprietor of Everglades Adventures. He had just promised that the skiff he had rented that morning would be returned in pristine condition, when Sanders walked up with a white paper bag in one hand and a small Styrofoam ice chest in the other. "We got vittles!" Sanders said with a self-satisfied grin. "Big sack of burgers and sodas, all American fare, thanks to this fine gentleman's wonderful sweet wife, Maggie. Man, am I starved."

The proprietor's demeanor softened a bit at Sanders' words, but he continued his pointed questioning of Sam. "So where did this weedeater come from, anyway?" he said, looking over the airboat. "I swear I've seen it before. Looks mighty familiar. And where did you pick up your passengers? There's nothing within twenty miles of here but gators, snakes, and fish. I thought you were goin' fishing."

Sam reached in his pocket and pulled out a hundred dollar bill. "Maybe this will answer some of your questions."

The proprietor eyed the bill. "That'd probably answer about half of 'em," he responded, quickly calculating the value of the cranky old ten horse motor that had been on the rented skiff, then tripling it. "When's the owner of that airboat going to be here to trade back?"

"Maybe never, in which case you will be the proud owner of a mighty powerful airboat," Sanders injected. "If he does show up, you can trade back and keep the cash. You can't lose on this deal. Just remember to forget you ever saw us."

Sam pulled another bill from his pocket and held it with the first. A broad grin spread across the proprietor's face. "I guess somebody must 'a tied that weedeater up there while I was out fishing," he said, pocketing the bills. "Shouldn't be a problem." He turned to go, then paused. "You boys enjoy those burgers now, but don't be eatin' 'em out there on that low end of the pier. Them gators, they kind'a developed a likin' for leftover burgers. Sometimes they climb plumb up on the pier after 'em."

Taking his advice, the three ate their hamburgers at a picnic table on the deck. Sam was pleased to note that Katrina had an appetite, despite her ordeal. She was certainly resilient. Sanders tossed a bit of hamburger into the water off the deck and watched as a small gator, not more than three feet long and as thick around the middle as a man's forearm, slithered out from under the deck and snapped up the tidbit with needle sharp teeth. The food made them all feel better, and as the sun began to sink toward the horizon, they made their way to their vehicle.

Sam pulled the Jeep Cherokee onto the long, straight, two lane road heading east toward Miami. The white ribbon of pavement stretched as far as the eye could see in both directions, with tall swamp grass and bullrushes bordering the canals on both sides. The setting sun reflected gold and red in the water of the canals, and towering white cumulus clouds dominated the vivid blue sky to the south and east. A distant storm cloud could be seen far across the glades to the north. The immensity of the Everglades was awe inspiring, a vivid reminder of the wonders of nature. Sam said a silent prayer that his Osage grandfather had taught him, blessing the earth and all that inhabits it. As the tension of the last few days began to ebb, a smile crept slowly across his face.

The tide was turning.

* * * * *

"So how in the world did you find us?" Sanders asked, as he reached behind the seat to pull out his bag of tricks.

"Nothing to it, really," Sam answered nonchalantly. "I remembered the Marco Polo device. I took a crash course in how to operate the thing and tracked you to the airport with it. Things got a little crazy there and for a while I thought I'd lost you, but then I saw the helicopter taking off and I figured you were on it. I just followed the helicopter into the Everglades using the Marco Polo device. I was barely able to keep you in range driving at top speed, but I managed to keep up, and when the moving dot stopped, I knew you had landed. I pinpointed the landing site on the map, then found a place to rent a skiff. When I got close to the island, I cut the engine and poled the last hundred yards. I just got lucky, finding the airboat tied up outside the lagoon. The rest is history."

"Damn, Sam, if I'd known you were so smart and resourceful, I would've recruited you for the Bureau long ago!" Sanders looked up from the Marco Polo device with a puzzled expression and added, "Have I said that before?"

"At any rate," Sanders continued, "you showed up just in the nick of time. I wasn't much interested in being alligator bait, especially one nibble at a time. And I'm sure they had some equally diabolical plan for sweet Katrina…Well, will you look at that!" Sanders said with satisfaction as he tuned in the Marco Polo device. "This thing still works—and it looks like they're on the move!"

Sam looked in the rearview mirror at his friend. "What do you mean…"

"I mean it looks like we got them on the Marco Polo again. When I was on the chopper, they made me empty my pockets, and I left my disk there in a pile of loose change. It must still be in the chopper. So, we can track them with the Marco Polo device as long as we're in range. It looks like they're coming this way. And fast."

Seconds later, the rhythmic thumping of a helicopter in flight could be heard in the distance. In the fading daylight, the same helicopter that had ferried Katrina, and later Sanders, to the hidden cabin appeared about a mile to the south, heading toward Miami, traveling at treetop height on a course that paralleled the highway. Katrina stiffened noticeably and looked at Sam with apprehension.

"They have no way of knowing this is us," Sam said optimistically. "They never saw this vehicle. They're probably heading into Miami for medical attention." He peered out the passenger window and noted that the chopper had changed its heading and appeared to be on a course that would intersect the highway just ahead.

"Famous last words, *amigo,*" Sanders said. "Looks to me like they're planning to head us off at the pass. Can't this jalopy go any faster?"

Sam pressed the accelerator to the floor, but he knew that the helicopter could more than double their fastest speed. "Best thing we can do is get back to civilization. There's no doubt that we're outgunned, and with the mobility of a chopper…" Sam watched the speedometer needle pass one hundred as the helicopter closed the last four hundred yards.

"Don't look now, Sam, and I mean that literally," Sanders said calmly, "but the side door of that chopper just opened and they're pointing something this way that does look a little bit like a rocket launcher…So brace yourselves, both of you, and get ready to hit the brakes on my command…Now!"

Sam mashed the brake pedal hard, and the antilock brakes did their job. The Jeep decelerated quickly, skidding only slightly. The chopper flashed past and a second later, the pavement fifty feet in front of the Jeep exploded into a wall of orange flame, which quickly dissipated in the gathering dusk.

"Yeeowee! That was too close for comfort!" Sanders shouted, as Sam gunned the Jeep and skidded around the flaming pavement, pushing the accelerator back to the floor. "Looks like they're coming around for another pass."

Sam gripped the wheel grimly and watched through the windshield as the chopper banked to the right and ascended, obviously circling back. In the distance, the twinkling lights of the city beckoned. If they could make it to the edge of civilization, surely their attackers would break off the assault.

Suddenly, the vehicle was filled with a rush of thick, humid air as Sanders opened the window. He produced from his bag a small pistol with a fat barrel that was nearly as wide as it was long. "Well, we're not going down without a fight," he muttered, as he slipped a shell about two and a half inches long and an inch in diameter into the chamber of the odd weapon. "Miniature magnesium flare," he said to Sam with a smile. "I always thought this would come in handy someday. You just never know."

"Bravo, Dave, Bravo!" Katrina exclaimed, pleased that they had some ability to fight back. Sam kept the needle pegged as the car ate up the last few miles to civilization.

Seconds later, the chopper was again approaching from the right rear. In the side view mirror, Sam could see that the sliding door of the aircraft was still open. He pressed harder on the gas pedal, but it was already on the floor. The heavy SUV flew solidly over the smooth, straight pavement.

"No need to wait for their move, Dave," Sam shouted. "This is not the OK corral. Fire at will!"

"Just trying to make sure this works…" Sanders muttered. *Bang!* An explosion reverberated in the speeding car and a second later, a brilliant white light burst forth in the darkening sky.

"Yes!" Sanders exclaimed. "Stuck it right on the old windshield! Whoever is flying that thing is going to be flying blind for the next couple of minutes."

The helicopter quickly pulled away and began to ascend, the bright magnesium flare still burning on its windshield. As the chopper continued to climb and assumed a heading to the southeast, it was clear that the assault was over.

Katrina exhaled an audible sigh of relief and then rested her head on the padded dashboard. "That was amazing," she said quietly, half to the others and half to herself. Sam thought she had taken the excitement remarkably well.

He slowed to sixty miles per hour as Sanders rolled up the window. After the harrowing high speed chase, it seemed as though the car was crawling. The lights of civilization were just a mile away.

Sanders again picked up the Marco Polo device. "Can you believe it? We've still got 'em on the Marco Polo! Maybe we should follow 'em and…"

"No!" Sam and Katrina both shouted in unison. Then they looked at each other and laughed. "No way, Dave, not tonight," Sam continued. "I think we've all had more than enough for one day. Make that a month. Tomorrow is soon enough. It's halftime and we're winning. We need time to rest and regroup."

"Wiser words were never spoken," Sanders responded solemnly. "Listen to him, Katrina, he's a smart guy. I've just got this heavy adrenaline rush going, you know, and I thought maybe…"

Sanders trailed off as Sam slowed and turned into the first major commercial development at the edge of the Everglades. A huge, garish neon sign lit the parking lot and announced "Creek Nation Casino Resort."

"Wow," Sanders continued with renewed enthusiasm. "This might be a good place to burn off some energy!"

"And to get some sleep," Sam added as he turned into a parking space. "Do you realize how long it's been since any of us got any good sleep?"

"Well," Sanders responded, "not counting when I was unconscious, for me, it's been…uh, a long time."

Sam looked at Katrina. "And you, Kate, how do feel?"

"I feel good, Sam, really good. I'm glad to be alive and not a captive of those evil people. I'm glad to be here with you…and Dave. I owe you both my life."

"Karmakov would not have killed you," Sam said softly.

"He might have, Sam. He is truly insane. If he did not kill me, I would have killed myself, rather than have my mind and spirit destroyed by torture and live in bondage," Katrina replied, a grim look on her face.

"Oh, well, enough small talk," Sanders interrupted. "Can we just go in here and get some good food and some beds or something? Maybe a few games of blackjack or craps, have a little fun for a change?"

"Great idea, Dave, I'm so glad you thought of it," Sam said, winking at Katrina as he opened the door. "Why don't you go get a couple of rooms on the quiet side of this place, while Katrina and I look for some clothes? I don't think we're very presentable right now." Sam looked at Katrina in the damp cotton shift clinging to her body and his own dirty blue jeans and tee shirt. "We'll find something for you to wear too, Dave. You just get the rooms."

"Your wish is my command, Sahib," Sanders said graciously as he turned and headed for the resort entrance.

* * * * *

An hour later, Sam stepped out of a steaming shower and toweled dry. He had managed to find a razor, and for the first time in days, he felt somewhat presentable. A quick look in the mirror revealed bruises, cuts, and a painful crease in his thigh, but nothing that wouldn't heal. He knew from experience that exhaustion would eventually catch up with him and then it would take a week to recover, but for the time being, he was still pumping a lot of adrenaline. Trying to sleep would be futile. *Dave is probably right*, Sam thought. *An hour or two in the casino will help take the edge off.*

"Sam, I'm heading downstairs," Sanders said through the bathroom door. "I'm going to check the restaurants in this place. Maybe we can find a decent meal for a change."

"Great. I'll wait for Katrina and we'll meet you downstairs in a few minutes. Save me a cold one."

"Ah yes, cold cervezas and hot Latin ladies, a warm tropical night and moonlight on the water, white sand and palm trees, tango and samba, what more could a man ask for…"

Sam could hear Sanders' ongoing soliloquy as the door closed behind him. Pulling on a clean white polo shirt and tan trousers, Sam gave his head a shake, then pushed his thick, dark hair out of his face. He dialed the room next door, and Katrina picked up on the second ring.

"Are you ready?" Sam asked.

"Yes. I am ready."

"Great. Meet you outside."

Sam stepped onto the wide, tiled balcony between their second floor rooms. The pale pink stucco walls and teal tile floor contrasted with the black wrought iron railing that was brushed at intervals by huge palm fronds blowing in the evening breeze. Below was the sandy beach of a nearby lake. Sam leaned on the railing and breathed deeply, absorbing the cool ambiance of the place, smelling the intoxicating aroma of tropical flower gardens borne on the heavy tropical air. The moon was nearly full. Bright silver moonbeams reflected on the surface of the lake like glittering pools of liquid mercury. He reveled in the perfect, beautiful scene, feeling connected to the earth and grateful to have an exquisite evening to enjoy. Grateful to be alive.

Two soft hands encircled his waist from behind, followed by lithe arms. Katrina embraced him briefly, then slid between Sam and the iron railing, both of them drinking in the incomparable scene before them.

"This place is so beautiful, Sam, this evening so perfect. I feel fantastic!"

"It doesn't get any better than this," Sam said, inhaling the fresh scent of her hair. "Life is full of surprises. Thank God we got a good one for a change." Sam raised a hand and pointed over the tops of the palms. "Hey! Look at those pelicans!" A flight of a dozen brown pelicans wheeled in the moonlight over the lake and skidded in for a noisy landing just offshore.

Katrina smiled and turned in the circle of Sam's arms, pressing herself against him. "The pelicans are quite charming, but isn't there something more interesting to you than birds here tonight?"

"Dinner!" Sam said without hesitation. "A big steak! Weren't we going out to dinner? Didn't you say you were ready?"

Katrina flashed a bright smile, with a mischievous glint in her eyes. "I did say I was ready, but I did not say for what." Without breaking eye contact, she took the front of Sam's shirt in both hands and slowly drew him back through the open door of her room.

The windows and double French doors of the spacious room were open to a private balcony and a fragrant tropical breeze filled the air. Sheer white curtains billowed in the breeze and the bright moon illuminated the room with enchanting silver light.

Katrina was clad in a man's white cotton shirt twice her size and a pair of men's trousers which were rolled up six inches at the cuff. She was barefoot. Without a word, she eased the shirt over her head and tossed it on the bed. Then with a deft movement of her hand, the loose trousers fell to the floor, and Katrina was free. For a moment, Sam gazed upon the lovely, soft curves of her body, cast in the undulating shadows of the intermittent moonlight, and he had the fleeting thought that she truly possessed the body of a goddess. Then quickly, she tugged his shirttail loose and slid her hands over the bare skin beneath his shirt. They embraced for a moment, then he pulled his shirt over his head and tossed it aside.

Suddenly, Katrina's body was molded against his and Sam felt her warm, soft breasts pressing against his chest. Her lips were reaching up for his, and when they met, they both trembled as though an electric shock coursed through their bodies. Sam felt himself sinking into softness, into a delicious delirium. The exquisite perfection of the woman in his arms, her anxious desire, his feelings of protectiveness for her and his triumph over their enemies all raised him to an unattainable level of white hot desire. Her yielding need fanned the flame even higher. Sam slid his hands over the smoothness of her back and hips, savoring the sensations, the passion, the building power of the moment.

They fell on the bed in a tangle of arms and legs as they fumbled to remove Sam's trousers. Then they were naked, clutched in a tight embrace. At once he felt both her softness and her strength and he knew without any doubt that she was his. As he hovered over her, moving slowly toward the consummation of their mutual desire, Katrina whispered, "I am ready, my love. I am ready for you."

Chapter 20

The landing gear of the Gulfstream G5 folded neatly into its belly as the sleek white airplane ascended rapidly from the private airport on the outskirts of Las Vegas. Crossing over the divided highway just past the end of the runway, the airplane banked to the east, giving passing cars an excellent view of the world's most luxurious business aircraft. At just over thirty-five million dollars, it was also one of the most expensive.

Vladimir Svetlanikoff settled into the rich leather cushions of a couch in the main passenger cabin, enjoying the acceleration of the takeoff. Beams of morning sunlight drifted across the walls of the plush cabin as the aircraft banked toward the morning sun. *A good decision,* he thought, *to purchase this aircraft.* It made him feel successful. Flying in the Gulfstream seemed to calm the insecurities and unruly fears that were his constant companions. Particularly during takeoff, Svetlanikoff could imagine that the rush of acceleration was propelling him away from all of his troubles and anxieties, and for a time, while the plane was airborne, he could imagine never returning to the world below. He would envision soaring endlessly from nowhere to nowhere until finally, the aircraft began to descend and the demons of his world invariably began to show their ugly faces again. He would have no choice, then, but to return to his position as the unchallenged leader of an immense international criminal organization with its roots in Moscow.

In recent years, Svetlanikoff had made a number of changes designed to reduce his vulnerability and engender a new aura of respectability. Taking up residence in Nevada, he had in effect purchased U.S. citizenship under an obscure immigration law that allowed residency status to be obtained by foreign nationals who invested half a million dollars or more in a U.S. business enterprise that created a number of new jobs. That had been easy. His first small casino had resulted in permanent residency. Then, through generous funding of a private university, he had obtained an undergraduate degree and later an honorary doctorate in business administration. Shortly thereafter, he was awarded dual citizenship. The Russian mobster relished the fact that he could manipulate the U.S. government as easily as he manipulated the minions of his criminal empire.

None of his efforts to alter his identity, however, diminished the fact that he was a Muscovite by birth and a preeminent boss of the Russian Mafia by trade. His work demanded frequent trips to Russia to maintain the complex relationships that were the foundation of his empire. Luckily, the new specially equipped aircraft made the flight from Nevada to Moscow nonstop. At times, Svetlanikoff dreamed of simply retiring in the States. It was only a dream, of course, and he knew it. No matter how much money he made from the illicit activities of his organization, he could never escape the Byzantine morass of criminal obligations. Relaxing his guard would lead to certain death. It was a fundamental rule of the jungle that those who grew complacent and allowed their support base to weaken would be attacked and brought down by even more predatory members of the criminal underworld, many of whom would welcome an opportunity to take revenge on him. The only choice, of course, was to be constantly vigilant and always to be stronger, richer, and faster than the pack. And this Svetlanikoff had managed to do very well for more than fifteen years, a feat unparalleled in the post-communist Russian crime world.

The son of a member of the communist party in Moscow, Svetlanikoff had been inducted into the Russian political aristocracy at an early age. As an ambitious young man with an excellent window on the world of politics, Svetlanikoff soon concluded that wealth and fear were the prime ingredients required to achieve a position of power. Intelligent enough to recognize the risks of entering politics in a Russia that was rapidly degenerating into chaos, and far too ambitious and impatient to work though the painful early growth of democracy, Svetlanikoff made a conscious decision to work outside the system.

With little more than his wits, some political contacts, a total disregard for the law, and a strict Machiavellian business philosophy, Svetlanikoff deliberately set out to develop his own personal base of wealth and power through criminal activities. Moscow proved to be a fertile field. From a small smuggling operation, Svetlanikoff and his partners rapidly progressed to selling Russian military arms that they procured through corrupt contacts to cash-rich international terrorist organizations. Pilfering Russian government assets was a mainstay of his business for years. Later, distribution of drugs, prostitution, and protection proved to be lucrative endeavors.

More recently, however, Svetlanikoff had sought ways to legitimize and protect his immense wealth, while still increasing it. He had turned his considerable intellect to studying the West and developing ways to secure and buttress his position. The incredible wealth of the Nevada gambling industry and the free-wheeling culture of that state encouraged him to quietly take steps to establish a beachhead in Las Vegas.

He was not in the least intimidated by the American criminal element that was well-entrenched in Nevada. Although his business and theirs had developed on different continents, the basic philosophies and rules of the game were the same. Devoting his wealth and human resources to the development of a new power base in Nevada, he planned to apply the same tactics that had made him one of the most feared men in the Russian underworld.

As his gleaming white aircraft reached altitude, he sipped espresso from a gold-rimmed porcelain demitasse and considered his position. It would be necessary to remove one of his new business partners soon to inaugurate his reign of power in America. Fundamental to Svetlanikoff's philosophy was the premise that wealth and fear together are the prime motivators in the world of organized crime, and neither element works without the other. The wealthy pay no deference to wealth alone, nor do criminals fear common thugs, no matter how violent or brutal. Only the combination of ruthless violence and great wealth could generate true power. His recent activities in Nevada, including his purchase of the Gulfstream with cash, had demonstrated his wealth, but the Americans knew of his ruthlessness only by reputation. It was time to prove himself.

Svetlanikoff thought briefly of some of the men who had been subjects of similar demonstrations in the past—a Turkish smuggler who failed to deliver the promised goods, a Russian competitor in the drug trade who rashly tried to expand his territory, a bodyguard who had fallen asleep on the job. Svetlanikoff usually had a reason to kill. It was not good for business to kill indiscriminately. But sometimes, it did not take much of a reason. Svetlanikoff recalled the Palestinian terrorist who had done nothing more than complain angrily about the quality of the arms he had purchased. Svetlanikoff had dispatched him on general principles, believing the man to be an odious individual whose insulting and derisive tone was intolerable. Generally, each and every execution was carefully planned and imaginatively gruesome, designed to deliver maximum notoriety. There was little practical benefit in exterminating vermin unless it put fear into the hearts of anyone who might choose to challenge him in the future.

Svetlanikoff knew that it would be necessary to kill, and kill again, simply to ensure that his power base was strong. So it had been, and so it would always be, for a man who had chosen to pursue vast wealth and power at all costs. He would be plagued by demons through all his days. And yet, he was satisfied with the course he had chosen so many years ago. The pressures of the job were great, but the rewards were truly incredible. Few heads of state flew in a sparkling new aircraft equal to his, nor could they boast a team of commandos better trained or better equipped than the group of hand-picked mercenaries who were presently drinking coffee in the aft cabin of the aircraft. Svetlanikoff felt certain that his men were equal to any crack team of Special Forces in the world. Again, Svetlanikoff felt a thrill of satisfaction, knowing that his new aircraft and the elite fighting force he commanded represented the epitome of power. He had reached the pinnacle of success.

His moment of self-satisfaction did not last long. When the plane began its slow descent, his immediate problem resurfaced. It was not a big problem, but an annoyance. He had ordered Karmakov to deal with a petty politician who opposed their plans, but Karmakov and his bumbling bodyguards had failed. Then a woman operative he had sent from Las Vegas to complete the job had also failed. Svetlanikoff was not accustomed to failure. Assassination was so simple in Russia. There was little need to create a diversion or to establish an alibi. The chance of a genuine investigation of a murder was small, and any investigation that was initiated would end up in a dusty file drawer of some bureaucrat on Svetlanikoff's payroll. America was different from Russia in many ways, but not all that different. He did not understand their repeated failures.

Considering this matter, Svetlanikoff realized he still had a lot to learn. For example, why was this particular public servant unwilling to reap the rewards of his office? In most of the world, provincial politicians were not well-paid and they used the influence of their offices to supplement their meager incomes. Huntington had assured Svetlanikoff that this tradition was alive and well in his state and that they would have no trouble obtaining the necessary approvals for the project. Huntington had been wrong, and he and Karmakov had both failed to solve the problems arising from their miscalculations. Someone would have to pay for their mistakes. Svetlanikoff saw before him an excellent opportunity to demonstrate his lack of tolerance for incompetence.

He poured another cup of steaming espresso and considered who would pay the price, and how. Karmakov's failures certainly merited his removal and his life was of no consequence, but for his musical ability. As a patron of the fine arts, Svtlanikoff had first met Karmakov in the cultural circles of Moscow. Attracted to the world of wealth and intrigue that Svetlanikoff inhabited, Karmakov had become increasingly involved in the business. Svetlanikoff knew him to be an intolerable egomaniac whose considerable musical talent was equaled, if not exceeded, by his bloodlust. He deserved to be extinguished, but as a true patron of the arts, Svetlanikoff was loathe to execute an accomplished Russian musician unless absolutely necessary.

Huntington was another obvious target, but he was also Svetlanikoff's primary contact in the state and the ostensible sponsor of the Greeenleaf Project. Millions of dollars had already been invested in Huntington and his project, which would undoubtedly be lost if Huntington was removed. Svetlanikoff was ambivalent. The matter of an execution would require careful consideration, but there must certainly be retribution for incompetence. His reputation demanded it.

When news of the troublesome failures of his operatives reached him, Svetlanikoff had decided to go to this province himself. It would do his men good to get out of the training hall, plus it provided him an opportunity to get out of Las Vegas. It would give him a chance to make a surprise visit on Huntington and ensure that the project remained on track.

Svetlanikoff's face hardened at the thought of Huntington. The man was getting on his nerves. At their first meeting, arranged by Karmakov, Huntington had been businesslike, short and to the point. He had proposed to join forces to develop a new power plant project. Pointing out dozens of ways to skim money from the public, which appealed to Svetlanikoff, Huntington had explained how the project would provide the perfect vehicle for laundering funds from other business activities, while assuring that all of the necessary permits and political approvals would be easily obtained. Obviously, he had seriously miscalculated.

In addition to showing incompetence in dealing with his own local authorities, Huntington had developed an overbearing demeanor in their last few conversations, failing to show Svetlanikoff the deference he deserved and required. Huntington appeared to have forgotten who was the master and who was the servant. Svetlanikoff considered whether Huntington's mistakes would prove fatal, and if so, what the repercussions to the project would be.

"Mr. Svetlanikoff, you may wish to buckle your seatbelt. We will be landing in approximately five minutes," the pilot announced over the intercom. "Your car is waiting at the airport."

Although he ignored the pilot's suggestion, the interruption helped him come to a quick decision. It was time for decisive action that would not soon be forgotten.

* * * * *

Huntington peered through the small, diamond-shaped panes of an old leaded glass window that overlooked the sweeping driveway of the country club. The room where they waited was of the same gothic decor as the club's dramatic vestibule. Heavy oak beams dominated the walls and ceiling. Ornate leaded glass windows punctuated the grey granite exterior walls on either side of a large stone fireplace. A deep oriental rug graced the aging hardwood floors. The room could have easily been located in a medieval castle or the Kremlin.

He looked at his watch for the third time in ten minutes, then abruptly turned toward Bandini, who was sprawled in an overstuffed chair against the wall. Olsen was seated in a straight-backed chair near the door.

Huntington cleared his throat, spat into the fireplace, then said, "Half an hour late. I shouldn't put up with this crap."

Bandini eyed his partner, but remained silent, wondering how long he would wait for the Russian. Huntington was not known for his patience and his fragile relationship with Svetlanikoff was strained. But there was much at stake. How would the Russian react if they were gone when he arrived? Was his lateness an intentional tactic designed to establish control? Bandini's active mind turned over every implication of the situation as he rose and moved toward the window. "Maybe we should give him a few more minutes, considering. Given the situation, he's probably not in a very generous mood."

"What's *he* got to worry about?" Huntington snapped. "We're the ones with our necks on the line. Who's going to pay the price if this gets exposed? Not the Russians, you can bet on that."

"Speak of the devil," Bandini replied, watching three men step out of a limousine under the portico. "There's Svetlanikoff with a couple of his trained Dobermans. Or should I say Russian wolfhounds?"

Olsen rose and slid his hand into his jacket, fingering the grip of his Glock automatic. Huntington caught the movement. "Keep your hand out of your jacket, boy, if you want to keep breathing. Don't give them an excuse. Now go greet our guests. Show 'em the way in."

Opening the double doors of the gothic room, Olsen stepped into the hall just as Svetlanikoff rounded the corner with one of his men in the lead and one at his side. Olsen stepped forward to greet the three and raised one corner of his mouth in a half-smile, but he quickly dropped his weak attempt at cordiality when it was not returned by the grim Russians. A muscular block of a man with short black hair and a jagged scar on his forehead uttered one word, "Huntington." Without speaking, Olsen turned and tipped his head toward the open door, then walked through it.

The scar-faced man entered the room behind Olsen, followed by his associate, an equally imposing figure, but much taller and with a lighter complexion and short blonde hair. Huntington and Bandini stood silently in front of the fireplace while the Russians scanned the room with handheld devices that resembled small cameras. Scar-face raised his eyes from the screen on the back of his device and looked at Olsen. Without moving his eyes from Olsen's face, he stepped forward, slipped his hand in Olsen's jacket, and withdrew the Glock. He stepped back and a smile spread across his face as he slipped the new gun into his waistband. In Russian, he declared, "this place is now clean." Svetlanikoff finally stepped into the room.

Huntington and Bandini watched the brief search and disarming of Olsen with little interest, having met with Svetlanikoff on previous occasions. They were well aware of his capabilities and knew that it would be useless to attempt to resist his security measures. Also, it was important to foster an impression of trust, regardless of their true opinion of the Russian.

When Svetlanikoff entered, Huntington greeted him with an appraising stare and an offered handshake. The Russian met Huntington's eyes and paused, as though reading his thoughts, before taking his outstretched hand. He released Huntington's hand almost immediately and made a cursory nod toward Bandini, who had risen and was standing by the conference table. He ignored Olsen entirely.

"I trust your flight was comfortable," Huntington said, attempting to open the meeting on an easy note.

"The flight was fine. In fact, it was very expertly handled by my own personal operatives, who do not make mistakes."

The scar-faced guard casually turned his head to the side and scratched his jaw with his forefinger, staring at Olsen, who stood against the wall, frowning.

"In fact, mistakes are not tolerated in my organization," Svetlanikoff continued in a louder voice. He turned to stare at Huntington.

Huntington stiffened, unconsciously responding to the challenge in the mobster's voice. "Mistakes are not tolerated in my organization either. And if you are implying that the current situation is our fault, you'd better think again."

Bandini winced and cast a secretive, sidelong glance at Svetlanikoff, who remained calm, his expression inscrutable.

"Then let us review the facts. I was told that you have ruled this state without challenge for forty years, yet today, a young politician and his lawyer friend continuously defy all of your power, and you are unable to either control or extinguish them. You have proven yourself impotent."

With immense effort, Huntington controlled his temper. His granite face revealed no emotion, but his eyes were piercing. "It was your boy, Karmakov, who failed in his mission. Your second operative, the woman, also failed. I thought you said that your operatives were the best in the world."

"And your guards? They could not keep a dying man from walking out of a hospital, and they were unable to capture him after he escaped! But none of this unpleasantness and publicity would have been necessary, if you had not overestimated your ability to control the situation from the beginning, a dangerous miscalculation."

Bandini quickly stepped forward, interposing himself between Huntington and Svetlanikoff to deflect the building animosity. "Gentlemen, let us refrain from recriminations," Bandini said formally, hoping to raise the tenor of the conversation to a more professional level. "We are business partners in this venture and we must work together in order to achieve our mutual objectives."

Both men turned their knife-edged hostility toward Bandini, who visibly shrank under the power of their combine glares. Yet he persisted, affecting a relaxed demeanor while raising an outstretched hand toward each man. "There is no point in quarreling among ourselves, my friends and comrades. There are always challenges in business. When this small problem is resolved, we will toast to our remarkable success."

Bandini's smooth tone seemed to soothe the hostility. Both men knew this was not the time or place for a confrontation. Svetlanikoff spoke, nodding toward the heavy walnut conference table. "Be seated please, gentlemen, and we will develop a new plan of action. This time, with my personal supervision, the operation will not fail."

As Huntington and Bandini took their places at the table, Bandini's cell phone rang. Opening it, he listened for several seconds, and then with a brusque "okay," he snapped it shut. "It seems that Littlehawk and the girl are headed this way," he said with grim satisfaction. "One of Barton's men was able to intercept a message from Littlehawk. What a fool he is, to come back here…"

"Do not continue to underestimate your adversaries," Svetlanikoff snapped sharply, cutting off Bandini. "Your disregard for your opponents' intelligence and abilities has already cost us dearly. Your vanity has caused the current situation. From this point forward, I will direct this operation. With luck, the project will be saved and you will be spared from personally bearing the full responsibility for a major loss."

Bandini shifted in his chair and licked his lips, while Huntington stared grimly at a point on the conference table, his arms folded across his broad chest, both men accepting the direct rebuke without comment.

"First, we must prevent further public exposure of the situation," Svetlanikoff said, seating himself at the head of the conference table. "There has been far too much publicity already, thanks to the melodramatic nature of Karmakov, who thought an assassination at the ballet would be most effective. I will deal with his stupidity separately."

Bandini swallowed hard as he silently recalled outlining for Karmakov his brilliant and dramatic plan to eliminate Angelletti and frame Littlehawk for the murder. He knew at the time that the drama of the murder at the ballet would appeal to Karmakov. Bandini had congratulated himself on disposing of the opposition in a clever and entertaining way, while putting all the risk on the Russians. Kidnapping the ballerina had been a bonus for Karmakov, to encourage him to adopt the plan. Apparently, Karmakov had not shared with Svetlanikoff the fact that the plan had been Bandini's from the outset.

"Second, we must quickly find and eliminate Angelletti, Littlehawk and the ballerina," Svetlanikoff said. "At this time, we do not know where Angelletti is. But we have been given a piece of luck. Now that Littlehawk has returned to this area, he will undoubtedly lead us to Angelletti, if your men do not lose Littlehawk again as they have done in the past."

"Littlehawk will not go to the authorities because he is still wanted for murder and several other charges. But if, for some reason, he does decide to surrender, your contacts among the authorities will prevent him from disclosing what he knows." Svetlanikoff again stared at Huntington, who returned his stare coldly.

"Mistakes have been made," Huntington interrupted, "but the blame is not ours. Your people got us into this mess. But I intend to get us out. My power in the police and judiciary is strong."

"So you have said. Now you have the chance to prove it. It is imperative that none of our adversaries ever to talk with the authorities. Therefore, I will dispatch two members of my personal contingent to handle the situation." He waved for the tall blonde bodyguard to come forward. "Now, Mr. Bandini, if you will be kind enough to arrange a rendezvous between our respective forces, we will assume control of this part of the operation." With a glance toward Huntington, Bandini motioned to Olsen, who moved to confer with Svetlanikoff's bodyguard.

"Finally, there is the project itself," Svetlanikoff concluded. "I will personally inspect the project site today, with your attendance. We are expecting the first delivery of cargo very soon."

"Cargo?" Huntington exclaimed, rising from his seat at the table. "But that part of the plan was deleted! We agreed months ago that there would be no dumping of toxic waste anywhere in this state!"

Svetlanikoff rose slowly, standing directly across the table from Huntington and fixing him with a cold stare as he flatly declared, "The plans have changed. We will receive the first shipment at the site tonight."

"You lousy son-of-a-bitch!" Huntington shouted, and instantly the scar-faced man appeared with a silenced pistol in hand, cocked and ready to fire, mere inches from Huntington's head. No one in the room moved. Seconds passed. Finally, Huntington again said to Svetlanikoff, "You lousy son-of-a-bitch," but this time he spoke with an air of resignation as he slowly sank into his chair.

* * * * *

The six men climbed into the stretch limousine in front of the club with Svetlanikoff in the front with his driver, his back to the bulletproof glass that divided the limo. Huntington, Bandini, and Olsen sat uncomfortably on the backseat facing two of Svetlanikoff's mercenaries. Half an hour from the club, they were bumping down a dirt road twenty-five miles west of the city and south of Skiatook Lake, on the southern edge of Osage County.

The limo turned off the dirt road and passed through an open metal gate, then drove another three hundred yards through a field overgrown with weeds, then through a second gate in a new eight-foot chain link fence that was topped with barbed wire. After a brief stop at a guard shack, it proceeded up a dirt track that climbed an immense mound of excavated rock and earth, finally arriving at a high vantage point from which the entire construction site could be viewed. The men piled out of the limo and climbed three steps onto a wooden observation deck perched on the north rim of a vast excavation.

The excavation was more than five hundred feet long and equally wide, and deep enough to hide a three story building. An earth ramp cut into the wall of the pit on the east end provided the only access to the bottom. A line of bulldozers, loaders, and enormous off-road dump trucks were parked at the west end. From their vantage point, the parked construction equipment, concrete mixing plant, construction office, and equipment storage shed in the bottom of the pit looked like toys.

Bandini had seen the site several months earlier, when a company in which he and Huntington owned interests had first acquired the old rock quarry. He had since developed a corporate structure that would prevent any identification of the site with its beneficial owners. As he studied the project site, Bandini noticed several changes. He nudged Huntington and pointed toward a series of trenches in the northwest corner of the excavation. "Those must be the footings for the foundation of the cooling tower. Zapata didn't slow down the construction any, just to wait for the commission to issue an order to proceed."

"Well they haven't poured any concrete yet, but it looks like they're ready to start, just as soon as the order is signed and filed. They didn't expect any delays in the approval of the project," Huntington said dryly.

Svetlanikoff stood within earshot behind Huntington and Bandini, flanked by his two bodyguards. "It will be necessary to pour some concrete very soon," the Russian said, "after the cargo is unloaded and placed in the excavation. Those footings you pointed out should accommodate one hundred drums. I assume that you will furnish a discreet crew to place the concrete in the foundation."

"Our crews are discreet," Bandini responded, "but we never planned to bury hundreds of drums of toxic waste in those footings, Svetlanikoff. It could undermine the foundation of the plant. You really should reconsider this. The deeper excavations for the larger buildings may penetrate the aquifer that flows under this area. There's no telling where those toxic wastes will show up in a few years."

"Relax, Mr. Bandini," Svetlanikoff said. "The consequences of pollution leaking from this site could not be any worse that the unfortunate results of the Chernobyl meltdown, from which our country is still recovering. Power companies, oil and chemical companies all over the world have a longstanding tradition of dumping toxic wastes. We are just profiting from a common practice of capitalists worldwide."

Svetlanikoff paused and looked directly at Bandini, who appeared ill. "Besides, the effects of this dumping will probably not be detected until you are a grandfather...if you live that long. By then, you will undoubtedly be retired and living happily in some tropical paradise far from this place."

Bandini remained silent, realizing too late the deadly results of the game they were playing with the Russian mob. Until this moment, it had never occurred to Bandini that there was a possibility that he and Huntington would lose control of the situation. Yet Svetlanikoff had seized the initiative, leaving them little opportunity to control the situation or affect the outcome. It dawned on him that they could be nearing the end of their usefulness to Svetlanikoff.

Huntington, who had been uncharacteristically quiet, ended his silence by addressing the Russian forcefully. "It's time we have an understanding, Svetlanikoff. This is *my* project, not yours. *I* will control it. You've provided some funding for this project, and as it turns out, little else that we could not have done without you. This is *my* state, not yours. If I say this project stops, not another shovel of dirt will be turned until I say so. Without me, your investment will be worthless. Do you understand?"

Huntington's tone was superficially commanding, but the usual ring of absolute conviction was missing. Bandini cringed and squinted in anticipation of a violent response, but Svetlanikoff only smiled slightly and regarded Huntington, who was staring out across the excavation.

"My friend, your time has passed," the Russian began in a patronizing tone. "I am sure that you have had an illustrious career and many brilliant victories. Now that time is over. From this moment forward, you will do as I say, or you and all of those who are close to you will die. Your attitude has not been helpful of late. Humility is a virtue. You must accept the fact that you are no longer in command."

Bandini watched Huntington closely. His partner's granite face bore no visible expression. With tight lips, he stood like a stone statue staring into space. Huntington clearly knew that Svetlanikoff had the ability, the capacity, and the willingness to dispatch them both on the spot. All that Svetlanikoff needed was the inclination. Yet Huntington had been willing to make this desperate gamble, this pure bluff, to assuage his stinging ego. Bandini wondered whether his partner was deluded enough to believe that he could intimidate the Russian Mafioso. Bandini had no such illusion.

"Now it is your time to decide," Svetlanikoff continued quietly. "You will agree to obey my orders precisely, or there will be more than toxic waste buried under the foundation of this project."

To Bandini, Huntington seemed to shrink visibly. He turned without another word, and with downcast eyes, he slowly descended the steps of the viewing platform and climbed into the backseat of the limousine alone.

Chapter 21

Jesse Jericho leaned back in an old metal lawn chair, hands clasped behind his head, worn cowboy boots crossed at the ankle, staring at a wasp nest hanging from the eve. During the past hour, he had finished reading the new Trade-a-Plane and tidied up the small, tan brick building that was the center of operations of the Hominy Airfield. It was a little cooler outside, and Jesse sat in his lawn chair just outside the open door, idly listening to the sporadic radio transmissions of a private pilot shooting his seventh touch-and-go at the deserted airfield. Before the day was over, Jesse would probably pump a tank or two of gas for afternoon joyriders flying their small planes around the lake area, and not do much else. And that suited Jesse just fine.

Hominy Airfield, like several other small airfields in the state, had been built as a pilot training and repair facility during WWII. Just forty-five miles west of Tulsa's International Airport and the Air Force operations there, it had once been an active training field for Air Force pilots. Now, in addition to two huge abandoned hangers, Hominy Airfield boasted nothing more than a long concrete runway and virtually no air traffic, which made it perfect for training local private pilots. Occasionally, a business jet would drop in for a few touch-and-goes and make Jesse's day. Otherwise, the place was pretty quiet.

"Hey, Jesse…Jesse, are you there?" the radio crackled though an ancient speaker mounted under the eve, next to the wasp nest.

Jesse let the old metal chair rock forward and slowly got to his feet. Stepping through the open door, he hit a button on the base of a large antique microphone. "This here's Jesse, who wants to know?"

"Jesse, this is Sam."

"Izzat Sam Littlehawk? What the heck you doin' up there, Sambo? Yer bird's still parked over in the hangar! I jest seen it there!"

"I'm coming in with a couple of friends, Jesse. They're going to drop me off and I'll hitch a ride out to the ranch. We'll be there in ten minutes. Do you suppose you could call the ranch for me and tell Danny or Red to come pick me up? And tell 'em to keep it quiet that I'm coming in, okay?"

"Why shore, Sam, no problem. I'll call 'em right now. And tell 'em to keep it quiet. Must be on some kind of a secret mission, huh?"

Sam paused for a second and then responded in a confidential tone. "Well, Jesse, no, it's…it's girl problems, you know?"

"No, I don't know, and I don't wanna know!" Jesse exclaimed. "Don't want to know about no girl problems. I *had* enough of them, thank *yew!* Just give me an old yeller dog any day. I'm gonna leave all of them wimmin problems to you city fellers. *Over and out!"*

* * * * *

Sam chuckled as the Cessna Citation began its final descent into Hominy Airfield. Jesse Jericho had taught Sam to fly in an ancient Luscombe while Sam was still in college. Jesse had always had an uncanny understanding of engines and mechanical devices of all kinds, but his understanding of the fairer sex was abysmally lacking. If Sam ever wanted to end one of Jesse's long-winded, one-sided conversations about some new aviation gizmo, there was an effective method—just raise the subject of women. But Sam always enjoyed Jesse's country humor and his priceless tidbits on every aspect of aviation.

The Cessna slipped over the threshold of the runway and settled lightly into a perfect landing. "Go ahead and taxi her over to the terminal, Sam," the pilot said.

"Thanks for letting me fly the right seat, Ross. That was fun. The Cherokee Nation has a sweet little aircraft here. And thanks for helping us out on such short notice."

"You've helped us enough, Sam. You just call if you ever need another ride."

Sam guided the aircraft to within a hundred feet of the small brick terminal and cut the engines. A couple of minutes later, he opened the door of the jet and extended its short stairway to the tarmac. Katrina descended the steps, followed closely by Sam. The pilot appeared at the door and waved.

"I'll drop Dave off in Tulsa. Good luck!"

"Thanks again, Ross. Hope to see you soon!" Sam waved, then he and Katrina walked quickly to the terminal. By the time they reached the building, the engines were spooling again and the sleek business jet was already beginning to taxi away.

Jesse was standing in front of the building, a broad smile on his thin, weathered face. His worn jeans and tattered denim cowboy shirt blended well with his surroundings, which had changed very little in fifty years. He grabbed Sam's hand and gave it a vigorous shake.

"Man, you do like to travel in style!" Jesse said in a slow drawl as they stepped inside the terminal. "I never know what to expect next from you, Sambo. That's some heavy iron! Bet you was flyin' the right seat, too."

Sam smiled and winked at his friend. They both knew that Sam wasn't certified in the Cessna, but his piloting was safe enough, with Ross in the left seat watching closely. "Jesse, meet Kate," Sam said, wrapping his arm around Katrina's shoulder. "She's a friend of mine."

Jesse turned his wide grin toward Katrina and said with deep conviction, "Well, any friend of Sam Littlehawk is truly a friend of mine, be he man or beast!"

As soon as the words fell out of his mouth, a crimson blush began to steal across Jesse's face, starting with his ears and continuing until his weathered face was deep red from the collar up. He began to stutter. "Oh, well...I mean...I didn't mean that like it sounded...I didn't mean nothin' by that...I just meant to say...say that...Oh, shoot!" Jesse turned away for a second, and then awkwardly reached for Katrina's hand and blurted, "It's real nice to meet you, ma'am."

Katrina smiled demurely and replied, "I am very pleased to make your acquaintance, Jesse. Any friend of Sam's is also a friend of mine. Sam has told me that you are a good friend to his family."

"Well, thank you, ma'am. The Littlehawks, they're real fine folks."

Jesse smiled and nodded at Katrina, and then turned again to Sam with a look of disgust. "I don't know when I'm gonna learn to jest keep my big trap shut. Never fails. Anyway, y'all got no luggage? Red ought to be here any minute. Can I get you a Coke or something?"

"Thanks, Jesse, but I think I hear the pickup coming now," Sam replied. He moved to gain a better view and saw the old green pickup rolling down the gravel road to the terminal in a billowing cloud of dust. "Looks like our ride's here. Thanks for making the connection for us."

"No problem, Sam. Ma'am." Jesse tipped his old straw cowboy hat. "Sure was nice to meet you, Kate. And you, Sammy, you'd better get back over here and do some flyin' sometime soon. Your bird's all gassed up and rarin' to go."

"Thanks, Jesse. I'll be seeing you soon. Right now we've got some business to attend to. But don't worry, I'll get over here real soon."

As Katrina stepped out the door, Jesse slipped closer to Sam and took him by the elbow. "Uh, Sam, I didn't want to say nothing in front of the lady, but did you know that the cops are out lookin' for you? It was on the news and everything. Sounded pretty serious. Sure hope you know what yer getting into."

"So do I, Jesse. So do I."

"Well, if there's anything I kin do to help, you jest let me know."

"Right now, Jesse, the only thing you can do is forget you saw us, okay?"

"Hell, I ain't seen nothin' all day, but a couple of buzzards," he replied with a wink.

"Thanks, Jesse," Sam said as he slipped out the door.

Jesse followed Sam outside and watched as the old green pickup pulled away from the terminal and bumped down the gravel road. When it turned out of the airfield gate, Jesse eased into his lawn chair and leaned back, crossing his ankles, just as the Cessna lifted off and banked to the east.

* * * * *

Red, Sam, and Katrina bumped down the rough gravel road of the airfield in the cab of a well-restored sixties vintage Ford pickup that Red cared for like an only child. The truck's windows were open and the warm summer air carried the smell of freshly mown hay, which was lying in windrows on both sides of the road, soon to be baled. Sam inhaled deeply, and silently he gave thanks for their safe return to familiar territory, his ancestral homeland. Here, Sam felt grounded and free of doubts.

"Where to, boss?" Red asked as they neared the airfield gate.

"Just take the old highway, Red. We'll drive by the lake. How have things been at the ranch since I left?"

"Well, the boss lady's been a little off her feed since you been gone, and Miss Emmie's sure wonderin' where you are. Told her you had to go away on business and we didn't know exactly when you'd be back. I reckon that was the truth, but it didn't set too well with that little filly, after the ruckus in the barn and the Sheriff comin' and all. You know, it'd sure do 'em both a sight of good, if you was to come on home. But I reckon you got other plans." The grizzled ranch hand glanced at Sam and at the same time took in Katrina, who was sitting quietly between them in the small cab. Red was a little rough from life on the range and not a big talker, but he was quite perceptive.

Sam dodged Red's question and answered with another question. "Do you have any protection at the ranch? Has Sheriff Fielding kept anyone there?"

"We been pretty much on our own since you left. Sheriff said he's just a phone call away. But everything's been quiet. And me and Danny's there."

"You two staying close to the house?"

"We been keepin' an eye on things, day and night. You know Danny, he sleeps like a cat. These warm nights, he's been sleepin' in the hammock on the front porch. Ain't nothin' could get past him. And I'm just across the road at my place."

Sam nodded, having complete confidence in the two ranch hands that he'd known most of his life. They were both cut from the same cloth—men who had chosen to live close to the land, forsaking the attractions of the modern world for a lifestyle that satisfied the spirit. They were men of honor with solid convictions and with deep loyalty to the Littlehawk family, for whom they had worked for many years. Both were quite capable with a rope and a gun. Some would say that their working ranch hand lifestyle was an anachronism, but they couldn't care less. Red and Danny lived the life they loved and they were good at it. Sam knew that Sheriff Fielding could not provide any better protection for his family than they could.

"That's good, Red. I guess you'll have to help us out a little longer, then this will be over."

"Figured as much," Red said. "You can't come home till you get a noose on them sorry polecats that whacked Tony. You just let me know what I can do to help."

"You're doing just what I need for you to do. Keep a close eye on Faye and Emmie and the ranch until I finish this job."

They puttered slowly along a two lane country road bordering the blue-green waters of Skiatook Lake for half an hour, then passed over the dam. Another few miles and they crossed the interstate highway, then continued east on a little used country road that would eventually lead to the international airport. Twenty minutes later, Sam directed Red to an access road that rounded the north end of the airport, then on toward the American Airlines hangar. Finally, the old pickup arrived at the guard shack in front of the massive hangar, and Sam hopped out.

It was mid-afternoon, and just as Sam had hoped, the guard on duty was the same man to whom he had tossed his car keys days before, just before his arrest. The guard looked up from his work as Sam approached the guard shack door and recognition dawned on his face. He grinned from ear to ear and pointed at the BMW roadster that was parked in one of the spaces along the fence.

"Man, I didn't know if I'd ever see you again, after what they did to you last week!" the guard said, peering at the fading bruises and cuts on Sam face. "You don't look all that much worse for the wear though, considering."

Sam grinned back. "Oh, I guess it seemed a lot worse than it really was. I just got bloodied up a bit, and a few bruises." Sam consciously suppressed the urge to rub some of the aching muscles that covered most of his body.

The guard shook his head doubtfully. "Well, I'm sure glad it wasn't me that state trooper decided to pound to a pulp. I thought most of the cops around here were pretty mellow, but you sure drew a bad one. I saw the whole thing. You didn't do anything to deserve that beating. That one dude just beat the crap out of you, while the others watched. It happened real fast. Maybe they didn't have time to stop him."

Sam cracked a smile and shook his head. "Don't remind me, I'm trying to forget it. Wasn't my best day. Say, did you get any use out of my car?"

"Man, that is a great little buggy!" the guard responded. "When the cops dragged you out of here, there was so much commotion, I guess no one ever thought about your car still being here." The guard looked a little sheepish. "You said you'd be back for it and I could drive it, so I did just what you said. I took good care of it, too. It's all polished up and full of gas. I guess you want it back now, huh?"

"Yeah, sorry I can't leave her with you for another week, friend, but I've got to have some wheels."

"Well, that sure is a set of wheels alright! Thanks for letting me drive her."

The guard stepped into the guard shack momentarily to get the keys, then turned back to Sam. "I guess you've got things all squared up with the law then?"

"Yeah," Sam responded truthfully. "They took me straight to jail, but the Judge let me walk out a free man."

"Well, I still can't figure out why you'd want to test a new sports car by running it across the airport with a load of security guards and cops in tow. But then again, I didn't see that it was cause for a beating, either."

Sam reached into his jeans pocket, pulled out a fifty dollar bill and handed it to the guard. "Thanks for taking such good care of my car, friend. Maybe we can just keep this between us, okay? This never happened and you never saw me before, right?"

The guard took the bill and poked it into his pocket. "What car?" he said with a wink as he stepped back into the guard house.

Sam opened the passenger door of the truck for Katrina to get out. Red cranked the engine over. "Sam, you know they'll spot you in that car. It's not safe."

"Don't worry, Red, I'm all over that one already. You just get back to the ranch and let Faye and Emmie know that you talked with me and I'm fine. Tell them I'm staying at the conference for a few more days and I'll call them later."

Sam slammed the door of the old pickup, then stepped back and waved as Red puttered out of the parking lot.

* * * * *

Half an hour later and three miles away, Sam and Katrina slid into the luxurious leather seats of a new Lincoln Town Car. "Thanks, Carlos," Sam waved to his friend, the car dealer from whom he had purchased a string of high performance sports cars over the past several years. "We'll take good care of it."

"Don't worry about the car, Sam, you just have fun with it," Carlos said with a strong Mexican accent. "I'll keep your car in the lot out back. And mum's the word." Carlos touched his lips and smiled as Sam rolled up the tinted, bulletproof windows and backed the car out. Carlos and Sam had agreed that the sleek black Lincoln was the safest car on the lot, under the circumstances, and the most inconspicuous. It had been a special order for a South American businessman Carlos knew and it was built like a tank. While it was on order, the buyer had left the state for greener pastures, or perhaps safer ones.

"You have a lot of friends, Sam," Katrina said as they pulled into the street, "and they all seem to trust you without question. That says a lot."

"It helps to have friends," Sam agreed. "I've been blessed in that way. Now it's time to go check on another one."

* * * * *

The Lincoln rolled slowly along Swan Lake Drive and turned into the driveway of Doc Robins' residence. After parking behind the high masonry wall, he and Katrina walked to the porch and rang the doorbell.

In a moment, Doc Robins answered, clad in a blue terrycloth bathrobe and slippers. "Well, I've been wondering when you'd show up, sonny," the old doctor said. He pushed the screen door open and immediately led the way to the kitchen, talking as he went. "Seems like everyone's been lookin' for you, sonny. You still living on the dodge, are you?" He slowly twisted his neck and peered inquisitively at Sam over his heavy bifocals.

"Well, Doc," Sam replied, "I guess it would be best for all concerned if you didn't mention to anyone that we were here."

The old physician's face lit up. "Don't you worry, sonny, this isn't the first time I've treated outlaws. You know, I've stitched up a few wild hellions in my time! Did I ever tell you about the time I was down in Muskogee and ran into the Carson brothers? They were all shot up and hiding out in the Rogers Hotel.

Hell, that was nearly fifty years ago…"

Doc stopped in mid-sentence and mid-step, and turned again to peer at Sam. "How the hell did you two boys come to be outlaws, anyway? You were always good boys. And why don't you just turn yourselves in? It's pretty obvious even to an old geezer like me that you didn't try to kill Tony. They can't get you for murdering someone who's standing right in front of them, can they! He's not going to press any charges."

"Too much to explain right now, Doc. One day soon, though, we'll go fishing and I'll tell you the whole story. But not right now."

"Okay, Sam, don't worry about it. It's okay with me. Just keep me in the dark. Probably better that way anyhow. I don't need to know anything about your dealings, strange as they may be. I'm just here to tend to the wounded. I guess you two came to look in on Tony."

"How's he doing, Doc?"

"The boy's improving slowly, but it takes a while when you've been through all that he has. He's got a mighty strong constitution."

When they rounded the corner into the living room, Tony was already on his feet. His head was still bandaged and he looked pale, but he seemed steady enough.

"Oh, man, you two are a sight for sore eyes!" Tony said, embracing them. "Thank God you're both safe! When I had a chance to think about what happened last Saturday night, I thought Kate must have been kidnapped."

Katrina and Sam exchanged a glance. "Thank God for your recovery," she replied quickly. "When we saw you last, we thought you…that you were… dead."

Tony touched the bandage and winced. "I was *nearly* dead, Kate, more than once. But thanks to Sam's quick moves and Doc Robins' expert care, I dodged the bullet. I'm getting stronger every day. Right now, I'm chomping at the bit to get out of here so we can take on those two-bit crooks…" Tony took two quick breaths and his eyes rolled back involuntarily. He began to list to the side and Sam stepped in to catch him before he crumpled. Sam eased him to the couch where he lay breathing heavily, eyes closed.

Doc Robins checked Tony's pulse. "A little bit too much excitement all at once. That concussion, followed by a very narrow escape with arsenic poisoning, left him weak. I had his blood analyzed, anonymously, of course, and there were still traces of poison. The boy's still got a ways to go before he's completely out of the woods. I'd give him at least a few more days."

Sam nodded as Tony's eyes fluttered open again. "Whew," Tony said, "that was just a little intense. I still get that light show in my head when I get a little worked up. Guess maybe I'm not quite ready to jump back into the fight."

"Don't worry, Tony, we've got it under control," Sam assured him. "You just rest easy here and get better."

"Yeah, thanks, buddy," Tony muttered, his eyelids at half mast. "But don't you let those dirt bags get anywhere near Katrina. You stay with her."

"Don't worry about that, *amigo*. Now that we've got her back again, nothing's going to come between us."

Something in Sam's tone of voice caught Tony's attention. He took a long look at Sam and Katrina, standing close together. A light slowly dawned on him as his eyes moved from one to the other. "So that's the way it is," he said simply.

Katrina glanced up at Sam, who silently communicated with his friend through a smile that was both serene and gentle. "Yep. That's the way it is," he said.

Tony clucked and shook his head, looking at them both like school children caught playing hooky. "Well, now, wouldn't you just know it. Things never change. Give 'em an inch, and they'll take a mile, every time. Just let you two out of my sight for an instant and look what happens…" Suddenly, Tony's face brightened. "Say, does Karmakov know about this new development? Maybe now I'll drop down a notch or two on his hit list, and you, Sambo, will step into first place."

"I'm already in first place, my friend. Our Russian comrades are gunning for me big time. We've had a couple confrontations while you were peacefully napping on Doc's couch. Someday soon, we'll go…"

"I know, I know," Tony interrupted, "we'll go fishing and you'll tell me all about it."

"Yeah, but right now, I don't have time." Sam gripped Tony's shoulder. "You just rest easy, *amigo*, and get better fast. Soon enough, we're going to need your help."

Chapter 22

"It's a good thing my cell phone was still in the roadster," Sam said to Katrina as he pulled the Lincoln back onto Swan Lake Drive. Scrolling down to a familiar number, he punched the send button and said, "We're back in business!"

"What happens now, Sam?" Katrina asked.

"Since you and Tony are safe and secure, we can draw a bead on Huntington and his entourage and blow them out of the water."

"And Karmakov?"

"I hope that he's left the country for good, but if he hasn't, then I have some special plans for him. Plans that I'm sure he will appreciate."

Katrina winced at the thought of more violence, but then her expression gave way to one of defiant determination. She would not soon forget the torture that she had suffered at Karmakov's hands, his taunting voice and his cynical manipulation and physical abuse. She had finally seen his true nature, and she despised it. Any compassion or sympathy she may have once felt for him was eradicated in Florida. Now she held nothing but contempt for the depraved villian.

As Sam wheeled the Lincoln through the manicured gardens of Woodward Park, a voice crackled on the cell phone. "Sanders."

"Hi, Dave! Ready to go to work?"

"Work, work, work. That trip to Miami wasn't much of a tropical vacation. The only things I saw in Florida were alligators and rattlesnakes."

"I hope you aren't describing those show girls you were dancing with in the casino. Now that you mention it, I heard that you and a certain lovely Latin lady danced the last tango in South Beach."

"Well, I guess *that* night wasn't so bad, come to think of it."

"I thought so. So, are you ready to go to work?"

"Just promise me Tahiti when we get this caper wrapped up."

"Done! *Now* are you ready to go to work?"

"Let's do it."

"Meet me at the sundial in the Rose Garden in ten minutes." Sam snapped the cell phone shut. "Yeah!" he said with satisfaction. "We're finally getting somewhere!"

* * * * *

The shadows were lengthening, but the rays of the setting sun still lit the thousands of rose blossoms creating a breathtaking rainbow spectacle as Dave Sanders entered the gate of the Rose Garden. He walked quickly to the bronze sundial located in a small alcove built into a huge wall of climbing red roses. Sanders checked his watch against the sundial and found that they agreed, it was seven-fifteen. Then he spotted Sam and Katrina waiting on a stone bench nestled between two large, blooming magnolia trees nearby. They rose to meet him.

"I see that you two have managed to find another place as beautiful and fragrant as the tropical gardens in Florida," Sanders said, inhaling the pungent scents of the magnolias and roses.

"We've enjoyed a few minutes of peace, but there will be more time for that after we've removed my name from the FBI's Ten Most Wanted list," Sam replied.

"And judging from the look on your face, I'll bet you have some ideas for how to accomplish that."

"The only way to exonerate me of wrongdoing and make the world a safe place for us is to expose the true perpetrators and present proof of their criminal conduct. Which brings me back to where we left off four days ago—the backup disk, the one I gave you at the Cherry Street Connection. Did you ever figure out what happened to it? That disk contains all of the evidence we need. And Tony and I risked our necks to get it."

Sanders drew his lips back into a thin line and shook his head. "Disappeared from my desk, Sam. I was only gone for a couple of minutes. I thought Smithson might have picked it up thinking it was something else and he would return it, but no such luck. When I asked, he had no idea what I was talking about."

A shadow of doubt entered Sam's mind for an instant, but it disappeared as quickly as it had come. Dave was too good a cop and a true friend. He had nearly lost his life saving Katrina. He might have lost the disk by accident, but he would never have given it away, even if he did think that they were in over their heads. There had to be some other logical explanation. The obvious one was that Huntington had friends in the FBI. Smithson may have taken it and lied about it, or someone else could have lifted it from Dave's desk. In any case, it would be impossible to track.

"Don't worry about it, Dave. We have a pretty good idea what they're up to, so it shouldn't be too tough to compile enough evidence to make a case." Sam was not nearly as confident as he sounded. He knew that in truth, they were back to square one, without the hard evidence they needed. "At least we still have Tony's audiotape of Aberson." Sam grimaced as he remembered telling Tony that the audiotape was not nearly enough evidence.

"Maybe it's time to go to the U.S. Attorney. There is quite a story to tell, with the kidnapping and all. If you, Tony, Katrina and I all lay it on the line, they'll have to listen."

"But what solid evidence can we show them, Dave? Do you think our story alone would be enough to convince him to take on Huntington and other major vested interests in this state, without a shred of documentary evidence? Do you think the U.S. Attorney is going to make a frontal assault on Southwest Energy based on nothing more than our story, even if three witnesses corroborate it? Not a chance. I can't think of a quicker way to end a promising career as a prosecutor. And that's assuming that the U.S. Attorney isn't on Huntington's payroll, like the local District Attorney seems to be. Besides, there's not a judge in this state who would authorize a search warrant against Southwest Energy based on nothing more than talk."

Sanders hung his head, a morose look on his face. "I really blew it, Sam."

"Well, I should have made another backup before I gave you the disk, but things were getting pretty hot at that point, as I recall. No point in beating ourselves up over it."

Katrina had been admiring the aromatic red rose blossoms on the hedge and watching the sunset while the men talked, but she had been listening. Touching Sam's elbow, she said, "Did you just say that this backup disk was in the computer drive when you were online, and the data was being downloaded from a remote location?"

"That's what we think happened."

"Do you think that the computer you were using is still at the Cherry Street Connection?" Katrina asked intently.

Sam and Dave both looked at her. "I wonder what's going on behind those gorgeous brown eyes," Dave mused. "I don't have a clue, but I'm betting that she's onto something. The wheels are spinning."

"Maybe, or maybe not," Katrina said. "Can we go there?"

"Now that presents an interesting challenge," Sanders replied. "You two are still the hottest property in town, and Huntington's gang surely knows you're back. He has eyes everywhere. Even if they don't know you're here, they'll be looking for you, through their police contacts and their own forces. Then there are the legitimate law enforcement authorities looking for you, Sam, as a murder suspect, and you, Katrina, as a kidnap victim. Depending on who spots whom first, they might just shoot you on sight, or arrest you. Neither option sounds good."

"Then Sam and Katrina won't go anywhere," Sam interjected with a telltale glint in his eye. "Harry and Maud will go instead."

Dave regarded his friend skeptically, then grinned and shook his head. "What the hell. In for a penny, in for a pound, I always say. Come on down to my place. I've got everything you'll need."

* * * * *

An hour later, a portly fellow with longish grey hair, a bushy grey mustache and a noticeable limp escorted a matronly lady with pancake makeup and a pile of greying brown hair to a black Lincoln sedan parked on the street in front of a townhouse on Riverside Drive. After seeing his companion safely into the passenger seat and closing her door, the old gentleman limped slowly around the car and opened the driver's door. As he eased his tired old body slowly into the car seat, he glanced at the window of the townhouse and waved.

Minutes later, Harry and Maud Whistler tottered into the Cherry Street Connection and approached the clerk manning the desk.

"Good evening, folks," the young man greeted them. "How can I help you?"

Harry leaned heavily on his cane, cleared his throat, and addressed the clerk in a gruff voice. "We want to try out one of your computers, young man. Might want to buy one. We decided it's time we learn something about them, so we can talk to our grandkids. Seems like they're talking a foreign language these day, talking all this computer gibberish all the time. How about we try out that one right over there?" Sam pointed at the station that he and Dave Sanders had used.

The clerk glanced in the direction Sam had pointed and shook his head. "That workstation has been having some problems, sir. Perhaps you should try another machine."

"Oh, no, that one will be fine," Harry said, as he and his companion walked to the station against the far wall. "I'm sure there's something we can learn from it, since we really have to start from the very beginning."

"But sir, I don't think that machine will even boot up. Maybe you should try another one."

Harry had already turned on the computer and was pulling up another chair for Maud. The computer was whirring, but the screen was still blank. Then a text box popped up on the screen, declaring "fatal error."

Maud turned to the clerk and in a wavering, high-pitched voice asked, "Young man, are all of your computers networked to a server?"

"Yes ma'am. Uh, sir, that machine is not going to do anything for you at all. I'm telling you—ever since some guys were on it a few nights ago, it's been completely down. The technician hasn't been able to get it to come back up at all. We've ordered a new one, but it's not in yet."

"We will try another machine, young man, and thank you," Maud said. She slowly lowered herself onto the chair in front of the adjacent machine, dropping the last few inches with a little "*Ooof.*"

"You missed your calling, Kate, you should have been an actress," Sam whispered, as the clerk walked to the front of the café. "You will make a wonderful grandmother some day."

Katrina ignored the jibe as she booted the computer, quickly logged on and began exploring the network, testing access to the other computers, while Sam watched.

"You're pretty quick on that thing. I didn't know that you were such a techie."

"Dancing is not the only thing I do. I have been studying computer programming for years. It is fascinating and good information to know. Computers are the future."

"Do you really think you can recover the information?"

"There is a possibility," Katrina replied. "But I doubt that we can do it here. I think it will take more time than we have…But wait, what is this?"

Katrina scrolled through a list of files on the network server. "This system is well equipped. It appears that there is a tape backup running constantly on the network. If we are lucky, the system may have backed up your CD on a tape drive while it was being downloaded. Some of the new systems automatically copy any information that is accessed and downloaded from a remote location. If such a program is in operation here, your information could be in the tape drive."

Sam continued to watch the screen while Katrina accessed the tape drive and began to search by date and time of file creation. "Do you know what time you were here, and how the work station was identified?"

"Bingo!" Sam exclaimed a minute later, as Katrina scrolled through the files that had previously resided on the lost backup disk. "You're a genius, Kate! Bravo! Now if we can just find a way to archive it."

"Your wish is my command," Katrina replied confidently, and with a flurry of fingers, she downloaded the files at lightning speed to a machine in the University's computer lab. "Now we will have the files at our fingertips when we need them," she continued. "And to keep them secure, I will encrypt them and save them under the password 'Mankiller'."

"'Mankiller?' That's an apropos password for a knock-out gorgeous woman like yourself," Sam said mischievously, eyeing the matronly disguise that made Katrina appear to be well beyond middle age and distinctly *not* gorgeous.

Katrina feigned a scowl at Sam's sarcasm, and then smiled. "Actually, Mankiller is the clan name of a renown Cherokee chief who happens to be a modern woman, and who I admire very much. Surely you know of her?"

Before Sam had a chance to respond, the clerk walked in their direction. "Do you folks need any help? I haven't heard a peep from you in half an hour. Maybe I could help with a few of the basics."

"I don't think that will be necessary, sonny," Harry responded as he leaned on his cane and slowly rose to a standing position. "Maud and I are about ready to give it up, at least for today. Maybe one day we'll let the grandkids teach us computers, after we learn to play Nintendo."

* * * * *

After removing a thick coating of make up, hair coloring and mid-drift padding, then showering and dressing, Katrina stepped out of the bathroom with a fresh, rosy complexion. Quietly stunning in white cotton slacks and a simple, light green blouse, she bore little resemblance to her recent alter ego, Maud. When she entered the living room of Dave Sanders' townhouse, the men's conversation momentarily stopped. After a long moment of reflection on the awesome and glorious wonder of nature that God created from Adam's rib, Sam summarized, "So all we have to do is to take up where we left off, build a strong case with the evidence we have, and find the right authorities in Washington to pursue the leads. Piece of cake."

"Sounds easy enough. Too easy," Sanders countered.

"There *is* one thing that's still nagging me," Sam replied. "We don't know who put Huntington up to all this. I can't believe that Huntington and Bandini developed this whole scheme on their own. It seems out of character. In the past, they've stuck to petty political corruption and draining the public coffers through marginally illegal means. They've never been involved in anything this ambitious."

"Yeah, and there's something else I really don't like about this," Sanders added. "Those websites the Bureau has been investigating are linked by secret pass codes. The Greenleaf Project is linked to sites that are promoting every known vice, from terrorist weapons to illegal drugs, to sex slaves. Something tells me that we've only seen the tip of the iceberg, which gives me a very chilly feeling, even when it's a hundred degrees outside, no pun intended."

"No doubt there's more to this than we've fathomed so far. But that just makes our work more challenging. We've got to smoke out the truth. This case could be the pinnacle of your career, Dave, a crowning achievement. It's a case that we can really get our teeth into!"

"Unless they get their teeth into us first," Sanders said. "But there's no choice at this point. First thing tomorrow, we'll tackle this tiger."

* * * * *

After half an hour of watching Huntington pace across his plush office and curse Svetlanikoff, it was clear to Bandini that Huntington was incapable of abdicating his position of power. More than forty years as the supreme commander had forged a steel that might break, but it would not bend. His depressed subservience the day before had been nothing more than the acting of a wily tactician.

"That Russian bastard must die, and fast," Huntington growled. "There is no other choice. You heard him, Bandini. I could not believe the gall of that sorry son-of-a-bitch. He threatened my life. He's far too dangerous to live."

Bandini had a sour taste in his mouth. This entire operation had gotten far out of control. Now Huntington was preparing to order a hit on a preeminent leader of organized crime—an action that could easily backfire. "Tom, this whole thing has gotten out of hand," Bandini said in a plaintive tone. "It was one thing to persuade that maniac Karmakov to take out Angelletti, then lay the blame on Littlehawk. We were just encouraging his own plan of action. It's another thing entirely to order a hit on Svetlanikoff. These guys are professional gangsters. They play for keeps. Svetlanikoff is well-protected. No telling what trouble will come from this." Bandini was having visions of bloody corpses floating in the Arkansas River, which did not set well at all on his squeamish stomach.

"What do *you* want to do, Bandini, hand him the keys to the city? If we give in to him now, from this day forward, we'll be his lackeys, under his control. The man is a menace. We've got to put an end to this right now."

"And what about Angelletti and Littlehawk?" Bandini worried.

"They dug their own graves," Huntington growled. "With luck, they'll be terminated before we hit Svetlanikoff. *But hear this.* There can be no delay. He must die, and soon."

* * * * *

Five blocks away, the Russian entourage was enjoying three penthouse suites at the Adams Mark Hotel. Svetlanikoff occupied the Presidential Suite, the most distinguished accommodation in the city. He clearly intended to remain in town until the current crisis was resolved. And to prove his mastery of the situation, he secretly planned to make an example of the incompetents who had botched the affair.

Svetlanikoff poured steaming espresso from a small silver pitcher into a china cup and wondered to himself why he had not executed Huntington at the construction site. It could have been easily done, and in the presence of Bandini and Olsen, it would have sent the message that he desired. But upon reflection, Svetlanikoff realized that he was not absolutely sure that he could complete the project alone. He was certainly not ready to abandon his large investment, and he might still need Huntington. Besides, he had not properly planned the assassination. A simple bullet to the head was too bland. No creativity. No drama. It would be more fun if he waited for Karmakov's ingenious and bloodthirsty imagination before deciding how to dispose of Huntington. There would be many opportunities to remove him after control of the project was well-established.

Then there was Karmakov. He certainly deserved to pay the ultimate price for his incomparable stupidity and incompetence. He had failed to eradicate the annoying politician, and he and his lawyer friend were still alive. Plus, he had bungled the kidnapping of the ballerina and allowed her to escape. Twice! A cold and sullen anger crept through Svetlanikoff. Perhaps it would be best to make a clean sweep. After all, it was equally important to let his own minions know that even his closest associates were not immune from his wrath. But Karmakov, like Huntington, had an integral role in the current crisis. In a moment of inspiration, Svetlanikoff decided how to deal with both men, and he felt a little thrill of satisfaction. It would be a colorful and memorable double execution that would be talked about for years to come, from Moscow to Los Angeles.

It was a good plan, in fact, a brilliant one. But it would not be executed for some time. It did nothing to satisfy his immediate thirst for bloody retribution for the incompetence he had witnessed within his organization. Someone must pay, and soon, for the many mistakes that had been made. It would take a life to set the balance straight. Like a rogue Siberian tiger, Svetlanikoff felt a compelling need to kill. He picked up the telephone and dialed the adjacent suite.

"Make ready the helicopter. We will inspect the project site from the air," he ordered.

* * * * *

An hour later, Svetlanikoff, his two bodyguards and Casey Sellers stepped out of a black Mercedes onto the airport tarmac and walked a few steps to a Bell Jet Ranger. One of Huntington's mercenaries was already at the controls of the helicopter, preparing to start the engines. Although the woman appeared slightly confused, she willingly accompanied the men onboard.

As the chopper rose from the airport apron and set a course in the direction of the project site, Casey considered asking Svetlanikoff again for the balance of her payment. She had completed her assignment days before, but instead of paying her on her return to Las Vegas, he had asked her to accompany him on this trip. As the helicopter flew low over the wide, sandy expanse of the Cimarron River, doubt began to grow in Casey's mind. No one had actually confirmed that her hit had been successful. Looking up at Svetlanikoff, she saw him staring at her with a predatory glint in his narrow grey eyes.

The helicopter followed the riverbed through nearly uninhabited territory at an altitude of five hundred feet. Its forward motion slowed as they approached an old bridge spanning the river at a height of about sixty feet above the sand-choked riverbed. The pilot expertly hovered a few feet downstream of the bridge and gave a slight nod to his boss.

Svetlanikoff's face had taken on a dark, malevolent look, and his eyes gleamed as he stood in the cabin of the helicopter. "It's a shame," he said over the noise of the helicopter engines, "that you failed in your mission, Miss Sellers. Now you must pay the ultimate price for your incompetence. Your fate will be a lesson learned by my entire organization. Please stand."

Until that moment, the cold-hearted woman who had ended so many innocent lives had seemed incapable of fear. But as the import of Svetlanikoff's words sunk in, she began to lose control of her body. Every muscle seemed to tremble. She attempted to stand, but her knees buckled and she dropped back into the seat, quaking with fear. Her eyes went wide and the blood drained from her face.

Svetlanikoff enjoyed a sadistic response to her terror. Her silent panic fueled his malignant cruelty. His only regard for her life was in the depraved pleasure he would experience in ending it. He stood and opened the sliding door, allowing the turbulent air to rush into the compartment.

Nodding to his bodyguards, they lifted the shaking woman to her feet. She stood mutely as Svetlanikoff drew an ivory-handled knife from his jacket pocket and nodded again to the guards, who each gripped one of the woman's forearms and hands, thrusting them toward Svetlanikoff, exposing her wrists.

"I am sure that your suicide will eventually be reported, but I doubt that anyone will care," Svetlanikoff said callously. Reaching forward, he slashed the knife deeply into each of the woman's wrists. She gasped and then shrieked from the intense pain. Svetlanikoff smiled. "And now it is time for you to go," he said brutally.

With blood spurting freely from her wounds, Casey Sellers was tossed from the hovering helicopter like a bag of rancid garbage. A long, horrified scream was torn from her lips until she slammed into the riverbed face down in two feet of muddy water. Svetlanikoff watched from the open door of the helicopter as opaque brown water filled the small crater created by the impact, temporarily covering the inert body. Finally satisfied, he turned and ordered the pilot back to the airport.

As he took his seat, Svetlanikoff felt a gratifying surge of power. Executing assassins was sometimes an ugly business, but it always made him feel omnipotent and invincible. With a thrill of triumph, he congratulated himself—a predator of predators, an assassin of assassins. No one could match his power and cunning. Svetlanikoff turned to the scar-faced guard, who was wiping blood from his hands with a cloth. "It is a shame that Karmakov missed that. He would have enjoyed it immensely."

* * * * *

"But how?" Bandini asked in response to Huntington's blunt statement. "Svetlanikoff is guarded better than the crown jewels. It would take more firepower than anyone we know could muster to take him out. Besides, ordering hits has never been part of my job description."

Huntington stood glowering next to the window in his office. He partially turned his head toward the third man in the room. "Barton, are you absolutely sure that there are no bugs in here?"

"I've been over this place a dozen times with a microscope, Mr. Huntington. This place is so clean you could do surgery on the floor."

Huntington scowled and continued with Bandini. "You know there are people with the necessary skills. You and Barton had better find someone, and find him fast. This thing is out of control. Svetlanikoff is a madman."

At that moment, the telephone on Huntington's desk buzzed. He picked up the receiver with a gruff, "Yeah."

"Mr. Huntington, this is Johnson at the security desk. Four men are here who say that they have a meeting with you. A Mr. Svetlanikoff and three others."

Huntington blanched. There were no plans for a meeting. After a few seconds, he said gruffly, "Send them up."

Bandini and Barton looked at one another. "Svetlanikoff and his men are on their way. I don't know why they're paying us a surprise visit. Don't say anything, just listen."

Seconds later, the door to Huntington's office opened and Svetlanikoff's two bodyguards stepped in, followed by Svetlanikoff and a fourth man, obviously another strong arm. Svetlanikoff wasted no time getting to the point. "After our little talk yesterday afternoon, gentlemen, I am sure that you are quite willing to cooperate with my command of this operation. We will now complete the removal of the troublesome politician and his friend, which both you and Comrade Karmakov were previously unable to accomplish. My forces are trained for such an exercise, but I will require your help in locating the targets. I understand that Littlehawk has returned to this city and that Angelletti has, to our knowledge, never left it. But their exact locations are unknown. This is an issue that can be easily resolved, and you will assist in resolving it."

There was no response from the three Americans.

"Huntington, your chief of security will contact Littlehawk's family. He will advise them that unless Littlehawk appears at a specified time and place, alone and unarmed, they will be summarily executed. Without doubt, Littlehawk is in contact with his family and will soon learn of the threat. I am told that he is a brave and loyal man. He will do what is necessary to protect his family. He will certainly understand that we have the capacity to carry out the threat, so he will appear at the appointed time and place. When we have him in our custody, he will reveal the location of Angelletti and the ballerina. Then we will have them all." Svetlanikoff ended with a flourish of his hand. "*Voila!* Problem solved."

Huntington eyed Svetlanikoff, considering this simple plan and again appraising the man who had proposed it, searching for any weakness in either. He found none.

Bandini, knowing that they had no choice but to cooperate, immediately seized on the Russian's plan, but sought ways to alter it slightly in order to turn the tables on Svetlanikoff. Like a judo artist, Bandini would allow the thrust of Svetlanikoff's plan to go forward, but at the last moment, he would sidestep and divert the thrust to accomplish another purpose. Bandini smiled inwardly, knowing that in the end, he would outsmart the Russian mobster.

Of the three Americans, only Barton was distressed. He had initially complied with Huntington's instruction to remain silent, but now it seemed that he was unable to contain himself. "What do you plan to do with those three when you get them?" he said nervously, knowing the answer before he asked the question. "I don't think that killing them would solve anything. It would just draw a lot more attention to us and put the whole project at great risk."

Svetlanikoff looked intensely at Barton, but spoke to Huntington. "Your chief of security does not seem to have the stomach for such work. Perhaps he should be replaced. I am sure that any member of my forces would serve well in his position. Unfortunately, this man knows far to much to be released."

Barton instantly realized his mistake and the huge risk he had taken. Huntington had been right. Nothing he could say would be of any value in this conversation and he should have kept his mouth shut. He had no choice but to try to correct the situation. "Oh, no, sir," he said submissively to Svetlanikoff, "I can do the work. I've been in this business for a long time. Mr. Huntington can vouch for me. Don't worry, I'll do the job. Whatever it is. Just tell me what to do and it's done." He nodded nervously several times and took a small step backward.

"So we have a clear understanding then," Svetlanikoff said with satisfaction. "Perhaps you, sir, will have the pleasure of performing the executions, although I am quite certain that Karmakov will not easily surrender that honor."

Barton looked as though he had just swallowed a live salamander, but he said nothing further, having learned to leave well enough alone.

"And speaking of Karmakov, he should be arriving here at any moment," Svetlanikoff continued. "He is in route from Miami, having completed a course of medical treatment necessitated by his unfortunate encounter with Littlehawk in Florida. His arm was seriously injured, but thanks to the miracle of modern medicine, it has been repaired and he is rapidly improving. His only desire is to exact revenge on Littlehawk and Angelletti. Lucky for you, Mr. Barton, if I know Karmakov, he will not willingly share the pleasure of visiting retribution on his enemies."

"Have you thought of a cover story?" Bandini ventured cautiously, not wanting to lead, but feeling compelled to discover the entire plan.

"Simplest is best, Mr. Bandini," Svetlanikoff instructed. "The three will appear to have died together in an accident. Perhaps an automobile wreck or a plane crash will suffice. It is inconsequential how they appear to have died. They will already be dead."

Bandini pressed the issue a little further. "But that doesn't square with the story that we fed to the police and the press, that Littlehawk tried to kill Angelletti over the girl and then kidnapped him from the hospital."

"That entire story was implausible from the start," Svetlanikoff declared. "I am surprised that Karmakov would think of such a plan."

"It could have worked," Bandini muttered, "If Karmakov's goons had done their job right. It was a good plan—no loose ends."

"Karmakov's men will pay a price for their incompetence," Svetlanikoff replied. "But now there are at least three loose ends to secure. And this time, nothing will be left to chance. Framing one for the death of the other was risky, and it failed. This time, we will use proven methods that do not fail. Follow my instructions precisely, and we will succeed. Is that understood?"

Svetlanikoff looked around the room for concurrence. Huntington's habitual scowl masked his thoughts. Bandini nodded, and Barton quickly responded with a terse, "Yes sir," nodding repeatedly while looking quickly back and forth from Svetlanikoff to Huntington.

Moving toward the door, Svetlanikoff spoke to Barton. "You, contact Littlehawk's most trusted associate and tell him that Littlehawk must be at the plant site tomorrow night at ten o'clock, alone and unarmed. That should allow plenty of time for Littlehawk to get the message. And be sure to tell him that if Littlehawk alerts anyone to this plan or does not comply precisely, his family will die. We are agreed?"

Without waiting for a response, Svetlanikoff walked briskly out of Huntington's office, followed by two of his men. As a matter of habit, the scar-faced man slowly backed toward the open door, only turning as he stepped through the doorway and closed the door behind them.

For a full minute after the door closed, none of the three said a word. Finally, Bandini said, "That Scarface is a creepy son-of-a-bitch. I wonder if he's former KGB. I bet he'd compete with Karmakov for the pleasure of killing Littlehawk."

"He's cold, alright," Barton added.

Huntington ignored the chatter. "He can't get away with this takeover. He cannot complete the project without me. He doesn't have the contacts." Huntington sounded as though he were trying to convince himself. "Besides, this is my goddamn state. I run the show around here." He glared at Bandini and Barton, as if expecting a challenge. There was none, but his words rang hollow.

Bandini responded quickly. "Don't worry, Tom, they're playing right into our hand. This is going to work out even more neatly than I had thought." A thin smile played across his lips. "Sometimes I'm shocked at my own genius."

"This had better be good, Bandini," Huntington said. "Your last scheme backfired. There's no more room for mistakes."

"But this is failsafe," Bandini replied. "We won't be able to set up the Angelletti faction to self-destruct with Karmakov's help, as I had planned. But I have a better idea. We need to eliminate both the Angelletti faction and the Russian faction, right? All we have to do is get Littlehawk, Angelletti and the ballerina, Svetlanikoff and Karmakov all in the same place at the same time, with lots of weapons. Instant conflagration. Some of them will be killed by the others. If there are any survivors, then from a safe distance, our sharpshooters will finish off anyone who's left. In the investigation, evidence will turn up that Angelletti was involved with the Russians in a drug deal that went sour. Happens all the time with the Russian Mafia. Remember those guys from Oklahoma City that were trying to build legitimate businesses in Moscow? They got tied up with the Mafia and when the deal went bad, they were found dead with their six bodyguards, full of about a thousand bullets."

"Don't remind me," Huntington said dryly as he pondered Bandini's proposal. "As I recall, you didn't think mob violence was an issue when we first met Svetlanikoff. Teaming up with him looked like a pretty good idea to you."

"And you had complete control of the Corporation Commission, too," Bandini replied, venturing dangerously close to making a remark critical of Huntington. "We've just got to roll with the punches. What do you think?"

"You're pretty short on details. It's going to take some major logistics to set up the meeting. It's dangerous. And we need to keep the project site free of any bloodshed."

"Do you have any better ideas?" Bandini pressed forward. "Once this is over, the project can go forward without delay."

Simultaneously, both men turned toward Barton, who stared back at them with reluctance written on his face.

"We'll need some triggermen," Bandini declared.

"Was what you said to Svetlanikoff all brag, or just fact?" Huntington growled.

Barton swallowed hard and decided that he had no choice but to cooperate. He was way too far in to try to back out now. He felt as though he had his life savings invested in a poker game and the stakes had just doubled.

"I can get you marksmen, sir. Soldiers of fortune. Just give me a little time. This is a lot different from planting a few electronic bugs in offices or putting the fear of God into some punk politicians."

"We've *got* no time!" Huntington exploded, releasing some of the stress of the last hour. "You're as much at fault in this as anyone, so you had better act fast if you want to save your own sorry hide. Now get moving!"

"Don't worry," Barton said as he headed for the door. "I'm on it."

A few seconds after the door closed, Huntington turned to Bandini. "Now it's time for you to think about the details," he said curtly. "Figure out a way to make this work, or we're all sucking wind."

Chapter 23

With obvious effort, Harry held open the heavy library door while Maud entered. Then, relying on his cane, he followed her into the hundred year old limestone building that had stood as the centerpiece of the University campus for a century. As inconspicuously as possible, the elderly couple made their way down the worn wooden staircase to the basement, which temporarily housed the University's open access computer lab. They walked past the front desk, which was attended by a single graduate student whose attention was directed entirely toward her studies. Without incident, they made their way to a small carrel in the recesses of the nearly deserted lab. Maud took a seat in front of the computer monitor and Harry pulled up a chair at her side.

"You know, we're getting entirely too good at this Harry and Maud routine," Sam said to Katrina. "This is so much fun, we may have to try it out in some more challenging venues like, say, the federal building? Southwest Plaza perhaps?"

Katrina was already logging onto the computer. "You make a fine old gentleman, *Harry*, but I will never be comfortable with six inches of padding strapped around my middle. I want to get out of this disguise as soon as possible."

"Actually," Sam answered, "now that you mention it, I do prefer you as Katrina. No offense, Maud." She turned and cast a look at Sam that could freeze hot coffee. "Okay, okay. Just a thought. But I still think you would make a wonderful actress."

"Thank you, I think," she replied, as the computer screen lit up. "Now, can we get on with the business at hand? We have work to do."

Katrina's fingers flew over the keyboard and in less than a minute, they were again scrolling through the documents that they had downloaded from the computer at the Cherry Street Connection. Sam was pleased with the amount of evidence that he and Tony had appropriated during their short visit to Southwest Plaza, but he was positively awed by the labyrinth of linked websites that Dave Sanders had uncovered. Luckily, the web browser that they had been using had recorded every site they had hit. Now they had a record of the sites, for as long as the sites remained in existence. Sam wondered if he would be able to put a case together fast enough, before the websites disappeared.

"How many hours can we work here?" Sam asked, as he selected documents and Katrina organized them in files and created an index.

"This place is open 24/7," Katrina responded. "It is open access for students and faculty, but not the public. But I doubt that anyone will question us. If they do, I have my student ID, but the photo does not look much like me." Katrina eyed the matronly body she had assumed. "I could have some trouble explaining how I gained sixty pounds and aged thirty-five years since the beginning of the semester."

"No problem," Sam replied. "We're student actors on our way to the drama department for a dress rehearsal. A class project. We stopped by the computer lab to complete an assignment. Hey, stranger things than that happen on campus every day."

"Well, I don't want to stay here any longer than necessary. We are both fugitives. But even worse, this disguise is getting more uncomfortable every minute." Katrina glanced over her shoulder, then adjusted the heavy bust line of her dress. "It's hot under all this padding!"

"Don't worry," Sam winked, "I'm as anxious to get you out of that rigging as you are to get out of it. So let's concentrate and get the job done!"

Nearly two hours later, Katrina wiped more beads of perspiration from her heavily powdered forehead, then hit the "Send" button, instantly transmitting a group of files to three e-mail addresses provided by Dave Sanders.

"That should get their attention," Sam said. "Surely someone in the FBI, the Justice Department, or Europol will be interested."

Katrina quickly downloaded the files to two new disks, then deleted their work from the computer. "It's a shame," Sam said, "that we could not go back to the websites to see how many are still there. But I guess it isn't worth the risk of giving away our position again."

"And I am more than ready to get out of this costume," Katrina added. "And, it is time for lunch. We have not eaten at all today."

"Food! Now you're talking my language! Let's get out of here!" Sam said, springing to his feet. Suddenly, he remembered his disguise and slowed his movements to the speed expected of an elderly gentleman, as together, they ambled down the hall and out of the building.

* * * * *

Sam sunk his teeth into a tuna sandwich and munched hungrily. He and Katrina sat at Dave Sanders' kitchen table, while Dave puttered in the small galley kitchen.

"It's a pretty unconventional way of approaching the authorities," Sam said between bites. "I doubt that the FBI's National Director of Investigations receives anonymous e-mails like ours every day. But it's best to keep your name out of this for now, Dave. Since the first backup disk disappeared at your office, it's hard to know who the enemy is."

"You would be amazed at all of the ways information comes into the FBI. There's no such thing as a 'normal' investigation. But we don't usually receive a case completely outlined, together with buckets of evidence, all tied up with a nice bow. I must admit, you put together a pretty convincing body of evidence. Too bad you couldn't take the credit."

Sam smiled between bites. "Yes, but if I did, I'm afraid their attention would turn from the real criminals to yours truly, who is, after all, a wanted man."

"You can say that for sure," Katrina said as she licked stray crumbs from her lips with a look on her face that was not lost on Sam.

Sam's cell phone rang. He opened it to the tense sound of Red's voice. "Sam, you'd best get back out here to the ranch. Things look to be heatin' up."

He instantly tensed. "What do you mean, Red?"

"Well, I just got a phone call. Don't know who it was, but he was a real mean dude. He said that you have to go out to that construction site where they're gettin' ready to build that new power plant tonight at ten o'clock, or they're gonna do in your whole family. Said if you call the police or don't come alone, same thing will happen. The guy was not joking. What are we gonna do, Sam?"

Sam drew in a deep breath and slowly exhaled, thinking fast. "Don't worry, Red, I was expecting something like this. I've got a plan, but I can't tell you everything right now. You and Danny take Faye and Emmie to the lake house, and you stay there with them around the clock. The people threatening us don't know about the lake house. Leave right now. I'll get in touch with you as soon as I can."

"You sure about this, Sam? You know the police are still lookin' for you? You sure it's not time to turn yourself in and deal with this through the law? I know you're a pretty good lawyer."

"If I did that, Red, I'd never make it to the jail, much less to the courthouse. The people we're dealing with want me dead. They're worse than I thought at first. You're just going to have to trust me to play out this hand. I've got an ace in the hole."

"Hope they don't have a full house," Red drawled. "Okay, we're headin' for the lake house, as soon as I can get us rounded up and outta here."

"Red, don't go straight there," Sam instructed. "You're probably being watched. Go to the Dogwood Marina first and rent a fast boat. Put it on my account. Cruise over to Ugly Jack's Marina and dock the boat, then go through the marina. Slip out the back as quick as you can and have Jack take you from there in his cruiser. Keep your heads below deck. That should put anyone following you off the track. If you need ground transportation, you can borrow a Jeep from Jack. Tell him I said it's okay."

"You're thinkin' every minute, Sam," Red said, his confidence restored. "You just keep it up now, until you get us out of this mess."

"Don't worry, Red, I've got a plan." Sam closed the cell phone, wishing that he felt as confident as he sounded. Another death threat against his family was all that he needed. And how would he deal with the ultimatum to appear at the plant site? His mind was racing.

"What was that all about?" Sanders asked, as he and Katrina both looked at Sam expectantly.

"Seems that someone wants me to make an appearance tonight at the plant site, alone. I wonder what in the world they want with me?"

"You know exactly what they want," Sanders said. "They want you dead. There's no way you're going out there alone, Sam. Did they threaten your family?"

Sam ignored the question and looked at his watch. "Two-thirty. That gives us less than eight hours before the meeting. Not enough time to bring in Washington, even if they got our e-mail and took it seriously. We only sent it an hour ago. They're too far away and they can't move that fast. And we can't rely on your office here, Dave," Sam said, looking at his friend and shaking his head. "Someone there is on Huntington's payroll and we don't know who. No, we've got to do this alone."

"Do what?" Sanders and Katrina both asked at once.

"With luck, we can use this opportunity to find out who Huntington is dealing with. Get an idea of some of their plans, maybe their schedule. Maybe we can even find out what sick mind is behind those websites."

Katrina gave an involuntary shudder. "Karmakov has some dangerous friends in Russia," she said. "He has dealings with Huntington. I think we must assume that his contacts in Moscow are now Huntington's contacts."

"The links between the websites bear that out," Dave said. "It's still just a little hard to believe that Southwest Energy could be involved with the Russian Mafia."

"Not so surprising, really," Sam said. "In this age of instant communication, the only issue is whether people have a common interest. Where they are physically located—even their nationality—doesn't matter. In this case, apparently Huntington and his new Russian contacts have a common interest in the Greenleaf Project, among other things. Besides, there's a longstanding tradition of organized crime being involved with public construction projects, in this country and elsewhere. Anyway, it's likely that Huntington's clandestine business dealings are not known to most of the management of Southwest Energy."

"So what about tonight?" Dave asked.

"If they want to talk, I'm ready."

"Who said they want to talk, Sam? I'd bet ten to one they're thinking shoot first, talk later. They're planning to use you for target practice."

"Unless I miss my guess, they'll want to use me first to find Tony and Katrina. Just killing me won't put an end to this. They've got to get us all. On the other hand, who knows, maybe they want to make some kind of a deal."

"I'm thinking that you need to get your head examined," Dave replied. "Sounds to me like you're actually thinking about going out there tonight."

"Got to, Dave. There's really no choice."

"And how's this supposed to help the cause?"

"We'll bait a trap," Sam said with a cracked grin. "Unfortunately, I'm the bait."

* * * * *

"Calling Huntington's office was a bold move," Dave said, as he strapped a bulletproof Kevlar vest around Sam's chest over a cotton tee shirt. "I'll bet he didn't expect to hear from you."

"Why beat around the bush?" Sam answered, shaking himself to adjust the stiff vest. "We both know what's going on here. I just wanted him to know that we're going to take him down. I wanted him to hear it from me, and I wanted to taunt him, to try to draw him out. With his ego, he won't be able to stay away tonight and we might be lucky enough to expose the whole criminal empire."

"You're pretty optimistic, Sam."

"It helps to be optimistic when you're getting ready to ride into the showdown at the OK Corral without Doc Holiday as back up."

Dave helped Sam slide a denim shirt on over the vest. "What if Huntington doesn't show? He might just send a messenger, or a trigger man or two." Dave glanced over his shoulder to make sure Katrina was out of earshot.

"Just gonna have to play it by ear, Dave. This is war. I know my abilities and limitations. I just have to do my best to respond to the circumstances as they unfold."

"Sounds pretty basic to me. The truth is, I don't know that there's any better plan, and if you handle yourself as well as you did in Florida, well, I guess maybe we've got nothing, or at least not too much, to worry about. I guess. Not too much. I hope."

"That's the spirit, Dave! Besides, who wants to live forever? We've got to face the enemy and spit in his eye." For emphasis, Sam kicked down hard on the starter of the dirt bike he was straddling, and the motor roared. He quickly shut it down and reached for his racing armor.

"With this stuff and the Kevlar," Sam said as he slipped the racing armor over his head, "it would take some heavy artillery to slow me down. That racing helmet has a layer of titanium inside. I'm a human cannonball."

"Just get what you need and get out. Keep your distance. If they start shooting, get moving fast. I'll be down the road in the empty field just past Woody's Corner. You know that I'd rather be in close, backing you up."

"Can't take that chance, Dave." Sam pulled his helmet on, fastened the chin strap, then donned thick leather gloves. "See you at Woody's Corner in an hour or so." Flipping his face mask down, Sam kicked the starter again. Then with a twist of his wrist, the bike roared to life, and he was gone."

"And don't tear up Tony's new dirt bike!" Sanders yelled, too late to be heard.

* * * * *

Sam enjoyed the half hour ride in the cool evening. He was beginning to wonder whether living on the edge could become a habit. The adrenaline coursing through his veins made every second seem like a minute, each minute, an hour. His senses were sharpened to a fine point, and in the evening light, the colors of the prairie flowers blooming by the roadside and the pungent aroma of the hayfields seemed more intense than usual. Sam liked being on edge. Warrior blood from two cultures on two continents coursed through his veins. *If this day is to be my last*, he thought, *well, it's a good day to die.*

Sam slowed the bike as he approached the entrance to the construction site, looking for any activity. Nothing caught his eye. He eased through the open gate and down the gravel road toward the huge excavation that was, in the night, a black abyss. Pulling up to the edge of the pit, he paused to study the site and the surrounding terrain in the dim light of the half moon.

A narrow perimeter road circled the top edge of the excavation. Bordering the road on the outside were nearly continuous, uneven piles of rock and rubble, which left a lane that was in most places just a little wider than a dump truck. There were a few scattered lights illuminating the bottom of the pit, two mounted on the concrete mixing plant, another on the front of a small shack opposite the plant, and two more on a long, tin equipment shed. The walls of the quarry were nearly vertical for the first thirty feet, then more gradually sloped near the top. The concrete mixing plant, which stood near the south wall of the pit, consisted of an elevator for dry concrete, a huge mixing vessel, and a tilted conveyor belt that carried sand and crushed limestone from the floor of the pit to the top of the mixer.

In the lit area around the concrete plant, heavy equipment parked at random cast inky shadows away from the lights. Instinctively, Sam knew that this was where they would be waiting. Without hesitation, he drove the dirt bike slowly down the wide, dark ramp that ran north to south along the east wall of the pit. At the bottom, Sam turned right and rode half the length of the pit until he was in the light in front of the shack. There he stopped and waited, with the engine of the bike idling.

He did not have to wait long. As he scanned the area for movement, a figure dressed entirely in black stepped out from behind one of the parked dozers and slowly walked forward. Even in the relative darkness, Sam could not mistake the long tangle of black hair framing the narrow, dark face. Karmakov! He walked to within ten feet of Sam and stopped. He was wearing a thin, waist-length jacket and both hands were in his pockets. The left arm of the jacket was thick and cocked at an unnatural angle, undoubtedly from a splint and bandages. Yet Sam was certain that Karmakov was armed and still very, very dangerous.

"So we meet again, Littlehawk," Karmakov said quietly. Sam noticed at once that Karmakov's defiant arrogance had been replaced with a flat, baleful tone that seemed all the more lethal.

"I had hoped that you had been a meal for the alligators, but no such luck, I see. Why don't you go find another place to play, Karmakov. You've worn out your welcome here."

"I would like nothing better than to leave this tragic wasteland forever. But you see, my business here is not quite finished. Before I leave, I must pay my respects to your friend Angelletti and to Katrina."

"You mean you want to finish the dirty work that your bumbling sidekicks fouled up. No, I'm not likely to hand you Tony or Katrina so that you can use them as objects for your sadistic pleasure. They've both had quite enough of you."

"I'm sure that you will reveal their locations and much more to us, before we are through with you. If you refuse, you will die an exceedingly painful death, starting now. The choice is yours."

"Come on, don't play me for a fool, Karmakov. Whether or not I give up Tony and Katrina, you won't let me go. Once you know where they are, you'll kill me, if you can. I know too much. And in any case, you'd kill for revenge, given the opportunity. Or just because you like to kill. Right now, in fact, you can barely restrain yourself from pulling that pistol out of your pocket and using it. You're an animal, Karmakov, a vicious killing machine with no humanity in your wicked soul."

Anger rose in Karmakov's face. Veins stood out on his forehead and Sam could see the whites of his wild, angry eyes. Pushing the maniacal Russian was a dangerous game.

Karmakov drew a small caliber nickel-plated automatic pistol from his pocket and extended his arm completely, aiming at Sam's chest. "So you have made your choice, then. You will die. But be assured, one bullet will not kill you. Yours will be a slow and excruciating death." Sam could see his finger closing on the trigger.

"Stop!" Someone shouted in Russian as another dark figure stepped out of the shadows. Karmakov froze, then slowly relaxed, keeping his weapon trained on Sam. Instantly, Sam realized that Karmakov's superior had intervened.

The speaker walked casually into the light and stood beside Karmakov. He was a man of medium build, a few years older than Karmakov and a few inches shorter, but with a commanding presence. His steel grey hair matched the color of his narrow eyes, which held a calm, cold stare, in contrast to the vitriolic hatred and hostility of his counterpart. Suddenly, Karmakov and his weapon were of little consequence. Sam waited.

"Mr. Littlehawk, let me introduce myself. I am Svetlanikoff. And you are my prisoner. You will do exactly as I say. You are under my control. Karmakov is my agent, but he is a Cossack and far too emotional. He would have killed you too quickly, and without getting the information that I require."

Sam said nothing. Obviously, Svetlanikoff was on a roll.

"You are right, of course. We cannot release you. You have already displayed your overt hostility toward our activities. You know far too much, and you do not appear to have the temperament to keep your mind on your own business. You must be extinguished. However, we can leave your family alone...*or not.* That will depend on you—on whether we acquire the information we seek. If not, the proud history of the Littlehawk clan will end. So you see, you really have no choice."

The coldness of the man and his bitter words hit Sam like a bucket of ice water. The death threat against his family awakened subliminal influences that stirred deep within his soul. The very land on which he stood resonated with centuries of sacrifice by his ancestors to protect their precious freedom. His response to such a threat was instinctive. He had no alternative but to fight to the death, if necessary. Another man might have thought it a noble sacrifice to give his own life to save his family. To Sam, his life and the lives of his family, his tribe, were all one. He was their chief. They would live or die together, as they had for a thousand generations.

"We always have choices," Sam responded coolly. "For instance, you could choose right now to leave this country forever and live a long and peaceful life in some tropical paradise, far from here. Or you could choose to continue your current course of action and watch me destroy your project and everything associated with it."

"Those are bold words for an unarmed man surrounded by enemies and doomed to die," the Russian replied. "Your audacity is refreshing. Nevertheless, you will tell us where your two confederates are, whether you intend to or not." He raised his hand and waved, and four armed men dressed in black battle fatigues stepped out from behind various pieces of parked equipment. "Make no mistake, you will tell me what I want to know."

"Well, I will tell you one thing, Svetlanikoff. Your days are numbered, and that number is a very small one. And you have already made one mistake. You said that I was unarmed."

With that, Sam reached with his left hand and whipped an Uzi from a holster hidden under his leg in the frame of the bike. At the same instant, he gunned the motor and the bike leaped forward, its front wheel in the air. In less than a second, the bike was launched into the space between a bulldozer and a loader, nearly knocking over one of the mercenaries. Without turning to look back, Sam swung his left arm wide and sprayed bullets in his wake. His shots were wild, but they accomplished the intended purpose of slowing the gunmen's progress. Gravel flew as the bike skidded around equipment and Sam found the road that crossed the bottom of the pit to the ramp.

Less than ten seconds had elapsed since Sam had drawn the Uzi, but he was already approaching the foot of the ramp, the only exit from the excavation. Svetlanikoff's gunmen had collected themselves after the unexpected dusting and Sam could hear the popping of their automatic weapons. Leaning low over the handlebars, he released another burst from the Uzi as he started up the ramp, with freedom mere seconds away.

A pair of headlights suddenly appeared at the top of the ramp. Sam skidded the bike to a stop a third of the way up. Both doors of the car flew open and armed men emerged, taking shelter behind the car doors, guns drawn. Trapped, for half a second Sam surveyed his surroundings, knowing that he had to keep moving—he was an easy target standing still. There was clearly no escape up the ramp, and the outside wall of the excavation at that point was vertical. Without hesitation, Sam gunned the bike again, the rear tire spun, and he shot over the edge of the ramp.

Momentarily, he was launched into open space. Holding the handle bars in a death grip while struggling to keep his feet on the pegs, he sailed through the darkness. Although it was only fifteen feet to the ground, a jump that would not be too difficult in the daylight, the floor of the pit was invisible in the dark. The impact came unexpectedly and the bike slammed down hard and unbalanced, but he managed to regain control. He raced across the flat, open floor of the excavation as the Mercedes that had blocked his escape spun its tires and skidded down the ramp in pursuit.

Sam took cover behind a stack of steel drums for a moment to think. In seconds, the gunmen would close in. There was no exit from the pit except the ramp, which was guarded by the Mercedes. Sam looked frantically around the perimeter of the pit, his gaze stopping on the concrete plant. An idea began to take shape. Although it was a long shot, he saw no other option and he acted on impulse. Bullets ricocheted off the steel drums as he gunned the engine. Gravel sprayed as the bike again shot forward.

Sam released another burst of fire from the Uzi as he circled the heavy equipment and aligned the bike with the concrete plant's inclined conveyor belt. The top of the conveyor belt ended about thirty-five feet above the ground and twenty feet from the wall of the pit. Just above that level, the wall began to taper back from vertical to a steep slope. If he could make it up the ramp and enter the jump with enough momentum, the bike just might reach the sloped wall and successfully climb out. If he missed, it would be a fifty foot drop onto solid rock.

"Well, I'm dead either way," he said, "Damn the torpedoes, full speed ahead!" He released a final burst from the Uzi in the direction of the gunmen, then booted the weapon and throttled the bike. Accelerating as he hit the base of the heavy conveyor belt, he sped up the steep incline. As the top of the conveyor approached, Sam wondered for an instant if he would have enough momentum to make the jump. He opened the throttle full and the bike roared with a last burst of energy.

Just as the bike cleared the conveyor belt and shot into mid-air, Sam felt two nearly simultaneous impacts, one to his upper back and the other to the back of his helmet, as though he had been double-kicked by a mule. The power of the impacts knocked Sam free of the bike, and in the next second, he and the motorcycle both collided with the steep rock slope, five feet apart.

Sam hit face first on the steeply sloping rock wall, fifteen feet below the lip of the pit. The force of the impact knocked the wind out of him, and for a moment, his consciousness began to fade. But as he felt himself sliding backward toward the vertical cliff just below, a surge of adrenaline focused his mind and he was able to grab an exposed rock outcropping to stop his slide. He held on and watched the bike, its engine still running, slide over the edge and fall, exploding on impact at the bottom of the pit.

In just a few seconds, the burst of flames from the gasoline was spent and darkness fell on the eerily quiet pit. The gunfire and shouting had stopped. Sam clung to his precarious position on the steeply sloped wall, panting. The soft crackle of flames on the burning motorcycle was punctuated by the sound of men running. Directly below him in the pit, a Russian shouted. Apparently, one of the gunmen had discovered that he was not with the bike. Sam knew that his situation was desperate. Gingerly, he began to climb the wall, but his movement released a small avalanche of rocks and gravel. There was another shout from below and a moment later a beam of light revealed his position. He was totally exposed and helpless, like a raccoon treed by a pack of baying hounds. Attempting to scramble up the steep slope, he slid back two feet for each foot of forward progress. A shot rang out and a rock near his left hand shattered as the bullet ricocheted away.

"Stop shooting, you fool!" Karmakov shouted. "We will take him alive! Capture him!"

With renewed energy, Sam struggled to reach the top. The spotlight flashed away and he was suddenly in the dark again, as the gunmen turned it on the lower wall in hopes of finding a way up. With ten vertical feet to go, Sam heard the sound of tires crunching on gravel above his position. His heart sank. The Mercedes had moved to block his escape. He froze, certain he was surrounded from above and below. The game was up.

"Well, what the hell are you waiting for, Christmas?" Dave Sanders shouted.

A wave of relief surged through Sam's body. "Dave, how…what…"

"Shut up and get moving, before they know you're gone!"

Sam felt a nylon rope drop over his shoulder. Without questioning further, he grabbed the rope, looped it around his hand, and held on. Sanders heaved, Sam climbed, and in a few seconds, he was reaching for Sanders' outstretched hand at the edge of the pit.

At that moment, the spotlight again moved up the slope, pinpointing Sam and Sanders in its light. Shouts rang from below. Sanders grabbed Sam's hand and pulled hard. They fell to the ground out of the beam of light, just as the gunmen released a volley of gunfire. Without another word, the two friends scrambled into the waiting Lincoln, Sanders behind the wheel and Sam in the passenger seat. As Sanders cranked the engine and hit the accelerator, Sam pulled off his helmet and tossed it into the backseat.

"Got to move it now," Sanders muttered to himself as he held the accelerator to the floor and fishtailed the Lincoln on the rough ground. "Time to get out of here." Accelerating along the perimeter road, Sanders tried to dodge the biggest obstacles as he headed back the way he had come, along the south edge of the pit. In another few seconds, they would round the corner of the pit and continue on the perimeter road along the east wall, past the top of the ramp. All other directions were blocked by mountains of rock that the Lincoln could not negotiate. Glancing out the car window into the pit, Sanders released a small, "Uh oh."

"What is it?" Sam asked.

Sanders reached to the floor of the car and handed Sam another weapon. "Looks like some of those yahoos are coming up to meet us." He pointed into the pit to their left, where the Mercedes was starting up the ramp, paralleling the course they had to take along the east rim. It was clear that the Mercedes would make it to the top of the ramp before they would reach the point of intersection. "Looks to me like we don't have much of a choice. This road doesn't go anywhere but straight ahead."

"You just drive, Dave." Sam rolled down the window and held the automatic in this right hand, outside the car.

As the Lincoln rounded the southeast corner of the pit and headed north along the east rim, the Mercedes cleared the top of the ramp at the northeast corner and turned south to face the oncoming Lincoln. Both doors of the Mercedes flew open and the occupants assumed their assault positions.

Bap, bap! Two rounds hit the windshield just in front of Sanders, who flinched, then smiled broadly. "Thank God for bulletproof glass!" Another spatter of gunfire hit the speeding Lincoln without causing any damage. Sam squeezed the trigger of the automatic three times, but was unable to see the effect of his shots in the dark. The Lincoln was bumping hard on the rough road at fifty miles an hour.

"Dave, I don't know if this car can squeeze through there," Sam said, as Sanders pointed the Lincoln directly toward the narrow space between the driver's open door and a pile of large boulders.

"Not gonna fit," Sanders agreed, as he gunned the Lincoln. A second later, the Lincoln slammed into the side of the Mercedes, tearing the door completely off its hinges and launching the man who was hiding behind it a hundred feet into the air. The force of the impact spun the Mercedes, which teetered on the lip of the pit, then toppled twenty feet onto the ramp below, where it came to rest upside down.

Without slowing to assess the damage, Sanders wrenched the heavy Lincoln around and sped out through the open gate of the construction site into the night.

Chapter 24

"This thing is built like a tank," Sanders said as he guided the damaged Lincoln down a country road, trying to dodge potholes with the light from one headlight. "Ripped the door right off that Mercedes, and it still runs like a top. Hardly a scratch on her that you can see in the dark."

"Carlos is really gonna be mad," Sam said mournfully. "He just got this car last week. Special order. He's proud of his fleet. This is gonna cost me big time."

"Ha! You think Carlos is gonna be mad? Just wait until Tony finds out you destroyed his new racing bike. I'll match that Italian against your Mexican buddy anytime."

Sam sunk a little deeper into his seat, then jerked as he twisted a tender spot in his back. "Well, better a broken bike than a broken back, I guess. And by the way, thanks for yanking me out of there when you did. Without your help, I wouldn't have made it."

"No thanks needed—I believe you recently saved me from becoming alligator *hors d'oeuvres*. Let's just call it even. But tell me, did you learn anything interesting from your little encounter with the enemy?"

"Svetlanikoff. Another Russian. He's the one controlling Karmakov and Huntington. He was there. Looked like Mafia to me, with a platoon of foot soldiers. I *knew* that there had to be a driving force in this besides Huntington. The name is about all that I got before the shooting started. Ever heard of him?"

"No, but I'll bet I know someone who has." Sanders pulled his cell phone from his pocket and hit a preset number for FBI information. When the line connected, he entered an extension.

"Angela, baby, this is Dave!" he said brightly. There was a pause, and then a frown pinched his brow. "No, no, Dave Sanders, from the Bureau. You remember me, *Dave*, from the Central Southwest Office. From the meeting in Vegas? It was *just* three months ago. Oh, well, yes, I have my identification number." Sanders scowled and repeated a series of numbers, then put the phone against his chest and rolled his eyes. "This chick's got a really bad memory. We were *close.*"

"Yes, Angela honey, that's me, Dave Sanders! You remember! All right, now we're getting somewhere! Yes, I know that it's midnight in Washington, but this is an emergency. I *know* everything is always an emergency, but could you do me just this one little favor, *please?* Could you see what we have on a Russian dude called Svetlanikoff? That's right, S-v-e-t-l-a-n-i-k-o-f-f, or something like that. And whatever you can find, would you transmit it to the secure e-mail in my office, pronto? Yeah, thanks a million, Angela. I owe you one. Maybe I can pay you back at the next techie conference."

He clicked off the cell phone. "*Not likely,*" he said with disgust. "Women! Am I *really* all that forgettable? Don't answer that…"

"How soon do you think she'll deliver the information?" Sam asked.

"Well, if she's as good at her job as she is at some other important things, I'd say that it's already there," Sanders replied.

* * * * *

Sam sat on the couch in Sanders' apartment, his finger sticking through a hole in the racing armor that he had been wearing two hours earlier. He rubbed his thumb over the crease in the titanium crash helmet and whistled. "Man, if that head shot had been an inch lower or to the left, it might have pierced this helmet instead of bouncing off. And thanks to your Kevlar, I only have a nasty bruise on my back."

"Any job goes better with the right equipment," Sanders agreed, as he studied the screen of his computer. "And lucky for us, Angela has the right equipment, too. She really got us the scoop on Svetlanikoff. Looks like we hit the jackpot."

With some effort, Sam rose from the couch and peered over Sanders' shoulder at the monitor. "See, we've got files from half a dozen different law enforcement agencies. He's definitely Russian Mafia. I wouldn't have thought that the CIA would have much interest in him, but there's a pretty big file. Nearly half a gig." He opened the CIA file and together they began to scan its contents. "Ah, yes, that's why the CIA is interested. He's got a long history as an arms dealer, selling Soviet-made weapons to terrorist organizations. There's also a Europol file. Looks like there's an ongoing attempt by law enforcement to infiltrate his organization."

Sam's eyes widened in disbelief. "Is this stuff real? How could you get all this information downloaded so easily to your home computer?"

"Nothing to it, really. I've been with the Bureau for a long time and I have a fairly high level security clearance. Also, I've loaded the Bureau's state-of-the-art encryption program on all of my computers. It's the same program, buy the way, that NASA uses to encrypt signals to satellites. Same one the major oil companies use to run equipment in oil fields halfway around the world. You probably didn't know that with the right codes, some guy with a laptop, sitting by the pool in his backyard in Texas, could turn a valve in Indonesia or Azerbaijan and dump a million gallons of oil into a pipeline, or shut down a hundred oil wells. That's just one tiny application of this program. There are a lot more sensitive applications, particularly in the military. The trick is the codes. It would take the biggest computer in the world a thousand years to break the codes this encryption program uses. Literally billions of bits of information make up the codes. Top secret information can be transmitted over regular fiber optic lines, or even broadband transmissions, but the signal is encoded. As long as the codes remain secret, there is very little risk."

"But you have all of this sensitive information right here in your living room! Isn't the FBI afraid that it will be compromised?"

"Well, they don't give security clearance to just anyone, you know. Angela obviously has a very high level clearance, and I've been an agent for seventeen years. Besides, it's the same information I have in my office. What's the difference? I could bring it home from the office in hard copy, just like you could bring home a court file. It's just a little more convenient this way."

"I'll say. So what was that part about someone infiltrating Svetlanikoff's organization?"

Sanders opened the file again. "Looks like the FBI has been cooperating with Europol in a joint effort to penetrate his business fronts. It says he's in Nevada, running his sham business operations from a casino."

"Wrong. He's in Oklahoma, trying to nail our hides to the wall!"

"Uh, yeah. I guess we could add a little note to this file. Tomorrow morning, I'll contact the agent in charge of the infiltration effort. Maybe we can help each other."

Sam stared at the screen for a few more minutes, then began to rub the back of his neck. He squinted hard at the screen before gingerly reclining on the couch, parking his head and feet on the low padded arms at either end. In a few seconds, his breathing became deep and slow.

"Another case of adrenaline overload," Sanders muttered as he continued to scan the screen. "Guess I'll have that whole pot of coffee to myself!"

* * * * *

Sam's eyes popped open. Slowly, they adjusted to the sunlight streaming into the room and he realized that he had slept for several hours on Sanders' lumpy couch. When he started to sit up, knots of stabbing pains in his back and legs stopped him short. With a groan, he eased back and relaxed for a moment longer to allow the pains to subside. More slowly, he lowered his feet to the floor and stiffly tilted to a sitting position. He was still wearing his jeans, T-shirt and motorcycle boots. Taking inventory of his strains and bruises, he realized it would take a little time to loosen up.

A few moments later, Katrina stepped into the room wrapped in Sanders' terrycloth bathrobe, carrying a steaming mug of coffee for Sam. *She is even more beautiful without makeup or footlights,* Sam thought. *More personal. More real.*

She placed the mug on the coffee table in front of him and sat at his side, taking his hand in hers. "Dave left early. You were sleeping so soundly, he did not want to wake you. He said to tell you that he needed to go to his office, but he will be back soon."

Sam nodded and took a sip of coffee. As he did, he looked into Katrina's deep brown eyes and saw a complex mixture of caring, concern, love, fear, and excitement. The stress of conflict and the exhilaration of victory had sparked a new fire in her. He could not remember having been in the presence of such an alluring woman.

"If you like, I will massage some of the soreness from your muscles. I am sure that your accident last night must have left you very stiff."

"I am pretty stiff this morning. A massage sounds great. But first let me shower. You don't want to grind in the grit and sweat. I can't believe that I fell asleep on the couch last night without even taking my boots off."

Ten minutes later, Sam stepped out of the bathroom wrapped in a large towel. "Dave didn't have another bathrobe," he said, as Katrina walked around the corner from the kitchen.

"You won't need a bathrobe for what I have in mind," she replied. Taking hold of his towel, she led him down the hall to a bedroom, her eyes coaxing, beguiling. "I plan to give you a massage that you will not soon forget," she said, and the bath towel slipped to the floor.

* * * * *

"Hello! Hello! Is anybody home?" Sanders called as he walked into the kitchen and dropped a sack of groceries on the counter. "It's lunchtime for all the hungry little munchkins!"

Sam emerged from the bedroom in his jeans and socks, pulling a polo shirt over his head and rubbing sleep from his eyes. "Hi, Dave. We were just catching a little cat nap. Katrina played doctor this morning. She fixed all my cuts and bruises and rubbed out some of the aches and pains. She's still snoozing."

"Does she know what happened last night?"

He shrugged. "After the meeting at the plant site, I stupidly wrecked Tony's new bike. Luckily, I was able to call you to bring me home. We're still a little vague on the details."

"So I guess you spared her the blow by blow of the shootout and your near-death experience. Does she know that Karmakov's back?"

"I didn't see any point in worrying her this morning. It wasn't the right time to talk business. She had other things on her mind. Anyway, she'll know everything soon enough. So did you learn anything at your office?"

"We hit the mother lode, Sam! We've got enough information on this Svetlanikoff and his outfit to write a novel. But the best part is that I managed to get in contact with the operative in Istanbul who's been tracking his operations in Russia and several other countries. Real deep undercover stuff. Code name is 'Oasis.' He handles a lot of clandestine operations in that part of the world. A friend in London hooked us up. Oasis said that if we share what we know with him, he'll fill us in on Svetlanikoff's Eastern European and Russian activities."

"Wow. That's amazing! How could you get that information so fast?"

"The network works incredibly fast these days, if you know the right people in the right places. But this really did involve a bit of dumb luck. When Angela's files revealed that there are operations against Svetlanikoff based in Turkey, I took a chance and called a guy I know at Scotland Yard who I met on an international bank fraud case a few years ago. I had heard that he'd been stationed in Turkey fairly recently. He happened to know the Europol guy in Istanbul who's been working the case. So we make a secure conference call, and a partnership is born!

Sometimes, believe it or not, intelligence agencies actually do cooperate."

"What a stroke of luck! Did he tell you anything interesting?"

"Lots of stuff. Svetlanikoff is worth a fortune from more than twenty years of illegal arms sales and other unsavory activities. And he's not a real popular guy. He keeps a heavy contingent of bodyguards at all times, real tough guys—former commandos, mercenaries and the like."

"Yeah, I think we already met some of them," Sam said with a grimace. "But maybe they're not as tough as they're cracked up to be."

"Wishful thinking. Anyway, lately, Svetlanikoff has been at odds with some of his best arms customers, terrorists of various stripes, especially a few of the Middle Eastern types. It seems that he and they have different ideas as to what's good business. Maybe they just don't like him, or he doesn't like them, or both. Anyway, that could be his Achilles' heel."

"What do you mean?" Sam queried.

"Terrorists don't have to fool around with warrants and indictments and such. If he crosses them too many times, they'll find a way to do him in, bodyguards or no bodyguards. They probably don't want to cut off a good source for arms, but if they get sick of his greed, double-dealing and other fine qualities, or if he cheats them, he could be history." Sanders paused. "Then of course, there are the other gangsters."

"You mean other cells of the Russian Mafia?"

"He apparently has many enemies in the underworld in Russia. Perhaps competitors is a better word. But there are also criminal elements in this country who are undoubtedly watching him because he's setting up shop in Nevada. By diversifying into the skin game, unregulated gambling, drugs and other rackets, he's breaking into territories that traditionally belong to particular domestic criminal organizations. The Internet is changing everything. As you saw from those websites, crime, like all other business enterprises, is globalizing. Territory, turf, is no longer sacred. He's likely to step on some pretty big toes soon, if he hasn't already. If we could just wait long enough, Svetlanikoff would probably self-destruct."

Sam shook his head. "Unfortunately, that's not an option. Svetlanikoff and Karmakov are hot on our trail. I'm sure that after last night, they'll redouble their efforts. By now, they might even have identified you, Dave. My family is at risk as long as those two villains are at large. I didn't worry too much about Huntington and his bunch murdering innocent people, but to these Russians, life is cheap. We've got to take decisive action, and fast!"

"Don't worry, Sam, I'm still with the plan. Uh…What's the plan?"

"Well, first things first. Let's eat lunch. I can't think on an empty stomach. Then we'll look at the information you've gathered and formulate a new plan. The old one is obsolete. It was based on the assumption that Huntington and his gang were in charge. Now that we know we're dealing with Svetlanikoff and we have some idea what his resources are, it should be a piece of cake to find his weak point."

"I've got to hand it to you, Sam. You're a true optimist!"

* * * * *

"Hah!" Huntington laughed, his face creased by the biggest smile Bandini had seen in years. "So the great Svetlanikoff fails to capture Littlehawk and loses two men in the bargain. That's rich! That condescending son-of-a-bitch isn't quite as perfect as he thinks he is."

"Well, his men aren't exactly lost," Bandini corrected, "but they'll be out of the action for a while. One of them took a bullet in the shoulder and the other one got pretty smashed up in a car crash, but he's still live. Littlehawk hasn't killed anyone yet."

"Have you identified his accomplice?"

"No, Olsen and Barton couldn't see much from the opposite side of the site, even with binoculars. You told them to stay out of the way and I guess they took that to heart, which is a good thing, considering it was like a war zone out there. In any event, Svetlanikoff's operation was a complete failure."

"So we're no better off than we were before," Huntington said, his dour expression returning. "Littlehawk is still on the loose and I'm sure that he's more cautious and determined than ever. We still haven't found Angelletti or the girl, and Svetlanikoff has declared himself king of the walk. That *sorry bastard!* We've got to do something fast or this whole thing will blow up in our faces. This has turned into a very dangerous game. What happened to your great plan to set Littlehawk and Svetlanikoff against each other, then take out any survivors?"

"That plan is still in the works. We just need to get them all in one place at the same time, then light the fuse and duck. Barton's getting some men together, as we discussed, to tie up the loose ends."

Huntington stared at Bandini and his eyes narrowed. "You get over there and meet with Svetlanikoff. Find out what they're plotting. They'll probably expect us to find Angelletti and Littlehawk, then blame us for this whole fiasco if we don't deliver them. You go meet with the Russians and come up with something fast. If you don't, then I *will* resort to my contingency plan, and it won't be pretty."

Bandini grimaced, then almost imperceptibly nodded.

* * * * *

Bandini took a seat in the Presidential Suite and tried to look comfortable. He wasn't, so he decided to seize the initiative. "Mr. Huntington asked me to meet with you," he began tentatively. "We want to help, of course, to ensure the success of the project. We will do whatever we can to stop Angelletti and Littlehawk." Bandini thought that those sentiments were safe. He stole a glance at the bruised and swollen face of Karmakov, whose eyes held a malevolent glow. "I came to ask what we can do to help."

Svetlanikoff stared at Bandini for a few moments without responding, measuring the sincerity of his words. "So Huntington has begun to understand his position, is that correct?" he asked skeptically. "I believed that he would not easily accept my taking command of the project."

"No," Bandini responded quickly, "he accepts your leadership, and we understand your position. We only want to remove the obstacles that have arisen and get the project back on a smooth track. The question now is how to flush out Littlehawk and Angelletti, after the events of last night."

Svetlanikoff gave Bandini another long, appraising look, then appeared to relax, a decision having been made. "Yes, that is the issue. Karmakov and I were just discussing that. What is your thought?"

Bandini saw his opportunity and spoke quickly. "Apparently, our threats did not work. Littlehawk was not willing to turn over his friends, even to save his family, who, by the way, have disappeared. Their ranch is deserted. Littlehawk knows that you could hit them months or years from now, but he has proven to be a risk taker. That makes threats a relatively ineffective means of motivation." Bandini looked from Svetlanikoff to Karmakov to gauge their response, but found no expression, so he forged ahead. "There is an old saying, 'If the stick doesn't work, try the carrot.' I think that we should offer him what he wants, and see if we can lure him that way."

"And what do you think he wants?" Svetlanikoff asked.

"He wants to make a deal. He has to. We have him now at a very serious disadvantage. We have the high ground. He is a fugitive. Huntington has a great deal of influence over the police, the judiciary, and the press in this state. Littlehawk and his family are in hiding and at great risk. We don't know where Angelletti and the girl are, but none of them can resume their lives until things change. The status quo does not favor them. Obviously, Littlehawk must want to make a deal."

Svetlanikoff's cold, inscrutable stare made Bandini uneasy, but he pushed on. "We need to propose another meeting, but on his terms this time. Let him think that we have reconsidered and we want out of this, that we have decided that the whole thing has become too risky. Tell him that we want to meet with him and Angelletti to work out the details. Let him choose the place. It really doesn't matter where we meet. Once we have drawn a bead on them, we can promise them anything, then we just keep them in our sights until they can be eliminated. And I'm certain that you have plenty of ways to handle that." He glanced at Karmakov and Scarface. "We just need to get them out in the open."

Karmakov's eyes narrowed at the thought of executing Littlehawk and Angelletti, but he said nothing, in deference to Svetlanikoff, who nodded slowly.

"Perhaps you are right," Svetlanikoff said. "Our meeting with Littlehawk last night may have had some benefit. Perhaps he now understands that his life is over, unless he can strike a deal with us. He may agree to another meeting, if he truly believes that we are willing to compromise the situation."

Bandini knew that once again, he was on a roll. His enthusiasm surged. "Just leave that to me, my friend. I'll contact Littlehawk and explain to him that we now recognize that he has the upper hand and we want to talk about a deal. Don't worry, he will deal. He has no other option."

"Huntington's prior mistakes have left us little choice," Svetlanikoff said dryly. "We must eliminate this threat to the project immediately. We have already received the first shipment of cargo at the site, and another is due tomorrow. The project must be resumed immediately. You have until tomorrow afternoon to contact Littlehawk. I want the meeting tomorrow night. And Angelletti and the ballerina must be there. Then we will finish this and all get back to the business of making money."

"Yes, sir!" Bandini said, as he quickly rose from his chair.

"And Bandini. You tell Huntington that if this plan does not succeed, my patience will be at an end."

Bandini was turning toward the double doors of the Presidential Suite when his cell phone rang. He pulled it from his pocket and flipped it open. No number appeared on the caller ID. "Bandini," he said curtly. There was a pause, then his eyes widened as he listened.

"We were just talking about you, *Littlehawk*." Bandini said the name with extra emphasis, shifting all attention his way. "I agree. There has got to be a way to work this out," he said, winking nervously at Svetlanikoff. "We've decided to pull the plug on the whole project. But for obvious reasons, we have little faith that you won't stir up trouble, even after the fact. For you and your friends to get out of this with your skins, there has got to be a deal."

There was a long pause, while Bandini listened. "Tomorrow night then, no later. We will expect you to name the meeting place by noon tomorrow. Any police or other authorities appear, and you're a dead man. And Angelletti and the ballerina must be there too, or there can be no deal. Okay, call on this number."

Bandini snapped the phone shut and turned with a smile. "No sooner said than done," he beamed.

"It is too convenient," Svetlanikoff said skeptically. "Why did he call you?"

"He has called me before. He knows the number. And that call just confirmed my prediction," Bandini said smugly. "Littlehawk understands that he can't win this game, nor can we, under the circumstances. He believes that we've reached a stalemate, and it's time to make a deal."

"And you understand the terms of the deal that we will make?"

"They couldn't be clearer," Bandini replied.

* * * * *

"Do you think that he went for it?" Sanders asked.

"Of course," Sam answered. "At this point, they'd promise anything to get Tony, Katrina and me out of the picture. They're desperate to contain the damage. I don't believe for a minute that they really intend to make any deal, but they might tip their hand a bit, if that's the only way they can get us into the open. I told Bandini that Svetlanikoff, Karmakov and Huntington all have to be at the meeting, or there's no deal. That gave him the chance to demand that Tony, Katrina and I all be there, too. This is going to be some meeting!"

"Yeah, and we better hope that your bright idea works. You've got to get in, get out, and protect yourselves during the meeting. Then leave the clean up to the authorities."

"The only question is, can we have the necessary forces in place in time? Washington isn't known for quick action in crisis situations—too many people to consult and political ramifications to consider."

Sanders looked at his watch. "A little more than twenty-four hours, and I'm supposed to field a battalion of forces without involving the local office. That's a tall order. So far, no one in Washington has even condescended to return my calls. I guess I've got my work cut out for me."

Katrina was sitting on the couch listening intently, but silently. Sam could see confidence in her calm demeanor. He looked at Sanders and shook his head with a grin. "Tony is going to love this plan!"

Chapter 25

On the back streets of Kabul, Afghanistan, a young teenage boy hurried down a narrow cobblestone alley in the old part of the city. His ankle length grey muslin caftan was dirty from travel, his thick, black hair tousled and dusty. He was tired, but he moved quickly, knowing that time was running out and his mission was important. He did not know the meaning of the message he carried, but he knew that its content was important to Sheik Mohammed Al Shadid, and he had been entrusted with its prompt delivery. He had been traveling steadily for nine hours from the camp in the desert mountains and he had not stopped to eat or rest, but he pushed on, knowing that his destination was near.

Finally, he arrived at the arched passageway he sought. Looking both ways and seeing nothing suspicious, he entered, then ascended a narrow stone stairway to an open air hallway that overlooked a courtyard. Following the explicit directions he had been given, he moved down the hallway to the third door, knocked in a curious pattern, then waited, praying silently that he had performed his duty well and he would be rewarded in paradise for his devotion to the cause. In a moment, the door opened and the boy entered.

Breathlessly, the boy handed the message to the dark-haired, dark-skinned man who opened the door. His face was thin and somber. He took the paper and read it quickly. He read it again and memorized its contents, than pulled a lighter from his pocket and lit the corner of the paper, which flamed briefly and disappeared. The man dropped the last burning fragment to the stone floor and stepped on it. Then he drew two silver coins from a pocket in his caftan and handed them to the boy. "You have done well," he said in Farsi. "Take this and go eat now in the city. You must be hungry after your travel. Then return to your master and tell him that the message has been delivered. Say nothing of this to anyone."

* * * * *

The boy bowed twice and silently exited the room. The man watched as he left and pondered the involvement of children in acts of terror. The boy was old enough to espouse a cause, but not old enough to understand it. He was probably fifteen years old. Already, he was a recruit of the virulent new terrorist organization that had no official name, but was simply called the New Jihad. The man shook his head and sighed. Some days he wondered why he continued in the eternal struggle. It would be nice just to retire to some green seaside town and try to forget. But then he would realize that he could never forget his family, the wife and children that had been slain by a terrorist bomb, nor could he forget the innocent people who would die at the hands of the New Jihad, if he did not act quickly and decisively. He could not leave the struggle as long as the fringe fundamentalists who had perverted the tenets of Islam for their own selfish political purposes continued to spawn new cells of terror. One day he would die in the struggle, but until that day, he would do what he could do, what he must do. Today, what he must do is continue to serve as a trusted lieutenant in the New Jihad.

It was already nearly noon, and the meeting was in four hours. He would have to hurry. Over his hooded caftan, he donned a heavier cloak against the cool of the mountain air. Walking quickly, he crossed the city on foot, then caught a local bus to an outlying community where a single water well and a few stone houses formed a small agricultural village at the edge of the desert. There, he quickly secured a horse and rode more than two hours into the deserted foothills, to a place known to only a few.

Approaching an ancient stucco and stone wall built against the base of a cliff, the man was challenged by a hooded guard who held an automatic weapon at the ready. Responding with the appropriate code words, the man was allowed to pass. He entered through a heavy wood door in the masonry wall, then proceeded along a path through a narrow canyon for some fifty meters. Rounding a stone outcropping, he entered a circular area perhaps forty meters across, surrounded by cliffs. In the center of the circle, a bonfire burned, sending flames and sparks high into the air. Around the bonfire a group of similarly dressed men, most of whom carried weapons, waited.

"Finally, brothers, we are all here." A tall man wearing a white turban, a finely embroidered caftan and a long grey beard walked toward the newcomer and raised his hand in greeting. The man's eyes were black under a dark brow, his faced lean and weathered from many years in the desert mountains. His age and bearing suggested that he was the leader of the gathering.

"Welcome, Omar. We have been waiting for you." The leader had a commanding presence, but he spoke quietly. Still, he could be heard easily in the enclosed area. As the newcomer took his place, the leader clapped his hands for attention, and when all was quiet, he addressed the group. "Brothers, our quest for revenge against the evil powers of east and west has finally reached maturity. You are the most trusted of our brotherhood and you should be the first to know of the great victory that is at hand. I called you together today to announce the accomplishment of a glorious act of war that will even the score with two of our enemies at once. Before the sun sets on Mecca tomorrow, these two enemies will suffer a grievous defeat."

There was a stir of approval among the men. The leader waited a moment for the random comments to subside, then continued.

"Some of you are already aware of this secret mission; some are not. As the leaders of the New Jihad, you must all be apprised of this great event which we are about to behold. As you know, we have long sought for a way to avenge the death of our brother Hakkid, who was killed without mercy by the infidel Russian arms dealer, Svetlanikoff. Many of you are aware that Svetlanikoff cheated our brotherhood by delivering inferior and defective arms he had stolen from the Russian government, after accepting high prices from us in both silver and women. The women were mostly kidnapped infidels, unruly and disobedient, and with them, he got what he deserved." There was a murmur of humor and agreement. "But the silver was very pure and precious. The Russian received full payment, and in return he furnished inferior weapons. When Hakkid confronted him and demanded satisfaction, he was tortured and executed, and his body left for the birds. The Russian must pay for this outrage to our brotherhood."

There was an angry outcry among the men, many of whom had known Hakkid, the Palestinian. The hostile outburst slowly subsided.

"We have long awaited the opportunity for revenge," Sheik Al Shadid continued grimly. "Svetlanikoff is always well-guarded, but no one can be permanently protected from the wrath of the New Jihad. We have waited for our opportunity, and it is now at hand!" Several of the men shouted encouragement. The anticipation of the group was growing.

"At the same time, we have long sought to reach the powerful hand of the New Jihad into the heart of America, to strike a blow avenging the acts of murder that have been visited upon our brothers in the Persian Gulf. The plan that has now been set into motion will accomplish both goals, and the world will know that the New Jihad's demands must be met!"

With this pronouncement, loud and strident support for Sheik Al Shadid and the New Jihad was shouted by every man. The power of the group was building to a familiar crescendo. "Tell us," a follower shouted, "what is this plan?"

The Sheik raised his hand for quiet. "One of our loyal contacts in Uzbekistan has managed to infiltrate Svetlanikoff's organization. He has recently learned that Svetlanikoff is making huge profits by burying deadly poisons in a construction site in America. So far, it seems that the Americans are ignorant of his activities. They have taken no action against Svetlanikoff. We have made a plan to take advantage of this situation to achieve two of our goals simultaneously."

"Even as we speak, agents of the New Jihad are secretly planting a powerful bomb in the construction site in America. When the bomb explodes, hundreds of barrels of deadly poison will be blown into the atmosphere. It will be, in effect, a chemical weapon of massive proportion. Thousands of our enemies will die. Svetlanikoff's project will be destroyed. The Americans will learn of the Russian's plan to bury tons of deadly poisons in their country, and he will become the enemy of America, pursued to the ends of the earth. Thus, we will have set our enemies against each other and will strike a deadly blow against two once. Then we will claim the glory."

Shouts of approval and encouragement rose from the gathered men, who unleashed a deafening barrage of gunfire into the air. "Long live the New Jihad! Long live Sheik Al Shadid, our great leader!"

Like the others, Omar joined the chant, yet even as he did, he planned the quickest route to his secure communications equipment.

An hour later, Omar was preparing to depart for Kabul, his new directive clearly defined by Sheik Al Shadid. He had never been an active participant in planning the acts of terrorism to be staged by the New Jihad. Instead, his job was to use his language skills as a liaison with other terrorist organizations and gather and analyze information shared among the loose network of terrorist groups across the globe. As such, he had become a close associate of the Sheik, a position that could quietly be used for his own purposes.

As he was speaking with some of the other men, preparing to depart, Omar felt a hand on his shoulder. It was the hand of the Sheik, who drew him aside and spoke softly. "Omar, it will be your honor to communicate the New Jihad's declaration of victory to the world. You must plan an announcement immediately, which I will review. Nothing can stop the wheels that have been set in motion. By tomorrow night, our enemies will feel the vengeful power of the Jihad. I regret that your role cannot be more direct. I know that you would gladly be a martyr for our cause, but your reward will be just as great in paradise. I will contact you in Kabul tomorrow."

Omar's face was partially obscured by the hood he had drawn over his head, but his black eyes glittered back at Al Shadid as he spoke. "The time is right for a strike, my Sheik. I'm sure there is nothing that can stop our plan. Long live the New Jihad!" Omar grasped Al Shadid's forearm for a moment, then he turned quickly and trotted down the path toward the ancient gate to the world of terror.

* * * * *

"It is good that our mission is well-funded by the Sheik's friends," Samir said as he watched the target they were tracking slide smoothly across the screen of the global positioning device he held in his lap. The small orange dot moved steadily across a road map of Texas, which scrolled vertically down the screen as the target's position changed. "It is much easier to follow the truck with this device."

Ali pulled their late model grey pickup truck into the left lane and passed a slow-moving van. "The land is flat, the road is straight, and the truck is less than one kilometer ahead of us. We could follow this truck all day without your expensive GPS device. What if it runs out of battery power? It is better to just stay close to the target. Mechanical devices can fail."

"It was good that we had it in the heavy traffic of Dallas," Samir countered. "If we had accidentally missed an exit or been forced to stop, we could have easily found the target again."

"But I did not lose the target, did I?" Ali replied haughtily. "Have I not told you that the old ways are the best? I trust my eyes and my hands. One day you will rely on this new technology and it will fail at a critical moment."

Samir decided not to argue further with his older brother, who was in one of his frequent bad moods. Since quarreling would not further the cause, he changed the subject. "Have you decided exactly where we will seize the truck?" Although the operation had been planned to the last detail, some discretion was left to the operatives for flexibility.

"We will wait until we are close to the destination. There will be less distance for us to drive the truck, less chance of discovery. There will still be plenty of time to make the transfer and arrive on time. Quit worrying me with such details. The plan is good."

They drove in silence for a while, then with youthful enthusiasm Samir return the conversation to his favorite topic. "Neddar told me the Jihad spent one hundred thousand U.S. dollars just to learn the time and place from which this shipment would be sent. That's a lot of money, Ali! Think what we could do with that much money! Think of the women we could buy!"

"Banish such thoughts from your mind, brother. We do this for the glory of the New Jihad, not for money! Your reward will be greater in paradise than any reward you could reap on this earth."

"True, but still, that is an incredible amount of money."

"That is not our concern. We will deliver the weapon without being detected, then bask in the glory of our triumph. Now quit bothering me with idle chatter of things that don't concern you."

* * * * *

Billy Butler parked his eighteen-wheeler at a Union truck stop three miles south of Beggs, Oklahoma. It had been a long haul from Houston, nearly ten hours on the road, and it was hot! The Peterbilt's air conditioning was on the blink and he had driven most of the way with the windows open and the dusty wind blowing through the cab. August in Texas was no place to lose the air conditioning. He pulled a dirty blue bandana from his back pocket and wiped sweat and grime from his face, then threw the door open and climbed down.

The cool air of the café was a welcome relief, and he stood under the ceiling vent just inside the door for a full minute before moving to the counter. He ordered a tall cup of ice tea to go, then drank a large glass of water while he waited. In an hour he would drop the load at its destination, then head for the Peterbilt shop in Tulsa. He had no intention of making the return trip to Houston without air conditioning.

After resting for a few more minutes, he picked up his tall cup of tea and headed back to his truck. As he neared his rig, he tossed his cigarette butt on the gravel, then took another pull on his iced tea. With the cup of tea in one hand, he climbed the ladder to the sleeper cab and slid into the driver's seat. He set the tea in a cup holder and was about to put the idling diesel in gear, when he noticed a strange smell in the cab. The odor was vaguely familiar, but nothing he had smelled in many years. He sniffed curiously as he shifted to release the emergency brake.

Suddenly, a hand reached forward from the sleeper cab and clamped a foul-smelling damp cloth over his nose and mouth. An arm was jammed behind his head, preventing him from turning or effectively resisting. Billy struggled for less than five seconds before his heavy frame went limp.

* * * * *

Fifteen minutes later and ten miles down the road, Ali pulled the hijacked eighteen-wheeler off the interstate highway onto a country road, followed closely by Samir in the grey pickup truck that they had driven from Houston. A mile off the road, both trucks came to a stop at a deserted intersection. No houses or buildings were visible in any direction. At Ali's command, Samir turned the pickup around and backed it up to within ten feet of the rear of the trailer. By the time the pickup was in place, Ali was already behind the eighteen-wheeler. Samir jumped out of the pickup and they conferred, then Samir began to walk toward the cab.

"Hurry, brother, if you want to live another day!" Ali shouted. "Someone could show up at any moment! If they do, the whole mission will be in jeopardy! Move quickly!"

Samir raced back with a heavy steel jack handle. He inserted it into the padlock on the back of the trailer and twisted hard. The lock was made of tempered steel and did not break. Straining his arms and back, he tried again to break the lock, with no success.

Ali impatiently pushed his brother aside. "There is no more time. I did not want to risk the noise and damage to the truck, but there is no choice." He pulled a small package from a bag hung over his shoulder and tore off a small piece of plastique. Molding it around the lock, he inserted a detonation trigger in the soft explosive. The two men stepped around the side of the truck and their eyes met for an instant. Ali held up a small triggering device in his hand and nodded to his brother. Samir placed his fingers in his ears. A second later, there was an explosion equal in volume to a small howitzer. The truck shuddered.

"Now use your pry bar to open the door. And do it quickly! The blast may draw attention. Someone might come to investigate soon!" In a moment, the doors of the trailer were open. Samir backed the pickup to within two feet of the open doors.

"First, the driver," Ali commanded. Looking furtively in every direction, the two men dragged the inert body of the driver from the sleeper of the cab and carried the heavy load to the bed of the pickup. Once there, they lowered it into a steel drum, then Samir secured the lid with a ring clamp.

"Now help me with the barrels!" Ali said. Grunting and straining, the two men removed two steel drums of toxic chemical waste from the fully loaded trailer and placed them in the bed of the pickup, replacing them with two steel drums from the pickup bed. Closing the trailer, Ali stood momentarily to survey their work. "Everything is secure," he said to the panting Samir. "The weapon is ready and the timer set. We must now deliver our cargo and if possible, escape. But if we are discovered," Ali paused, casting an intense look at his brother, "we must be willing and ready to sacrifice our lives for the cause. You understand that is our duty, do you not, my brother?"

"Of course I understand," Samir responded glibly, while secretly doubting his commitment to martyrdom. "How many times have we been told that our lives belong to the Jihad?"

Ali nodded and pulled from his pocket an electronic device that was no larger than a pack of cigarettes. "This is the trigger that can detonate the bomb instantly, if necessary. The bomb will destroy everything within a hundred meters. But the poisons that will be released and spread by the explosion will destroy or fatally contaminate everything within a hundred kilometers, and maybe much more, depending on the wind. We will do what must be done. It is time now to complete our mission."

* * * * *

Sam pushed the throttle of the high performance aircraft to full power and held it there for a second before releasing the brakes. Immediately, the tiny tail wheel of the half-size P-51 Mustang replica lifted off the ground. The four-hundred-horsepower engine roared through the straight exhaust pipes and the nimble aerobatic aircraft began to speed down the runway. In the length of a football field, the plane was airborne and climbing at the rate of four thousand feet per minute. At an altitude of two thousand feet, Sam leveled off and banked to the east.

He enjoyed the exhilaration of the takeoff and at altitude, he drank in the beauty of the crystal clear blue sky and the green pastures sliding by beneath his wings. Although his ancestors had never seen the land from this perspective, they had loved its enchanted forests, rolling hills and expansive plains, just as Sam did. A pair of bald eagles circling a thousand feet below reminded him that some of his ancestors might be sharing his birdseye view of the land after all.

Sam banked left, then right, carving a long serpentine curve in the sky, catching views over the low wings. Although he considered looping the aerobatic plane once or twice just for fun, he resolved not to get distracted from his mission. Instead, he settled for a couple of precisely executed aileron rolls. Like a slowly twisting drill bit, the plane bored an invisible hole in the sky while revolving twice on its longitudinal axis.

Sam's headset crackled. "Hey, Sammy, that was a real smooth move! A perfect maneuver. But you might give me a little warning next time," Jesse Jericho griped from the backseat of the tandem cockpit. "Dang near slammed my head into the bulkhead. I'm gonna remember to wear a helmet next time I fly with you!"

"Sorry if I rattled your gourd. I thought you'd already learned that lesson. In fact, you're the one who taught it to me!" Sam grinned into his microphone and winked over his shoulder at his friend. "Keep your hat pulled down if you don't want it blown off. I'm taking her down for a closer look."

Sam banked in a gentle dive toward the brown smudge on the horizon that was the excavation of the Greenleaf Project. "Why don't you take over, Jesse, so I can get a better view. I want to snap a few pictures. Just take her in low and slow so I can get a good look."

Jesse took the dual controls and throttled back, lining the aircraft up on a glide path that would dissipate speed and bring the plane in as if for a landing in a field just south of the construction site. As they approached the imaginary airport boundary, Jesse throttled the plane and stopped their descent. They cruised over at eighty knots and four hundred feet.

Sam surveyed the site. He noticed a black scar near the concrete plant where the motorcycle had burned, but the remains of the bike were gone. There was construction activity in several areas of the excavation. Focusing on the stockpile of steel drums that had provided cover during the firefight, he felt certain the pile had grown. He snapped half a dozen pictures through a telephoto lens. As the Mustang circled, workers on the site shaded their eyes to stare at the unusual aircraft overhead.

"One more time around, then home," Sam said over the radio.

On the next pass, Sam focused on a matrix of smaller, deeper excavations in the northwest corner of the pit, into which about a hundred steel drums had been moved. The camera clicked and whirred and another dozen pictures were recorded. Sam put the camera down and took one last look at the site as it receded. "Okay, I've seen enough. Let's get out of here."

"Roger, Captain." Jesse banked the Mustang and began a slow climb. Then the radio cracked again. "Uh, don't look now, Sam, but I think our airspace is being invaded. There's a black helicopter at one o'clock high, headed this way."

Sam peered out the canopy and saw the chopper, a Bell Jet Ranger, coming in fast directly toward the site.

"Well, I wonder who that could be," Sam said, with little doubt in his mind. "What would you think about going in for a closer look?"

"You're the Captain," Jesse answered. "Why don't you take back the stick. I just came along for the ride."

"Thanks, buddy. This time, just hang onto your hat."

Sam nosed the Mustang to a heading that would pass within two hundred feet of the chopper. Seconds later, he glimpsed the shocked look on the scarred face of the pilot as two aircraft passed at a combined airspeed of nearly three hundred miles per hour. As soon as they had passed the chopper, Sam pulled the stick back hard and the nose of the Mustang rose until, looking up, Jesse saw the earth above him. Hitting the left rudder and throwing the stick to the right, Sam brought the plane smartly upright at a higher altitude, several hundred feet above and behind the chopper and headed in the same direction.

"Well done, *amigo*!" Jesse crowed. "That was a nice about-face, just like I taught you! You may amount to something after all."

"I want to go back and take another look," Sam said as he pushed in the throttle and threw the plane into a dive that threatened to redline the airspeed indicator as it closed on the helicopter.

"Let's try to keep the wings on her, Sam," Jesse cautioned. "This here's a fast bird, but even a peregrine falcon has limits."

Sam leveled off at the same altitude as the chopper and bled some airspeed, as much to get a better view of the chopper as to appease his friend. This time, the plane was passing the chopper on its right and the difference in their relative airspeeds was only about twenty knots.

As the Mustang closed on the chopper, the side door of the chopper slid open and Sam saw more than he had expected. Buckled into a seat facing the rear of the chopper, holding a heavy automatic weapon, was Karmakov, his long, dark hair whipping in the wind. There was an instant of recognition when the eyes of the two adversaries met, then at virtually the same instant, Karmakov released a burst of machine gun fire and Sam jammed the stick of the Mustang forward. The high performance airplane bucked and its two occupants were thrown against their restraining harnesses as he sent it hurtling toward the earth in a steep dive.

"Eeeeeeeyow-wow!" Jesse yelped into the radio. "You damn near left my brains plastered all over the top of the canopy that time! Give us some warning when you're gonna do that, son!"

"Sorry, Jess, but this thing's not bullet-proof or armed for combat. Since we don't have a pair of fifty millimeter guns, I think it's time for us to make a graceful exit." He banked to the north, then pushed the throttle in, quickly accelerating and putting distance between the Mustang and the chopper. "We've got what we need. We'll just let 'em think we're heading north for a minute, then we'll come around and head back to the base."

"Roger that. But if you decide to turn any more corkscrews, just let me know, okay?"

* * * * *

"I can't believe it," Sam said incredulously, as he studied the photographs of the site. "It's hard to believe that anyone could be deranged enough to intentionally poison the land and everything in it for the next thousand years. On the other hand, it's right in line with the other miscreant activities Svetlanikoff is involved in."

"Could be a lot longer than a thousand years, based on the tests of the substances we scraped off your boots last night," Dave Sanders said, handing Sam a report from the testing lab. "You guessed right. Some of those barrels you were hiding behind in the pit must have been leaking. That black ooze on the soles of your boots was a real witch's brew. It's a good thing we discovered this before they buried the stuff. Too bad you tracked it all over my new carpet."

"I *hope* we discovered it before they buried any of the stuff," Sam replied. "But how can we know for sure?"

"We can't," Sanders said, flipping through the pictures on the table. "But it looks like they've placed steel drums in four new holes, and there doesn't seem to be any evidence of recently buried excavations. They haven't started pouring concrete yet. But maybe that's just wishful thinking. I guess we won't really know until after we get control of the site and do thorough testing."

Sam shook his head and began to flip through the photographs again. "I'll bet that's another load of waste being delivered," he said as he paused to study one of the pictures. "That looks like an eighteen-wheeler coming in through the front gate." He handed the picture to Sanders. "I wonder how many more truckloads of death are on the way to Oklahoma right now."

The telephone rang and Sanders rose to answer it, while Sam continued to study the photographs. Sanders listened for two full minutes in silence. When Sam looked up, wondering who was on the other end of the line, Sanders' normally placid visage wore an expression of shock and disbelief. He cast a meaningful look at Sam as he simultaneously hit the speaker button on the telephone and activated a recording device attached to it. Instantly, a heavily accented male voice filled the room. "Our contact in the New Jihad is well-placed and very reliable. There is no doubt that an attack is imminent. According to our source, the strike is intended to embarrass Svetlanikoff and destroy his operation there, while punishing America for its military actions in the Middle East. A fairly clever plan, in a demented sort of way."

"Do we know what type of weapon it is or how it's supposed to be delivered?" Sanders asked.

"No. Like most terrorist organizations, information is disseminated in the New Jihad on a need-to-know basis. We learned only that the operation is in progress and the weapon is intended to blow a thousand drums of poisons into the atmosphere. Based upon what we know about this New Jihad, I would expect a very potent weapon. This is a virulent group, well-funded and with powerful connections."

Sanders and Sam stared at one another with wide eyes as the incredible news began to sink in.

"And one more thing," Oasis continued, "the terrorist leader said that the bomb would explode 'before the sun sets on Mecca tomorrow.' How long before sunset, he did not say. That was several hours ago. It was evening in Afghanistan then, but it was early morning here. We don't know whether he was speaking literally or figuratively, but obviously, time is of the essence."

"Who else knows about this?"

"My first call was to the CIA, only ten minutes ago. Tactical anti-terrorist units will be scrambled, but that will take time. Since we don't know what type of weapon it is or how it will be delivered, preparing a response will be difficult. The team will require contingency plans and equipment to deal with many possibilities. They will need to be prepared for toxic chemicals. Langley is beginning preparations, but it will undoubtedly take some time to prepare. They may be too late."

"What about the local authorities? Has anyone contacted them?" Sanders asked.

"The CIA will decide who to notify. You must talk with the CIA. I will provide a contact person there. I am sure that there are protocols that the CIA uses in dealing with local authorities in America. But considering Svetlanikoff's usual practice of bribing local officials, which he has done in many places, you may not want any local authorities involved. There could be a great deal of confusion when a terrorist threat is added to the tangled web Svetlanikoff has surely woven."

"That's affirmative," Sanders responded, nodding at Sam. "We just need to know who you've already contacted."

"I've spoken with no one except the CIA since I received the call from our contact in the New Jihad half an hour ago. Immediately after concluding my report to Langley, I called you. You and your associates are the closest to the situation and you have some knowledge of Svetlanikoff and his activities in your region. You have seen the site where the bomb will be delivered. I hate to say it, my friend, but you may be the only ones who can prevent a disaster of historic proportions."

Sanders looked grim. "Anything more that you can tell us?" he asked.

"I'm sorry. As you can imagine, it is very difficult and dangerous to obtain information from inside the terrorist groups. This is all that I can tell you."

"Any suggestions?" Sanders asked.

"Stay in contact. I may have more information later. But don't expect too much. Our contact in Afghanistan is scheduled to announce to the world the success of the operation and to claim responsibility on behalf of the New Jihad. We have been told that he is scheduled to deliver the announcement from Kabul tomorrow. The situation is moving very quickly. There is no time to lose."

There was a pause as the men considered the enormity of the situation. "Okay, you know how to reach us. Please let us know immediately of any further developments."

Sanders broke the connection and turned to Sam, who had risen and was pacing the floor, limping slightly from the previous night's encounter with a rock wall. It was clear from the determined set of his brow that he intended to take action.

"The gods are smiling on us," Sanders said. "It's a lucky thing that we got in touch with Oasis yesterday. Otherwise, he wouldn't have known that we were here. After our conversation, he must have put two and two together and concluded that the Greenleaf Project is the toxic waste dump that the terrorists are planning to blow up. He sure hit the nail on the head."

Sam winced at Sanders' words as much as at the pains in his back and legs. "Doesn't sound like we have much time, Dave."

"No time. We need to move right now. You got a plan?"

Sam rubbed his temples. "Give me five more minutes. Then I'll lay it out."

"Good," Sanders said. "That will give me time to scare up a few hundred more rounds of ammunition. I'm afraid we're going to need them."

"And while you're at it," Sam said, "call Tony and tell him to get dressed, I'll be there to pick him up in fifteen minutes. We're going to need all the help we can get, and he's been gold-bricking long enough! Tell him it's show time!"

* * * * *

"So that's it," Sam said. "Any questions?"

Sanders, Tony, and Katrina all began to chatter at once, none yielding to the others. After a few seconds, Sam waved his hands, then made a time out sign. Slowly, the clamor subsided.

"Okay, okay, you're right. We don't know where the bomb is. We don't even know for sure that it's at the site. We don't know what it looks like or when it is supposed to detonate. We don't know what Svetlanikoff has up his sleeve, other than knowing that he plans to kill us all at the first opportunity. We don't know where Karmakov is, or when or where Huntington and his contingent will turn up. I realize there's a lot that we don't know."

A pregnant silence filled the room, so he continued. "But there are a few things we *do* know. We know that a few miles from here, there's a huge dump of toxic waste that will be blown sky high by a terrorist bomb within a few hours, maybe sooner, if we don't stop it. We know that this act of terrorism could kill thousands of people. If that isn't enough, we also know that until we face these Russian gangsters and put and end to this mess once and for all, we'll continue to be fugitives, running for our lives. There's nothing certain about this. One or all of us could die today, from a gangster's bullet or a terrorist's bomb. But if we don't do something, thousands of innocent people *will* die, slowly and painfully, while the perpetrators walk away from a poisoned land, *our* land."

"The hell with that!" Tony flared. "They can't get away with this! And I can't sit on my hands waiting for the CIA to get their act together. This whole corner of the state could be destroyed at any minute!"

"You and Katrina could beat feet out of here until this is over," Sam said. "You could head for the Arkansas border."

"And leave all the fun and excitement to you?" Tony shot back. "Not a chance."

"I feel responsible for getting you all into this," Katrina added. "I must see this through to the end."

"You did not get us into this, but if you want to help get us out, we can use you. We'll need all the help we can get," Sam replied.

"Well, I just can't believe that you expect to leave me here," Sanders said sourly. "You're going to need me, too."

"Not until you've made contact again with Oasis and coordinated our plan with the CIA. Managing the operation is as important as being on the front line."

"And Dave," Katrina said, gripping his forearm, "if we do not make it in time, there must be someone alive who knows what has happened—someone with credibility who knows the whole story."

Sanders scowled and stared at his hands. "I just hate being left behind. I'll be there as soon as I can."

"So we're set then," Sam said with finality. "Let's move like the wind! A lot of lives are depending on us."

Chapter 26

Dave hit the redial button for the third time and listened as the Bureau messaging equipment went through a long litany of commands. Since it was Saturday afternoon, his personal contacts at FBI headquarters weren't available. Relegated to the standard access lines, after what seemed like an interminable wait, he finally reached the regional desk for Oklahoma, which patched him through to the duty officer, Agent James Brett. Dave was delighted to learn that Agent Brett already seemed familiar with the file.

"Yes, Agent Sanders," Brett said in a formal tone, "I've been reading that file all afternoon. An incredible saga, I must say. And it seems that you have played a key role in it."

"A very insignificant role, really," Sanders said, feeling a sudden sense of distrust. Something in Brett's tone put him on guard. Sam's report had minimized any references to his involvement, and he began to wonder who else had contacted Bureau headquarters. Moving cautiously, he waited for Brett to thrust as he prepared to parry.

"There have been some other reports filed in addition to the so-called Littlehawk report," Brett replied, as if reading Dave's mind. "In fact, your own field office issued a brief communiqué just this afternoon. It seems that some of your superiors think that you greatly overstepped your authority in this matter, using Bureau assets in your own private investigation, after being prohibited from having any involvement in the matter."

Dave cringed, not liking the direction the conversation was going, but knowing that the urgency of the situation dictated complete candor on his part, even if Brett was already prejudiced against him. There was no time to play games. "Okay, perhaps I did take a few liberties with Bureau property," he admitted, "and I do have a personal interest in this case. But it was all absolutely necessary under the circumstances. And I am calling to tell you and anyone else who will listen that every word in that Littlehawk report is true and there is a doomsday scenario playing out right now, right here in Oklahoma. We need your help, and we need it immediately!"

There was a moment of silence on the other end of the line.

"Agent Sanders, why are you calling this office directly and not following the proper chain of command?" Brett's voice held a distinct note of suspicion. "Any request for assistance should be coming from the Director of your state office."

"I thought you said that you had read the report. It clearly explains that we don't know who all is implicated in this…"

"The report that I've read, which, by the way, *did* come through the proper chain of command, clearly explains that you, Agent Sanders, are believed to have been harboring and consorting with known felons, including the author of this anonymous report, who it appears is a personal friend of yours. Now that may or may not be true, but I think that we had better look into some of the allegations through the proper chain of command, before we talk about dispatching a strike force to Oklahoma."

Sanders rolled his eyes in frustration and grimaced silently, knowing that minutes were precious and his chances of securing any help from the Bureau were rapidly diminishing. "Agent Brett, I appreciate your desire to follow the proper procedures, and I recognize your authority in the present situation," Sanders said in a solemn tone, hoping to mask his disgust. "But would it be possible for me to talk directly with the Regional Director?"

"Regional Director Hammett just left for the golf course a few minutes ago. He left me in charge of this investigation. He told me that he was sure that I could handle anything that came up, at least until he has finished eighteen holes. He was really quite pointed about that."

"So you have no intention of sending help?"

"I think that in this case, discretion is the better part of valor, Agent Sanders. And I have to exercise my discretion in this case in favor of the report of your superiors. I'm sorry, but until a few of these points are reviewed, I'm not ordering a battalion of agents to descend on Oklahoma. I will, however, give Chief Hammett your message and ask him to call both State Director Walton and you just as soon as he can. I'm sure that he'll get this straightened out in short order."

"His golf game could cost the lives of thousands of people!" Sanders said, finally exploding with frustration.

"I will give him your message without fail, and as soon as reasonably possible. In the meantime, I suggest you call your Director Walton and discuss the matter with him. He certainly wants to have a word with you."

Sanders dropped the receiver on its cradle and slammed his hand down hard enough to make the water glasses jump on the table. Pompous young bastard! Something had to be done, and fast! Even now, his friends were walking into the jaws of certain death, and he was helpless to do anything about it. He snatched the phone again and dialed another number. He would find *someone* who would listen, or die trying.

* * * * *

Huntington was cooler than he had been in weeks. Standing in his penthouse suite with a site plan of the Greenleaf Project spread on the table, he was the consummate battlefield commander, taking charge and giving orders. Where conniving and manipulation had failed, he knew that direct action would succeed, and the execution of his plan was imminent. He had devised a role for everyone and his orders carried the authority of a papal edict among his followers. Barton and Olsen, dressed in khakis, stood by, while Bandini lounged in an armchair, his feet resting on an ottoman.

"There, Barton, there!" Huntington spouted, pointing to the intersection of two lines on the site plan. "Two men right there, and two more men over here." He hit the map with the tip of his index finger. "Get 'em in a crossfire! From the high ground on the edge of the pit, with infrared scopes, it will be no problem to pick 'em off, if your men are as good as they say they are. There will be fewer than a dozen targets and they will all be shooting at each other. They won't know you're there until it's too late."

"How do we know that?" Barton asked nervously.

"As soon as the first shot's fired, I guarantee there will be a free-for-all. Your first shot may even trigger the shootout. They won't know where the bullets are coming from. Your men just have to make sure that no one is left standing."

"Won't it look kind of suspicious, I mean, that they all killed each other, that no one survived at all?"

Bandini pushed up from the armchair. "Not after a few drums of gasoline explode. There won't be enough evidence left to piece together anything. Besides, the investigators won't know how many more escaped."

"But what about the…the 'cargo' that's down there? Won't the gasoline fire burn that stuff and…wow!" Olsen exclaimed, as the import of his own words sunk in.

"Don't worry," Bandini said lightly, "the drums of fuel are next to the shack, quite a distance away from the drums of waste. I doubt that anyone there will get too close to those toxins. They all know what it is."

"But isn't it an awful risk, Mr. Huntington, to bring the authorities down on the site when it's full of…that stuff? Gun battle and all?"

"It's one *hell* of a risk, you idiot! And we would never *be* in this position if *some* damn fools had done their jobs right!" Huntington's face was flushed and heavy with anger as he looked back and forth between Barton and Olsen. "But we've got an out-of-control situation and this is the only way to deal with it."

Bandini interceded. "The authorities are not going to question much, after we tell them what happened. They'll be sympathetic to Southwest Energy, an innocent bystander. And remember, this is the Russian Mafia. It was a big drug deal gone sour. This stuff happens all the time."

"Not with the Russian Mafia in Oklahoma," Olsen mumbled.

"The place will be locked up as a crime scene, giving us time to clean it up," Bandini instructed. "We'll find a way to get rid of the toxic wastes. We've just got to regain control of the situation and eliminate Svetlanikoff and the others. Then we can put a lid on it."

Huntington's face was a mask of iron determination. He turned to his two unlikely field commanders, Barton and Olsen. "Just make sure you keep your heads down, leave no evidence, and get out fast after the job is done. *Completely* done."

Barton looked queasy. He swallowed slowly, hesitating, the muscles in his jaw flexing involuntarily, before he answered, "Sure thing, Mr. Huntington. There won't be any slip-ups this time."

"Get into position, then," Huntington said, dismissing Barton and Olsen with the wave of a hand.

* * * * *

An hour later, Huntington and Bandini were still sitting in the living room of the penthouse, concocting and rehearsing a story for the authorities and a separate version for the press, who would undoubtedly be at the site shortly after the discovery of the gun battle. Bandini was in the middle of a sentence when the doorbell rang. "Now who could that be?" he asked.

Huntington strode to the door to look through the peephole. Casting a dark look at Bandini, he opened the door. Svetlanikoff and two men dressed in black fatigues entered the room.

"To what do we owe this surprise visit?" Bandini asked quickly as he walked toward the visitors, hoping to defuse any further confrontation.

Svetlanikoff was relaxed, almost casual, as he regarded Huntington and Bandini. "The two of you will accompany us to our meeting with Littlehawk," he said. "You may be instrumental in brokering a deal. Your presence may be useful in a number of ways."

Bandini's pulse quickened as his mind raced through the myriad ramifications of Svetlanikoff's simple statement. What could they possibly add to the negotiations, since there weren't going to be any? There would only be the quick executions of Littlehawk and Angelletti, and probably the girl. He knew that he and Huntington had no role at the meeting and he wondered how much their lives were worth to Svetlanikoff at this point. Was his comment pure fiction, intended to keep them guessing as they were driven to their own executions? And if Svetlanikoff did not kill them, would they be shot by their own forces, who had just been instructed by Huntington to make sure no one was left standing?

Bandini's stomach was in a tight knot as he sank into a chair and pondered the possibilities. Suddenly, he wondered if they could create an opportunity. Maybe a deal actually could be brokered! He began to search furiously for some reason why they should talk with Littlehawk and Angelletti, some value that they could offer to Svetlanikoff in exchange for their lives. Outwardly, Bandini remained calm, but his mind was churning as he said, "Really, I don't see how anything could be added by our attendance. I'm sure that you know exactly how to deal with these radicals."

For once, Huntington wisely held his tongue.

"There are several reasons why you both must join us," Svetlanikoff answered. "We don't need to discuss them now. I do, of course, have a plan for dealing with the opposition. Karmakov will enjoy compelling them to reveal the identities of those with whom they have spoken about the project, and what has been said. Karmakov is truly a creative genius at the art of interrogation. He is currently making ready his tools." He glanced at his watch. "It is past four-thirty. Time for us to go."

Svetlanikoff's cold grey eyes turned briefly toward his henchman. Scarface, who had stood quietly next to his boss during their brief encounter, drew an automatic pistol from his shoulder bag, then slipped the gun behind the bag where it was hidden, but instantly accessible. Without saying a word, he had made it perfectly clear who was in control of the situation.

How quickly the tables turn, Bandini thought ruefully as the five men stepped out of the suite and into the elevator.

* * * * *

Fifteen minutes later, Huntington and Bandini found themselves being escorted into the cabin of a black Bell Jet Ranger helicopter. The pilot was already at the controls and takeoff was imminent.

"So you see," Svetlanikoff lectured, as the turbine engine of the helicopter spooled up and the rotor began to turn, "your feeble attempt to gain control was doomed to failure even before it began. I have been working with the criminal element for many years. I was, of course, expecting your duplicity. Surely you did not think that I was so gullible?"

Huntington and Bandini sat silently on a bench seat facing the Russian and his two armed henchmen.

"Even now, my ground contingent is approaching the site by surface transport and will secure it prior to our arrival. Your men will be neutralized. I will then take a commanding position, a grandstand seat, if you will, on the very platform from which we assessed the project two days ago, which offers an excellent view of the entire site. Then, like Caesar at the Roman games, I will watch my gladiator champion, Karmakov, eviscerate the annoying vermin who have dared to threaten me."

Bandini stared across the helicopter cabin at Svetlanikoff. The Russian was truly mad, even more so than he had imagined, or perhaps the current circumstances were driving the man to new heights of insanity. He was more egocentric and grandiose than Huntington by a double measure, if that was possible, with absolute confidence in his own invincibility. Bandini had experience dealing with megalomaniacs, but how could he take advantage of the present situation before he and Huntington became a meal for the lions at Svetlanikoff's demented gladiator games?

"So where is Karmakov, anyway?" Bandini asked.

"In the other helicopter," Svetlanikoff replied, glancing out the window at the Jet Ranger flanking theirs. "I expect that by the time we have found our grandstand seats, Karmakov will have captured Littlehawk and his friends. Then the fun will begin."

Bandini cringed, wondering whether he and Huntington would play an active role in the nightmarish "fun" that the Russians had planned, and feeling with great trepidition that he knew the answer.

* * * * *

The oppressive heat of the August afternoon poured in invisible waves over the rock walls of the excavation and settled in the pit, where the eighteen-wheeler was being unloaded. The intense heat was strangely comforting to Samir—it reminded him of the deserts where he and Ali had spent most of their childhood.

He was content knowing that their mission was nearing an end. A few more hours and they would be celebrating victory in the desert of Central Mexico.

As Samir watched a rough terrain forklift raise the last pallet of steel drums, he checked his watch. Four forty-five. The bomb was set to detonate at six o'clock. That would give them more than an hour to clear the area. With luck, they would be thirty miles away by the time of detonation, close enough, perhaps, to hear the explosion, but far enough away to avoid contamination. Since the prevailing wind was from the south, they would head southwest toward the Mexican border.

Samir thought of the beautiful women he had seen in the coastal villages of Turkey and in Constantinople, where they had received their final training by the Jihad. Armenian gypsy girls, Persian belly dancers, European women on vacation, all were intriguing to Samir. The financial reward for successful completion of the mission would allow for many months, maybe even years of leisure, before he would again be asked to risk his life for the New Jihad.

As Samir dreamed of the women and the good times to come, his vision of the cause became cloudy. Although trained to maintain a completely clear focus on the mission and the cause, exactly what "the cause" was had never been totally clear to him. He had been just fourteen years old when his father gave him to the Jihad. His duty was to assist and support his older brother, Ali, whose intense commitment to the cause was an inspiration for many. For nearly four years, he had tried to develop a great commitment to the cause like his brother, but the gregarious Samir was not meant for the solitary life they led. His longing for female companionship was a constant distraction.

In the rising heat waves, Samir envisioned the lithe figure of a young woman in veil and pantaloons of the sheerest fabric, swaying and coaxing silently, flashing enchanting dark eyes over her bare shoulder in his direction. Soon, he would find himself in the arms of a beautiful young Mediterranean woman…

"Samir!" Ali hissed. "What are you doing? Keep your focus on the mission! How long has the truck been unloaded?"

Samir's attention snapped back. "How long…?" he muttered, looking again at his watch, he quickly answered, "Not long, brother, only for a minute or two…"

"Then move!" Ali said harshly. "There is not one minute to spare! Close the back of the trailer and get in!"

Samir quickly followed his brother's orders and climbed into the high cab of the Peterbilt.

* * * * *

The Ford pickup went airborne as it topped a rise on the two lane country road at eighty miles an hour. Landing hard, Sam corrected for the fish-tail and again stomped on the accelerator.

"We can't stop any terrorists if we don't get there alive," Tony shouted over the noise of the engine, while Katrina braced herself with both hands on the dashboard. "This ain't no BMW, y'know!"

Sam shot a quick glance at his two friends and eased up a little on the accelerator.

"It's almost five o'clock," Tony continued in a slightly lower voice. We must be pretty close. Have you had any more bright ideas, or are we just going to ride in and shoot up the town?"

"It's going to be a fluid situation," Sam said noncommittally.

"Meaning we haven't got a clue what we're doing," Tony replied.

"Of course we know what we're doing. We're going to evaluate the situation, take control of it, kick the bejeezus out of the Russians, then find the bomb and defuse it. What did you think we were going to do?" Sam looked at Tony like he had just asked which shoe to put on first.

"So we really don't have a clue," Tony insisted.

"It's like this—truth and justice are on our side. We have no choice but to trust fate. We'll let the spirit guide us. Get my drift?"

"Nothing like walking into the jaws of death with a blindfold on, huh?"

"Actually," Sam replied, "we're *riding* into the jaws of death in this here pickup truck and we've all got our eyes wide open."

"Aw, now you're just trying to make me feel better," Tony said.

"Will you two just *stop it*!" Katrina burst out in frustration. "You sound like we are going to a…a *rodeo* or something!"

Sam grimaced. He and Tony had a long history of taking risks together, from sky diving to bull riding to ski jumping, and their alliance had always involved a heavy helping of gallows humor. Katrina didn't understand that grim comedy was their way of relieving tension.

Acknowledging his second thoughts about placing her in harm's way, Sam said, "Katrina, maybe it would be best if we drop you off somewhere before…"

"No way, Sam. You and Tony will need my help. You do not know what we are facing. And besides, you must not forget who saved your sorry behind at the airport!"

"She's got you there, buddy!" Tony chortled gleefully. "Say, Kate, you're picking up on our Okie lingo pretty good! Saved his 'sorry behind!' Hah! That's good! But from what I hear, it was more than his 'sorry behind' that you saved!"

"Okay, okay," Sam said. "I give. You're right, you saved my skin. Maybe you'll do it again. Just be careful, Katrina. This is no Sunday afternoon picnic. And I hope you're ready for it, because it looks like we're here." Sam slowed the truck and cranked the wheel of the pickup to the left as they turned into the entrance to the project.

"Now stay loose and move quick," Sam said with a sudden calmness. "Follow my lead and we may just come out of this alive."

Chapter 27

Sam pulled up by the guard shack and stopped, rolling down his window as the guard walked around the front of the truck to the driver's side.

"Hey!" Sam said, "We've got a piece of equipment to deliver." He cocked his head toward a blue plastic tarp wrapped around something long and flat in the bed of the pickup. "We're supposed to unload it by the building down there in the pit."

The guard looked at the blue tarp and frowned. "No one said anything to me about a delivery of equipment this afternoon. You got any paperwork?"

"Well, no, I guess they didn't think they needed to send any…"

At that moment, Sam's attention was drawn from the guard to a tractor-trailer rig that was topping the ramp some eighty yards away and turning in the direction of the guard shack. Its engine was racing as the driver double-clutched, having some trouble putting the big machine through its gears. The drive wheels of the Peterbilt tractor were spinning, throwing showers of dirt and gravel as it belched black smoke from its double stacks. The guard turned to follow Sam's gaze.

"What the heck is he doing with that truck?" Sam asked, hoping that the guard would forget the question about the paperwork.

"Oh, those camel-jocks don't know how to drive trucks," the guard said, as the trailer finally cleared the ramp and began to roll more smoothly. That driver was double-clutchin' and jake-brakin' all the way down the ramp an hour ago. They're gonna blow up that truck."

As the truck drew nearer, accelerating as it came, Sam could see the dark countenance of the driver, and the deranged look on his face sent a chill down Sam's spine. A sudden realization swept over him, and a quick glance at Tony confirmed his suspicions.

"You'll have to take out the guard," Sam whispered, turning his head away from the open window, "but try not to hurt him. When I hit the gas, Tony, you jump. Katrina, hang on tight!"

Without a second of hesitation, Sam gunned the engine and cranked the wheel to the left, spinning the tires and throwing the pickup into the path of the eighteen-wheeler, blocking the gate. At the same time, Tony jumped out of the passenger door and rolled wide to stay clear of the massive truck. The driver of the Peterbilt instinctively slammed on the brakes to avoid a collision, skidding to a stop five feet from the passenger side of the pickup. In seconds, Sam was out of the pickup and climbing the short ladder to the Peterbilt's cab.

For a brief moment, the terrorists were frozen by surprise and indecision. Then, with a defiant cry, Ali slammed his foot back down on the accelerator and popped the clutch, at the same time reaching for a weapon. The Peterbilt roared forward, belching black smoke as it rammed the pickup broadside and slowly pushed it sideways through the gate.

In the next second, Sam, clinging to the outside of the cab, reached through the open window and slammed his fist into the side of the driver's head, connecting hard with his left ear and jaw. Ali reeled, but in a second came up with an automatic pistol in his right hand. Holding fast to the steering wheel with his left hand, he tried to bring the pistol to bear, but Sam quickly leaned in the window, grabbing the pistol with one hand and Ali's throat with the other. Sam squeezed hard and the man's eyes bulged, his face slowly turning dark red. As they struggled over the weapon, a burst of fire from the automatic pistol shattered the truck's windshield.

Still in the passenger seat, Samir was scrambling to unsheathe another weapon. As flying shards of glass and bullets filled the cab of the truck, he opened his door and leaped out, rolling on the ground as the Peterbilt continued to slowly grind its way into the pickup truck. At the same moment, Katrina jumped from the open driver's door of the pickup and ran out of the path of the twisted, groaning metal monster that was advancing slowly through the gate.

Sam let go of the terrorist's throat just long enough to stun him with three quick jabs to his left eye. He took advantage of the moment by dislodging the gun with a sharp, chopping blow to the wrist. As the gun dropped to the floor of the cab, Sam dragged open the door. Grabbing the man by his hair with one hand and his shirt with the other, Sam threw himself backward, and the two combatants tumbled eight feet to the ground. The Peterbilt, still in gear, finally died in the gateway with the hulk of the pickup truck twisted around its front bumper.

Pushing away from the Peterbilt as they fell, Sam maintained his balance and found himself straddling the terrorist's chest on the ground. Ali was stunned, but not unconscious. Quickly, Sam rolled him over so he was face-down on the ground and twisted his arms behind his back.

"What the hell is going on here?" the security guard shouted as he fumbled with the leather catch on his holster. The entire fracas had taken less than a minute, all of which time the guard had spent dodging the trucks and bullets while trying to comprehend the unexpected situation.

"Nothing that you need to worry about," Katrina said, as she poked a pistol into the guard's back. "There is not time enough to explain. Now please lay on the ground and you will not be hurt." Katrina looked toward Sam with a question in her eyes and Sam gave her a quick nod of encouragement.

"I've got this one under control," Tony yelled from the other side of the Peterbilt. He walked the young terrorist around the truck with a strong forearm around his throat and his arm cranked tightly behind his back. "What shall I do with him?"

Sam thought fast. "Put him next to this one. Keep that gun on both of them. If either of them moves, shoot 'em. Katrina, you get those two big rolls of duct tape from the floor of the pickup. We've got to work fast."

At that moment, a two-way radio hanging on the guard's belt squawked. "Hey, Bobby, you ready to head for the house?" The noise startled Katrina.

Sam's attention was momentarily distracted and the terrorist felt his grip relax. With a mighty jerk and a piercing yell, he wrenched himself free from Sam's arm lock and they both tumbled again on the ground, arms flailing, kicking and wrestling in the dirt. Suddenly, Ali broke away and jumped to his feet. Reaching into this pocket, he produced a small metal object. "Stop!" he shouted, "Or I will detonate the bomb now! We will all die!"

Sam froze, staring at the tattered, panting man, who was clearly desperate to complete his mission.

"This is a trigger to the bomb!" he shouted, waving the metal object. "We are prepared to die *for the glory of the Jihad*," he added through gritted teeth, spitting dirt and blood as he spoke.

There was a moment of silence.

"What the hell is he talking about?" The dazed security guard asked from the ground. "What the hell bomb is he talking about? What Jihad? Who the hell *are* you people?"

"No, Ali!" the younger man blurted, his neck still locked in the crook of Tony's heavy forearm. "Do not do it! I *do not* want to die for the Jihad! Not now!"

"But we will live forever in paradise, as the Mullahs promised!" Ali shouted.

An instant later, there was a sudden crack, and Ali's upraised right arm jerked back, his forearm appearing to explode in a spray of blood. Ali was spun by the impact of the bullet, his lifeless hand releasing the triggering device, which fell to the ground. Sam lunged forward, snatching the device as Ali screamed with pain and clutched his shattered arm. For an instant, all was still. Then with a wild scream, the enraged terrorist charged Sam, who stood warily with the triggering device in his hand. This time, Sam was ready. As Ali rushed forward, Sam spun and planted a well-timed back thrust kick squarely in the terrorist's solar plexus, stopping his momentum in mid-stride. Ali dropped to the ground with a surprised look on his face, immobilized, gagging, and trying unsuccessfully to inhale.

Sam turned to Katrina, who was holding a smoking pistol.

"That was some shooting," he said with a measure of awe.

"Muscle control," Katrina shrugged. "I practiced shooting in Russia."

Tony shook his head in wonder. "That was a hell of a chance you took!"

"What choice did I have?" Katrina shot back.

"Don't ever underestimate this one," Sam said to Tony.

Sam nodded to Tony, and the two men restrained Ali while they bound him hand and foot. Sam wrapped duct tape tightly around his broken arm, binding the wound and stopping the profuse bleeding. When he was done, he bound the younger man's hands, then he sat them back to back on the ground and wrapped several loops of duct tape around them. As an afterthought, he threw a few more loops of duct tape around their throats and foreheads, so that by the time he was done, they were beginning to look like a pair of grey mummies.

"I know you're ready to die for your cause, my friend, whatever it may be, but it won't be on *your* terms. You'll be tried by a court of law and punished on *our* terms, if any of us live that long. Now you will tell me how to find the bomb," Sam said, "or I will remove your skin one strip at a time, starting with your ears." He pulled a hunting knife with an eight inch blade from a scabbard on his belt and pointed it menacingly at Ali.

Ali sneered at Sam, his face a mask of hatred. "We will never tell you anything, American dog! We will *all* die here in a few minutes, just as I said. The woman's lucky bullet will *not* prevent the fulfillment of our mission. You could *never* find the bomb in time! But try, please, try," he mocked. "If you find it, you will still die!" Ali ended his soliloquy with an evil laugh of triumph.

His partner's countenance showed genuine fear, not hatred. "He is right," the teen said to Sam. "The bomb will explode very soon. We will all die, if we do not get away from here fast."

Sam stared hard at the young terrorist. "It would be worth your life, son, if you will tell us how to find the bomb and defuse it."

"Say nothing, Samir!" Ali hissed. "You cannot jeopardize the mission!"

"The mission would take my life, Ali," Samir said miserably. "Next week I will be eighteen. I have not yet lived, and I am not ready to die! I want to live like we have always planned. I want to go Mexico and Turkey, to finally see Mecca! I want to live! I do *not* want to die!"

"Then tell us!" Sam said forcefully. "Tell us how to find the bomb and defuse it! There might still be time!"

Samir closed his eyes and shook his head, racked by internal conflict. "The bomb is in a grey steel drum with red paint sprayed on the top," he said, anguish and despair evident in his voice. "It is stacked with the other drums we delivered. But it cannot be defused. If you attempt to do so, it will detonate. The only hope for us is to be far away from here when it explodes. Please, take us away now," he pleaded. "There is not much time."

"What time is it set to go off?" Sam demanded urgently.

"Six o'clock. In less than half an hour."

"That might just be long enough," Sam said, a kernel of hope beginning to grow.

"Six o'clock," Tony echoed thoughtfully. "That rings a bell. Isn't that about the time the Russians are due to arrive?"

"I don't think we have that long to wait," Katrina said. Still holding the pistol with both hands, she nodded toward the county road, where a pair of Hummers were slowing as they approached the entrance to the site.

Chapter 28

"Now what, Sam?" Tony asked, staring at the two Hummers turning off the county road two hundred yards away. They all knew that it held a squadron of hostile mercenaries with a carload of small artillery.

"What the hell is this all about!" the security guard yelled again, more than a little exasperated at his inability to get any answers.

Again, Sam ignored the question, but he took some pity on the guard. "If you want to stay alive, friend, you'd best get out of sight and stay there," he responded. "They don't pay you nearly enough for this duty. Now give me the keys to your truck."

"The hell I will!" the disarmed guard shouted, glaring at Sam. But when Katrina turned her gun from the subdued terrorists and pointed it ominously at the guard, his tone changed. "Keys are in the ignition," he said scowling, but without further comment.

"Get in quick!" Sam yelled to Katrina and Tony as he dashed toward the guard's truck, parked near the guard shack just inside the gate. Tires spun, and the truck with the three conspirators on board skidded toward the pit, gaining speed. As the Hummers slid to a stop outside the blocked gate, the pickup truck cleared the lip of the ramp and descended into the pit.

"Well, there's one good sign," Tony said, as the truck bounced down the dirt road on the ramp. "The shock troops didn't come in shooting. They'll lose some time getting through the gate and trying to figure out what the heck happened up there. Maybe those three at the gate will scare them off with talk of a bomb."

"Don't count on it," Sam said grimly. "Those guys working for Svetlanikoff are professionals, trained by the KGB, or maybe the Mossad. They're tough and efficient. They'll think it's a diversion to throw them off balance. I doubt that it will slow 'em down more than five minutes."

"Then we must work fast," Katrina interjected. "But how can we find the bomb, and what will we do when we find it? He said that the bomb cannot be defused."

"One thing at a time, please," Sam said as the truck turned off the ramp onto the floor of the pit. "We have to find it first."

Ahead, a rough terrain forklift was being driven into a long equipment shed. Sam skidded to a stop behind the forklift as the driver climbed down from the machine. As he turned to see who was driving so recklessly, Sam jumped out of the truck.

"Did you just unload a bunch of steel drums from that trailer that just left?" Sam demanded without introduction or explanation.

"Sure did," the driver said. "What about it?"

"Can you show me where the drums are?"

"Yeah, I could," the driver said, skepticism creeping into his voice. The driver looked at Sam's battered condition, blood dripping from cuts on his face, and his dusty and torn clothes.

"Well, where are they?" Sam pressed urgently.

The driver frowned. "I could show you, but I don't think I want to. I don't know who you are or why you're here, and I don't think I like your attitude. Why didn't Bobby up at the gate answer my radio call a few minutes ago? He should've told me, if anyone was coming down here. And what was all that noise up there by the gate? Sounded like someone was shooting."

Sam shook his head in frustration and then swiftly drew a gun from his waistband behind his back. He pointed it directly at the driver's nose at point blank range. "I wish I had time to explain this, friend, but I don't. Just show us where those drums are and then get out of here fast. There's a bomb about to go off."

The driver's back stiffened and his eyes widened at the sight of a forty-five automatic inches from his face. "Okay, okay, since you put it that way, the drums I just unloaded are stacked behind that big pile of blue drums over there." The guard pointed to a large stack of steel drums fifty yards north of the equipment shed, near a deep hole in the floor of the pit. "The new drums are mostly grey. They're still sitting on the pallets they came on. You aren't serious about a bomb, are you?" the driver added uneasily.

"Just get out of here now, and fast," Sam said. "But first, do you have the keys to any of this other equipment?"

"The keys are just hanging in the ignitions," the driver said. "Help yourself. It ain't my equipment anyway, and they ain't paying me to be no guard. I'm gone." The driver jogged to a pickup truck parked by the end of the equipment shed, climbed in, and tossing a worried frown back over his shoulder at Sam, he spun his tires and fled.

"So far, so good," Sam said, turning back toward the pickup truck. "Tony, you and Kate drive over to that pile of drums and see if you can find a grey one with red paint on top. And keep an eye out for the Russians. They could show up at any minute. I'm going to borrow this front end loader and meet you there."

Sam stepped over to an enormous off-road Caterpillar loader that could easily scoop up a small house in one bite. He noticed with satisfaction that the steel plate of the bucket was a good two inches thick. Scrambling up the ladder, he found the key hanging in the ignition, as promised, and the huge machine's twelve cylinder diesel engine rumbled to life. An infectious smile spread across Sam's face.

"I think the man's got an idea!" Tony shouted to Katrina over the roar of the loader's engine. "Get in the truck. Let's get over there!" They jumped in the pickup and headed toward the stack of steel drums.

As he studied the controls of the machine, Sam checked his watch. Twenty-three minutes to six. He silently prayed that the clock on the bomb was accurate and that the terrorist had not been lying or mistaken about the time. Although no one could hear him over the roar of the engine, he howled an Osage war cry as he threw the machine into gear. Adrenaline pulsed as he stood on the accelerator and the steel behemoth lurched forward.

By the time Sam arrived at the stack of steel drums, Tony and Katrina were waiting. "I think we've hit pay dirt," Tony shouted from his perch twelve feet above the ground, three pallets high. "There's a couple of barrels here that meet the description."

Sam lost no time raising the loader bucket to Tony's level and advancing it to within two feet of the drums. After setting the brake on the loader, he left the engine idling while he quickly climbed to meet Tony. A glance at his watch showed they had twenty minutes left. It was going to be close!

Tony began to tip one of the drums to move it into the bucket, but Sam stopped him. "Let's make sure we've got the right ones. It would be a terrible waste to go to all this trouble for the wrong barrels."

Sam quickly removed the metal collar from the top of the first drum, and holding his breath, he gently lifted the lid a crack and peeked in. He frowned and lifted the lid further, exposing the top of a balding head. Tony's eyes widened at the sight of the corpse, as Sam quickly dropped the lid and slid the collar back on the barrel.

"Whew! Definitely the wrong barrel," Tony said with a grimace. "Wonder who that poor sucker was?"

"We'll worry about that later. Let's check the other one."

This time Tony released the catch that sealed the steel drum and lifted the collar off. Sam raised the lid an inch. An ominous whirring sound filled the air. He raised the lid another inch, and sufficient light entered the barrel for Sam to see some kind of mechanical device strapped to a plastic container that nearly filled the barrel. An electronic timer ticked off sixteen minutes and a few seconds in large orange numbers. Sam quickly checked his watch, which was about one minute ahead of the timer.

"I don't know what's in there," he said, "but if it's as potent as some plastic explosives, this could be enough to blow a square mile to kingdom come. I have no idea how to defuse a bomb. Let's just get it out of here fast!"

He clamped the lid back on the barrel in seconds. They were moving the drum into the bucket of the idling loader when Katrina shouted. The two looked up to see her pointing at figures dressed in black taking up positions on opposite rims of the excavation. Even at a distance of a hundred yards or more, Sam could tell that the weapons in their hands were sniper rifles. From their positions on the rim, they commanded the entire scene. Two more figures dressed in black were stationed at the top of the ramp, preventing any escape.

"Holy Jesus," Tony said as he saw the mercenaries. "They've got us in a cross fire. We're sitting ducks down here!"

"Doesn't look like they came to talk," Sam said as he nimbly jumped from the raised bucket of the loader to the enormous engine cover. "But it doesn't matter anyway. There's no time for palaver. We have to get this bomb out of here fast. If it goes off anywhere in this pit, the terrorists will have accomplished their goal."

"Don't look now, Sam, but I think they've got us boxed in. How we gonna get this steel monster out of here?"

"Drive it," Sam said with determination. "There's no other choice. You and Katrina get out of sight. Go back to the equipment shed and hide under one of the dozers. The heavy steel will protect you from gunfire. I'm going to drive this thing right up the ramp and out of here. I'll keep the bucket raised for protection."

"Sam, that's suicide! They'll pick you off before you even get close to the ramp!"

"Maybe they won't. Maybe they'll want to know what I'm doing."

"Sam, please!" Katrina shouted. "There must be another way! I don't want to lose you now!"

At that moment, a bullet ricocheted off the loader bucket where Tony still stood. Another bullet hit the instrument panel of the machine just in front of Sam, showering him with pellets of glass.

"Go!" Sam yelled, as he knelt on the loader. "We've got to do this now!"

Sam's eyes met Tony's for an instant over the top of the bucket, and Tony could see his raw determination. It was time to trust fate. Tony jumped from the raised bucket as another volley of gunfire hit the loader.

* * * * *

Sam crouched on the deck of the loader to get out of the line of fire, released the brake, and backed away from the stack of drums. He silently prayed that he would be impervious to bullets until he had moved the bomb a safe distance from the mountain of toxic waste. Then he could die, if necessary, but not now. Too many lives were at stake.

As he shifted gears, preparing to begin a fatal dash up the ramp, Sam heard the unmistakable sound of helicopters at close range. The loader's loud diesel engine had previously drowned out all other sound, but now, looking up, Sam saw two black choppers closing fast on the construction site. In a moment, the lead chopper was swinging over the pit, headed for a raised earthen pad behind the shack. Through the open side door of the chopper, Sam caught a glimpse of Karmakov, his face a grim mask, ready for action and obviously bent on revenge.

As Sam turned to locate the second chopper, which was settling on the rim of the pit, the loader was peppered with a new volley of gunfire. Suddenly, he was knocked off the deck and falling. He hit the ground hard on his face and right shoulder, wrenching his neck in the process. Gravel dug into his right cheekbone, but the pain in his face and neck was nothing compared to the searing pain shooting through his right arm. It felt as though he had been struck just below the point of the shoulder with a medieval mace, a wicked weapon cleverly designed to both break bone and tear flesh.

Sam rolled over and sat up, reaching with his left hand to touch the back of his right shoulder. He found the flesh ripped open and a gaping hole quickly filling with blood. The pain and shock of the bullet wound made his head swim for a few seconds, but he instinctively clamped his left hand over the wound and breathed deeply to clear his head. He looked at his watch—twelve minutes left! *Time for a miracle*, Sam thought.

He rolled under the loader to regroup. The machine's engine had died, leaving a strange quiet in the pit. The choppers' engines were winding down and the shooting had stopped. Sam leaned against the inside of the big wheel of the loader, breathing deeply and struggling to think through the pain.

"Sam, are you alright?"

Sam heard Katrina's voice nearby. He leaned forward and peered around the loader tire to find Katrina and Tony under the pickup a short distance away.

"I'm okay," Sam said, trying to stanch the flow of blood from his shoulder wound. "How about you?"

"Great," Tony answered, "considering we're trapped like rats on a sinking ship. What are we gonna do now, *kemosabe*?"

Sam didn't answer. His head was getting foggy again, like a punch drunk boxer on the ropes. There was no time to waste, yet his mind spun helplessly, wanting desperately to find an answer, but finding nothing but agonizing pain.

In the relative quiet, they heard Karmakov shout to the men on the rim, "They are at our mercy now, comrades. We will take them alive."

Sam looked toward Karmakov who was standing near the helicopter parked on a elevated pad a few dozen yards away. A desperate plan began to take shape in his pain-clouded mind. "Katrina, toss me that pistol and try to keep out of sight. Tony, can you drive this loader?"

"If it's got wheels and a motor, I can drive it!"

"The controls are simple, just like an old John Deere. When I head for the chopper, you get up on the loader and keep low. They might not even see you since their attention will be on me, but even if they do, they may follow Karmakov's order to take us alive. I'll create a diversion. When you see an opening, dump the bomb in the chopper. I'll take care of the rest. Got it?"

"Got it!"

Sam looked at his watch. "We've got ten minutes. Give me the gun!"

The automatic pistol landed in the loose dirt at Sam's feet. Without a moment of hesitation, he snatched the pistol, crawled from under the loader, and stood.

"*Via con dios, mi amigo*," Tony shouted, as Sam sprinted toward the idling helicopter and a final confrontation with his nemesis.

* * * * *

Topping the sloped bank of the earthen pad where the chopper had landed, Sam found himself standing in the open, a scant fifteen yards from the chopper. Karmakov was near the open door of the chopper shouting orders at the pilot, who was still seated at the controls.

Sam raised his weapon and took quick aim at Karmakov. He squeezed the trigger. Nothing happened. He squeezed again, to no avail. Jammed! The mechanism was jammed! Sam threw down the pistol just as a hail of gunfire began to make dust dance at his feet. The commandos on the rim had seen his threat to Karmakov and were reacting, trying to stop his attack without killing him.

Summoning an inner reserve of strength, he charged toward the chopper, which was less than a dozen steps away. Hearing the gunfire, Karmakov turned to see Sam launch himself in a flying open field tackle. Before the Russian could move, Sam's good shoulder caught him dead center. Karmakov's ribs cracked audibly and the force of the impact drove both men through the open door of the chopper, where they tumbled in a struggling pile on the floor.

Karmakov had not foreseen the attack, but he reacted instantly, gouging and clawing in an effort to gain the upper hand. Sam had come up on top, and ignoring the intense pain in his shoulder, he fought for his life and the lives of many others. He landed two hard blows squarely on Karmakov's face, breaking his nose again and blackening his right eye. The force of the blows knocked Karmakov senseless.

Suddenly, an intense white light exploded in Sam's head and he was thrown against the seat of the chopper. Without knowing what hit him, he was spun into a sitting position on the floor, his head leaning limp against the seat cushion. His eyes were open halfway and he was facing the front of the aircraft. Through blurring vision, he could see the pilot watching him, a smoking gun in his hand. Slowly, it dawned on Sam that he had been shot again. His head seemed to be splitting apart and he could vaguely feel the wet warmth of blood dripping down the left side of his face and neck. He stared at the pilot with a fixed gaze through unblinking eyes. His thoughts were confused, but in his peripheral vision, he saw a pistol on the floor near Karmakov's leg.

Certain that Sam was finished by a shot to the head, the pilot turned his attention to the stunned Russian. The pistol was within Sam's reach, and with more speed than seemed possible, he seized the gun, aimed and shot. The pilot crumpled to the floor next to Karmakov, a neat hole in his right temple.

For thirty seconds, Sam sat still, catching his breath and letting his head clear. But he did not have long to recover. He heard the roar of the loader's diesel engine as it rolled up to the chopper's open door.

Sam struggled to stand. Although he was bleeding steadily from a deep scalp wound and dizzy from the glancing impact of the bullet, he was alive. On his feet, he steadied himself and took three deep breaths, then stepped to the door of the chopper. His head was clearing and he could see Tony at the controls of the loader. The bottom of the loader's bucket was only a foot from the floor of the chopper, ready to deliver the deadly cargo.

Sam pushed hard on the side of the heavy steel drum to tip it up, then managed to roll and scoot it into the chopper. Bursts of pain were shooting through his head. He forcibly suppressed the pain and caught a glimpse of his watch. Seven minutes left! The instant the drum was off the loader, he motioned to Tony to move the machine back, and Tony quickly complied.

Sam moved to the chopper's controls, starting the engine as he set the autopilot controls for an immediate takeoff and a climbing course to the southwest. Would there be enough time? He looked at his watch. Five minutes to go. It would be close! He engaged the engine, pushed in the throttle, and as the rotor began to turn, he glimpsed Tony jumping off the loader and running toward the truck where Katrina was still hiding. Commandos were closing in on the truck from three directions, guns at the ready. Katrina didn't have a chance, but Tony was running to her aid. Sam felt a quick pulse of fear for his two friends as he leaped toward the door of the chopper.

Karmakov caught him in mid-air, tackling him at the knees. He went down hard in the open doorway, his injured right shoulder and arm hanging outside while Karmakov gripped his legs. He heard the engine whining and felt the increasing wind from the spinning blades overhead. The chopper would be off the ground in seconds!

Rolling, he twisted in Karmakov's grasp and came face to face with the most shocking and sinister vision of evil that he had ever seen. Thick, dark streams of blood and mucus hung from Karmakov's broken nose, covering his open mouth, teeth and chin with a bloody veil. His black eyes were wide and wild, showing white all around. Muddy bruises on his cheeks and tangled ropes of hair completed the picture of a man gone totally insane. Karmakov was obviously in a manic fury, beyond the reach of any human feeling, harboring only an insatiable thirst for violence and revenge.

Although shocked and repulsed by the hideous specter, as Sam felt the helicopter lighten and begin rise, he suppressed his revulsion, knowing that he had mere seconds to escape. Karmakov still restrained his legs, but Sam struck a glancing blow to the Russian's head, which loosened his grip. Yanking his left leg free, Sam began pushing and kicking, battering Karmakov's head and shoulders. Suddenly, without warning, Karmakov let go, and the power of Sam's kick sent him rolling backward out the door of the helicopter. He found himself hanging from the landing skid of the chopper, his left elbow hooked over the welded aluminum tube. Looking down, he could see that they were more than fifty feet above the ground and rising. The chopper was slowly leaning into its preset course.

Looking up, Sam saw Karmakov standing in the door of the chopper staring down at him, blood dripping from his face and head, a malevolent gleam in his eyes. "Now you will die," Karmakov said simply, and he drove the heel of his shoe into Sam's exposed elbow. Searing pain shot through his left arm and shoulder. For a moment he held fast, but a second blow to his elbow completely deadened the nerves and his grip slipped. With a final kick, Karmakov triumphantly broke his grip, and Sam slid away from the rising chopper, falling backward toward the hard rock pit below.

* * * * *

The tin roof of the equipment shed broke Sam's fall. On impact, the flimsy framing at the front snapped and the roof tilted, allowing Sam to slide relatively unharmed to the ground. Lying dazed on the metal incline, he watched the chopper continue to rise, with Karmakov still standing in the open door. Though it was more than a hundred feet above the ground and accelerating quickly, he could see Karmakov's triumphant grin fade as he realized that Sam had survived the fall. The Russian lifted the dead pilot's pistol and squeezed off a few shots at Sam, but the moving helicopter was an unstable platform and his aim was inaccurate. With a curse, Karmakov disappeared from the open door of the chopper. In a moment, he was in the pilot's seat, trying to take control of the aircraft. Sam was glad that he had pulled the key from the autopilot. Without the key, the course could not be changed. The chopper was rising faster, passing through two hundred feet of altitude.

Sam struggled to raise his arm enough to see his watch. Three minutes remained. His vision blurred, and he closed his eyes. Incredibly intense pain clouded every thought. He touched the deep scalp wound above his left ear, where the pilot's bullet had glanced off his skull, and his fingers came away covered with fresh blood. He wondered idly whether he would bleed to death before the advancing commandos had a chance to kill him.

Ten seconds later, Sam heard the crunch of shoes on gravel. Slowly and painfully, he opened his eyes to see three operatives with automatic weapons escorting Tony and Katrina toward him. He struggled to his feet, shaking and wobbly, but erect. He was surprised that no major bones seemed to be broken. Katrina rushed to his side and steadied him to keep him from falling. Sam glanced at his watch, then leaned over and spoke a few quick words into her ear. She immediately turned and whispered to Tony.

"No talking!" one of the mercenaries said roughly, jabbing Katrina with the barrel of his weapon.

In his dazed state, Sam had not noticed the second helicopter lifting off the rim of the pit and landing nearby. Svetlanikoff and two more armed men joined the others and formed a ring around the three captives. More henchmen watched from the rim of the pit.

Svetlanikoff fixed his steely gaze on Sam and stated, "Your resistance was useless. Karmakov is an excellent pilot. He will return shortly and administer the punishment that you so richly deserve. It will be a pleasure to watch as he drains life from you one painful drop at a time."

"Karmakov is not coming back," Sam croaked. "And this game is not over yet. Take a look. Karmakov is about to jump." Sam pointed toward the rising helicopter, several hundred feet high and beyond the perimeter of the site.

All eyes automatically turned skyward. Karmakov was standing in the open door of the chopper, waving his arms frantically.

As the Russian leader and his henchmen stood staring at Karmakov, wondering what he was trying to communicate, Sam's wristwatch alarm began to quietly beep. The small, innocuous sound went unnoticed by the Russians, but Sam, Tony, and Katrina all turned their faces downward and slowly raised their hands to cover their ears.

Five seconds later, a blinding flash of light appeared in the sky as the helicopter and its contents were vaporized by the detonation of two hundred pounds of plastic explosive. Sam, Tony, and Katrina instantly dropped to the ground, still covering their ears, while the Russian mobster and his henchmen stood blinded and in shock, their retinas temporarily seared by the intense, magnesium-bright flash. A second later, the shockwave from the blast rolled over them like a tidal wave, toppling everything in its path. For several more seconds, the blast reverberated through the pit, bouncing off the solid rock walls like artillery fire at point blank range.

Svetlanikoff and his commandos lay dazed and helpless on the ground. The instant the shockwave passed, while the echoes of the blast were still reverberating, Tony and Katrina jumped to their feet and picked up loose weapons dropped by the falling commandos, while Sam painfully stood and surveyed the scene. It only took a few seconds for the trio to be fully armed.

Two of the commandos had managed to hold onto their weapons when they were knocked over by the blast, but they sat stupidly on the ground, disabled and vulnerable from temporary blindness. Sam motioned to Tony, making a knife hand strike in the air, and Tony nodded.

"This is going to hurt you more than it does me," Tony muttered as he clubbed the blinded commandos who still held weapons. In less than a minute, they had made a pile of pistols and other weapons and the commandos were fully disarmed. Slowly, the mercenaries began to come to their senses, shaking their heads and rubbing their eyes and ears.

"Watch them like a hawk," Sam said to Tony and Katrina. "We've got to hold…"

Before Sam could finish his sentence, a bullet slammed into the breech of the weapon in his hands and he dropped it like a red hot iron. They instinctively looked up to see who had fired the shot and saw three armed mercenaries advancing along the rim of the pit with a clear field of fire.

"Into the shed!" Sam shouted. He scooped up two of the automatic weapons from the pile on the ground, and with a weapon in each hand, he sprayed a hail of bullets in the direction of the mercenaries on the rim, who ducked for cover.

On the run, Tony and Katrina each grabbed more weapons from the pile and the three dashed into the equipment shed. They took refuge behind the blade of a bulldozer and took stock of their limited ammunition.

Sam peered over the blade of the dozer and saw one of the commandos in front of the shed, pointing and motioning to his comrades on the rim. Sam's gun chattered and the commando fell backward and lay still. Instantly, a hail of bullets peppered the blade, as he dropped behind it and joined his two friends, who had crawled under the big machine. Both were panting and filthy, with scrapes and bruises, but miraculously, neither had been hit in the melee. He drew in a deep breath. "We've got to get…" His words were again cut short as an explosion directly above them removed an entire section of the shed's metal roof. Twisted sheet metal and smoking boards rained down around the dozer as the three huddled under the crankcase between its massive steel treads.

"Move, now!" Sam urged, pointing toward a motor grader parked thirty feet away against the far wall. Pointing an Uzi over the blade of the dozer, he released another long burst, sweeping the weapon from side to side. Without a word, Tony and Katrina ran under Sam's covering fire and dived behind the smaller blade of the grader.

Standing behind the heavy dozer blade, Sam heard a *clink* and turned to see a hand grenade bounce off the tread of the dozer and fall to the ground on the side opposite the grader. Instantly, Sam leaped in the direction of the grader and hit the ground face down, just as the grenade exploded. The force of the explosion was deflected by the heavy steel of the dozer, and he managed to struggle to his feet and stumble the few remaining steps to the grader, falling behind its low blade with the others.

Sam looked around as he coughed and gasped for breath, trying to bring his fogged mind into focus. He slowly realized that they were out of options.

"For a minute there, Sam, we had 'em," Tony said. "At least we got rid of the bomb. That was the main thing."

Sam looked at his friend's dusty, sweat-streaked face and tried to smile. "Gave 'em hell," he coughed, blood dripping from his lips.

"I want you to know, Sam, that it's been...well, I mean, we always had a winning hand, didn't we?"

"Shut up, Tony!" Katrina said. "We're not dead yet!"

At that moment, they heard a *clunk* on the shed roof directly overhead. Their eyes met for an instant, and then all three hit the ground face down, covering their heads. A second later, a deafening explosion ripped through the ruins of the equipment shed and the roof section above them collapsed in a rain of wood and metal.

Knowing that another grenade would drop through the roof at any second, Sam shouted, "Back to the dozer!"

Then, as they crouched to run toward the smoking ruins of the dozer, a new sound filled the air—the loud, deep, rapid-fire of a much heavier caliber machine gun. They could hear large caliber bullets ricocheting off the rock wall behind the ruins of the shed. Another burst of heavy machine gun fire dug a trench in the dirt in front of the equipment shed. At the same time, they could hear a heavy *whump, whump, whump* that Sam vaguely recognized.

The roof of the shed was all but gone, and in a second, the three desperate heroes saw two huge Army National Guard helicopters swing out over the pit at low altitude. The sides of both choppers were open and mounted machine guns were firing from each door. In the doorway of the nearest chopper, they could see Dave Sanders directing fire at the rock wall above them.

At that moment, time stood still for Sam. Standing in the smoking remains of the equipment shed, flanked by Katrina and Tony, he looked up at a surreal vision. Everything seemed to move in slow motion as he watched the olive green National Guard helicopters floating in the air overhead, orange flames bursting from the barrels of their guns, but he could no longer hear the sound of the gunfire. He saw black-clad figures tumbling off the wall of the pit, and then suddenly, all that he saw was clear blue sky. A single white cloud was floating in blue sky. The next moment, everything went black.

Chapter 29

Svetlanikoff was barking orders at his five remaining henchmen, pressing them to storm the equipment shed, when the two National Guard helicopters came into sight. The master gangster immediately realized that the operation was at an end and he had only a minute or two to make an escape. He also knew that leaving the three witnesses alive was not an option.

"You three men," he ordered, "must go finish our enemies in the shed! We are out of time. The grenades were ineffective. You must *charge* them! It must be done immediately! *Do it now!*" As the three mercenaries dashed away to carry out their orders, he turned to the remaining two men and commanded, "Get the hostages into my helicopter and prepare to depart. We must escape while we still have the chance. Now move!"

The two remaining figures raced to prepare the Jet Ranger, while Svetlanikoff hid momentarily behind a stack of steel drums to see his orders carried out. Instead, he saw his three commandos pinned down by a merciless hail of gunfire from above. With the National Guard helicopters pulverizing the area, Svetlanikoff dashed for his helicopter.

* * * * *

Bandini and Huntington watched from behind the chopper as two mercenaries in black fatigues raced headlong toward them, with Svetlanikoff not far behind. "What do we do now?" Bandini asked weakly. "Maybe it's better to try to make a run for it in the helicopter with Svetlanikoff and his men. If we could just get the hell away from here, maybe we could..."

"Are you totally insane?" Huntington shouted. "Leave with that murdering gangster? That son-of-a-bitch will kill us later, if he doesn't do it right now! This is our chance to make a break! We have to run for it. Now move!"

Huntington put a hand on Bandini's back and gave him a shove, and the two men ran away from the chopper. By the time Svetlanikoff and his men arrived, they were out of sight, hidden among the parked construction equipment. To their relief, Svetlanikoff and his henchmen boarded the chopper to leave immediately. As the sleek black helicopter gained altitude, National Guard troops were surrounding the few remaining mercenaries, who were surrendering their arms. The short battle was over.

* * * * *

By the time Dave Sanders reached the equipment shed, Katrina was kneeling over Sam's prostrate body. His bloody head rested in her lap and her face was close to his as she listened for his breathing. She looked up as Sanders approached.

"Dave! Thank God you arrived in time! Another minute or two and we would have all been dead!"

"But none of us are?" Sanders queried, looking at Sam.

"He is still breathing," she replied in a tremulous voice. "He has a deep wound on his head and another in his shoulder. He has lost much blood and is still bleeding. We must take him to a hospital fast!"

"The Colonel has already called MedEvac. The Life Flight helicopter could be here in less than ten minutes."

"I pray that he will live that long." Katrina's eyes clouded and her tears began to fall on Sam's face, making small streaks in the dust on his cheek and forehead. "He saved my live, Dave!" Katrina said, quaking with emotion. "He saved me from kidnapping and torture at the hand of Karmakov. Today, he saved many thousands of lives. Now we must save his life! We *must!*"

Sanders nodded and knelt to take Sam's pulse at the jugular vein. At first, he could feel no pulse, causing a moment of panic, but then the pulse was there, irregular and weak. "Sam's a tough bird," he said grimly. "He'll just have to hold on. He has to."

* * * * *

He felt, more than heard, the rapid drumming of many hooves beating the ground behind him, but he could see nothing at all. His eyes were squeezed shut tight against the blinding dust and wind. Racing through a dust cloud, he clung to his bareback steed, doubling his fists in its mane and urging it on, faster and faster.

His pursuers were close behind, and they were many. They were coming very fast. He wanted to turn and look, to stand and fight, but he could not. They would have no mercy. Running like the wind was his only chance. He leaned forward until he felt the sting of his mount's long mane whipping his face.

The beast he rode was strong and brave, with the heart of a warrior. It would run an untold distance until it dropped. They must press forward with all of their strength. He felt the surging power of the animal, the rhythmic rolling of its massive shoulders between his knees. Its breath rushed in and out, deep, hard and fast, as it galloped flat out across the plain. It could outrun them all. But they were many. He was only one.

Suddenly, out of nowhere, a black limb loomed ahead. It was the arm of a giant, or an ancient god, or a tree. He did not see it with his eyes, but he knew it was there, nonetheless. There was no time to stop or to turn. In an instant, it struck him square in the chest and he was falling, falling, until he landed hard, flat on his back on the ground.

For a time, all was blackness. As awareness returned, he noticed that there was no pounding of hooves. All was quiet. It seemed strange at first, then he felt only a calm peacefulness.

His eyes finally opened to the clear sky above. There was no dust, but a single, brilliant white cloud drifting in a perfect azure sky. The cloud was exquisite in its gently undulating shape, its white edges sharp against the turquoise heavens. It was a light summer cloud, companion to the soaring eagle.

The air was filled with the fresh, fragrant aroma of freshly mown clover. The wind had dropped to a gentle breeze that carried a hint of wild roses.

A golden border appeared at the edge of the slowly moving cloud, as the sun sought to emerge from behind it. It was impossible to look on the brightness of the sun, but it was impossible not to look. Its brilliance was mesmerizing. He felt at once drawn to the light, but rooted to the ground. He could not move, nor could he take his eyes from the warming light of the sun. He was transfixed. It was enough. He closed his eyes and for a time, there was nothing but the gentle, warming rays of the sun on his face. He felt no pain, only a pure and complete inner peace.

A drop of rain, then another, hit his face. He felt the dampness of each drop trace a line across his cheek and forehead. Slowly, regretfully, he opened his eyes. Another drop of rain fell from the white cloud, which had again eclipsed the sun. The perfect cloud had retained its golden rim, but it had taken a new shape. It was larger, closer, obscuring the sky and the sun.

"Sam, can you hear me? Stay with me, Sam, I love you! You must not die! Please, God, let him live!" The pleading, familiar voice invaded his mind.

He blinked, and the ethereal cloud began to resolve itself into something more substantial. A gentle hand touched his cheek.

"Katrina?" he whispered through parched lips.

She cradled his head in her hands and gently kissed his cheek. More tears fell on his face as she held him and wept. Then there was nothing.

* * * * *

"Move aside please," the medical technician said as he gently separated Katrina from Sam's unconscious body. Tony took her shoulders in his hands and helped her to her feet, while the two technicians hoisted Sam onto a stretcher.

"Be careful!" Katrina pleaded with the medics, reluctantly allowing them to take him. "Please act quickly or he could…" She did not finish the sentence. Turning, she buried her face in Tony's shoulder as he fought for composure.

"Don't worry, Katrina, he's going to make it. He's way too tough to give up the ghost now." Tony tried to buoy her spirits, but the mist in his eyes revealed his own misgivings.

They watched from where they stood as the medics lifted the stretcher into the Life Flight helicopter that had landed a short distance away. As the door slid closed, they could see that an IV was already being connected. The MedEvac unit quickly lifted off and set a course for the city.

Tony took a deep breath and blew it out, releasing some of the intense emotion he was feeling, then turned to Katrina. "We'll head straight for the hospital just as soon as we can," he said gently, "but right now, we've got some business to attend to. There are still people around here who would like to use us for target practice. We have to talk with Dave and make sure the situation is under control and this place is secure. Then we'll have to give a statement to the authorities. The full story can wait, but we've got to set the record straight now, before someone turns the tables on us again."

Katrina looked up at Tony. A deep sadness was evident in every line on her face. It was as sincere, as poignant and as expressive as any dance she had ever performed. Tony felt a pang of sympathy for her and he shared her deep feelings of distress and concern. But then suddenly, he was inexplicably filled with an upwelling surge of confidence. He turned to Katrina and squeezed her shoulders with both hands.

"I *know* Sam, Katrina. And I know that he *will not die!*"

Chapter 30

Beams of late morning sunshine streamed through the high east windows of the oak-paneled courtroom, a reminder to the small crowd seated on the long benches that it was still mid-summer in Oklahoma. The temperature was near eighty in the courtroom and it was not yet eleven o'clock. It had been scarcely sixteen hours since the assault of the Air National Guard on premises thought to be owned by one of the state's major public utility companies. Most of the press, public officials and others in the courtroom were still very much in the dark, trying to piece together what had happened at the construction site. A very few of those in the courtroom already knew.

Tony, Katrina, and Dave were seated together at a long walnut counsel table located in front of the bar. At the other counsel table, speaking together in low tones, were Huntington, Bandini, and two other prominent lawyers. One of them was District Attorney Tom Wallace. The other was a well-known criminal trial lawyer. Three more members of their legal team were seated behind them. It was clear that Huntington and Bandini intended to make an early show of strength. The jury box was filled with members of the media, while a few dozen spectators had gathered in the gallery. Inconspicuous among the crowd was a visibly shaken and unhappy Pug Aberson. A subdued murmur filled the courtroom.

"All rise!" the bailiff commanded loudly from his position standing beside the Judge's raised bench. With a noisy scraping of chair legs on the floor, the crowd rose.

"District court is now in session, the Honorable Chief Judge Mickelson presiding," the bailiff continued in a stentorian tone. A door behind the Judge's bench opened and the black-robed form of Judge Mickelson entered and ascended the bench. He settled himself and leaned forward, surveying the crowd through eyes that seemed even more jaded than usual.

"Be seated," he said as he scanned the crowd, peering over his reading glasses. He scratched his grizzled chin and looked at the group of attorneys as if he were appraising their mettle. He mentally noted the attendance of the District Attorney, the members of the various media, and the young Public Utility

Commissioner, who sat at counsel table. As the Judge was silently taking roll, a tall, middle-aged man in a military uniform entered through the back door of the courtroom. He paused, then walked quickly to the front, through the bar, and took a seat at counsel table next to Dave Sanders.

"Well, are we all here now?" the Judge asked in a deprecating tone, directing his comment at the newcomer as though he were a tardy school child. Colonel Ripkin of the Air National Guard sat up in his chair, familiar with the tone of authority, but uncertain as to the degree of deference that he should show in this setting. He elected simply to remain silent and nod.

The Judge then looked at Tony and frowned. "I thought that they said you were dead, Mr. Angelletti," he declared, as though Tony's continuing existence was a disappointment.

"No, your Honor, I'm very much alive," Tony responded.

"Yes, I can see that," the Judge agreed.

Lowering his voice, Judge Mickelson spoke to his clerk, a young woman seated at a lower level in front of the bench. "Okay, Betty," he said, "I guess we'd better get this on the record." The diligent clerk was already poised at her reporting machine.

"For the record," the Judge began, his voice edged with irritation, "this is not how I usually spend my Sunday mornings. Normally, I would be enjoying a leisurely breakfast and reading the Sunday paper at this hour. However, last night I received about a dozen urgent phone calls in the space of eight hours, the very hours when I would otherwise have been sleeping." It was clear from the Chief Judge's dour expression and his tone of voice that he did not like his sleep to be interrupted. "The fact of the matter is, in more than twenty-eight years on the bench, I have never convened court on a Sunday. This is a first." The Judge paused to make sure that his words were sinking in. He had the undivided attention of the entire courtroom.

"At any rate," he continued, "as near as I can tell, it appears that some major crimes have been committed. What is *not* clear to me is *what* crimes have been committed, and by whom. There has been loose talk of a dozen different felonies, up to and including capital murder, which is not all that unusual. What is unusual is the involvement of the National Guard in a major military-style assault on a public utility company in my district. There has also been talk about deadly and widespread public health hazards, which concerns me. Everyone seems to want to enjoin someone else from doing something or other, and to have someone arrested, but there are a dozen different stories, and it's damned hard for me to make heads or tails out of any of it. So I called you all here in hopes that you could enlighten me."

The Judge paused and looked around the courtroom. The entire audience waited expectantly. A few were poised on the edges of their seats.

"Well? Who's first?"

Simultaneously, Tom Wallace, Bandini and Tony all jumped to their feet and began to talk rapidly, none willing to yield the floor to the others.

"Whoa, whoa, hold it now," Judge Mickelson quickly interrupted, holding both hands up to stop the onslaught. "One at a time." He eyed Tony. "Since it's Sunday morning, I think it would be apropos to start with the one who has apparently risen from the dead. Commissioner Angelletti, I was given to believe by our esteemed District Attorney that you were murdered by your close friend, Sam Littlehawk, who I do not see in this courtroom this morning. Perhaps you could start by satisfying my curiosity as to how it is that you are appearing here in the flesh, when you're supposed to be dead."

Tony smiled and took center stage with the natural aplomb that had served him well on the campaign trail. "It's a long story, your Honor, but I can assure you that I was never the object of any evil plot or death threat from Sam Littlehawk. To the contrary, Sam saved me from assassination by the agents of Southwest Energy and its shills, Huntington and Bandini, who were conspiring with Russian mobsters to rip off the citizens of this state and to kill me and a few other people!"

There was a loud outburst in the courtroom as Wallace, Bandini, and Huntington all jumped to their feet in vehement denial. The press began to hurl questions from the jury box in all directions, and general pandemonium ensued. The Judge leaned forward and pounded his gavel loudly on the bench.

"Order! Order!" he shouted. "I *will not tolerate* disruptions in this courtroom! Come to order! Now! Come to order!" Slowly, the commotion subsided. Huntington, Bandini and their associates grudgingly sank back into their seats. Tony and Tom Wallace remained standing.

Without waiting for any further comments from Tony, Wallace abruptly seized the floor. "I object, your Honor! I object to false accusations being leveled against two of our city's leading citizens and a well-respected public corporation that has done so much for this state! The accuser is obviously guilty of numerous crimes…"

"*You object?*" the Judge interrupted in an incredulous tone. "You object to what? This isn't a trial. There is no jury here. You *can't* object! I am just trying to get some information in an expeditious and orderly manner. Now, Mr. Wallace, if you would just sit back down and keep your peace, *maybe I can get to the bottom of this!*"

Wallace scowled as he dropped into his chair and turned to whisper to the other attorneys with him.

"As you were saying, Mr. Angelletti?"

"Well, as I was starting to say, your Honor, it was mainly Sam's idea to get the goods on the power company. I was the object of their bribery attempt. They tried to pay me off to get me to vote to approve the Greenleaf Project, and when I refused to take their money, they tried to have me assassinated at the ballet. I was clubbed over the head and left for dead. I guess that was all in the press. But Sam was the one who put together the evidence. Then he figured out that they were involved with the Russian Mafia, who were the ones who tried to take us out again last night…" The words were tumbling out of his mouth too fast in his rush to get the story told.

Bandini's nerves were raw from the stress of recent events. For twenty years, he had defended Southwest Energy against all comers and he could not resist denouncing Angelletti now. He jumped to his feet, his usual perfect composure shattered. "Judge, this is absolute nonsense! There is no proof of any of these wild accusations. The fact of the matter is that Angelletti and his friend, Littlehawk, were involved in a major drug deal that went bad last night. We have no idea why they chose to use the new power plant site for their dirty business. Yes, there were some bodies found on the site, but that had nothing to do with the company…"

It was clear that Bandini was improvising and not doing a very good job of it. Wallace put a hand on Bandini's shoulder and pulled him slowly down into his chair, while the Judge glowered at him from the bench.

"Mr. Bandini," the Judge said scornfully, "I thought that Angelletti was supposed to be dead and Littlehawk was supposed to be a kidnapper and a murderer, not a drug dealer. Which is it? Maybe you should get your story straight."

"Well…he's probably both…" Bandini stammered from his chair, stopping in mid-sentence upon receiving a sharp elbow jab from Huntington.

"If I may, your Honor," Wallace said, rising from his chair and beginning again on a more even note. "Perhaps I should take a moment to put things in perspective."

"That's what we're here for," the Judge interjected. Tony scowled and slowly took his seat, temporarily yielding to the District Attorney.

"As you know," Wallace continued, carefully feeling his way forward, "Sam Littlehawk has been indicted on a number of criminal charges, not the least of which is escape from your jail." He paused for emphasis, hoping that this simple fact would strike a chord with the Judge, who stared at him with unblinking eyes.

"You may or may not be aware, your Honor, that both Littlehawk and Angelletti committed burglary and grand larceny by breaking into the offices of Southwest Energy and stealing files and papers in an illegal attempt to fabricate false charges of bribery against the company and its officers and legal counsel. And there were several witnesses to this heinous crime. There is undisputable evidence against them!" Warming to his subject, he seized the opportunity to flog his opposition. "In their effort to denigrate the reputation of Southwest Energy, and for their own criminal purposes, these disreputable characters have conspired at every turn to place this respected company in the worst possible light. It has been their consistent goal to blame the company for their own misdeeds."

Tony grimaced at Katrina and Sanders, but remained seated.

"The fact of the matter is, your Honor, that these two fugitives selected the Greenleaf Project as the site for a major drug deal, which literally blew up in their faces last night. We will soon present evidence that a large quantity of crack cocaine, heroin, and other controlled substances was discovered near the bodies of the slain Russians who were found at the construction site. There is no question that Littlehawk and Angelletti were behind it all. The police already have plenty of evidence on that score, too."

There was a murmur from the crowd in the courtroom, but the Judge held his silence. Tony's back was ramrod straight and his black eyes were burning like coals of fire. Still, he held onto his self-control and squelched his intense desire to leap onto the crooked District Attorney and throttle him.

Wallace whisked the reading glasses from his beak-like nose. "May I remind you, your Honor, that these two felons are both attorneys, officers of the Court who are sworn to uphold the law. Yet by their actions they have disgraced the law and their positions of public trust, and nothing they say should be countenanced by this Court."

That was far more than Tony could take. In an instant, he was on his feet again, this time fighting mad and pounding the table with his fist.

"That's a pack of lies!" he shouted. "Lies, your Honor! All lies! *They* were the ones in cahoots with the Russian mob! They were going to poison this whole country for money! You can go out there to the project site right now and find a thousand barrels of toxic waste they were dumping there!"

Dave Sanders was standing at Tony's side. "It's true, your Honor, I can vouch for what he's saying."

Judge Mickelson leaned forward and his stern stare settled on Sanders. "And who, may I ask, are you?"

"Agent Dave Sanders, FBI," he said in his most respectful voice.

"So you must be the FBI agent I heard about. Are you the one accused of abuse of process, misappropriation of government property, dereliction of duty, harboring escapees, and about a dozen other violations of the law and the policies and procedures of your own agency? Are you *that* Agent Sanders?"

Sanders looked sick, as though he had just swallowed something that did not go down easily and was about to come back up. He said nothing.

"Be seated, Mr. Sanders."

Sanders slid back into his seat with a grim expression on his face.

"Now, Mr. Angelletti, I thought that I had made myself perfectly clear about interruptions in my courtroom. *I don't permit them.* If you will just sit down until Mr. Wallace finishes, then I *may* give you another chance, *if* I think there's anything left that I need to know. And maybe we can get through this before dinnertime."

Tony slowly lowered himself into his seat as Wallace cleared his throat. "As I was saying, your Honor, before I was so rudely interrupted, there are more charges to be leveled against these people. Our preliminary investigation suggests that there were weapons grade plastic explosives at the site. It seems that their illicit dealings with the Russian Mafia include not only drugs, but weapons sales. There is plenty of evidence, your Honor, to hold Angelletti, Littlehawk, and all of their accomplices, including this Agent Sanders and that young woman there, on both drug and weapons charges and complicity in several homicides! And I suggest that you do just that. Hold them in jail until the evidence is fully developed. They are definitely a flight risk."

"That's preposterous!" Tony shouted, again jumping to his feet. "This is not a bail hearing! We haven't even been charged with anything!"

"But you soon will be!" Wallace crowed triumphantly.

"Order, order!" Judge Mickelson was on his feet, shouting and slamming his gavel down hard on the bench several times. "I have half a mind to put you *all* in jail for contempt of court! Then at least I'll know that I have the guilty party, until I can get this thing sorted out. That includes you, Wallace."

Judge Mickelson was standing behind the bench, surveying the courtroom, gavel in hand like a weapon, when his eyebrows arched in surprise. Members of the press seated in the jury box followed his gaze to the back of the courtroom. The expressions on their faces caused Tony and the others to turn and look, too. A wave of shock and incredulity passed through Tony at the unlikely specter he saw. Limping down the aisle of the courtroom was Sam, his right arm in a sling, a large white plaster patch on the left side of his head, and a wide grin on his battered face. One by one, all eyes in the courtroom turned to follow him.

Quiet fell over the courtroom, in sharp contrast to the commotion that had just prevailed. Sam made his way to the front of the courtroom, pushed through the bar and shuffled up to Tony, who stood speechless, amazed that his friend, who had been unconscious and seemingly near death twelve hours earlier, was standing before him.

"A quart of blood, a quart of milk, and a good night's sleep will sure do wonders for a tired soul," Sam said, still grinning through a face full of cuts and bruises.

"But you were in intensive care!" Tony said.

"What? So you think you've got a corner on the market for medical miracles?" Sam replied mockingly. "It was nothing but flesh wounds, anyway. Never hit a vital organ. Not even a busted bone, just a few cracked ribs, cuts and a concussion."

"They did *not* let you just walk out of there," Tony said doubtfully, eying the row of stainless steel staples holding together the skin at Sam's hairline.

"Don't you remember our recent course on hospital escape procedures?"

"So you *did* walk out of there."

"Red came to check on me. With a little more coaching, he could be an expert at evading hospital security."

The silence in the room had been replaced with a low buzz of conversation. "Hey, Sam!" one of the reporters in the jury box yelled, "Did you really blow up a helicopter out there? And who called out the National Guard?"

"Order!" Judge Mickelson said harshly, slamming down his gavel a few times. "I did *not* give anyone the floor! I will ask the questions here!" The Judge pointed toward the jury box and swept his arm back and forth accusingly. "You reporters can wait until later to ask your questions. This is not a press conference. I only let you in here as a courtesy, and I can just as easily excuse you. And don't think I won't, if there are any more interruptions." Judge Mickelson smiled inwardly, knowing that he would not stand for election again before his upcoming retirement.

Having soundly rebuked the offending member of the press and everyone else in his general vicinity, the Judge dropped back in his seat and looked sternly at Sam, who returned the Judge's stare with a serene and innocent smile on his face.

"So, Mr. Littlehawk, you seem to be at the eye of this particular tornado. What do you have to say for yourself?"

"If I may approach the bench, your Honor, I have something for you."

Judge Mickelson's brow furrowed. "You may approach."

Sam walked the few steps to the bench and handed to the Judge's clerk a small packet that had gone unnoticed in his hand. The clerk handed the packet to the Judge, who opened the plastic cover and began to examine the contents, which included a micro-cassette tape, a compact disk, and an inch of papers.

"That, your Honor, is evidence," Sam said, comfortably taking the floor and assuming control of the courtroom as he would for a closing argument. "You have in your hands hard evidence of a multitude of crimes involving Southwest Energy and the Greenleaf Project. Identical copies were sent to the FBI headquarters in Washington and to the CIA yesterday. Additional copies are now in safekeeping, just in case. The packet in your hand includes irrefutable and conclusive evidence of a massive conspiracy to use the Greenleaf Project to siphon off public funds and to line the pockets of corrupt public utility executives and the politicians they control."

"That's a bold statement, Mr. Littlehawk."

"It was a bold plan, your Honor, but it has been thwarted by the quick, decisive and brilliant action of one of our elected public servants and a patriot, Tony Angelletti, and two individuals who helped him, Agent Dave Sanders, who you have met, and this Russian foreign student, Katrina Petrovna." Sam motioned in the direction of Katrina, who caught the Judge's eye and smiled demurely.

Sam had seized the initiative. Judge Mickelson was listening intently. Wallace and his cadre of attorneys knew that any interruption at this point would be met with a quick and dreadful response from the Judge. They remained silent.

"Go on, Mr. Littlehawk," the Judge said. He closed the packet of evidence that he had been examining and leaned back in his chair, folding his hands over his ample belly, ready to hear the story.

"It's a sordid tale, your Honor, of international criminal intrigue and unexpected consequences," Sam began, immediately hooking his audience. "It began with simple self-dealing by power company executives, who sought to bribe or force members of the state Public Utility Commission to approve the building of an unnecessary power plant, the Greenleaf Project, which was to be used as a vehicle for skimming public funds. The power company executives and their associates were so confident of approval that they began construction on the site even before approval was obtained. Commissioner Angelletti threw them a curve, however, when he refused to vote for the project, which he saw as an enormous waste of money. He then rebuffed their repeated attempts at bribery and ignored their attempts at coercion. In the process, Mr. Angelletti began to look into the dealings of the power company, and he learned of a hidden alliance between the company and organized crime. It seems that the management of the power company had come under the influence of a malignant cell of international thugs that had its origins in Russia, but now has put down roots in Nevada. The so-called Russian Mafia and the power company had conspired to use the Greenleaf Project to make and launder dirty money in a dozen different ways, all of which can be easily proven, your Honor."

The courtroom was completely quiet. Sam instinctively turned toward the press in the jury box as he continued.

"We do not know who first formulated the plan to use the Greenleaf Project as a dumping ground for deadly toxic wastes. Common sense suggests that it was the criminal organization and not the public utility executives. But money talks, and the irrefutable fact is that the project site has been used as an illegal toxic waste dump. Your Honor, you have in your hand a report of tests that were performed two days ago on samples taken from the site. The samples contain traces of some of the most insidious and deadly toxins known to man. At this moment, there are still hundreds of drums of liquid death stored at the site. You need to take immediate action, sir, to safeguard and prevent the removal of these drums, which constitute not only evidence of very serious crimes, but also a major public health hazard. These toxic wastes will have to be removed and disposed of properly and safely, and at the expense of the perpetrators of this crime."

The Judge looked sternly at the group huddled around Huntington and Wallace. Huntington sat stoically with his arms crossed in a defensive posture. Bandini's black eyes flickered constantly from Wallace to Huntington, the press and the Judge, measuring all of their impressions. The Judge nodded for Sam to continue.

"Industrial wastes have been hauled in from sites outside this state," Sam continued. "The intent of the conspirators was to bury the wastes under the new power plant without detection, which would have created a long-term health hazard for the entire region, due to migration of toxins into the aquifer. But for the vigilance and quick action of Mr. Angelletti, the scoundrels might have gotten away with it, and we would not have known until long after the damage was done. If they had succeeded, the citizens of this region would have been subjected to unknown health hazards for decades, possibly centuries, never knowing the source. The criminal perpetrators would have reaped a tidy profit from industrial companies whose executives chose to pay the price and look the other way, in order to get rid of the deadly byproducts of their operations. What no one anticipated, however, was the possibility of a revenge strike by a Middle Eastern terrorist group that had a bone to pick with the Russians."

Sam turned to stare directly at Huntington and Bandini. "What these people did not know, your Honor, and what they are learning now for the first time, is that we were literally seconds away from a thousand barrels of deadly toxins being blown into the atmosphere by a terrorist's bomb!"

Huntington sat rigidly straight in his chair. Bandini slumped, staring at a point on the table with a despondent look in his eyes. Wallace's brow furrowed as he began to wonder whether he had bet on the wrong horse.

"While investigating the Russian Mafia figures involved in this plot, your Honor, we learned that they had double-crossed a Middle Eastern terrorist organization in an arms deal. The payback for their deceit was to be the destruction of the Greenleaf Project, in which the Mafia boss has invested heavily. The terrorist group would reap a double reward, striking a crippling blow at the heart of America, and at the same time destroying their enemy's project and his prestige in the criminal underworld. A strike was carefully planned by the terrorists. In fact, your Honor, the bomb that could have killed and sickened tens of thousands of people was already in place and was only minutes from exploding, when it was discovered and neutralized by these people sitting in front of you. The bomb was removed from the site and it detonated harmlessly, away from the toxic wastes. That explosion that you all heard yesterday evening was the detonation of the terrorists' bomb. It was only through the brilliant, heroic and selfless action of these people, your Honor, done at great personal risk, that a monstrous catastrophe was averted."

The Judge nodded almost imperceptibly as the doomsday scenario painted by Sam soaked in. Sam had the floor and held it. "The involvement of the National Guard was crucial to save the lives of those few who had risked everything for the greater good, your Honor. They were under heavy hostile fire from Mafia gunmen. Colonel Ripkin and Agent Sanders only did what was necessary to protect them. The situation was out of control, and the National Guard brought it under control as quickly and efficiently as possible. The Governor was not available to consult and the situation was critical. Colonel Ripkin made a command decision, which turned out to be the right decision."

"Well," Judge Mickelson said, "I'm not going to get into any jurisdictional issues between the various law enforcement agencies and the National Guard. What's done is done. It will be up to a higher authority than me to sort that out. You folks can discuss that with the Governor." The Judge looked over his spectacles at Colonel Ripkin and Dave Sanders, then he glanced back at Sam. "Go on, Mr. Littlehawk."

"What you *must* do now, your Honor, is protect the public health and welfare by placing a strict quarantine on the project site, and appoint an independent special prosecutor to investigate this matter. It is essential that the investigative team and the special prosecutor be totally *independent* of the political system in this state."

"That's about it, your Honor," Sam said as he stood behind his friends, his good hand on Tony's shoulder. "We all have these people to thank for risking their lives to prevent a monumental disaster that would have resulted in enormous loss of life and untold suffering in this state. They not only averted disaster, they also captured the terrorists. Their actions were nothing short of miraculous under the circumstances. And we should be very grateful to Agent Sanders and Colonel Ripkin for their quick response and successful intervention in a desperate situation, without which we would not be here today. My only regret is that the central perpetrator of the entire conspiracy, the Russian Mafia kingpin, Svetlanikoff, seems to have escaped."

The Judge removed his glasses and rubbed his eyes, then looked back up at Sam. "Thank you for the briefing, Mr. Littlehawk. I think I've heard enough. First, the project site must be secured to protect the public safety and preserve the evidence until a proper investigation can be made. Colonel Ripkin, I recommend that you take immediate direction from the Governor in that regard. I believe that the National Guard would be the appropriate authority to quarantine the site, unless the Governor disagrees. I'll be available to speak with the Governor if he so desires. Second, given the credible allegations of a conspiracy involving public institutions, I think there needs to be an independent investigative task force put in place..."

The Judge's words were interrupted as Tom Wallace rose to his feet, his beaked face unusually red, with beads of sweat visible on his forehead and bald pate. "Your Honor," he began, "before you take any such action, don't we get an opportunity to be heard? You have only heard the ludicrous statements of these indicted criminals..."

"*Mr. Wallace!*" the Judge bellowed in a tone that stopped the District Attorney in his tracks. "Are you interrupting me? Didn't I tell you that this is not a public hearing? So you do *not* have an opportunity to be heard here today, unless I say so. *And I don't say so!* You and the others sitting at your table will have an opportunity to be heard tomorrow morning at nine o'clock in this courtroom, when I will consider who will be appointed to the task force that I will establish to investigate this entire matter and bring any appropriate indictments. Obviously, your office cannot conduct the investigation due to your well-known political alignment with some of the parties involved and your blatant prejudice against others. I will find another prosecutor by tomorrow. And I suggest that you consider employing your own personal legal counsel."

Wallace's swallowed hard and slowly sank down into his chair.

"For the record, this is not a hearing," the Judge continued to the courtroom at large. "There have been no petitions filed, no legal notices given, there is no pending proceeding, and I am not deciding any issues here today. I am only gathering information and making a few comments and suggestions on how to best protect the public safety and hopefully to keep a lid on this situation until it can be properly addressed by a panel of independent authorities who have no personal ties or relationships which could prevent impartiality. And that ain't you," the Judge declared, pointing his gavel at Wallace.

"Notwithstanding the serious allegations that have been made on both sides, I do not consider anyone in this room to be a flight risk or an imminent threat to society. I will not order that anyone be arrested, and I will in fact release each of you on your own recognizance. No one may leave town. If you do, I promise that I won't take it lightly. By this time tomorrow, I will have assembled a task force of independent state and federal authorities to fully investigate this bizarre matter. I expect to see you all back here at nine o'clock tomorrow morning, prepared to give sworn testimony. Do you all understand?"

There was a general nodding of heads in the courtroom.

The Judge leaned forward and peered over his glasses at Wallace, Huntington and Bandini, who appeared ready to bolt for the door. "And gentlemen, bear in mind that if anything whatsoever happens to Mr. Littlehawk, Mr. Angelletti, or anyone associated with them, I will know exactly who to look to in that regard. You had better hope that all of the witnesses stay healthy. Do you understand?"

With a look of trepidation, Wallace nodded, then Bandini followed suit.

"Court is dismissed until nine in the morning." The Judge rapped his gavel, then quickly stood and turned to exit the courtroom.

"All rise," the bailiff intoned hastily, as the Judge's flowing black robe disappeared.

As the door closed behind the Judge, reporters piled out of the jury box and began to shout questions at all of the participants at both tables. Huntington, Bandini, Wallace and company made a hasty exit without responding to any questions. Sam put his good arm around Tony's shoulders and gave him a squeeze, then turned to give Katrina a long and close embrace.

"That was absolutely brilliant, Sam! I didn't know you had it in you!" Dave exclaimed, gripping Sam's hand. "Until you showed up, I was starting to think that we were all going to jail!"

"He is a silver-tongued devil," Tony said, beaming from ear to ear.

"He is a true hero," Katrina smiled, wrapping her arms around him.

The cluster of reporters standing around the close group of friends could contain themselves no longer. They began to fire questions at Sam and the others faster than they could be answered.

"Mr. Littlehawk, sir, was a helicopter really shot down by the National Guard?"

"How did you know that a terror attack was coming?"

"Does this mean that the Russian Mafia has a foothold here?"

"Can you give us a blow by blow of the action at the site?"

"How did you know that you wouldn't be killed by the bomb or the Mafia?"

"Mr. Littlehawk, what made you all risk your lives like that?"

Sam smiled at the last question and winked at Tony. Turning to the reporter, he said, "We just did what had to be done."

Chapter 31

Four weeks later, the bandages and sling, stitches, cuts and bruises were gone. All that remained as physical evidence of the gun battle that Sam had endured was a red scar starting on the left side of his forehead and disappearing into a patch of shorter dark hair. Sam was dressed in an immaculate navy suit, and the scar went unnoticed by the panel of senators and congressmen sitting on the Joint Congressional Committee for Homeland Security, before whom Sam had been testifying for the past two days.

"Do you believe, Mr. Littlehawk, that the emergency funds being used to remove and properly dispose of the wastes and clean up the site will be fully reimbursed from the assets of the criminal enterprise?"

"The short answer, Senator, is yes. Although Svetlanikoff was able to transfer most of his liquid assets out of the country within hours, his companies owned a number of casinos and other businesses and real estate that could not be moved and were essentially debt-free. Our preliminary estimates suggest that the net value of the assets that will be recovered will be in excess of fifty million dollars, which should be more than enough to pay for the clean-up and to convert the site to a useful purpose."

"And Agent Sanders is overseeing the seizure of these assets?"

"Yes sir. His prior investigation into this criminal organization gave him a good head start. After the seizure of assets is complete, he wants to continue to pursue the investigation of this international criminal organization and he particularly hopes to stop the trafficking in slaves and arms, along with the other crimes they are committing."

"Has Agent Sanders been exonerated of any wrongdoing in connection with the investigation?"

Sam smiled. "It seems, sir, that his immediate superiors in the local FBI office who were complaining about his conduct are now busy defending themselves against charges of conspiracy, obstruction of justice, and criminal negligence. Their complaints against Agent Sanders have been dropped."

"And do you feel that the special prosecutor and task force sorting all of this out are truly independent?"

"I do, sir. Judge Mickelson personally recruited and interrogated at length each member of the task force. The Governor reviewed the appointments. I understand that Judge Mickelson has agreed to postpone his retirement until after the task force disbands, so we will have him continuing to supervise the group. With Mr. Angelletti chairing the task force, no stone will be left unturned."

The Senator made a few notes, then looked up again. "Mr. Littlehawk, based upon the testimony of all of the witnesses concerning this affair, it is clear that your actions were extraordinary. At enormous personal risk, you acted quickly and decisively to prevent a catastrophic disaster and stop a ruthless act of terrorism against our country, while exposing a major criminal organization in the process. On behalf of this Committee and the American people, I want to congratulate you for your success and thank you for your selfless efforts. America is a better, safer place because of individuals like you."

Sam smiled and flushed at the high compliment. "Thank you, sir. We just did what had to be done."

"Can we count on you, Mr. Littlehawk, to continue to be our window on this process and to report back to us periodically?"

"I would be honored to serve, sir."

"Very well. This hearing is now concluded. You may step down."

Sam remained in the hearing room for several minutes, receiving personal congratulations from various committee members and spectators, then prevailed upon a staff member to provide a car to the airport. It was already mid-afternoon on Friday, but with luck, he still might make it.

* * * * *

"It's too bad Sam can't be here," Tony said to Dave Sanders as they took their seats in the orchestra section of the Performing Arts Center. "I know that it's killing him to be missing Katrina's last performance here."

"That offer from the Vienna ballet was sure a surprise," Sanders replied. "Must have been all the publicity. Mix a world class ballerina who's already a big sensation with an international terrorist plot and you've got a story! The tabloids are still going bananas."

"Well, regardless of the publicity, she deserves Vienna. She's the best."

"They don't come any better, or any braver, either."

The two friends settled into their seats as the lights dimmed in the performance hall and the orchestra tuned their instruments.

* * * * *

There was a short screech as the tires of the aircraft made contact with the runway. Sam opened his eyes and realized that he was home. He had been lost in a recurring dream in which he was lying on the ground, looking at a dazzling white cloud in the sky. The sun was behind the cloud, giving it a brilliant gold lining. Vestiges of the dream remained, leaving him peaceful and calm.

He smiled and felt the tension of the day and the long flight ebbing from his body. It had been a good week, despite the unwelcome news that Katrina would soon become a prima ballerina with the Vienna ballet.

Sam deeply regretted her leaving. They'd had little time to sort things out between them. From the minute Sam walked out of the hospital and into Judge Mickelson's courtroom, they had been caught up in a maelstrom of activity. Two trips to Washington for Sam, many hours with the task force, and endless interviews for both of them. In fact, their entire time together had been filled with constant activity. There had been no time to really get to know each other.

With longing, he recalled the one afternoon and evening that they had spent together at the cabin on the ranch. The sunset had been spectacular. It had been a long time since he had experienced such intense intimacy, and he yearned to take up where they had left off that night, when Katrina had been kidnapped.

The plane arrived at the gate and Sam was the first one up the ramp, running through the terminal to the taxi stand. With luck, he would be there in time.

* * * * *

The entire audience was on its feet applauding enthusiastically. It was the third curtain call. At center stage, Katrina smiled sweetly as she was handed another large bouquet of red roses. The troupe all bowed in unison again and again. Finally, they took two steps back and the curtain dropped.

Katrina handed the bouquets to a stage hand and was embraced by several other dancers offering their congratulations. It had been a brilliant performance and a moment of true joy for her. But in her joy, there was a hidden reservation, a bittersweet feeling, knowing that Sam was not there. Knowing that within just a few days, she would be leaving for Vienna. She prayed that he would return before her departure.

Katrina broke away from the crowd in the wings and made her way quickly to her dressing room, feeling both the glow of a successful performance and a longing that she had never felt before. She had wanted Sam to be there to see her performance, and she needed to see him one more time. Her life in Russia, her classical training, had all been filled with stoic forbearance. She had denied herself, and she had been denied so many things. She had learned discipline, not to want things, to simply accept what she was given.

So much had changed, and so quickly. She had glimpsed another way of life, one in which her own desires mattered and could be satisfied. Success was haunting her now, pursuing her, changing her life dramatically. She was delighted and excited, but confused. There were so many unknowns in her new world. She needed to talk with Sam. He would help her understand what the future would hold.

Katrina stepped into her dressing room and closed the door. Pausing for a moment, her hand still on the knob, she took a deep breath, releasing the tension of the stage. She smiled, closing her eyes and remembering the performance. In her heart, she knew that it had been superb.

"Katrina."

She turned quickly, startled by the unexpected voice in her dressing room. Standing across the room was Sam, with a smile on his face and a sparkle in his eye. In an instant, she was in his arms. They met in a long and passionate embrace, then they kissed and he held her tightly, kissing her cheek, savoring the moment, inhaling the intoxicating incense of her hair. Finally, he pulled away.

"Your performance was incredible," he said.

"You were there? You saw it?"

"You didn't think I would miss it, did you?"

"I wanted you to be there more than anything." Katrina's eyes filled with tears. She laid her head on his shoulder and again she held him tightly. "What now, Sam?" she whispered. "What does the future hold?"

The future was too big for Sam. He could only think of the moment, which he was enjoying very, very much. "Let the future take care of itself," he said gently. "For now, let's just take up where we left off. Let's go spend the next few days alone together at the cabin, watching the sunset."